Since winning the Catherine Cookson Prize for Fiction for her first novel, *The Hungry Tide*, Val Wood has become one of the most popular authors in the UK.

Born in the mining town of Castleford, Val came to East Yorkshire as a child and has lived in Hull and rural Holderness where many of her novels are set. She now lives in the market town of Beverley.

When she is not writing, Val is busy promoting libraries and supporting many charities. In 2017 she was awarded an honorary doctorate by the University of Hull for service and dedication to literature.

Find out more about Val Wood's novels by visiting her website at www.valwood.co.uk

D1079322

The Harbour Girl

Val Wood

PENGUIN BOOKS

TRANSWORLD PUBLISHERS
Penguin Random House, One Embassy Gardens,
8 Viaduct Gardens, London SW11 7BW
www.penguin.co.uk

Transworld is part of the Penguin Random House group of companies
whose addresses can be found at global.penguinrandomhouse.com

First published in Great Britain in 2011 by Bantam Press
an imprint of Transworld Publishers
Corgi edition published 2012
Reissued as a Penguin edition in 2022

A CIP catalogue record for this book
is available from the British Library.

ISBN 9781529177299

Typeset in 11.5/13.5pt New Baskerville by Jouve (UK), Milton Keynes.
Printed and bound in Great Britain by Clays Ltd, Elcograf S.p.A.

The authorized representative in the EEA is Penguin Random House Ireland,
Morrison Chambers, 32 Nassau Street, Dublin D02 YH68.

Penguin Random House is committed to a sustainable
future for our business, our readers and our planet. This book is
made from Forest Stewardship Council® certified paper.

To my family with love, and for Peter

ACKNOWLEDGEMENTS

Special thanks are due to Dr Robb Robinson who kindly and generously gave me permission to use his informative and interesting book *Trawling: The Rise and Fall of the British Trawl Industry* (Exeter University Press), and to thank him, too, for his patience in answering my ingenuous questions on the subject of fishing.

Also to Jim Porter of The Bosun's Watch and Chris Petherbridge's Hull Trawler site: Hull Trawler – Smack to Stern, www.hulltrawler.net.

The Scarborough Maritime Heritage website is a most excellent site and I give my sincere thanks to the archivist for allowing me to use the information therein. In particular, I must mention the factual details regarding the Great Storm of October 1880 in which many ships and lives were lost and which I was able to incorporate as part of my fictional story.

CHAPTER ONE

Scarborough, 1880

The door in the wall had been bricked up for many years, long before Jeannie was born. There had once been a shop there and the door had been regularly used, but when the shopkeeper died the building was turned into a rooming house and another door opened up, rendering the original obsolete. It had been blocked roughly and hastily and wasn't level with the wall, leaving a niche about a brick and a half deep, a space just right for a small thin girl to shelter in. From inside this narrow refuge Jeannie could see her mother's back as she sat deftly mending nets, and watch the harbour.

Had her mother known she was there, she would undoubtedly have told her to go back home to Sandside, or sent her to buy bread or call on Granny Marshall with a message, and Jeannie didn't want to do any of those things. She wanted to wait for Ethan Wharton to sail into harbour in his father's fishing smack. Ethan was twelve, four years older than her, and he would know that she was there, watching him, so would make a great show of bringing in the vessel without a scrape and tying up with assumed casualness below the castle hill, close by the warehouses and the boat builders' slipway.

There she is, she thought, her keen eyes picking out the *Bonnie Lass* as she nosed her way through the waterway, screeching herring gulls following in the wake. Jeannie's mother turned her head.

'Jeannie!' When Mary spoke the name it sounded like Jinnie. She had chosen the name Jeannette, after her own Scottish grandmother. 'Jeannie,' she called again, 'come here. I know you're there. You can't hide from me, bairn.'

'How did you know I was there?' Jeannie asked from behind her.

'Ah! Your mother knows everything.' Mary Marshall looked up from beneath the shawl which covered her red hair to smile at her daughter. 'Go now and tell Josh Wharton to go home immediately. There's news waiting for him.'

'What news?'

'Never you mind.' Mary's eyes went back to the nets. 'He'll know. And come straight back; I need you for a message to your gran. Don't dally talking to Ethan. He's plenty to do without you bothering him.'

Jeannie opened her mouth to reply, but her mother waved a swift hand so instead she ran barefoot towards the slipway, avoiding the nets and ropes and lobster baskets, to where she could see Ethan, his older brother Mark and their father bent low over their catch.

'Mr Wharton,' she piped. 'You've to go home straight away.'

Josh Wharton looked up, pushed back his sea-stained hat and grinned. He said something to his two sons, then stepped quickly off the *Bonnie Lass* and ran to the cliff path, up the narrow streets and alleyways of Sandside towards the cottages clustered below the castle walls, which seemed from down below to be built one on top of another, their red roofs overlapping.

Jeannie walked towards the smack. 'Hello, Ethan,' she said shyly.

He nodded, felt for something in his pocket and beckoned her closer. 'Here.' He held out his hand. 'Da said I'd to give you a penny.'

She took it. 'What's it for?'

He shrugged. 'Bringing the message, I suppose.'

'Why did he have to go home?'

He lifted up a pail and turned his head away, a flush creeping up his neck. 'To see Ma, I expect. She's having a babby.'

'Oh,' Jeannie said. 'I didn't know.' She was cross that she didn't know. She would have liked to announce that his mother had been delivered of a baby girl or boy. But maybe that was why her mother hadn't told her, knowing that she would blurt out the news.

'Did you get a good catch?' she asked, and he nodded. They'd gone out last night, when the sea was calm and there was a moon; it would have been a good night for fishing. Not like the night two years ago when her father had gone out and hadn't come back. She only just remembered him. A Scarborough man born and bred, her mother was proud of saying, as his father and grandfather were before him, though his grandmother, Alice, came from a Hull whaling family.

Jeannie's mother had been a Scottish fisher

11

lass who had come down from Fraserburgh to Scarborough following the herring fleet; she'd met Jeannie's father, Jack Foster Marshall, and never went home again. Mary was never short of work: she was swift and sure when mending nets, and during the herring season – between October or November to March – she went back to her old job on the quay, gutting and curing the 'silver darlings', and filling and rolling the huge storage barrels. Best of all were the times when the Scottish fisher girls arrived, for her own mother still came with them and Mary could catch up with news from home.

She had not stopped working after the tragedy of losing her husband to the sea, for she had a young family to feed. Jeannie had been only six, a year younger than her brother Tom. Tom wanted to go to sea like his father, and had already been promised a job with a family friend as soon as he was twelve.

If Mary was worried that her son might suffer the same fate as Jack, she never showed it. They were fisher folk, the sea was in their blood, salt in their spittle and seaweed in their hair. There was no other calling.

Now Jeannie walked slowly back to her mother and stood in front of her. The sun warmed her through her thin frock though it didn't touch her toes, which she curled and wriggled against the wet paving. She breathed in deeply, embracing the salty smell of fish and wet hemp from the nets draped across her mother's aproned knee.

'Will you teach me?' she said. 'I'm old enough.'

Mary nodded. 'To gut or to mend?'

'Both,' Jeannie said, and was rewarded with a warm smile.

'Aye, I will, but you must go to school until you're twelve at least. You must have an education, Jeannie. Your father always wanted that for both of you, though it's hard to keep Tom there.'

Jeannie's brother hated being at school. He couldn't wait to leave and earn a living on the boats. He was forever playing truant, and although he avoided the area where his mother worked he could usually be found somewhere around the harbour, doing jobs for the fishermen and generally knee deep in water.

The best time was during the herring season when Mary, busy working from morning to night with the other herring girls, turned a blind eye to Tom's activities as he and other boys waited for the men to bring the catch to shore in baskets and crates. The lads would rush to gather up any fallen herring and race off with a boxful to sell round the narrow streets. Everyone knew they were stolen but even the fishermen didn't begrudge the boys a few fish or the pennies they sold them for.

Jeannie could run as fast as any of the lads and would have liked to join them, but they told her it wasn't a job for girls. Only Tom allowed her to sell some, for when they saw her waiflike face, thin frame, bare feet and curly brown hair the housewives they targeted couldn't resist her innocent charm, or the chance to buy her herring at a cheap price. On these occasions, Tom always kept a few fish back for Granny Marshall. She too mended nets, but she did so outside her own front door, the steep path up from the harbour being now too difficult to climb with her arthritic legs.

When Jeannie told her mother Josh Wharton had

given her a penny, Mary suggested she take it up the hill to Castlegate and give it to her gran. 'She needs it more than we do,' she said. 'And tell her I'll be up to see her tomorrow. Talk to her for a wee while,' she added. 'She likes the company.'

But Jeannie was still pondering the issue of school. 'It's a long time till I'm twelve,' she said. 'Do I have to stay at school all that time?'

'Yes, but on your ninth birthday I'll show you how to mend the nets, and then on your tenth birthday I'll show you how to gut the herring. The knives are sharp, and right now, lassie, you don't stay still long enough to handle one. If you sliced off your fingers now, there'd be no work for you when you're grown.'

Jeannie saw the sense in this and said she would try to be patient.

'Childhood is fleeting, bairn,' her mother said softly. 'Make the most of it. Time enough to grow up.'

Later that day, when she had come home to cook supper, Mary said the same thing to Tom, but as she sat by the table slicing bread she had to wrap her legs round his to keep him still.

'You'll go to school and that's the end of it.'

'Don't want to,' Tom muttered. 'Shan't! Who said I have to?'

'Wanting has nothing to do with it,' she answered calmly, 'but if you don't go, your poor auld ma'll go to jail.'

Tom gave a small gasp. 'Why?'

'Because it's law.'

'Who made the law?'

Mary sighed. 'I think it was Mr Gladstone when he was prime minister; and then Disraeli agreed,

14

and now we've got Gladstone back again he says you've definitely to go to school.'

'He doesn't know me,' Tom said defiantly.

'I think he does.' Mary put the bread on a plate and unwound her legs from Tom's knees. 'He knows all the children. Now, wash hands and face and come to the table.'

'My hands are clean,' he objected, but his mother just pointed to the stone sink in the corner of the room, where Jeannie was already holding her hands under the pump. It wasn't that Jeannie was exceptionally obedient – in fact she was quite a rebel at heart – but she was hungry and knew from the long experience of her eight years that her mother would win in the end. Supper wouldn't be put on the table until hands were clean and faces were washed and she and Tom were sitting quietly waiting for it.

That night, in the bed they shared with their mother, Jeannie woke to the sound of a howling wind, thinking that she could hear voices. She lifted her head from beneath the blanket. Tom was asleep at the foot of the mattress, but her mother was gone from her side and was standing by the small square window looking out towards the sea.

'Ma,' Jeannie said sleepily. 'Is it a storm?'

'Aye, it is.' Mary turned away and came towards the bed. 'Go to sleep, bairn. It'll soon abate.'

Jeannie sighed. Her mother often woke in the night, especially if the wind was blowing hard, and she always went and stood at the window in her long white nightdress with her dark red hair hanging down her back. Jeannie thought she looked like an angel, like pictures she'd seen in story books, except that angels didn't weep the way her mother often did.

She looked out of the window herself the next morning and saw the mass of ships in the harbour being tossed about by the high-crested sea as if they were made of matchwood. Scarborough lay between the Tyne and the Humber, and ships caught between the two great waterways would race towards it if gales threatened. It was not an easy haven to enter and many ships dipped and plunged beyond the harbour walls, sheltering as close as they could, their skippers praying that the lifeboat would reach them in time to save their crews. There was a flag fluttering on the lighthouse on Vincent Pier, but last night it would have been showing a warning light.

It was raining as Jeannie and Tom trudged to school, but by midday the sun was making a valiant effort to come out from behind heavy cloud. When they left in the afternoon, Tom raced ahead and said he was going down to the harbour. Jeannie shouted after him to go home first, but her words were tossed away by a gusty wind and he either didn't hear or chose not to. He probably chose not to, she thought, knowing that he and his pals liked to climb into the coggy boats that were tied up by the landing stages and pretend they were at sea as they rocked and bucked on the waves.

'Where's Tom?' her mother asked when she got home.

'Don't know,' Jeannie said. 'Down at the harbour, I think.'

'Go and fetch him,' Mary said. 'Tell him I want him back here right now. There's another storm brewing and I want him where I can see him.'

'He might not come.'

'He'll come. Tell him there's a belting if he doesn't.'

Jeannie draped a shawl over her head and went out again to look for her brother. She knew why her mother was anxious. Tom and his mates usually played on the sands, leaping in and out of the sea when the tide was full and the waves were high, but they also ran up and down on the pier, a dangerous game when the sea lashed over the wooden structure and they could so easily be washed over.

But there's no danger now, she thought. The sea was grey, though there was a heavy swell; she had seen it in much angrier moods. Why is Ma so bothered? In the harbour she could see boats being prepared for a night's fishing and some smacks already on their way out.

She caught sight of a group of boys on the sands and screwed up her eyes to find Tom among them. She couldn't see him but shouted anyway.

'Tom! Tom Marshall! You've to come home now.'

Some of the boys looked up and waved their hands negatively. Another shouted back but she couldn't hear him, then one of them pointed in the direction of the castle headland and she exhaled impatiently. She walked along the sands as far as the pier and then went up on to the road, past the stalls which during the day had been selling fish, crabs, cockles and winkles but were now shutting up; past the quay where the fisher lasses gutted the fish and down towards the bottom of Sandside where warehouses and mast builders and boat building yards were situated and she knew she'd find Tom.

He was in a rowing boat on his own, rowing up

and down the inlet and turning in circles whilst a couple of men looked on.

'Tom,' she called. 'Ma says you've to come home.'

'Aw, heck,' he complained. 'Why do I have to?'

'Cos your ma says so,' one of the men laughed. 'Don't you know you've allus to do what your ma says? Even when you're grown. Go on, you can come another day.'

Tom rowed back to the shallows, taking a long time to do it, made the boat fast and climbed ashore. 'You allus spoil my fun,' he grumbled.

'Not me; Ma said,' Jeannie retaliated. 'Besides, I've had to look all over Scarborough for you and I could've been at home.'

He muttered all the way until they reached the sands, where he saw his pals playing and raced ahead to join them. Jeannie set her lips and turned her back, heading for home, but in a minute he sped past her, reaching the doorstep before she did.

'Now then, Ma,' he said cheerfully. 'Is there owt to eat? Dunno where our Jeannie is.'

'Get inside, cheeky little beggar.' Mary hid a rueful grin. 'Come on, Jeannie. Supper's ready.'

'Why'd I have to come in?' Tom spooned a mouthful of stew into his mouth. 'It's not dark.'

'Because!' his mother said. 'Because I said so.'

'But why?' he whined.

Mary heaved a sigh. 'Because there's going to be a storm.' She looked towards the window and remembered that it was on such a day as this, two years before, that a sudden squall had sprung up as darkness fell and her life had changed for ever. 'I can feel it in my bones.'

CHAPTER TWO

Jeannie thought her mother was wrong. The morning dawned bright and clear although a stiff breeze was blowing; the ships which had been out overnight had come in safely and there had been a good catch, or so she heard as she went off to school. Tom didn't walk with her and she thought he might be playing truant again.

Yesterday when she had visited her grandmother and given her Mr Wharton's penny, the old lady had bid her sit down and talk. Jeannie had wriggled about on the cold doorstep and watched the nimble fingers of her father's mother as she mended nets. Women whose husbands were fishermen brought them to her when they had an odd penny to spare, for there was no other who could mend so fast or as neatly as Aggie Marshall.

A coarse apron covered her black dress, and with her greying hair tied in a severe bun at the back of her neck she looked much older than her fifty-odd years. She'd perched straight-backed on a wooden chair and gazed at Jeannie. 'Well,' she had said. 'What have you to tell me? What's your brother up to? He nivver comes to see his old gran.'

Tom was more important than she was. Jeannie

had garnered that knowledge from her grand-mother a long time ago. He was a boy; he would grow into a man and earn a living to support them all, including Jeannie until such time as she would marry a seaman or fisherman who would keep her and any children that they had. Family was essential to keep women from poverty. Aggie had lost two sons and a husband to the sea, and although she had three daughters she relied more on Mary than on any of them. Two of her daughters had married out of the fishing trade and the other was a widow.

'I'm going to learn to mend nets,' Jeannie had told her, 'and when I'm ten I'll learn to gut. Ma's going to learn me.'

Aggie nodded. 'Good. And Tom? Is he still wasting time at school?' She had no truck with education. She'd never had any, she often boasted, and it hadn't stopped her from catching a seafaring husband.

'Ma says he has to go. She says that our da would've wanted him to.'

Aggie snorted. 'Aye, our Jack had all sorts of daft ideas and look where it got him. Bottom of the sea, that's where.'

Jeannie had chewed on her lip. She'd heard this before from her grandmother, but she could never work out the connection between schooling or lack of it and her father's death.

'Your ma should let him go to the boatyards and learn about boat building till he's old enough to go to sea. That's all the edication he needs. He doesn't need to know how to read or write to be able to catch fish.'

'I like reading,' Jeannie ventured.

Her grandmother raised her eyebrows. 'And when

do you think you'll have time to do that when you're grown and with a houseful of babbies? Go on, be off with you. Don't be wasting my time with your idle chatter.'

She'd escaped thankfully, and now, as she sat in the classroom with her slate and chalk in front of her and the tip of her tongue protruding, she copied the words written on the blackboard.

'Where's your brother, Jeannie Marshall?' the teacher asked. Jeannie went hot and then cold. 'And don't tell me he's sick.' Miss Jennings glared at her. 'I saw him this morning down on the sands.'

'I don't know, miss.' Her cheeks were aflame. 'He left home before me. He said he didn't want to be late.'

'Then tell him he can look forward to the cane when he does come in. I'll not tolerate truancy.'

'Yes, Miss Jennings,' she muttered and contemplated on the unfairness of getting into the teacher's bad books just because of Tom.

Miss Jennings stood behind her to read what she had written. 'Good,' she said. 'But what have you forgotten?'

Jeannie stared at her slate and then at the blackboard. The words were the same, she was sure of it, and she'd tried to write neatly in spite of the crumbly chalk.

'The date, girl,' Miss Jennings barked. 'You've forgotten the date! Who else has forgotten the date?'

Several hands were reluctantly raised and they were told to write it three times so that they wouldn't forget another time: 27 October 1880.

*　　*　　*

Jeannie asked her mother if she could go and see Mrs Wharton's new baby. Mary hesitated for a moment and then said she could and that she would go with her. She finished making supper, washed her hands and face, brushed her hair and told Jeannie to do the same.

'Where's our Tom?' she asked. 'Has he been in school?'

Jeannie shrugged. 'Haven't seen him. Miss Jennings asked where he was and said he'd get the cane when she saw him.'

'Did she?' her mother said grimly. 'We'll see about that.'

They walked up the hill towards the cottage where the Wharton family lived. Jeannie hoped that they would see Ethan and was pleased when he opened the door to their knock.

'Ma's poorly,' he said, when Mary asked if they could see his mother and the baby. 'Parson's been this morning as well as the doctor. Shall I ask if you can come in?'

'Please,' Mary said. 'Ask if there's anything I can do.'

Josh came to the door. 'I'd ask you in, Mary, but . . .'

'I'm sorry. Is she . . .'

He looked haggard and unkempt. 'Babby's all right, it's Lizzie that isn't. Parson's been to church her – you know, cleanse her, in case— Daft idea I call it, but Lizzie insisted. It's a boy,' he added as an afterthought. He scratched his beard. 'I should be going out but I daren't leave her.'

'Do you want me to stop with her? I don't mind, but . . .' She paused. If Lizzie was in danger he should stay at home.

He shook his head. 'No, I'd best not. If owt happened – I'd . . .'

'I know,' she said sympathetically. He was a good man. 'You'd always regret it. Let me know if there's anything I can do. There's a storm brewing,' she added. 'You're best at home anyway.'

'Our Mark'll go and mebbe tek Ethan. And he'll tek a couple of lads who know what they're about. It'll be a bit of a blow, but nowt much. He needn't go out far beyond the harbour. There's plenty of fish about.'

And that was the top and bottom of it, Mary thought as they stepped out down the hill again. If there was plenty of fish, the fishermen would sail. They couldn't afford not to.

The wind continued to howl throughout the night and as they lay in bed they heard the rattle of drainpipes and the crash of slates falling off the roofs of nearby cottages on to the road below. Then the rain began and lashed against the window and even Tom, always a heavy sleeper, woke up and slid between his mother and sister.

Mary prayed. Dear God, have mercy on those poor souls. For those in peril. She wept silent tears as she thought of her own husband, lost overboard in a gale not as violent as this one threatened to be.

'Ma!' Jeannie whispered. 'Do you think Ethan has gone out with his brother?'

Mary hoped not. Ethan hadn't the experience to battle with such forceful weather and his brother Mark was only nineteen, though he had been a fisherman since he was twelve. Men who owned their own vessels didn't always take their sons with them, but apprenticed them to other ship owners. The loss of fathers and sons in one ship would be devastating to a family, leaving them destitute.

It was not yet dawn, but Mary heard the mutter of voices and the thud of scurrying feet down the steep steps of the passageway at the side of their cottage. Others too had been awakened by the storm and were heading down to the shore to watch and wait. Lifeboat men and the coastguard would be preparing for action in case of foundering ships. Most of the community of this bottom end of Scarborough had some connection with the sea; practically everyone would have a family member or a friend out at sea this night.

But it was not only local ships and men who were at risk; ships crossing the North Sea from Holland, Norway, Sweden, Scotland and the south of England too would be making for this safe harbour.

Tom got out of bed and began to dress. 'Where do you think you're going?' his mother asked.

'I'm going to watch,' he said, stepping into his breeches and buttoning up his shirt.

'No you're not. Get back into bed.'

'Aw, Ma! I want to see the lifeboat launched.'

'Get back in! You're going nowhere.' His mother's voice was sharp. 'You'll be in the way and I know you'll be up and down the shore getting under everybody's feet. This is not a game, Tom. There are lives at risk.'

He heaved a sigh and unfastened his breeches but kept his shirt on and climbed back into the bottom of the bed. 'I just wanted to watch.'

'We'll go as soon as it's daybreak. Now go to sleep.' And although the children did fall asleep again,

Mary didn't, but lay awake until a small patch of light showed through her window. She rose, and drawing the curtain back from their sleeping area she built up the fire, prepared gruel for Tom and Jeannie and swung the kettle over the flame.

She was sitting quietly with a cup of tea clasped in her hands when someone tapped on her door. When she opened it she found Ida, one of Josh Wharton's daughters, standing there, holding another smaller child by the hand.

'Da says can you come, please. He says to tell you that Ma's gone and babby's cryin'. He's gone down to the shore.'

'Did Mark sail last night?' Mary took pity on the girl with her tear-stained face. She guessed she was about Jeannie's age, and the little one about four or five.

The child nodded. 'And our Ethan as well.'

Dear God, Mary breathed. Not both of them. 'I'll get the bairns up and come straight away,' she told her. 'Do you have a gran you can go to, or an aunt?'

'We can go to Aunt Ginny, but Uncle Ned's out in his boat as well so she'll not want the bother of us.'

'All right,' Mary said. 'Go home and I'll be up there as fast as I can.'

She woke the children and hurried them through their washing and dressing and breakfast. She put Tom into his father's sou'wester and raincoat, tucking up the too-long mackintosh and fastening it with a belt.

'Now!' She shook an admonishing finger at him. 'You can go along Sandside. You are *not* to go anywhere near the slipway or pier or the lighthouse. Do you hear me?'

'Yes, Ma.' He looked up at her from beneath the brim.

'Promise? I shall hear of it if you do and you'll get a strapping that you'll remember all your life.'

'I promise, Ma. Honest!'

'Go on then.' She ushered him out of the door. 'Jeannie, you'd better come with me. There might be errands to run.'

'Where's Mrs Wharton gone, Ma?' Jeannie had caught Ida Wharton's husky words.

'To heaven if she's been good,' Mary said vaguely. 'Put your boots on, and an extra shawl.'

Mary put on the clogs that she used when working on the herrings. They were heavy wooden things but they kept out any wet and wet it was when they stepped out of the door. She unfurled a black gamp. Two of the spokes were broken but it gave them a little shelter from the pelting rain as she held it close over their heads, though it flapped so much because of the howling wind that it was in danger of flying out of her hands or turning inside out.

'How would she get there, Ma?' Jeannie asked.

'What?'

'Mrs Wharton? How would she get to heaven?'

Mary sighed. 'Erm – an angel would fetch her soul but leave her body behind.'

Jeannie fell silent. That's what she'd thought, or what she'd been told, and she believed it. So there would have to be a funeral for the body. She clenched her teeth as they climbed the hill and the even steeper steps. I hope Ethan hasn't drowned, because if he has there'll be two funerals from one house. Then she reconsidered. Unless of course they didn't find him. Her own father hadn't had a funeral

26

because he wasn't found. I'll cry if they don't find Ethan, she thought as they neared the Whartons' door. Because he's my bestest friend. Which she knew was rather odd, because he hardly ever spoke to her, but even so he was, and she thought that he knew it too.

They were glad to be inside and out of the pouring rain, but there was no fire lit. This cottage had a separate bedroom and the door was firmly closed. Susan, who was about eleven, was holding the crying baby and rocking it in her arms. Mary took him from her.

'What a little scrap,' she murmured. 'What a wee mite.' She turned to the girl and asked her if there was any kindling, and Susan said there was and she would have made a fire if she hadn't had to nurse the baby.

'I think he needs feeding,' she told Mary. 'He's only had water. Ma wasn't able to feed him. Doctor said he'd try 'n' find another nursing mother but he's not been back.'

Mary knew of one young mother who had given birth about a week ago. 'Make a fire,' she told her, 'and I'll try to find somebody to nurse this babby.'

It was a risk, she knew, to take a newborn child out in this weather, but to wait for the doctor to come back was not a good option. There was a blanket on the back of the chair and she draped it over her shoulder and tucked the child under it, close to her body, leaving an air hole so that it didn't suffocate. She told Jeannie to wait with Susan and that she would be back as soon as she could.

As she puffed her way further up the hill, she pondered on the big gap in age between this child and his brother Mark. Six bairns without a mother, or maybe fewer, she thought sadly, if the boat has foundered. Please God it hasn't. To lose wife and sons together would be too much for Josh Wharton to bear.

She knocked on the door where she thought the young mother lived and recognized the older woman who answered. 'Can your daughter give this child a feed?' she asked. 'His ma's died and he's fearful hungry. He's been baptised,' she added, knowing how superstitious some folk were, 'and his ma was churched.'

She was invited in. Sitting in a chair by a good fire was a young woman of about eighteen, nursing a child. The house was well furnished, with polished Windsor chairs and a wooden table, and she guessed it belonged to the older woman.

'If you could feed him for a day or two?' she asked the girl. 'I'll try to arrange for him to have a bottle. His da's down at the harbour; he's got two sons out in a smack.'

Both women expressed sympathy, and the older woman said, 'Sally's got plenty o' milk. She's been well fed. Her da said she had to have onny the best, even though he was not well pleased with her for having a child out of wedlock.'

'Ma,' the girl whined. 'There's no need to tell everybody.'

'I expect everybody'll find out anyway,' Mary told her. 'You can't keep a bairn secret, not unless you lock it away, and you won't want to do that. They're a blessing when all's said and done.'

Mary told them who the child was and where his father lived and sped off back down the hill. She was getting anxious now about her own son. Tom was a rascal, and although he had promised not to move from the sea front she knew that he would follow the crowd if there was any hint of excitement or drama.

There was a fire blazing in the hearth at the Whartons' cottage and the children were sitting at the table eating bread and cheese. Susan had been well taught, Mary thought, and complimented her on her efficiency. She suggested they wait indoors until their father came back, gathered up Jeannie and headed once more down towards the sea where already a large noisy crowd was gathered along the foreshore. Adding to the din was the constant screech of the herring gulls flying overhead.

Mary pushed her way through to the front, dragging Jeannie by the hand. The waves were high, even in the harbour, and maybe twenty or so battered fishing boats and ships had made their way safely to port. But out of the harbour mouth and beyond there were many others, their sails full set, desperately battling gusting winds and rough seas to make their way in. She looked southwards beyond the harbour, along the Foreshore Road and towards the Spa. Several ships were in difficulties; one, a brig, was being washed by the massive waves flooding its deck, and as she watched its broken mast keeled over, dipping into the turbulent sea. A great shout went up as the lifeboat was launched to help the crew of another ship, a schooner, breaking up under the pressure of heavy seas.

'Ma! Ma! I'm over here.'

It was Tom's voice, though she couldn't see him. 'Where? Where are you, Tom?'

He was standing by the pier road leading to the

lighthouse. He had heeded her words and not gone down, but was perilously close to it.

'Ma,' he shouted hoarsely. 'Mr Wharton's about to put off in a fishing boat. He's seen the *Bonnie Lass*. She's turned over and Ethan and his brother are in the water.'

CHAPTER THREE

'What?' Mary said. 'How do you know, Tom? Who said?'

'I saw him rush past, Ma. He was with two other fishermen and I heard 'em. Look!' He pointed northwards beyond a group of warehouses to a slipway where he often could be found playing in the boats. 'They've gone over to the boatyard. I heard them tell him that the *Bonnie Lass* had keeled over and that everybody was in the water.'

'Both of you stay here. Don't move from this spot.'

Mary pushed her way back through the crowd, ran past the wharf where they brought in the herring barrels and headed towards a slipway where berthed fishing smacks and rowing boats were being tossed about on the water; a group of about four or five men with coils of rope in their arms were about to release a smack from its mooring.

'Stop!' she cried. 'Wait. Wait.'

They all looked up, but one of them – she was sure it was Josh – jumped into the smack.

'Don't,' she said breathlessly as she reached them. 'Josh. Please don't. You can't leave your bairns without a mother *or* a father. What'll become of them if you go down?'

'What's she on about, Josh?' one of the men asked.

'Did he not tell you?' she gasped. 'His wife died this morning and there's another mouth to feed.'

Josh straightened up. 'We're wasting time,' he bellowed. 'My lads are out there. I've got to go to them. The *Bonnie Lass* has foundered. I've got to save my lads.' His voice broke with emotion. 'Come on!'

'Nay, Josh. Tha can't,' another fisherman broke in. 'Mary's right. Tha can't leave them motherless bairns to fend for the'selves.'

Josh pressed his hand to his head and took a deep breath, then looked out to sea. 'I have to, Ted. I can't just leave 'em out there,' he choked.

'Get out of the boat.' Another man reached for his arm. 'Come on.' He hauled him out and stepped into the boat himself. 'Come on, lads. Bear away. We've enough manpower to manage.'

Within seconds the *Castle* was free from her mooring and they were pulling away, the sail unfurled and filling as the gusty wind carried them out to sea.

'Do they know where she is?' Mary asked softly.

Josh nodded; it was an effort for him to speak. 'Just outside the harbour.' He pointed. 'You can just see her.'

Mary narrowed her eyes. 'She's not capsized,' she said. 'There's somebody on board!'

Josh put his hand to his forehead and stared. 'She must have righted herself. No! She's gone again! Her mast is down. Dear God, what a nightmare. I can't see her – she'll be drifting towards the harbour. If she hits the wall they're done for.'

He began to run back to the harbour and turned

towards the lighthouse pier. Mary followed him, her long skirt clutched in her hand so that she didn't trip. She prayed that the smack would be in time to save the crew, but what sickened her more than anything was that when she had spotted the *Bonnie Lass* she had seen only one figure clinging to the broken mast.

The smack was heading for the stricken vessel, but they too were struggling to keep from capsizing and at one point were perilously close to crashing into the *Bonnie Lass* as they were lifted high by the billowing breakers and then plunged down into the depths.

'I should've gone with them,' Josh muttered. 'An extra pair of hands—' He broke off as his ship dipped into the angry swirling foam and disappeared from sight. He put his hand over his mouth to stop himself from crying out and Mary saw tears in his eyes before he dashed them away.

The wind was tearing at her hair and skirt and it was difficult to keep upright. She looked back to the crowd on Sandside to see if she could spot Tom and Jeannie and saw them wave to her. She lifted her eyes up to the castle headland, where another group of onlookers was gathered. They would be members of fishing families on the lookout for their own men; their eyes would be turned towards the North Bay and the Scalby sands where there was no safe anchorage. Any ships struggling there would have to make their way through the surging turbulent waters round the foot of the castle hill, avoiding the hidden rocks as they headed for the harbour.

Another shout went up from the south as the rocket launcher was fired towards a ship in distress. The line must have missed its mark, for another was immediately launched. A cheer went up as the lifeboat *Lady Leigh* hit the water in an attempt to reach the stricken ship, but it was followed by another shout of dismay as the ship they were heading for keeled over under the pressure of the enormous waves.

Mary turned back to gaze into the middle distance where she had last seen the *Bonnie Lass*. 'Can you see her?' she asked Josh, who was standing silently with his back to her, both hands clasped over his head.

He turned to her and there was anguish written on his face. 'No,' he said. 'I can't. Nor the *Castle*. I think they've both foundered.'

She looked beyond his shoulder. The sea was raging; she had never in her life witnessed such terrible power. Beyond the harbour and along the coastline for as far as she could see, even beyond the Spa, hundreds of ships and small boats were being tossed around like corks by the ocean's massive strength and destructive fury.

Even so, some vessels were managing to enter the harbour and Mary curled her fist, making a circle with her thumb and forefinger to focus the view. She said nothing to Josh as she watched; he had crouched down, his chin in his hands as if he was garnering his strength to face what was to come.

She caught her breath. A smack was making good progress towards port and she was almost sure . . . was it . . . or not? There were possibly five or maybe more on board. As it came nearer she saw that it was the *Castle*. But who was on board? The crew might have picked up anyone from a stricken vessel – or plucked somebody from the sea.

Finally she exclaimed, 'Josh! Look up.'

He lifted his head and glanced at her. She nodded towards the harbour and he slowly got to his feet. He gave a gasp, and as the smack came nearer he whispered, 'Is that our Ethan? It is! It's Ethan! Thank God.'

Ethan lifted a hand but it wasn't a joyful wave, and Mary knew with a sinking heart that his brother was probably lost. And Ethan himself had yet to learn that his mother was dead.

The smack took several attempts to tie up, for the water in the harbour was turbulent, but eventually after several crashes into the pier a rope was thrown and the boat secured. All the men were soaked to the skin, and Ted said they'd feared for their lives. Two of them had been thrown into the water and had to be rescued before an attempt could be made for the *Bonnie Lass*.

He clapped his hand on Josh's shoulder. 'I'm right sorry about thy other lad, Josh, and the other two crew. But we were too late. They'd gone overboard by the time we got there. I don't know how yon young lad survived. Sheer willpower, I'd say, for he'd been under water several times. He was clinging to the mast by his fingertips; it looked as though someone had tried to tie him to it but the ropes hadn't held.'

Josh had his arm round Ethan's shoulder. He could hardly speak he was so choked, but eventually he said, 'I'm grateful to you all. I'll thank you all my life for what you've done today in saving my lad.'

One of the other men spoke up. 'You'd have done the same for us. But there'll be some sorrow in the town afore long. This storm isn't finished yet. Best go home, young sailor,' he said to Ethan, 'and get

35

into some dry clouts afore you catch your death. You did well today. You're a brave lad.'

Mary watched and listened and thought that Ethan, though trembling and trying to keep back tears, seemed to grow in stature with the fisherman's praise, but he was looking towards his father, who nodded and in a voice thick with grief said, 'That he did. He'll have his own ship yet.'

It was close on midday when Mary collected Tom and Jeannie, and they were both shivering with cold. Even Tom made no fuss when their mother said they'd go home for some warming broth. She asked Josh and Ethan if they'd like to come back with her. 'There's plenty of soup,' she told them, 'and bread.'

Josh shook his head and Mary guessed that he would be bracing himself to break the news to Ethan about his mother and tell his daughters about Mark.

'Susan's lit a good fire,' she said, 'so you can get warm and dry, Ethan; and the babby's being fed. What name have you given him, Josh?'

Josh looked at her vaguely. It was as if he had forgotten about the child, and even his wife, for he blinked rapidly and then his face crumpled. 'Stephen,' he said huskily. 'It was what Lizzie wanted.'

Ethan glanced questioningly at his father and Mary turned away, ushering the children in front of her. Josh Wharton had a double sorrow and his wife's burial to arrange. Whether he would ever find his son was in the lap of the gods. Mark could have been washed out to sea, never to be seen again, just as her own husband had been, but she dearly hoped that the boy would be found and they could put him to rest next to his mother.

The storm continued to rage all the rest of the day and all night, and the following morning Mary went down to the shore once more. There were still many onlookers on the cliffs and the headland as well as those on the sands. Those down by the water were mainly fisher families, hoping against hope that their men would be saved, but there were other townsfolk too, and there was much praise for the lifeboat men who had risked their own lives. The coastguard, too, was praised for launching the rocket apparatus in their attempts to save the ships' crews.

Vessels had foundered all along the east coast and lay wrecked not only near Scarborough but along the sands of Burniston Bay, Cloughton, Robin Hood's Bay and Filey, or so she gathered from the people who waited, many of whom had been there all night. But the storm was not yet done. The angry seas were to claim even more lives before it blew itself out, but there were tales of great bravery as men such as the crew of the *Castle* and others like them battled against the force of nature to save lives.

When she returned home, Tom, who had been unusually quiet since they'd returned the previous day, asked her if he could go down to the sands.

'I'll be careful, Ma,' he volunteered. 'I'll not get in the way.' He'd pressed his lips together. 'I just want to watch the rescue.'

'All right, Tom,' she agreed, thinking he seemed pensive. 'Wrap up warm.'

He nodded, and then said, 'Do you think that Ethan'll go fishing again?'

'Why yes,' she said. 'It's his living. What else would he do?'

'Dunno,' he muttered. 'He must've been scared, mustn't he?' He lifted his eyes to his mother's. 'Being in the water! I would've been.'

She sat down and pulled him towards her and tenderly tucked a muffler into the top of his raincoat. 'Of course you would,' she said softly. 'Everybody is at some time, even experienced fishermen and seamen. The sea has to be treated with respect. That's why I'm always on at you to take care when you're messing about down by the slipway. If a boat should escape its moorings and drift out to sea, what would you do?'

He hung his head. 'Don't know, Ma.'

'When you reach ten I'll ask about and maybe some of the men will show you the rudiments of sailing and rowing, just to give you a taste of what it's like.' She kissed his cheek and said softly, 'If your da hadn't been lost he would have taught you, just like Josh Wharton's taught his sons.'

'He's still lost one, though, hasn't he? Mark's lost at sea.'

'Yes,' she said. 'But none of us can escape danger no matter what we do, Tom. And there are old men who've been going to sea all of their lives and have come to no harm.' She smiled at him. 'You might become one of those.'

'You mean like Josh Wharton?'

Mary laughed. 'I don't think he'd want to be called old, Tom, but yes, just like him.'

After Tom had left, Mary thought back over their conversation. She'd always thought that Josh Wharton was perhaps a few years older than her, maybe about thirty, but then she remembered that Mark had been nineteen and reasoned that he must be older, unless of course Mark wasn't his son and Lizzie Wharton had been wed before. She thought again about the age gap between Mark and his siblings: seven years between him and Ethan, the oldest of the five.

She shrugged and got on with cleaning their room and preparing food for midday. There would be no mending of nets today as the weather was too wild, but tomorrow, if the gale eased, there would be plenty of work on the damaged nets, and soon the Scottish herring girls would be coming down to Scarborough. Her mother Fiona and two others would stay with her; she'd give her mother her own place in bed with the children and she and her friends would bed down on the floor and she'd listen to the news from home.

CHAPTER FOUR

The residents at the bottom end of Sandside remarked to each other that it was the worst storm they could remember, and the following week several families were still waiting for news of their menfolk. Numerous ships had been wrecked, but many lives had been saved and the lifeboat crew, who had risked their own lives during the rescue, had saved more than twenty-five seamen. Seven from the brig *Mary*; five from the *Black-Eyed Susan*; five more from a Plymouth sloop and several others. Some bodies were washed up on the shores of the North Bay, Cloughton and Scalby, but some were never seen again, like Josh's son, Mark Wharton.

Mary had gone to see her mother-in-law, who was fretting that she couldn't get down to the shoreline to see what was happening.

'You don't need to go down,' Mary told her. 'It's enough that you know how it is. No sense in bring-ing back sad old memories.'

'Aye,' Aggie sighed. 'You're right. Fifteen years since Herbert was lost, four since Bob, and two since our Jack. It's not summat you ever forget. I don't need another great storm to remind me.'

Jeannie, watching and listening, noticed that her

grandmother's tongue was never sharp with her mother in the way it was with her. It seemed that she held back her caustic opinions when speaking to Mary.

On the way back down the Bolts, one of the narrow sets of steps which led to Sandside, she questioned her mother on this issue.

'Gran doesn't shout at you the same as she does at me,' she said, clip-clopping down. 'I've heard her telling off other grown-up folk, but never you. Why's that?'

Mary hid a wry smile. 'Once she did,' she told her daughter, 'when I first came to Scarborough and met your da. But I told her straight that I was going to marry her son and if she was going to cause trouble I'd persuade him to leave town and come back to Scotland wi' me.' She laughed. 'That did it. She'd lost one son already and didn't want to lose another, although of course' – her voice dropped – 'she did eventually. But you're onny a bairn, Jeannie. You must be polite to her and not answer back. She doesn't mean half of what she says in any case, so don't mind her too much.'

And, Mary thought, the old tyrant would be lost without me, which is why she's careful not to cross me. She sighed. I never thought that she'd become so reliant on me. And she remembered Aggie's comment when they spoke of Josh Wharton's losing his wife and eldest son on the same day.

'He'll be looking for a wife to look after his bairns,' Aggie had said. 'His eldest girl is hardly old enough to take on the household, not when there's another mouth to feed.'

'The babby's being looked after until he's able to

41

take a bottle,' Mary told her, 'and Susan is doing a grand job with the other bairns. He'll not want a wife yet a while.'

'Aye, well you watch out,' Aggie had warned her. 'Don't get yoursen drawn in there. You've enough on wi' your own bairns to clothe and feed.'

Mary had said nothing, but she knew what the old woman was thinking. If Mary should marry again into another family, she was afraid that there'd be no one to look after her. But she needn't have worried. The fisher families always looked out for each other.

'Can I play out for a bit, Ma?' Jeannie asked. She'd spotted Ethan sitting on a bollard by the harbour.

'Aye, for a wee while,' Mary said. She turned towards the quay on the West Pier to collect some fish for supper and called back, 'If you see Tom tell him to come home with you.' Tom had once again played truant from school.

Jeannie walked up to Ethan, who was gazing out into the harbour. He looked up but didn't speak.

'You all right, Ethan?' she asked softly.

'Yeh. Why wouldn't I be?'

Jeannie shrugged. 'Just asking, that's all.'

Ethan gave a big sigh. 'Folks keep on asking me all the time.'

He didn't seem cross, Jeannie thought. Just fed up, and rather miserable. 'It'll be because of your ma and Mark, I expect,' she said. 'And because you nearly drowned.'

He turned to look at her. 'But I didn't, did I? It was our Mark that did.'

She nodded silently, and then murmured, 'I'm glad you didn't. I think I would've cried if you had.'

'Would you?' He gazed at her. 'I know my ma

would have cried. She'd have cried for Mark as well, but she didn't know cos she'd died already.'

She let a moment elapse before asking, 'Were you scared? On the ship, I mean? I would have been.'

He let his gaze drift seawards again. 'When I was on my own I was,' he answered softly. 'It was exciting until Jed and Sammy went over and then it was just me and Mark. I was scared then. Mark helped me tie myself to the mast. It was that what saved me. If it hadn't been for him—' He broke off.

'He was a hero then, wasn't he?' she said. 'He saved your life.'

Ethan pressed his lips together, and then spoke in a choking voice and she knew that he was close to crying. 'Aye, he was. My brother a hero.'

Jeannie tentatively put her arm round his shoulder. It was what her mother did if she knew that Jeannie was upset about something and it always helped; it somehow made her feel comforted, but she wasn't sure it had the same effect on Ethan for he suddenly stood up, gave a loud sniff and wiped his nose on his sleeve.

'It's my ma's funeral on Monday,' he said. 'And Da says I have to go. He says I've to go and repor— erm, represent Mark, cos he was the eldest son and now I am. My da wasn't Mark's da,' he added. 'Mark's da used to work on the railway. He was run over by a train.' He turned to walk away. 'Be seeing you then, Jeannie.'

And for some reason those few words made her feel warm inside and she smiled and nodded and went in search of Tom.

*   *   *

The Scottish herring girls were due to arrive the following week and Jeannie was hopping with excitement. She was fond of her Scottish grandmother, who always brought them shortbread and rich fruit cake and told ghost stories in bed; such scary stories that even Tom hid under the blanket.

'Can I have a day off school?' she begged her mother. 'Like last time?'

'We'll see.' Her mother was non-committal. 'Your education is important.'

'But if I'm going to be a herring girl, I need to watch what you do.'

Mary smiled. 'Plenty of time,' she said. 'Don't be in a hurry to grow up. Life is short.'

Jeannie wasn't in a hurry to grow up. She didn't object to school generally; she was quick with numbers and good at reading. What she didn't like was to be indoors when the sun was shining and the golden sands and glittering sea beckoned and rock pools were warm and crawling with crabs; in the summer months and school holidays she and her friends used to race down the sands to see the fashionable visitors who had come to the Spa to take the medicinal waters, or peep at the ladies as they were driven down to the sea in bathing huts from which they would descend to dip their toes in the water, squealing at the coldness of the sea before quickly immersing themselves up to their necks and then rushing back to their huts to dry themselves. Jeannie and her friends, who were all perfectly at home in the water, would position themselves so that they could observe the antics of these strange creatures. The sight of the maid within the hut waiting with a large robe or towel to wrap the returning bather in sent the children into shrieks of laughter.

But now the town was preparing for the herring girls who followed the fishing fleet down the coast. They were not rich and they worked long hours for the money they earned but they were not afraid to spend it; bakers bought in extra flour and prepared to make large quantities of bread and cake and the hostelries polished their brasses, for where the girls were, so were the men. The girls took lodgings with the bottom-enders of the old town who opened up their homes for as long as they were there, usually about a month or until the fleet moved on to follow a shoal; then they packed up their possessions, their oilskins, boots or clogs, into their wooden trunks and moved down the coast to another port, to Lowestoft or Yarmouth.

Mary opened up her old wooden trunk and shook out her oilskin apron, and stood her wooden clogs by the door in readiness. Although she wasn't on an official agent's list, she was regularly employed by a local curer, who also took on her mother and one of her friends and put them to work as a team. Mary was going to ask them if she could do the packing of the barrels this time, as she thought she had lost some of her skill and speed with the gutting knife.

She walked Tom and Jeannie to school, making sure that Tom went through the door and didn't sneak out when he thought she wasn't watching. Then she went on to the railway station to await the train bringing her mother and the other herring girls.

The train steamed in and within a minute the platform was a seething hub of women and noise as they descended from the train, many of them carrying their trunks on their shoulders and others with packs on their backs, for these were strong and independent women. Mary craned her neck to seek her mother. She looked out for Fiona's red hair, brighter and more fiery than her own, but greying, she'd noticed the previous year.

She heard her name called, saw an arm waving and then another, and at last made out her mother and her friends Nola and Nell coming towards her.

Mary gave her mother a hug, and a big welcoming smile and a pat on the shoulder to Nola and Nell, whom she had known since childhood. 'Did you have a good journey?'

'Aye, well enough, but I'm fair weary now,' Fiona answered. 'These two have blethered all the way here. A guid cup of tea is what I'm after, lassie.'

'The kettle's on the fire and the teapot's on the table.' Mary laughed, shouldering her mother's box. 'Don't I know what you always want as soon as you get here?'

'Aye, you do. Where are the wee bairns? I thought they'd be here to greet me.'

'They would have been had they had their own way. They're in school,' Mary told her. 'You can have a rest before they come home, for you'll have none once they set eyes on you.'

'School!' her mother said benevolently. 'Well there's a thing. Tom too? Is he not too big for school now?'

'No, Ma. He's only nine. Three more years and then he can leave.' She led the way down the hill towards her cottage. 'He wants to finish and go fishing,' she said. 'Or at least he did,' she added thoughtfully.

'We had a big storm. A lot of boats were wrecked and he's not mentioned it since. I think he got scared.'

'Aye, and well he might,' Nola chipped in. 'Poor bairn. We heard about the storm. It ran havoc right along the coast. Held up the fishing – we were without work for nearly a week.'

Mary made them tea when they got home and Fiona drank hers down in seconds and then went to lie on the bed.

'Ah dinnae ken why I'm so weary,' she complained. 'I'm pure done in.'

'You'll feel better after a rest,' Mary told her. 'Sleep now and I'll keep Nola and Nell quiet; mebbe we'll go out for a wee stroll. The bairns'll wake you when they come home.'

Her mother heaved a sigh. Turning over, she tucked herself into her shawl and instantly fell asleep.

'It's hard on the old women,' Nola said softly. 'Not the gutting, they're as fast as anybody, but the travelling gets them down.'

'She's not old!' Mary exclaimed. 'She's not yet fifty. She's got years of work in her.' The thought of her mother giving up her work horrified her. Who would look after her? Mary's father was dead and both her brothers had large families to look after. 'She'd have to come and live here with me if she gave up work,' she thought aloud, and her companions glanced at each other.

'She'd never do that,' Nell said. 'Not in a million years.'

'She's tired, that's all,' Nola said. 'We all are, but we'll be fine in the morning. Come on now, let's go out. I want to buy a present from Scarborough.'

47

CHAPTER FIVE

Few of the children from the fishing families attended school during the first few days of the herring season. The boys positioned themselves as near as they dared to where the herring boxes would be deposited and shuffled about, nudging one another, ready to dart forward as soon as they saw any of the silver fish drop to the floor.

Jeannie cosied up to her grandmother. She was still sleepy, for they had been up since five o'clock and down at the harbour half an hour later, ready and waiting for the boats. Her grandmother, like the other herring girls, was decked out in her long rubber apron and boots, her head wrapped in a shawl which wound round her neck and fastened at the back leaving not a single red hair showing. In her hand she held her gutting knife.

'Don't come too close, lassie,' she told Jeannie. 'If I give you a nick with the blade you'll bleed to death.'

Jeannie took a step back. Her mother was always warning her about the gutting knife, but her grandmother's threat seemed especially grim.

'I just want to watch how you do it,' she said in a small voice. 'So that I'll know.'

'We'll teach you, have no fear,' Fiona told her. 'But

not now, you skinny malinky, not when we're about to start work. Look at my fingers. Why have I got them bandaged, eh? So that I don't cut myself, that's why.'

Jeannie nodded. She did know. All of the herring girls bandaged their fingers to avoid cutting themselves and to prevent the salt which was used for preserving the fish from entering a cut and stinging them or even turning them septic.

They were still waiting at half past six and everyone was becoming impatient.

'Come on, laddies, where are you?' Nola shouted. 'We're wasting the day.'

'And money,' another girl called. 'We've to get our quota in before the day is out.'

'Here they come!' someone else called. 'The lads are coming.'

All eyes turned to the fishing fleet, the Fifies and the Zulus, coming towards the harbour; a cheer went up and some of the girls broke into song.

'Wha'll buy my caller herrin' / they're bonnie fish and halesome fairin' / Wha'll buy my caller herrin' / new drawn frae the Forth.'

Mary smiled at their enthusiasm, though she felt emotional at being once more with her Scottish companions. They were jolly women full of laughter and anecdotes and worked hard all day often in difficult conditions; it was not always sunny as this morning was. If it was raining they continued as usual, trying their best to earn enough money to pay for lodgings, food and a ticket home at the end of the season.

The herring were unloaded from the ships' baskets, tipped into troughs and covered with rough salt so that they weren't so slippery to handle, and the girls began their job of sizing and gutting each fish, a task which took only seconds. In their team Mary had taken on the role of packer with her mother and Nola as gutters and hoped she hadn't lost her skill as she arranged the herring in tiers, slit bellies uppermost and heads towards the barrel edge, and sprinkled each layer with salt. Each barrel held about seven hundred fish, and the cooper who was watching Mary as she worked ensured that all the barrels were properly packed and salted.

Jeannie made herself useful by going on errands for the girls; sometimes running to the bakery to buy them bread or scones, fetching water from the pump, or carrying messages from one to another. Tom, she knew, was with the other barefoot lads, dashing to pick up the fallen fish and scooting off to hawk them.

At the end of the day, when they had packed thirty barrels of herring, Fiona's crew, as she called them, packed up for the night. It had been a reasonably good day, they agreed, but maybe it would be even better tomorrow. They rinsed off their aprons and boots and hung them to dry outside Mary's door, then went inside for supper.

Jeannie climbed into bed at Tom's side at about seven o'clock. They were both tired after the early start, but Tom was jubilant for he had made a shilling from his catch.

'I'll give you a penny to spend, Jeannie,' he said sleepily, 'and I'll keep tuppence cos I was the one to work for it, 'n' I'll give the rest to Ma.'

'Thank you,' she said, and as she drifted into sleep the last thing she heard was her grandmother saying, 'Have ye not found another man to wed,

Mary?' and her mother's reply: 'No, Ma. I'm not looking. Have you?'

Fiona glanced towards the bed. Seeing the children asleep, she said softly, 'Aye, as a matter of fact I have.'

'What!' Mary said, and Nell and Nola both grinned. 'You're joking!'

'No, I'm not.' Fiona flushed a little. 'I said I'd give my answer after this trip and I will. It'll be aye, I will; so this will be my last season with the silver darlings.'

Mary was speechless; then she swallowed. 'Who?' she said. 'Who are you going to marry?'

'Andrew Duncan. You don't know him. I met him at a ceilidh about three years ago.'

'A ceilidh! Three years ago?' Mary was aghast. 'What do you know about him?'

Fiona laughed. 'Wheesht, lassie. He's not marrying me for my money, that I can tell you.' Then she patted her daughter's knee. 'You're a long time deid, Mary, and I'm getting tired,' she said soberly. 'I can't keep on with this work for much longer. Andrew wants me to give it up and live with him. He's got a nice little croft with a few sheep and a mite o' money put by. Enough, he says, to last us out our days. He's nice,' she added. 'You'd like him.'

Mary was astonished. Not only that her mother was considering marrying again, but also that she had been at a ceilidh when Mary would have thought her dancing days were over.

'Did you two know?' she asked Nell and Nola.

They hummed and hawed. 'We guessed,' they said in unison.

'So you don't have to worry about me any more,'

Fiona added, 'for I know that you do. And the wee bairns can come and stay with us sometimes.'

'Don't worry,' Nola whispered as they bedded down for the night. 'We'll report back to you on how she is. We'll still be coming with the fleet, and the three of us can be a crew.'

But it means I shan't see her again, Mary thought the next morning as she checked the previous day's barrels and topped up those that had settled. The only time I get to see my mother is when she comes for the herring season; I can't afford to visit her in Scotland, any more than I can send the children. She felt happy for her mother, but sad for herself as the last link with her homeland seemed to be dissolving.

When Tom reached twelve he told his mother he would rather be a boat builder than a fisherman. He had been out on a few fishing trips and been very sick. The skipper who had offered him a place with his crew had expressed his doubts to Mary.

'If he's sick when the weather's calm,' he explained, 'he'll be a liability when it's rough. I don't want to disappoint the lad – I know he'd set his heart on following in his father's sea boots, so to speak – but I think you should talk to him about it.'

She asked Tom plainly what he wanted to do.

'I'm sick as a dog, Ma,' he said. 'Last time I went out we got as far as the Dogger Bank and I thought I was going to die! I'd rather build boats than sail in 'em.'

'You'd still have to go out in them to try them out, surely.'

'Aye, I would, to make sure they were seaworthy,

but not so often, not like fishing for a living and staying out at sea for a week or more.'

It turned out that Tom had already been to a boatyard to ask if he could do any work after school and had been given odd jobs of clearing up and polishing brasses. He had been complimented on his ability and it was suggested that his mother went in to see the owner.

'You're not mad at me, are you, Ma?' he asked. 'Not disappointed that I won't be a fisherman like my da?'

She ruffled his hair. 'Not a bit.' She smiled. 'It'll be one worry less if I know you're safe on dry land.'

For Jeannie's ninth birthday Mary had given her a pair of scissors and a mending needle and then a lesson in how to pick up the broken strands of torn net and loop and knot the new twine to repair the hole. At first Jeannie had found it difficult and the net heavy but eventually she mastered it; her mother had been pleased with her progress and the fact that Jeannie would have some means of earning money when she was old enough. Then, as she had promised, when Jeannie was ten she taught her how to gut fish. 'The secret is a very sharp knife,' she told her daughter as she showed her how to bind up her fingers. 'But that can slice fingers as well as fish bellies, so you have to be very careful.'

Mary's mother had married her Mr Duncan and Mary had received a postcard from him, saying that he hoped he would meet her one day and that she and the children were always welcome to visit them, at which Mary had sighed, knowing that she never would.

Nell and Nola had come the following year for the

herring, but they hadn't seen Fiona since her marriage and so had nothing to report.

'Wish someone would come along and tek care of me,' the unmarried Nell had complained when they returned to Fraserburgh. 'I'd have him like a shot.'

'But you don't want to wait until you're forty,' Nola had said, 'so out on the town we'll go tonight and find a couple of Scottish fisher lads.'

Which they did, and married them, but they still came to Scarborough for the silver herring.

Jeannie joined her mother and Nola when she was fourteen and made up the third in the crew, for Nell was pregnant with her second child. She was now quite swift with the knife and also adept as a packer, and out of the herring season she sat with her mother by the harbour and mended nets. When she was fifteen she began to walk out with Ethan.

It happened quite naturally. He never asked her especially to meet him, but whenever all the girls and boys congregated around the harbour or the sands the two of them paired off instinctively. He never held her hand as they walked, as she had seen other boys do with their girls, and she was too shy to take the initiative herself. He had never kissed her either, and she wanted him to do that too.

At nineteen he was tall and blond, with blue-green eyes and dark lashes. She knew that she loved him, but deduced that he had no feelings for her except for friendship. And I suppose, she thought hopelessly, I'll have to be content with that. But it was not enough; that much she knew.

'Is Ethan your beau?' her mother asked her one day as they sat together mending nets.

Jeannie gave a little shrug but didn't meet her

mother's eyes. 'He's a friend,' she murmured. 'Always has been.'

'He's a good lad,' Mary responded. 'Very steady. Very reliable. His da says he'll soon have his own smack.'

'I know.' Jeannie looked up this time. The sun was warm on her head and she gazed at the tossing white crests as they washed up on the sandy beach. 'But . . .' She didn't want to put her feelings into words, not to her mother, that Ethan, although she cared for him, didn't respond to her in the way that she wanted him to. He didn't show any emotion. 'I don't know how he feels about me,' she added lamely. 'He never says.'

'He's probably shy,' her mother said. 'Some lads are, even with girls they've known a long time. You've to beware of men who are all promises and kisses and other things to sweet-talk a lassie.'

Jeannie shook her head. 'Well, that doesn't happen with Ethan, Ma, so you don't need to worry about it.'

Mary hid a wry smile. She hadn't really been worrying about Ethan Wharton, just thinking that the calm and constant lad was an ideal prospect for her daughter. He was reliable and bound for a worthwhile life, according to his father, and she really hoped that Jeannie was prepared to wait for him to declare himself. And that really was the worry; for Jeannie, despite appearing to be placid and self-possessed, had, she felt, inherited her own youthful waywardness as well as the headstrong determination of her father.

CHAPTER SIX

The bracing air at Scarborough was considered to be beneficial to health, and as well as the gentry who came to take the medicinal waters, listen to the music in the Spa Hall or walk by the mere and flower gardens, the employees of manufacturing companies in the West Riding towns enjoyed a day at the seaside for their works outings. Men polished their boots and looked out their straw hats or bowlers; women and girls dressed up in their best hand-me-down gowns and decorated their hats with ribbons and flowers. They paddled in the sea, the men rolling up their trousers to their knees but never removing their hats, and the women drifting down to the edge in groups, egging each other on to lift up their skirts as far as their knees to splash in the ice-cold water. Often they strolled towards the Spa, where there might be a travelling show on the sands, or else visited the harbour to see the ships and watch the women mending nets, and stopped to buy a dish of cockles, or a crab or a lobster or a smoked herring to take home.

Mid-afternoon one day in the summer of 1887, Mary broke off her work to take a stroll along the quay. Jeannie stayed where she was; sometimes visitors stopped to talk and she enjoyed listening to the different forms of speech: the friendly charm of the West Riding folk who called her *luv*, the blunt tone of farmers' wives from the North Yorkshire Moors, and the softer flatter style of the East Riding. All of us from Yorkshire, she mused, and all sounding so different.

She put her head back and breathed in deeply, closing her eyes. A slight breeze fanned her face; the herring gulls were screeching overhead and she could hear their wings flapping as they swooped. They seemed to know when the visitors were here and spent more time searching for the titbits they threw for them than they did wheeling over the sea.

A shadow fell across her face and she opened her eyes. Someone was standing over her and it wasn't her mother. She put her hand to her forehead to see who it was. It was a man. A young one.

'Sorry,' he said, moving to one side. 'Were you tekking a rest?'

Jeannie picked up the twine again. 'No,' she said. 'No time for that.'

'Wish you'd mend my nets!' His voice was teasing.

'Bring them then and I will. For a price,' she added, looking more closely at him. He wasn't anyone she knew and he wasn't wearing working clothes so she guessed he was a visitor.

'Too far to come, though I reckon it'd be worth it.' He grinned down at her and she smiled back.

'How do you know?'

He crouched down beside her and handled the net, brushing against her hand. 'Looks pretty good to me.'

'Are you an expert then?' She gazed at him, so

57

close to her. He was dark-haired and clean-shaven, with brown eyes and a smiling mouth, and as he stood up she saw he was of medium height and strong build. He was also weather-browned and she guessed he might be a fisherman, but not from round here.

'Expert? Well, in a manner o' speaking I am, not on mending nets but on filling 'em.'

'Where are you from?' she asked curiously. 'Where do you fish from?'

He continued to look at her and she turned her eyes away from his scrutiny and began working on the net. 'Hull,' he said. 'That's my home town and where I earn my living.'

'Having a day off, are you?'

'Aye. 'Ship's being overhauled so I thought I'd tek 'train and come to Scarborough for 'day. I've not seen it from 'land side afore. I like it,' he added. 'Though I don't reckon there's much work when 'visitors have gone.'

'There's the fishing,' she told him. 'And the herring season.'

'Oh aye, I know that. Are you a herring girl?'

'I am.'

'Can you gut?'

She looked up at him. 'What a lot of questions. Course I can!'

He grinned. 'I'm just considering whether you'd mek me a suitable wife.'

She gasped at his cheek and put down her mending. 'I'm not old enough,' she said pertly. 'Even if I wanted to. I'm not yet sixteen.'

He appeared to consider. 'Will you tek a walk wi' me later on? What time do you finish?'

Jeannie looked towards the quayside and saw her mother coming back. 'Not till about six.'

'You didn't say no, then?' He grinned. 'So will you?'

She licked her lips. 'Dunno.' Should I? she thought. 'All right then. Do you . . . erm, do you know where the Grand Hotel is?'

He laughed. 'Oh aye!' He winked. 'I stop there every year! Where is it?'

'You can't miss it,' she said, glancing again towards her mother, who had stopped to speak to somebody. 'Walk back down to the end of the Foreshore Road and it's the biggest building you'll see; it's got four domes and is set back on St Nicholas Cliff. I'll meet you near the entrance, about half past six.'

He hesitated for a minute. 'You will come?' he said. 'It's just that I've to get 'train back at ten past eight.'

She swallowed. She felt strangely excited. 'I'll come.'

I didn't ask his name, she thought as he left. She felt rather guilty as her mother came back and sat by her side.

'Everything all right?' Mary asked.

'Yes.' Jeannie put down her net. 'I think mebbe I'll take a walk now,' she said. 'Just to stretch my legs. Shan't be long.' She set off in a casual manner away from the harbour and towards the Foreshore Road. She was curious to know if the stranger was alone, and where he would go next. She had suggested the Grand Hotel because it was a long way from the haunts of anyone she knew, especially Ethan, who would be down by the harbour later, preparing to sail.

And there he was in front of her, the stranger, walking with two other young men towards Blands Cliff which led up to the town, no doubt in search of a hostelry in which to quench their thirst.

Mary watched Jeannie, wondering where she was going. As she'd walked back from her break she had seen the young man talking to her and had deliberately slowed her steps, stopping to speak to an acquaintance.

She works hard does the lassie, she mused, turning her eyes away as she saw Jeannie start to head back; she deserves a little fun. But who was he? Not a Scarborough man, not one that I know at any rate, unless he's from up town. I bet he's a visitor come to flirt with the local girls. Still, no harm in that. She smiled as she recalled Jack's flirting with her on her first visit to the fishing port. Little did he know that I was determined to have him right from the start. He didn't stand a chance.

The afternoon seemed to drag for Jeannie. She made several mistakes with her knotting and had to undo her work and begin again, and at half past five she began to pack up.

'I've had enough for today,' she told her mother. 'I'm going home.'

Mary nodded. 'All right. I'll just finish this and then come up. Put the kettle on to boil and we'll have a cup of tea.'

'I'm not hungry,' Jeannie said. 'I might go for a walk and have supper later. Shall I get a crab? I've got some change.'

'Yes, good idea. Tom can have some cold beef when he comes in.'

Jeannie bought a crab from the fish market and

dashed up the hill towards home. She didn't want to tell her mother that she was going to meet someone but neither did she want to lie to her. But I won't, she persuaded herself. I *am* going for a walk. Just not by myself.

She put more wood on the fire and swung the kettle over it, then quickly washed her hands and face and brushed her hair, which was tangled from the wind, and changed her skirt. She always wore a heavy apron but sometimes the nets caught her skirt hem and left a black mark. She knew that she probably smelled of fish. Would he notice, she thought, or if he was a fisherman perhaps he wouldn't?

She had a quick cup of tea and a piece of bread and then told her mother, 'I'll eat later. Save me a bit of crab. Shan't be long.'

Mary smiled at her. 'Have a nice time.'

Jeannie stopped with her hand on the door. 'I'm only going for a walk, Ma.'

'But you might meet someone nice to talk to,' was her mother's rejoinder. 'Ethan stopped by, by the way. He asked where you were.'

'What did you say?'

'Just told him you'd gone home.' And he said nothing more, Mary thought. He just nodded and went to his boat and yet I felt that he was surprised that Jeannie wasn't there as usual, as if her absence had changed his day from its usual routine. As if he took it for granted that she would be sitting there, as if she were part of his life, and yet, she mused as Jeannie went out of the door, he has never, to my knowledge, asked her to share it.

Jeannie wasn't late for the meeting but she still hurried, anxious to be there first so that she could watch out for him. What if he doesn't come? she thought, and gave a mental shrug. No harm done. At least no one will know me up there, and nobody will know I've come on a fool's errand. But he was there already and standing on the hotel steps with his hands in his pockets as if he owned the place; as if he wasn't concerned that it was reputedly the biggest hotel in the whole of Europe.

He saw her from across the road and waved, then ran down the steps towards her. He took hold of both her hands. 'You came!'

'I said I would.'

'I bet fellers ask you out all 'time, don't they?'

'Maybe,' she said. 'Sometimes.'

'Do you want to go in for a drink?' He signified the hotel behind them by a toss of his head. 'Or go for a walk?'

She pretended to consider even though she knew they would never be allowed in. Carriages were drawn up outside and elegant women and important-looking gentlemen were being ushered into the hotel by uniformed lackeys.

'I'd rather go for a walk,' she said. 'I'll show you Scarborough if you like?'

He put his arm round her waist and drew her near. 'All right. Show me all 'best bits.'

She wriggled a little. 'The best bits are by the harbour where I work; up here is where the visitors come. But we could walk by the Spa; there might be music playing and the gardens are lovely. And if you haven't much time . . .'

'Let's do that,' he said. 'We can watch 'sea and listen to 'music and you can tell me all about yourself.' His thumb stroked her hip bone and she moved away from him. 'Don't you like that?' he murmured.

She flushed and shrugged. It was rather nice but she thought he was being forward. 'I've only just met you. I don't even know your name.'

He smiled. 'Harry,' he said. 'Harry Carr. What's yours?'

'Jeannie. Jeannette Marshall.'

He put his arm about her again. 'So now that we've been introduced, Miss Marshall, is it all right to do it?'

She couldn't help but smile. She'd never met anyone like him before. 'As long as that's all you do,' she said archly.

'Oh – oh!' He stood back and perused her. 'What else might I do?'

She was embarrassed now. Did he think she was being bold? That wasn't her intention.

He saw her confusion and was contrite. He held her hand. 'Onny teasing,' he said softly. 'I won't do owt that you don't want me to. Come on, let's walk.'

They walked down the hill, taking the path past the squares with their elegant houses and private central gardens and dropping down to the footpath to the Spa. They could hear music and the muted cry of sea birds, and the sea was gently lapping on the rocks below. Jeannie thought it was the most beautiful place she knew.

'Don't you think it's lovely?' she asked. 'Is Hull like this?'

He shook his head. 'Hull's nowt like this. Hull's a busy lively town. It's a grand town to live in, if you're in work. And there're lots o' shops if you like that sort o' thing, and history, loads o' history. This is nice, though,' he conceded. 'If you like living near 'sea. Bet it's cold in winter!'

'No more than anywhere else. It's very bracing. So what's special about Hull?'

'Well, it's home isn't it? It's where my family live, where my mates are, where 'fishing is. If you're a fisherman in Hull there's allus work.'

'Same here,' she said.

He suddenly turned towards her and pressed her against the sea wall, both arms round her. 'Let's stop talking, shall we?' He bent his face towards hers. 'I want to kiss you,' he said. 'I don't want to talk about everyday things.' He kissed her mouth hard, taking her breath away.

She pushed him away. 'Not here!' she said. 'People will see!'

'What people? I don't see any people.'

'I live here,' she said, turning her head away. 'It's broad daylight. Someone might see.'

'Hoity-toity! Don't Scarborough folk kiss?'

She held his hand tight, for he was about to hold her round the waist again, but she could see that he was laughing at her.

'Course they do – I expect, anyway. But not where their friends or family can see them.'

He grinned at her. 'That's 'first time you've been kissed, isn't it? Didn't you like it?'

I did, she thought, but said, 'It was all right.'

'Come on!' He grabbed her hand and began to race her back towards the Foreshore Road.

'Where?' She laughed, exhilarated. Was this what being wayward was like?

'I'll show you!' He ran with her, dodging people

coming in the opposite direction. 'I found some-where earlier, a cut-through!'

Jeannie wrinkled her eyebrows. What was he talk-ing about? But he raced on, dragging her with him.

'Here,' he said. 'In here.'

'What about it?' she said. 'There are lots of them. They're short cuts up from the sands to the town.'

He pulled her into a narrow alley with a steep flight of steps at the end of it. 'Yes,' he said softly. 'And out of sight of prying eyes. We've got them in Hull too; they lead from one street into another, except in Hull they don't have steps. Come on. Nobody'll see you in here – it's too dark.'

'But . . .' Residents used these passageways all the time, but at this time of day most of them would be at home eating a meal, as she should have been doing.

'But nothing,' he murmured, taking her face in his hands and putting his lips close to hers. 'Kiss me, Jeannie. Kiss me now, cos I've a train to catch.'

CHAPTER SEVEN

And so she did. She kissed him as passionately and fervently as he kissed her until she was dizzy and breathless and wondered at herself for never having guessed that it could be like this. If she had ever thought of Ethan kissing her, and she had, often, it had always been a tender and loving kiss, not full of fire and longing as these kisses were, so much longing that her legs felt weak and her body melted.

'I've got to go,' he gasped at last, pulling away. 'I'll miss my train. Wait for me, Jeannie.'

'How long?' she whispered. She swallowed, and licked her swollen and tender lips.

'Until I come,' he murmured in her ear. 'Just wait.'

They ran up the steps and she hurried with him through the town to the railway station. His friends were already there, and two girls with them. The men called to Harry to hurry and Jeannie felt their eyes upon her. One of them grinned and the other winked as they drew near, and she didn't know what they meant by it. Harry kissed her again, murmuring once more that she must wait, and dashed aboard as the guard waved his flag and the train got up a head of steam.

She waited until the train steamed out. The two

girls glanced at her as they walked past. She didn't know them. Town girls, she thought, noting their rouged faces and scarlet lips. Their gaze moved from top to toe as if they were assessing her, and both wore a cynical grin.

'Night, darling,' one of them said. 'Time you were in bed.'

Jeannie thought they were drunk for they cackled with laughter, rolling from side to side with their ridiculous bustles swaying on their vast behinds and the feathers fluttering in their hats.

She walked slowly back home and cut down the Bolts on to Sandside. She had used these familiar passageways most days of her life; they were quite dark now as the light was fading and there were no gas lamps, but she had never been afraid, and now these ancient rights of way held a special signif-icance for her. She knew that from now on whenever she cut up or down them she would think of Harry. Wait for me, he had said. And she would.

'Where've you been, lassie? I was beginning to worry.' Her mother got up from her chair to cut some bread. 'You must be hungry. I saved you some crab.'

Mary's glance was keen. Something's happened. Jeannie's face was flushed, animated. She's been out with a lad, Mary surmised. But not with Ethan, for I saw him set sail.

'Have you been out with friends?' she asked. 'You're not usually so late.'

'It's only half past eight, Ma. That's not late.' Jeannie knew her mother would expect some kind of explanation. 'I met a friend. We walked to the Spa and then up town. We were just talking.'

'Would this be a new friend?' Mary took the kettle off the fire and made a pot of tea as she talked. 'You'll be careful, Jeannie?'

'Of what?' Jeannie washed her hands at the sink and sat at the table. 'I said we were just talking.' And kissing, she thought, her eyes glazing.

'It's just – well, if you don't know somebody very well, you have to learn to trust first.'

Jeannie looked up at her mother and licked her lips. Could she tell? Does she know by my face that I've been kissing someone?

'When you first met my father – how did you feel?' she asked. 'Did you know that he was the one you were going to marry?'

Holy Mother, Mary thought. Is it worse than I thought? She's only fifteen! And you were seventeen, a voice in her head reminded her.

'He was the one I hoped to marry,' she said softly. 'I was completely bowled over by him, but I asked around, tried to find out about him, asked who knew him and of course everybody did. Every lassie who lived on Sandside wanted him.' She smiled. 'But he wanted *me*, and nobody else!'

She gazed at her daughter, who was picking at the crab in a desultory way. 'I thought that you and Ethan . . .' she murmured.

Jeannie nodded. 'So did I,' she said. 'I care for Ethan, but he never says anything. Perhaps he thinks I'm too young.'

'Which you are,' her mother agreed. 'Does he see any other girl?'

Jeannie shook her head. 'I don't think so. I'd know if he did.' But I think it's too late, she thought. If Ethan had kissed me in the way that Harry did and

68

asked me to wait for him, I would have done; but not now. There was a tinge of regret in the thought, for she felt that Ethan would have been true, whereas Harry . . . She heaved a sigh. I know nothing of him. He might be married already – except he did ask me to wait. Was he just fooling around with a girl from another town? I hope not, cos I'll wait anyway.

And so she did. All of that autumn and winter too, past Christmas and into cold January, but he never came. Ethan suspected something, she thought, for once or twice she found him looking at her in an enquiring way when she made an excuse not to go for a walk when he suggested it.

'Is there something wrong, Jeannie?' he asked at last.

'No.' She shrugged. 'It's too cold. Don't feel like going out.' And it was true, she didn't. The air was no longer bracing, but cold and raw, the sea no longer sparkling but dull and grey, reflecting the low sky.

In February she turned sixteen. The day was bright and sunny and bitterly cold and she made the decision that she would wait no longer. He wasn't coming, that was certain. I can't waste my life waiting for someone I don't know. Someone who has a life that I know nothing about.

There wasn't much work on the nets just now, not enough for her and her mother, so Jeannie applied for a job at a ship's chandlers. It was warmer working indoors and she soon familiarized herself with the marine hardware, the navigation rulers, pumps and anchor chains which she couldn't lift without assistance. She knew most of the customers and enjoyed the banter, and so one March Saturday as she left the shop at four o'clock she had more of a spring in her step than she had had for a long time.

She walked home along Sandside with her eyes on the sea as always; the sun had almost set and its rays suffused the waves, turning them to a sparkling flush. She turned her gaze landwards, and there he was.

'Jeannie!' He looked as she remembered him. The same grin, the same dark eyes, and the full mouth which had so enchanted hers.

'I'd given up on you,' she said softly.

'Don't do that, Jeannie. I said I'd come.'

'You didn't say when.' She wanted to cry with relief that he was here.

'I couldn't. Work, you know.'

She did know. Fishermen had little time off. 'You could have sent a postcard,' she said weakly.

He pursed his lips. 'I didn't know your address. How would it have found you?'

'Everybody on Sandside knows me.' Except the postman, she thought. We hardly ever get letters.

He took hold of her hand. 'I'm here now. Are you pleased to see me?'

'Yes,' she murmured. 'I am; it's just been a long time.'

'Have you reached sixteen?' His eyes stayed on her face.

She nodded. 'Last month.'

Jeannie suddenly dropped his hand. Ethan was striding towards her from the harbour. Her mother always said that he looked like a Viking and he does, she thought. He wore a beard in the winter; it was thick and fair, and his long hair was the same.

'Jeannie?' Ethan spoke to her but looked at Harry. He towered over the two of them.

'This is Harry Carr, Ethan,' she said nervously. 'He's a fisherman from Hull.'

Ethan put out his large hand to shake Harry's. 'Looking for work?' he asked and his eyes were like steel.

'No, no. Just here for 'day. Ship's laid up till tomorrow.'

That's what he said last time, Jeannie recalled. Does he lose pay when that happens? To her knowledge, Ethan was never without work. If his boat needed repair then he usually worked on it himself.

Ethan nodded and turned back in the direction from which he had come. 'See you later, Jeannie?' There was a question mark hovering and she gave a slight nod.

'Is he your feller?' Harry asked, gazing at Ethan's broad back.

'I've known him since we were bairns,' she said casually. 'We're really good friends.'

'Aye.' Harry looked at her. 'I can see that. But he thinks you're his girl.'

She laughed, nervously. 'I don't think so. He's a bit shy is Ethan. He probably feels comfortable with me.' Those were her mother's words coming out of her mouth. In truth she still didn't know what to make of Ethan and his feelings towards her.

'So are you mine?' he asked, drawing her close.

Jeannie felt her body melting, her legs weak and her mind numb. She nodded. 'I said I'd wait, didn't I?' she said softly. 'And I have.'

He bent and kissed her cheek. He smiled. 'Good. Come on, let's tek a walk.'

She held his hand along Sandside and didn't really care who saw them; they stopped for a plate of cockles which Harry chewed and then spat out. 'Yuck,' he said. 'Never did like them.'

Jeannie laughed; her spirits had been raised sky-high. 'Staple diet on Sandside. Cockles and crabs – and herring, of course.'

He put his arm round her. 'We won't live in Scarborough then. We'll have to live in Hull.'

She felt as if the breath was drawn from her body. 'What do you mean?'

'When we get married.' He grinned down at her.

'You'll have to ask my mother first.'

'All right. Now?'

'No – not today! I've got to think about it.'

'Fair enough,' he said. 'But don't tek ower long. I'm an impatient man. I want you, Jeannie,' he said softly. 'Don't mek me wait.'

Her mind worked swiftly. Her mother wouldn't be pleased. She'd want to know all about him and what his prospects were, but Jeannie was determined to marry him. She thought of St Mary's church up by the castle. That's where she'd like to be married. A simple wedding, of course: they wouldn't have much money. She imagined coming out on Harry's arm and seeing her home town spread out below.

'I won't. I want to marry you, Harry,' she said shyly. 'Would you like to take a walk up to the castle? There's a fine view from up there. You can see the North Bay as well as the South.'

'All right,' he agreed. 'But I mustn't miss my train. I'm catching an earlier one. I've been hanging around all afternoon looking for you.'

'Are your friends with you?'

'No.' He seemed to hesitate. 'I came on 'spur of 'moment this time. They're all in work.'

72

She looked questioningly at him.

'What I mean is,' he qualified, 'they're on different ships from me. I might look for a different company to work with when I get back.'

'I think you should,' she said. 'You need to be sure the vessels are seaworthy. It doesn't sound to me as if the one you're on is!'

He squeezed her waist. 'Listen to 'expert!' he teased.

'I'm serious,' she said. 'My brother Tom's an apprentice boat builder. I listen to him telling us how important it is. We all know the sea has to be taken seriously.'

'I know that,' he said sharply. 'I've been working on ships all my working life.'

She'd touched a raw nerve and was puzzled, but said nothing more on the subject. They continued their walk up towards the castle, taking all the short cuts through alleyways and up steep steps, and she made him laugh when she said they were in Paradise. He stopped and took a breath and then kissed her passionately on the mouth. An old woman shouted at them to move on, and they laughed and continued.

'I'll know when I'm in paradise, and it won't be here in full view of everybody,' he whispered in her ear, and once again she felt weak at the thought of what he was suggesting.

They paused by St Mary's church. 'This is an ancient church,' she said solemnly. 'My parents and grandparents were married here.'

Harry glanced at the clock on the tower. 'Come on. We haven't much time before I'm due back at 'station.'

She was disappointed that he hadn't said that

here, then, was where they would be married too. But perhaps, she thought, men are not as romantic as women about continuity.

They reached the castle grounds and headed towards the edge of the cliff to look down. Jeannie pointed out the North Bay, accessible by a pathway down the cliff, and the red-tiled roofs of the town in the South Bay.

'It's the best place in the world,' she sighed.

'How do you know?' He laughed. 'Where else have you been?'

'Nowhere,' she said. 'But I still know.'

'You must come to Hull,' he said, his arm round her waist. 'You'd like it there.'

She allowed him to lead her back across the grass towards the ruined castle and they entered its broken walls. 'I'd like to come,' she said, and didn't object as he unbuttoned her blouse. 'Wh-whereabouts do you live?'

'Hessle Road,' he murmured, fingering her nipples. 'All 'fishing community live there.'

Jeannie swallowed. 'I don't think you should do that,' she whispered.

'Why? Don't you like it?' He gently pushed her down on the grass and ran his hands over her belly. 'I'm sure that you do, Jeannie. It's what you want, isn't it? Say that you do and you'll make me a very happy man.'

His hands roamed her body, beneath her blouse, beneath her skirt, touching her flesh so that she wanted to moan. There was no one to see or hear; not another single person was there, only the two of them and the sea birds and the family of rabbits she could see from her position on the grass.

'I do like it, yes,' she breathed. 'But – I think we should wait.'

'I've waited.' His voice was hoarse. 'Waited and waited and I want you, Jeannie. Do you know what that means?'

'I think so.' She could barely speak.

'And you needn't think that I'll change my mind about marrying you, cos I won't, but I need you now. I'm desperate for you, Jeannie. I need to show you how much I want you.'

He pressed himself upon her and his warm moist mouth found hers, his tongue found hers and his fingers found places that she hadn't known were there.

She cried, 'I love you, Harry.'

'I know,' he said. 'I know. So everything will be all right, Jeannie. Everything will be all right.'

CHAPTER EIGHT

Ethan called at their house the following morning. Mary opened the door. 'Won't you come in, Ethan?'

The two families had become quite close since the death of Ethan's mother. Susan had taken on the role of mother to her sisters and baby brother Stephen and Mary had helped as much as she could, but it was quite unusual for Ethan to call unless for something specific.

'Will Jeannie come for a walk?' he asked, hovering on the doorstep. 'I need to talk to her.'

Jeannie appeared behind her mother. 'I'll just get my shawl,' she said nervously, and Mary looked from one to another. They were both tense, and Jeannie had hardly spoken last evening when she had come in late from work. Had they had a quarrel? she wondered.

'Where do you want to go?' Jeannie asked, once they were outside.

'Don't mind,' Ethan said. 'Up to the castle if you like?'

'No,' she said quickly. 'Not the castle. Let's go up to town.'

She couldn't bear to go to the castle, not after yesterday. She would always think of it now as her and Harry's special place. He hadn't allowed her to accompany him to the railway station, saying that he hadn't much time and would have to run, but she hadn't gone home immediately. She had sat by the sea taking deep breaths and thinking of how wonderful it had been with Harry; she had been nervous and doubtful but he had been tender, though persuasive, constantly assuring her that it was perfectly all right because they loved each other.

She and Ethan walked in silence for a while until at last Ethan said, 'How do you know Harry Carr?'

'Oh, erm, I met him last year. We just got talking, you know how it is. And then we bumped into each other again.'

'No, I don't know how it is,' Ethan muttered. 'He seemed very familiar considering you've only met twice.'

'We – seemed to have things to talk about,' she said lamely.

'He was holding your hand,' he said, 'and he kissed you. I looked round and he was kissing you.'

He stopped walking and turned to her. It seemed that he was waiting for a response.

Jeannie looked away from him. She couldn't meet his eyes. 'Yes,' she murmured. 'He did. Several times.' When she thought of Harry's lips on hers, his hands on her body, she trembled. 'I wanted him to.'

It was as if she had struck him, for he gave a small gasp. Then he took her face in his hands and turned her towards him so that she had to look at him.

'I thought that we – that you and I – that we were a twosome – I took it for granted that we were.'

She took his hands away from her face and shook

her head. 'Took it for granted?' she whispered. 'Without a word to me? You never so much as hinted that that was what you wanted, or asked me how I felt.'

'We've known each other since we were bairns, Jeannie! Was there ever any need for words?' There was pain and bewilderment on his face. 'Surely you knew that I always cared for you? That one day, when I had my own smack and was earning money and you were old enough, we would be wed?'

She wanted to cry. If she had known . . . but if she had known and still met Harry, would it have made any difference? She didn't think it would. Harry meant desire and excitement, and temptation to which she had succumbed. Sensible Ethan would always be dependable and loyal and she still cared for him, but not in the same way. Not any more.

'You should have asked me, Ethan,' she whispered. 'I didn't know, and – and it's too late now. Harry wants to marry me and I've said that I will.'

He put his hands to his head. 'I can't believe you're telling me this, Jeannie.' His face was a picture of misery. 'I can't believe it. Don't *want* to believe it. You're shattering dreams I've had ever since I was a lad.'

'I'm sorry, Ethan.' And she was. She tried to take his hand but he pushed her away and began to walk off, but then he turned back.

'I'll walk you home,' he said. They went back down the hill in silence.

'Something the matter?' Mary asked when Jeannie went in the house. 'You've not been long. There's no trouble, is there?'

'No. At least – yes.' Jeannie felt regret that her long

78

friendship with Ethan was broken and she burst into tears.

'What is it, lassie? Something's wrong. Can you not tell me about it?'

'I saw Harry again yesterday.' Jeannie saw the question on her mother's face. 'I met him last year, remember? He came looking for me after work yesterday. He wants us to be married, Ma.' He didn't actually say will you marry me, she thought. But that's what he meant. 'And I want to.' She wiped her wet cheeks. 'And Ethan saw us together and came over and I introduced them and that's why Ethan came just now. He wanted to know about him, and – and I told him and he's upset.'

She began to cry again. 'I didn't want to hurt Ethan, but what could I do? He said that he thought – that he thought that he and I would get married when I was old enough. But Ma, he never ever said! He took it for granted that I knew. And I didn't.' She wept. 'I didn't.'

Her mother sat down. 'And are you sure that you want to marry this Harry? Are you sure that he hasn't sweet-talked you? Is he going to come and see me? Cos you know you can't be married without my say-so.'

Jeannie snuffled. 'I know, and he said he would come and see you, but I wanted to think about it first. And I have thought about it and I do.'

Her mother took a breath. 'So,' she said slowly. 'When is he coming again so that we can talk about it? You're only just sixteen, Jeannie. It's a big step to take with someone you hardly know. What do you know about his background, his family? Is he in regular work? All these things might not seem

79

important when you meet someone you think is special, but believe me they are when you're bound to someone for the rest of your life.'

'He didn't say when,' Jeannie said. 'It'll be when he has another day off, I expect. He's a fisherman. We know what it's like. If there's fishing to do then that's what they do. He has to earn a living.'

But it was different in Hull, from what she had gathered. The fishermen of Scarborough were mostly self-employed, or at least if they didn't own their own boat they often had a share in one. In Hull, so she had heard, there were big companies with several vessels and men were employed to work them. They were also away for longer periods, sailing to Arctic waters for deep-sea fishing.

The joy she should have felt was somehow eroded because of Ethan's misery, and although she didn't try to avoid him they didn't meet, not even accidentally. She still went about her daily business and joined her mother down by the harbour as before, but her path never seemed to cross Ethan's.

'Have you seen Ethan, Ma?' she asked one night. 'I want to talk to him. I still want us to be friends.'

'I don't think that'll happen, Jeannie,' her mother said quietly. 'He's hurt. He's licking his wounds. He'll talk to you when he's ready.'

One morning Mary saw Josh and called him over. 'There's trouble between our bairns,' she said.

'Is there?' Josh looked puzzled. 'Is that why Ethan's like a bear with a sore head? I've not had a word out of him for days.'

Mary told him the story as she knew it as she continued knotting and splicing the net on her knee. Josh crouched down beside her.

'I always thought that they—'

'Aye, so did he, but ne'er a word to Jeannie. This is the trouble, Josh,' she said, glancing at him. 'If nothing is said how is anyone to know?'

He straightened up. 'It's been hard, Mary. Very hard, bringing up bairns without a mother. A double tragedy for Ethan, losing Mark on the same day. No wonder he says so little.' His face softened. 'And my poor Susan, she's lost her childhood trying to be a ma to the little ones, and raising Stephen.'

'She has,' Mary agreed, and wondered if Josh had ever noticed the occasions when she had looked after his younger children for a few hours so that his daughter could have some time to herself or with friends. Susan was eighteen and her hopes, if she had ever had any, of having a husband of her own must be rapidly fading with so little opportunity to meet people. Her younger sister Ida was courting a fisherman. The youngest girl, and Stephen, who was now eight, no longer needed constant attention, but Susan's role of housekeeper to her father and surrogate mother to her siblings was a duty it would be difficult for her to abandon.

'You should have married again, Josh,' she murmured. 'It would have been best for you all.'

Josh nodded. Like Ethan he was not communicative; he kept his worries close to his chest. 'Mebbe I should. But what woman would've taken on a man with a house full of children?'

She smiled. He was a handsome amiable man. 'A few, I should think, but your bairns are almost all full grown now, and maybe Susan won't want to relinquish her position.'

'But Ethan,' he said. 'What to do about him?'

'Nothing,' Mary replied. 'There's nothing to be done. Jeannie has set her sights and her heart on this fellow Harry. I only hope she's not making a big mistake.'

Josh heaved a sigh. 'I hope not too, but Ethan's heart will be broken, I know that. I know my lad.'

March turned to April and the days were getting longer, the evenings cool but pleasant. Jeannie took to taking rambling walks after work, to parts of Scarborough which she normally wouldn't visit. She walked beyond and above the Spa, admiring the rose gardens and the tree planting that was taking place for the benefit of visitors coming to the resort. Sometimes she walked in the parks, or gazed through the railings at the locked square gardens to which only the private householders had a key.

Sometimes she climbed the hill overlooking the North Bay and stood gazing at the power of the sea as it hit the rocks, or watched the ships dipping between the watery ridges of the choppy ocean. This eastern coastline was notorious for its shifting currents and the vagaries of its weather, which could change instantly from bright sunshine to enveloping sea mist, from gentle breeze to gale-force wind.

She made her way down the cliff and walked along the sands almost to the boundary of Scalby before turning about and returning home. There were times when she wished she could take out a boat and row or sail in the bay and round the headland towards the harbour. There was talk of a road or promenade being built to join the north and south bays, but it had come to nothing, though plans were being drawn up for pleasure gardens and landscaping and work had already begun to clear a woodland ravine.

Jeannie needed these walks alone as she slowly began to realize that there was a possibility that Harry might not come back; that what he had told her, of his love and of their marriage, might not be true. She had given him her address so he could no longer claim not to know where she lived, as he had said last time.

By the end of May she was becoming anxious and towards the middle of June she was decidedly so.

On the longest day of the year Mary rose and with a shawl over her nightgown began the breakfast; she took the pan of porridge from the fire where it had been simmering all night, stirred it, salted it and poured it into three bowls on the table, then riddled the coals and placed the kettle over the heat.

'Come on, Jeannie,' she called. 'Six o'clock. Time you were up.'

Jeannie rolled out of bed and within a minute was heading for the outside privy. Mary heard the retching and placed a hand over her mouth.

'Dear God,' she muttered, 'please. No. Not that!'

'I knew that crab was off,' Jeannie gasped as with watery eyes she stumbled back through the door. 'Tom! Was that one of yours?'

Tom had purchased crab and lobster baskets which he took out at weekends. He was doing well with the boat-building company and at seventeen was assured of a regular job. He had also conquered some of his fear of sailing and the baskets were a sideline to bring in a little extra money.

'Nowt wrong with my shellfish!' he said. 'Anyway, I had some and so did Ma and we're all right.'

Mary said nothing, but her hand shook as she dished up the porridge and beckoned Jeannie to sit down.

Jeannie wiped her hand across her mouth. 'I'm not hungry,' she muttered. 'I've definitely had something that disagreed with me.'

'Yes.' Her mother's voice was subdued. 'I would say that you had.'

CHAPTER NINE

For Mary there appeared to be only one possible explanation for Jeannie's nausea, and when she thought back to the day her daughter, so flushed and wide-eyed, had told her she wanted to marry the Hull fisherman, the interpretation seemed totally plausible.

As she walked down to the harbour to work on the nets she felt weighed down with shock and anxiety. What will we do if he doesn't honour her and the child by marrying her? When Mary had first met Jack and they had fallen instantly in love with each other, he had treated her with respect and never asked her for more than she wanted to give.

But this Harry! We don't know who he is; he could be married already. The thought of Jeannie bringing up an illegitimate child without the support of its father filled her with fear. Trying to earn a living is hard enough; we're barely able to make ends meet as it is. And in a few years' time she would lose Tom's small contribution. Although he had not yet completed his apprenticeship, he was courting the daughter of one of his colleagues and already talking of marriage and saving to set up a place of their own once he was earning a living wage. Yet despite everything, the idea of having a small child tottering about and playing in the house also gave her a frisson of pleasure. By the time Jeannie was six she had wanted more children, but her husband's tragic death had put an end to that possibility.

We'd manage, I expect, she considered, and not a word of censure penetrated her thoughts. Only the practicalities of dealing with the problem concerned her.

Granny Marshall will have plenty to say, she thought as she arrived at the harbour yard where the nets in need of repair were draped on racks; she nodded and raised her hand in greeting to the fishermen and the other women who were also starting work. Aggie had become even more difficult over the last few years and nothing anyone did or said ever pleased her.

At midday Mary left the yard and took a walk towards the harbour. A fleet of drifters was coming in, and Josh's boat was among them. He and another fisherman had recently bought the *Bonnie Lass Two*, which could hold about sixty drift nets. They had also invested in a steam capstan which made hauling the full nets on board a little easier, although it was still hard work and they needed a crew of seven or eight, but the bigger catch meant it was worth it.

Josh called to her from the deck. 'Everything all right?'

'Yes, thank you,' she lied. 'As right as can be. All right with you? A good catch?'

He nodded. 'Pretty good.' He grabbed a couple of herring from the deck and leapt off the boat. 'Here.' He handed them to her. 'Fresh as they come. Ethan seems to be more settled. He's not as morose as he was. Mebbe they're seeing each other again – him and Jeannie, I mean.'

She thanked him for the herring and then said, 'Don't think so.' She didn't meet his eyes. 'I think we can forget about that.'

He gazed down at her for a second before saying, 'Pity.' He turned to go back on board, where the other men were filling the baskets ready to send them to the curers, but then he paused. 'I was wondering – now that we've got a bigger boat would you consider working on our nets as a regular job? These nets are thinner and they snag quite a bit. Simon and I will do the soaking, shan't expect you to do that, but if we knew that somebody reliable could do the mending it would free us up.'

'Yes, I would,' she said, delighted to be offered regular work. She was hardly ever idle, but there were lots of women just as capable as she was of mending and braiding and it would be a comfort to know she need not worry about slack periods any longer.

Fishermen were very particular about their nets and many preferred linen or hemp over cotton, but sea water rotted them all and, to prevent this damage, they were soaked in vats of chemical solution to deter further disintegration.

'You wouldn't mind if I worked on anybody else's, would you?' she asked, mindful that they would need as much money as it was possible to earn. 'If yours were finished? Yours would be the priority, of course.'

'No, course not. If you like I'll ask Ethan and his partner if they'll give you theirs on a regular basis too.' Ethan had shares in a boat and seemed to be making a reasonable living.

She accepted gratefully, feeling less downcast than she had been, and tried not to dwell on the future and its problems.

The next morning Jeannie was up first and immediately went outside, where she could be heard retching.

'What's up with Jeannie?' Tom asked. 'Has she caught summat?'

'I think she has,' his mother admitted.

'Hope it's not catching,' he said. 'We've the launch of a new coble in a couple of weeks and I can't take any time off.'

'I shouldn't worry about that,' Mary said dismally, and when he had left for work and Jeannie was toying with her gruel she decided that the time had come for discussion.

'Are you going to tell me, then?' She sat down opposite Jeannie. 'What's making you sick?'

Jeannie's face was white, and her lips were pale as she faced her mother. 'I don't know, Ma.'

'Don't you? Can't you guess?' Mary took a deep breath. 'You must have some idea, Jeannie.'

Jeannie's eyes filled with tears and her mouth trembled. 'I've missed my flux three times,' she whispered. 'Ma, I'm frightened. Am I pregnant?'

'Are you asking me, Jeannie?' her mother said quietly. 'There's only one way to get pregnant and you are the only one likely to know. Did you and Harry . . .'

She couldn't bring herself to ask outright if Jeannie had allowed this stranger to debase her. Had she been willing, or had he committed an outrage? She's just a bairn, she thought. Just a wee bairn.

But Jeannie was nodding her head and reaching

for a handkerchief to wipe her eyes and blow her nose. 'I loved him,' she wept, rocking to and fro. 'And he said he loved me and that it would be all right. But now he's gone and I don't know if he's coming back.'

Mary privately thought that there was no chance in the world that he would come back, and beneath her breath she cursed him with all the vile words she knew but never uttered.

'We'll wait another month so that we're sure,' she said. 'And then we'll think of what we can do.'

'I'd want to keep it,' Jeannie cried.

'That you will,' her mother agreed. 'We'll have no back-street abortion. It's a life we're talking about, if in fact you have been caught.' She sighed and stood up. 'We'll wait and see.' She raised her head. 'Now, get ready for work. You've a living to earn.'

'Yes, Ma,' Jeannie said meekly. 'I'm sorry. I'm so very sorry!'

'You'll not be the first,' Mary said. 'Nor the last.' Her eyes too were moist and her voice trembled. 'But I never thought it'd happen to you, Jeannie. I feel as if I've failed you in some way. That what's happened is my fault for not keeping you on the straight and narrow.'

Jeannie stared at her mother. 'It's not your fault, Ma. It's mine – and Harry's too. But I didn't think of the consequences, I was just – just . . .' How could she possibly explain to her mother how she had felt about him, how he thrilled her to her very being and that she had wanted him as much as he wanted her – or, she amended, as much as she had thought he wanted her. Perhaps, she thought miserably as she set off for the chandler's shop, he didn't feel the same way she did. Perhaps he only wanted the thrill of the chase, and not anything permanent.

There was plenty of work on the nets, so Jeannie gave in her notice at the chandler's. She saw Ethan several times and he always came over to speak to her, but she found she had nothing to say, nothing that would heal the breach between them.

Her sickness eased but she felt sluggish and lacking in energy, although she suspected this was because of her worry over the non-appearance of Harry rather than anything physical. Her shape remained the same and each morning she ran her hands over her waist and belly to check if there was any sign of swelling, but there wasn't; yet still her flux didn't appear and she was convinced that she was carrying a child.

Mary took Tom aside one evening just before he went out. 'I want to talk to you, Tom.'

'What have I done?' he exclaimed, seeing his mother's serious expression.

'It's not what you've done but what you might do,' she said. 'Sit down. I want to discuss something.'

Obediently he sat, glancing at the clock on the wall. 'I'm meeting Sarah soon,' he said.

'It's about Sarah I want to speak,' Mary said, and Tom's mouth dropped open. 'It's my duty as your mother to make sure you are treating her with respect. I know that you love her, but I want to say . . .' She took a breath. This was something a boy's father should do, not his mother.

'I want to say that you must always treat her honourably—'

'Crikey, Ma! I've known Sarah since I was six!' Tom broke in.

'I know that,' she said, 'and all the more reason why you must show her regard and not familiarity.'

Tom's cheeks suddenly crimsoned as he understood his mother's meaning.

'What I'm saying, Tom,' Mary went on, 'is that it's all right to have a kiss and a cuddle, but nothing more than that. Do you know what I'm saying?'

'Yeh! Course I do,' he mumbled. 'And I won't. Crikey,' he said again. 'Have you seen the size of her da? He'd have my guts for garters if I did summat I shouldn't.'

'Good,' she said with a heave of breath. 'That's all right then. So long as you know. It's not a good way to start a marriage if you've to wed in a hurry.'

He stood up and towered over her. 'What brought that on?' he asked. 'You know I've been courting Sarah since she turned sixteen.'

The same age as Jeannie, she thought, and look at what's happened there. She shook her head. 'Just thought it needed mentioning, that's all. I dare say Sarah's mother has said the same thing to her.'

He gave a little shrug of his broad shoulders. 'She might have done, but Sarah's never said. But she's never needed to, Ma,' he said gently. 'She knows that she can trust me.'

Mary held back her tears until he had gone and then gave way to them; she was just composing herself when the door opened and Jeannie came in. She was flushed and windswept, her thick brown hair wild and tangled, but she looked beautiful, Mary thought.

Jeannie smiled at her mother. She seemed relaxed

yet buoyant, more cheerful than she had been for some weeks.

'Ma,' she said, 'I've made a decision. I'm going to Hull. I've enough money for the train fare. I'm going to look for Harry.'

CHAPTER TEN

Jeannie had decided that evening, as she set out on her usual walkabout, that she would confront the demons which were holding her fast, and to this end she took the steep hill up to the castle. She entered the gateway and walked across the rough grass to the edge of the rocky promontory and gazed down at the well-loved view of the medieval town which had been built close to the harbour and now climbed up the precipitous limestone cliffs. The town had been founded by and named after the Viking raider Thorgills Skarthi, though Jeannie remembered being told at school that the castle had been built by King Henry II, who had granted charters to the town.

A fleet of fishing cobles and smacks was putting out to sea on their way to night-time fishing, and she wondered if Ethan was sailing tonight. From this distance she couldn't see either the name of his ship, the *Scarborough Girl*, nor the flag that it flew.

She turned round and walked back through the open walls of the castle, tracing her hands over the rough stone and remembering the last time when she had been here, with Harry. So much must have happened between these walls, but we know nothing of the human emotion, only the history we are taught at school. In a hundred years' time, she thought, no one will know of me or of the anguish I'm suffering now.

She sat on a low wall and deliberated. But if I carry this child safely, then in another century there could be some other person connected to me who'll walk on this grass and look at the view below and wonder how they got here. Just as I do sometimes. She thought of her mother coming from Scotland; of her father's grandmother coming from Hull to live in Scarborough and marrying a Scarborough man; and now here am I, carrying the child of a Hull man.

And it was this thought which had decided her. She would go to Hull and seek him out, and if he rejected her she would return to Scarborough, brave the scorn and contempt, and bring up the child alone, or at least with her mother's help, for she knew in her heart that her mother wouldn't fail her. And if Harry did indeed honour his promise, then she would stay with him and live with him wherever he wanted to be.

'Will you go alone, bairn?' her mother asked anxiously. 'Or shall I come with you?'

Jeannie shook her head. 'I'll go by myself,' she said. 'And I'll decide what to do when I get there and if I find him.'

'Do you have his address?' her mother said practically.

'Hessle Road,' Jeannie said. 'I don't know whereabouts it is, but if it's where the fishing community live, then anyone will know it and him, just as we do in Scarborough.'

Mary was doubtful. Hull was a very large town, much bigger than Scarborough, but she didn't say so. Jeannie had enough problems to contend with without her adding to them.

'When will you go?' she asked, and then added, 'Will you return the same day?'

'Tomorrow,' Jeannie said, 'but I don't know when I'll come back. That's why I want to go by myself. I might have to stay awhile. Harry could be away at sea and I'll have to wait for him. But I will see him,' she said determinedly. 'I have to know his intentions.'

'You're a brave wee lassie,' her mother said, and put out her arms to enfold her. 'And you know, don't you, that come what may I'm always here if you need me. But you must tell me, Jeannie. Don't leave me in the dark. Don't let me worry that something has happened to you.'

Jeannie hugged her mother tight. 'I won't, Ma. If I don't return straight away then I'll write as soon as I can. You understand, don't you? I have to do this. I have to know one way or another. I can't live a half life, wondering constantly if he'll come back and if he really meant what he said.'

Early the next morning Jeannie set out for the railway station. She had waited until Tom had left for work, and her mother had told her that she would tell him about the child when he returned that evening and swear him to secrecy.

As Jeannie climbed the hill from their cottage to reach the main street she was appalled to see Ethan coming towards her.

'Hello, Jeannie. Where are you off to? Are you not mending this morning?'

'Erm, no. Not today.' She saw a small frown crease

above his nose and worried that he would ask her why. But he just gazed at her from his blue eyes, and she added, 'Did you not sail out last night?'

'No, I didn't.' He was almost as uncommunicative as she was until he said, 'The ship's gone in for repair. Didn't Tom tell you?'

She was anxious to be off. 'No. You know Tom. He doesn't discuss much.'

He continued to look at her. 'You know I named the boat after you, don't you, Jeannie?'

The *Scarborough Girl*! No, she didn't. She gave a nervous smile. 'Lots of Scarborough girls about, Ethan.'

'Not for me there aren't,' he said steadily. 'There's only one.'

'Ethan, please!'

'Has he been back? He's no good for you, Jeannie. You must know that.'

'I have to go,' she said. 'I'm sorry.'

'I'll be here when you change your mind.'

She nodded and turned away. You won't be when you hear, she thought. When you hear that I've behaved like a harlot and am carrying a child. You'll run away as fast as you can. You won't want to hear of me then. And who'll blame you? Not me and that's a fact.

She hurried off but ducked into a shop doorway in case Ethan should turn round as he had done on a previous occasion; she peered out and sure enough he looked back, hesitated and then walked on, and she rushed on up Eastborough in the direction of the railway station.

But there was no hurry. She had a twenty-minute wait for the next train, and as she sat on the platform she thought that if her journey hadn't been so vital she might have enjoyed the outing. She had been on a train only once before, when she had been taken with a party of other school children to Seamer Fair. They hadn't enjoyed it, for it had rained and their clothes had got damp and their boots muddy. Their teacher had told them that it was St Swithun's Day, and tradition had it that if it rained on that day it would rain for forty more.

She taught them a song which they sang all the way back to Scarborough. 'St Swithun's Day if thou dost rain, for forty days it will remain / St Swithun's Day if thou be fair, for forty days 'twill rain no more.'

Jeannie sighed as she remembered. It was not so very long ago that she had been that child and now she was grown up expecting a child of her own. How stupid I've been, she thought. How could I have been swayed so easily? And yet she knew that if Harry really did mean to marry her she would follow him and love him and be happy.

On the train she watched the passing scenery with only mild interest, though she craned her neck when they arrived at the seaside and fishing towns of Filey and Bridlington. The sunny day turned cloudy as the train reached Hull, and when she stepped outside the concourse the rain was coming down steadily. She looked about her. Which direction should she take? She could see a theatre building and a row of shops and a huge amount of traffic: carts and carriages, broughams and traps, omnibuses and waggonettes. A horse cab for hire drew up but she turned away. She'd no money for such luxuries.

A man carrying a bag was coming out of the station and glanced at her. She summoned up the courage to speak.

'Excuse me, sir. Can you tell me the way to Hessle Road?'

He waved a hand vaguely across to his right.

'Do you happen to know a man by the name of Harry Carr?' she asked. 'He lives on Hessle Road.'

The man frowned and looked at her as if she were mad. Then he laughed. 'Is this 'first time you've been to Hull?'

'Yes,' she said.

'Well, I can tell you this,' he said brusquely. 'Hessle Road is a long road, and no I don't know anybody down there. It's where all 'fishing folk live, and I'm from East Hull on 'other side of 'river and that's as different as can be!'

He went off in a great hurry and she wondered what he'd meant by the other side of the river. If he meant the Humber, then surely the land on the other side was Lincolnshire not Hull.

She turned right as he'd suggested and walked to the end of the road, where she asked a woman for directions. The woman looked her up and down. 'You a stranger here?'

'Yes,' Jeannie said. 'I'm looking for a friend. She . . . she was supposed to be meeting me. She lives on Hessle Road.'

The woman gave her general directions, then said, 'You're going to get wet. It's a fair walk.'

Jeannie thanked her and set out again. The town was much bigger than she had imagined, with tall buildings and many roads which criss-crossed each other. She asked someone else for directions to the docks, but when she was asked which one she couldn't say.

The woman shrugged. 'There's so many docks: Humber Dock, William Wright, St Andrew's . . . Why do you want to be there?'

Someone else asking her a question instead of a direct answer. 'I don't,' she said. 'I'm looking for somebody – he's a fisherman and lives on Hessle Road.'

The woman looked at her pityingly, she thought, but suggested she went on to Hessle Road and asked in a shop. Again she was given directions, and after traversing Great Thornton Street and Walker Street eventually found the road she was looking for, but was aghast when she saw the length of it.

There had been huge growth in Hull in the last forty years, especially on the west side, and an immense housing project had been built to accommodate the families of those who worked in the successful trawling industry, and those who had come to work on the railway.

Jeannie stood at the bottom of the long straight road and then, taking a breath which she immediately regretted as she drew in the stench of fish oil, began to walk. She passed streets with names that sounded strange compared with those she knew in Scarborough – Strickland Street, Wassand Street, Walcott Street – and noticed that some of them had other streets and terraces running off them.

I'll never find him without asking, she thought. I'll have to pluck up the courage to go into a shop. But there was no help forthcoming from the first one, a fishmonger, nor the second, an ironmonger; it wasn't until she went into a bakery that the woman behind the counter said, 'I know his gran.' She laughed. 'If you want Harry you'd best call in at 'Wassand Arms. They'll know where he is, unless he's gone to sea.'

'Do you know where he lives?' Jeannie asked. 'Or where his gran lives?'

The woman huffed out a breath and shook her head, but then called out to the queue of women waiting to be served. 'Anybody here know where Nan Carr lives?'

There was muttering among the women. They were all dressed in similar fashion in dark skirts and shawls round their heads and shoulders and without exception they all looked careworn; then a child piped up, a boy of about seven wearing a cap that was too large for him, a torn shirt and ragged trousers.

'I might know,' he said, and wiped his runny nose on his sleeve.

'Yes?' Jeannie's hopes were raised.

The boy gazed at her. His face was pasty and he was breathing with some difficulty through his mouth.

'He'll want a copper for telling you,' the woman standing next to him said. 'He'll not tell you owt for nowt, not Stan.'

Jeannie nodded. 'Can you take me?' she asked him. 'I'll give you a penny if you will.'

The boy licked his lips. 'Tuppence an' I'll tek you to 'door.'

'I'll wait for you outside,' Jeannie said, and added to anyone who might be listening, 'Thank you.'

She heard a chorus of muted laughter as she went out and wondered what they were laughing about. Was it because the boy had got the best of the bargain, or was it because they all knew Harry's whereabouts but were unwilling to share the information with a stranger? In Sandside they would have done the same if a stranger had asked about a local resident. They were loyal if nothing else, and she thought that the Hessle Road residents were probably the same. Everyone looked after their own.

She'd noticed the public house, the Wassand Arms, as she'd walked along the road, but she dared not go in. Such places were not for women or girls like her.

The boy came out of the shop and muttered, 'I've gotta tek 'bread home first or me mam'll bray me.'

Jeannie nodded and followed him further up the road until he turned off into a narrow terrace.

'Wait 'ere,' he said. 'Don't follow me or it'll cost you more.'

She waited as instructed and watched as he raced up the terrace and turned into a gateway. All the houses had a patch of soil in front of them but none as far as she could see were cultivated. In the nearest one, weeds flourished among decayed cabbages. She waited what seemed an interminable time and wondered if perhaps his mother wouldn't let him come out again. She thought of what her mother might have done if a stranger had asked Tom for directions when he was a child. Jeannie knew for certain that she would have come out to inspect the enquirer before letting him go anywhere with someone she didn't know.

Presently the boy came out again. He walked nonchalantly, biting into an apple core.

'Is it all right?' she asked. 'Your mother doesn't mind you taking me?'

He stared at her, his mouth half open as if to bite the apple. 'I didn't tell her,' he breathed nasally. 'She'd've wanted more'n tuppence and she'd've kept it.'

They walked away from the terrace, and when out of sight of the houses he turned towards her. 'I'll 'ave 'money fost.'

Jeannie felt in her deep skirt pocket, brought out a penny and held it out to him.

'I said tuppence!'

'A penny now,' she said firmly, 'another when we get there and I know it's the right house.'

He grabbed it from her. 'It is 'right house. I know 'lad who lives next door.'

Jeannie nodded. 'That's all right then, but you'll still have to wait for the other penny. Are we going or not?'

He seemed to hesitate, as if wondering whether to scarper with the unearned coin or make an effort to earn another. 'Yeh!' he said at last. 'Come on then, it's not far.'

She followed him back in the direction from which she had come until he turned off down the road marked Walcott Street, which had a large church on the corner. She was encouraged to believe that he probably did know the house and the family, for it was close enough to his home for him to have a friend in the vicinity.

The street was lined with terraced houses, their front doors opening on to the pavement. Halfway down Stan stopped and pointed. 'Next but one to 'bottom.' He waved a finger to the right side. 'That's where they live.'

'Who lives?' she asked cautiously.

'Harry Carr. That's who you said, wa'n't it?'

'Yes,' she murmured. 'It was.'

She gave him the other penny and he scooted off without a thanks or goodbye, leaving her to walk alone past the windows of the other houses, wondering if anyone was looking out inquisitively at her.

She came to the house he'd indicated and timidly knocked on the door, waited a second and then knocked more firmly. She waited, shivering, wet and cold, and was about to knock again when she heard footsteps on wooden boards. The door opened a crack and she saw an eye peering out and a grey head.

'Yes?' It was a woman's voice.

'I'm – I'm looking for Harry Carr.'

The door opened wider and an old woman stood there, and for a second Jeannie felt that she was looking at her own grandmother Aggie Marshall. The same iron-grey hair tied in a knot, the same thin lined face. But this woman's expression was granite hard; her eyes were cold as steel and her mouth was set in a thin narrow line. Her voice when she spoke was harsh.

'An' who's askin'?'

CHAPTER ELEVEN

Jeannie swallowed hard and pushed her soaked hair away from her face. 'I'm Jeannie Marshall, a – a friend of Harry's.'

'Oh aye.' The woman gazed at her. 'And what d'ya want him for?'

'I – I want to speak to him, please.'

'He's not in.' The woman made as if to close the door, but Jeannie moved forward.

'Oh, but please, can you tell me where I can find him?'

The woman narrowed her eyes. 'You're not from round here. How d'ya know him?'

'I'm from Scarborough,' Jeannie told her. 'I've met him twice, last time in March.' She hoped the woman wouldn't add up the months and shut the door in her face.

'In March? Where?' The questions were harsh and the woman frowned. 'He's nivver been to Scarborough.'

'He has,' Jeannie said. 'Twice, like I said. I just need to speak to him, please.'

She was scrutinized severely and unblinkingly, and was just beginning to think she ought to turn tail and run when she was told, 'You'd better come in.'

The outer door opened straight into a room which was clean but barely furnished and she was led through another door, past steep and narrow stairs leading up to another floor and into a kitchen where she saw a gleaming black cooking range with a shabby easy chair next to it, a scrubbed wooden table and two spindly chairs. Hanging from the ceiling was a lamp with a gas mantle. There was another door which she supposed led to a scullery and the yard. It was a much larger house than their old Scarborough cottage and she wondered who else lived there.

'Sit down an' dry yourself afore you get your death.' The woman pointed to the easy chair.

'Thank you,' Jeannie said. 'I am very cold.'

A grunt was the only verbal response but tea leaves were put into a pot, the simmering kettle was swung round and hot water was poured on them. After what seemed to be an interminable time the old woman lifted the teapot lid and swirled the tea vigorously with a metal spoon, and Jeannie watched mesmerized as she produced two tin mugs from a cupboard and poured tea into them.

'D'ya tek milk?'

'Yes please, if you have it.'

A minute drop of milk was poured from a brown jug and the mug of tea handed to her.

'Thank you,' she said. 'I'm very grateful.'

'So you should be. I'm not in 'habit of pouring precious tea to folks I don't know.'

Jeannie nodded nervously and took a sip of the hot weak liquid; there was no answer she could give.

One of the spindly chairs was placed across from her and the woman picked up her mug and sat down. She took a gulp of black tea, sighed and said, 'So what's this about? Lasses don't usually knock on my door asking for Harry. They know I won't stand for it.'

Jeannie took another sip before replying; she could feel the warmth coursing through her, giving her strength.

'Are you a relation of Harry's?' she ventured. She was fairly sure the woman must be his grandmother and not his mother; she looked much older than Fiona and even older than Granny Marshall. Perhaps the whole family lived together.

'I'll ask 'questions.' The answer was terse. 'But yes, I'm his nan. His da's mother. He lives here wi' me. This is my house.'

'W-will he be back soon?' Jeannie risked another question. 'Or is he at sea?'

Mrs Carr frowned. 'Did he tell you he went to sea?'

'Yes. He said he was a fisherman.'

'What d'ya want wi' him?'

Jeannie clutched the mug with both hands. 'I'd rather speak to him.'

'Who brought you? Did you come on 'train?'

Jeannie bit her lip. She hadn't expected to be interrogated. 'I came by myself. On the train. When will Harry be home?'

Mrs Carr took a deep breath, her thin chest rising and falling. 'It's a long way to come just to see somebody. Are you expecting?'

Jeannie gasped. 'I don't – I want to speak to Harry.' Tears began to fall. She was cold, wet and miserable and she didn't want to talk to this horrible old woman.

'Did he say he'd marry you? Did he mek any promises?'

Dumbly Jeannie nodded and took another sip of tea; her teeth chattered on the metal lip.

'Stand up,' Mrs Carr ordered and Jeannie thought she was going to order her out of the house, but she obeyed and the old woman barked out, 'Turn about.'

Jeannie stared at her but did as she was bid. Mrs Carr nodded and then took the mug from her and refilled it from the teapot, though she didn't offer any milk this time. She pointed a thin crooked finger indicating that Jeannie should sit again.

'How old are you? How far gone?'

'I'm s-sixteen. I last saw Harry in March.'

'Five months, then. We're still in August, aren't we?'

'Where is Harry?' Jeannie said. 'I need to talk to him.'

'So do I,' his grandmother said grimly, and Jeannie noticed that she had screwed the hem of her apron into a tight ball in her bony hand. 'I'll have summat to say when he gets in. He'll feel 'sharp end o' my tongue an' no mistake.'

'Where is he?' Jeannie asked again. 'I don't want to miss my train home.' She felt that she would have to go home; that she would get no satisfaction here.

'You can stop here for 'night,' Mrs Carr said unexpectedly. 'He'll probably be late in. If he's not found work then he'll be in 'pub 'avin' a game o' doms.'

For a moment Jeannie didn't grasp what she was saying. What did she mean? *Inpub*? Then she blinked. In the public house? Having a game of dominoes!

'I see,' she said. 'And you think he'll be late?' Surely, she thought, if he hasn't any work then he

107

won't waste time and money drinking and playing dominoes. Anxiety washed over her. Is this what he was like? Was he often out of work? Would she be better going home and living out her shame where she was known?

There was a sudden crash as if a door had been flung open and a second later the door from the scullery opened too and Harry, his face flushed and his hair tousled, stood there grinning.

'Hey up, Nan! I said as I wouldn't be late, didn't I?' He didn't seem to notice Jeannie sitting by the fire, though she had turned her head towards him. 'There's nobody much about so I thought I might as well come home.' He began to untie the laces on his boots, trying unsuccessfully to bend down without falling over and grabbing hold of the table.

'Happen everybody else is in work!' his grand-mother said sourly. 'Have you been down to 'docks?'

He straightened up and as he did so caught sight of Jeannie, her face almost level with his. His mouth opened as if he were about to speak, but he seemed to be dumbstruck and licked his lips instead.

'Hello, Harry,' Jeannie murmured. He looks like a naughty schoolboy, she thought, caught out in some misdemeanour. 'Remember me?'

'Jeannie!' he breathed. 'What 'you doing here? How did you find me?'

'With difficulty,' she said. 'I had to ask several people.'

'So . . .'

He was trying to ask why she had come, she thought, but didn't know how to frame the question.

'You asked me to wait for you,' she said quietly. 'You said—'

'You said you'd marry her,' his grandmother butted in. 'Is that right?'

'Well, aye,' he blustered. 'But not yet. I've no money, have I? No job.'

'We'll put 'banns up then. She's pregnant.'

He took a gasping breath. 'Pregnant!'

Jeannie nodded. 'That's what happens, Harry,' she said. 'When two people . . . You said you wanted me to marry you and come to live in Hull.'

Harry hung his head and didn't look at her and scratched the back of his neck. Then he was almost knocked sideways as his grandmother stood up and hit out at him.

'You great daft ha'porth!' she shouted. 'How could you think o' bringing a bairn into 'world when life's difficult enough trying to scratch a living and you wi' no job?'

'I didn't think, Nan,' he muttered. 'I didn't think about having a bairn.'

She reached out again and slapped him and he flinched but didn't retaliate.

'Well, you'll marry her if she still wants you,' she bawled at him. 'I'll not have folks talking about me and saying my grandson is a ne'er-do-well who doesn't honour his commitments.'

Jeannie was astonished. For support to come from such an unexpected quarter as this mean-faced, sharp-tongued woman completely flummoxed her. But her share of censure was yet to come as Nan Carr turned on her.

'And as for you, young woman, if this is how you carry on in Scarborough, then shame on you. Did your ma not tell you 'difference between right and wrong? Were you a virgin?' she snapped.

'Or did all 'lads in Scarborough know you?'

Jeannie was stung by the question and began to cry. She stood up and picked up her damp shawl. 'No, they didn't,' she said between sobs. 'I'd never been touched by a lad before. Harry was the first and I went with him because he said he loved me and wanted to marry me.'

'Loved you,' the old woman sneered. 'Aye, he loves you all right. He'll have to love you for 'next forty years. Then you'll know what love is!'

She stormed out of the kitchen and into the scullery, banging the door behind her, and could be heard clattering pots and pans.

'She's got her dander up,' Harry remarked. 'Don't worry. She'll calm down in a bit.'

'Harry!' Jeannie snuffled. 'Didn't you mean it when you said we'd be wed?'

He rubbed his hand over his chin and Jeannie noticed that he hadn't shaved. 'Well.' He hesitated. 'I suppose I did at 'time.' He glanced at her. 'You look right bonny, Jeannie. You've put on a bit o' weight.'

She took a breath. 'I'm pregnant, Harry, that's why.'

'Oh, yeh! Do you mind?'

Jeannie gazed at him. He looked sleepy, which she guessed was from drinking, but he was still very appealing. 'About the bairn? Not if you don't. But I won't hold you to marriage if you really don't want to. I'd get a bad name in Scarborough, but I'd manage somehow.'

He came towards her and kissed her cheek. 'You were lovely that day up by 'castle,' he murmured. 'I've never . . .' He paused.

'What, Harry? Never what?'

110

'Oh, nowt,' he said. 'It was your fost time, wasn't it?'

She pulled away from him. 'Yes,' she said. 'You know it was. But not yours, was it?'

He shrugged. 'Got to get experience somehow, haven't we?' He reached out and ran his hands over her hips, then drew in a breath. 'By, you look good, Jeannie. If Nan wasn't in 'next room . . .'

She backed away again. 'But she is,' she whispered, and was glad that the old woman was within hearing because she knew that otherwise she would be tempted. She swallowed and licked her lips. What was it about him that attracted her so irresistibly? He wasn't handsome, not the way Ethan was handsome, but he was very fetching with his cheeky grin and eyes that seemed to swallow her up.

'Don't,' she said. 'Harry, be sensible. I've to think about the bairn. Are we to be married or not?'

His eyes roamed her face, her body, even down to her feet. 'Course we are. Nan said, didn't she?'

CHAPTER TWELVE

Jeannie pondered Harry's remark as she travelled back to Scarborough the following morning. He had escorted her to the railway station and seen her on to the train. His grandmother had curbed her temper the day before and come back into the kitchen to tell him that he must put up the banns the next day and that she would go with him to make sure that he did. She told Jeannie that she should go home and ask her mother to send a letter saying she gave her consent to the marriage, and that Harry would send her a postcard telling her when the marriage was to take place. She also said that after the ceremony she and Harry would live with her.

Nan had taken her upstairs. The top step led straight into the front bedroom. She pointed out the double bed and told Jeannie that she would share with her that night. 'I'll have no carryings on in my house,' she'd said grimly. 'You'll wait till you're wed for that.'

Then going from that room she'd opened a door to show her Harry's tiny room with a single bed and nothing more and told her that she would try to buy a larger second-hand bed once they were married.

Jeannie had spent an uncomfortable night sleeping in a strange bed with a woman she didn't know, aware that Harry was only on the other side of a thin wall.

It's not what I want, she thought as the train steamed back to Scarborough. I don't want to live with her. But reason told her that she would have to. If Harry hadn't regular work then there'd be no money for a place of their own. It would be the same in Scarborough, she knew. We'd have to live with my ma and I don't suppose he'd like that either. But at the back of her mind was the anxious thought that Harry was only marrying her because his grandmother had said that he must. Would he have agreed to it if old Mrs Carr hadn't insisted?

I know nothing about him, she thought. I don't know any more now than I did before I came. She wasn't filled with joy as she felt she should have been; rather, she was downcast and desolate to think that she was leaving home and all that was familiar. As she stepped off the train in Scarborough the sun was shining and the air felt fresh; it had been dull and raining in Hull when she left.

'It won't always be raining,' her mother reassured her when she told her. 'When the sun shines Hull will look as good as Scarborough.'

'It won't, Ma.' Jeannie burst into tears. 'Am I doing the right thing? Tell me. Please.'

Mary shook her head. 'I can't, lassie. You must decide. If you want to marry Harry, then you'll live with him wherever the work is. And think of this. Mebbe his grandmother needs him to live there, to help pay the rent. It can't be easy for her.'

'It's a bigger house than ours, Ma.' Jeannie wiped

her tears. 'It's got an upstairs and a yard with a privy. And gas light.'

In their cottage they still had oil lamps and candles. Their landlord hadn't updated any of his properties, but as Jeannie looked round now and imagined the prospect of leaving, she thought it was perfect.

'It sounds just fine.' Her mother smiled. 'And Harry's grandmother seems like a very sensible woman.'

In truth, Mary was relieved. The knowledge of there being an older woman in the household slightly allayed her fears about her daughter's marriage. She had told Jeannie she would support her if she wished to bring up the child alone, and she had meant it, but she could not deny that she was glad the child would be legitimate.

'I'll send a letter today,' she assured Jeannie, 'one they can give to the parson. And listen to me, bairn.' She squeezed Jeannie's hand. 'I'll come with you to see you married, and so will Tom, and he can give you away. We'll be witness to your marriage. We'll show this new family that your own folk will always be there to support you.'

A week later, Jeannie received a badly written postcard with many crossings out, saying that the wedding would take place on the first Saturday of October, signed with the letter H. She showed it to her mother, who nodded and thought privately that it would be just in time. Jeannie's pregnancy was beginning to show, and she was sure that people they knew were looking curiously at them.

I'll have to see Ethan and explain, Jeannie thought. She had avoided him as much as she could, although he still came over to speak to her when she was working on the nets. She always kept her shawl loosely around her and her back to him, speaking to him over her shoulder, and she didn't think he had noticed anything different about her.

She was on her way down to the harbour early one morning when she saw him walking ahead of her and took her courage in her hands to call to him. He turned and gave her a wide smile, and for just a moment she felt a tinge of regret.

'Ethan,' she began, 'can you spare a minute?'

He nodded and gazed at her. 'Any time; you know that.'

She pressed her lips together. 'You're going to be upset with me,' she said. 'You'll be angry.'

He gave a little laugh, though she felt it was forced, and took her arm so that they could lean on the railing and look out across the beach where the sea was far out and the sand was soft and golden.

'I'll never be angry with you, Jeannie,' he said softly, his eyes on the ocean. 'I might be angry over circumstances, or frustrated over things which I can do nothing about.' He turned towards her. 'But not with you.'

She looked up at him. 'I'm going to be married,' she said. 'To Harry.'

He flinched and his eyes seemed to spark. 'When?'

'In October,' she whispered. 'It's all arranged. We're to be married in Hull and that's where I – we'll live.'

He leaned on the rail and put his head in his hands and she watched as he shook it slowly as if disbelieving what he had heard.

'I'm sorry, Ethan,' she said quietly. 'I'm really sorry. I said you'd be angry.'

He turned his head to look at her. 'I'm not angry,' he said, but she knew that he was for his voice was bitter. 'I'm – I'm – devastated. Hurt,' he added, 'and – I want to kick something – or myself, for not telling you before how I felt, rather than thinking that you always knew.'

'I didn't know.' Her voice broke as she spoke, for she didn't like to see him like this, so sad and unhappy. 'But even if I had . . .' She stopped, knowing it was unfair to tell him how she had felt about Harry.

'You still wouldn't have wanted me, not after you met *him*, with his sweet talking and persuasive ways!'

And as if he had guessed after all and in a totally uncharacteristic manner, he grabbed at her shawl, revealing her swelling belly. His mouth turned down and his eyes were moist, whether with tears or anger she couldn't tell.

'You're pregnant,' he said accusingly. 'Did you go with him willingly or were you forced?'

'I wasn't forced, Ethan.'

He turned on his heel and walked away, down towards the boatyard, and lost himself among the crowd of boatmen, fishermen and net braiders.

She cried then; cried for the loss of a friend, for the life she was leaving behind and with anxiety over the one that was to come.

She hadn't much to take with her, only a few clothes, two shawls and her spare pair of boots, but her mother had found the money from somewhere – she wouldn't say how or where – to buy her a blue striped skirt and matching bodice with long sleeves. Jeannie used her final week's money to buy a blue bonnet trimmed with white lace.

'I might never wear these again, Ma,' she said guiltily. 'I'm being reckless.'

'Never mind about that,' her mother said, her voice choking. 'We want it to be a day to remember and I don't want anyone to think we can't afford a wedding dress for my only daughter.'

Jeannie put her arms round her mother and hugged her. 'Tom's hardly spoken to me since you told him,' she said. 'Do you think he'll come?'

'He'll come,' Mary said. 'He's embarrassed, that's all. You're his baby sister, don't forget.'

Jeannie had never thought of Tom in that way. She had always felt that she was a nuisance to him when they were younger. She was always sent to fetch him back from wherever he was, interrupting his games when he was wanted at home.

On the day, the three of them caught the early train to Hull. Tom had been allowed a day off work and wore his only suit with a clean white shirt which his mother had starched so much that the high collar cut into his neck and he had to turn it over. He carried a bowler hat that had been his father's and his mother had kept. Mary wore her best skirt and fitted jacket with a paisley shawl, and a straw hat trimmed with a herring gull feather which she had dipped into squeezed blackberry juice so that it had become a rich vibrant purple.

A young man, who Jeannie thought looked vaguely familiar, met them as they came off the platform.

'Are you Jeannie?' he said. 'I'm Harry's mate, Billy Norman. I'm his best man.'

Jeannie recalled then that she had seen him at Scarborough station the first time she had met Harry. She nodded and gave a nervous smile.

'This is my mother and my brother Tom,' she said, and was glad that Tom was there, so tall now and broad.

'I'm to look after you till 'wedding,' he said. 'Harry's nan said it were bad luck for 'groom to see 'bride afore 'wedding.'

'What nonsense,' Jeannie heard her mother say beneath her breath. But Mary added in a louder voice, 'So what are we to do until eleven o'clock? We can't stand here all morning.'

'There's a pub near St Barnabas's church. We can wait there,' Billy said. 'That's where we're going after. They're putting on some victuals for us.'

'We're not going to wait in any pub,' Mary said decisively. 'My daughter isn't in the habit of frequenting alehouses. How far is it to the church?'

'Not that far.' Billy Norman's face dropped, and they all guessed that he had been looking forward to a pre-nuptial drink. 'Twenty minutes, mebbe.'

'Then we'll walk slowly,' Mary said. 'It's a nice day and you can tell us about Hull and the fishing and the church where they're to be married.'

Billy Norman gazed at her in astonishment. Beneath his hat his hair was greased for the occasion and he was wearing what looked like his Sunday suit; beneath his jacket he sported a bright waistcoat.

'It's 'fishermen's church,' he said. 'St Barnabas. That's where all 'fisher folk get married or go when they die.'

'Good,' said Mary positively. 'Well chosen, seeing as we're all fisher folk.'

'Aye,' he agreed. 'It'll be Nan Carr that's chosen it, I reckon. She's 'one who says what's to be done in that household.'

Jeannie glanced at her mother. Tom and Billy were walking in front of them and they could hear Tom asking about the ships in Hull. They heard Billy reply that many of them were built in Beverley and Hessle.

'Don't be browbeaten by anybody,' Mary told Jeannie. 'Stand up for what you believe in. Be your own self.'

'I will, Ma.' Jeannie's eyes gleamed. The sun was shining and it was a warm pleasant autumn day and she suddenly felt a lurch of happiness. She was going to marry Harry and she was going to have his child. She'd be patient with his grandmother and try to be accommodating towards her. It was her house, after all, and she was inviting a stranger to come and live with her.

Granny Marshall had only been told that Jeannie was to be married to a fisherman from Hull and was going to live in that town, and she had replied that the girl was going back to her family roots. Fiona had written with her good wishes and sent her a fine grey wool shawl which she was wearing now, draped over her bodice.

It was going to be all right. Her only regret was Ethan's misery, for Tom had told her that he'd said he would never look at another woman. But I can't help him, she thought. There's nothing I can do. I'm going to marry Harry, who loves me as much as I love him. I know it's so, because he told me and Ethan never did. Not until it was too late.

They walked slowly up Hessle Road and saw that some of the houses were in a dilapidated state of repair; they gazed at the long rows of shops: butchers, bakers, fishmongers, cobblers and a post office. There were several churches and many public houses and alehouses. Horse trams trundled along picking people up and dropping them off, which was a good thing, Jeannie thought, as it was a very long road.

It was just striking eleven o'clock as they arrived at the church of St Barnabas which was situated at the junction of a wide avenue. Waiting at the door were several people, including Harry's grandmother and Harry himself. Jeannie took a deep breath. Here then, like it or not, for better or for worse, was the start of her new life.

CHAPTER THIRTEEN

The ceremony was short and soon over, but as Jeannie repeated her vows she lifted her eyes to see the sun shining through the stained-glass windows of the chancel, filling the church with rainbow colours.

'Happy the bride the sun shines on,' her mother had whispered to her before she took Tom's arm to walk down the aisle, and as she stood by Harry's side she did feel very happy.

But the rain began as they left the Wassand Arms after their wedding breakfast. Nan Carr had arranged a good spread of beef and chicken and roast potatoes, with apple pie to follow and copious jugs of tea, and ale for the men, to wash it all down, but when they emerged from the public house they all had to run their respective ways to avoid getting soaked. Mary and Tom took a horse cab to the railway station, while Jeannie, Harry – whose best man had kept him well supplied with ale – Nan, and two young women, one of whom turned out to be Harry's sister, went back to Nan's house.

Mary had hugged Jeannie before they left and Tom had pecked her cheek and whispered, 'Let me know if there's any sort of trouble,' but her mother had said, 'I think it'll be all right, Jeannie, and you'll have a ready-made friend in your sister-in-law.'

Jeannie had doubted that, although she didn't say so, for Harry's sister Rosie had eyed her up and down on meeting her and then murmured something to her friend, who had lowered her eyes and pressed her lips together in a smile.

Rosie would have been pretty, Jeannie reflected, with her fair hair and blue eyes, if it were not for her sulky mouth, but as for her friend Connie Turnby, Jeannie had never seen such a plain girl, with her bony face and sharp protruding chin above a long thin neck. Her only redeeming features were her large brown eyes and long lashes.

Nan Carr was dressed in black and Jeannie wondered if it was because she considered the marriage a cause for mourning rather than celebration, but then she checked herself as she thought that the old lady was probably wearing her best and didn't feel the need or couldn't afford to buy something new.

Harry offered Jeannie his arm as they walked back and gave her a sideways glance. He was well oiled, she realized as he turned to the friends who had been present at the wedding. 'Are you coming back?' he slurred. 'We'll get some jugs in.'

'No you won't,' Nan called sharply. She was walking in front, striding out in her black boots, umbrella held high. 'Party's over,' she added. 'They've had their fill at my expense.'

'Aw, Nan!' Harry said. 'It's my wedding day!' He turned to Jeannie and gave her a wet kiss. He had aimed for her mouth, but she moved her head to receive it on the cheek.

'Aye, well, happen it is,' Nan said brusquely. 'But

now we get back to normal and we need to talk and I'm not doing that wi' your drunken pals listening in.'

Jeannie doubted whether even if his friends listened to the conversation they would remember much of it the next day. They accepted what Nan said, however, and all of them, with the exception of Billy, turned about at the top of Walcott Street and staggered back in the direction of the pub. Billy would have gone with them but for Harry's grabbing his arm to stop him. Harry tapped the side of his nose and said in a loud whisper, 'You'll be all right, Billy. She don't mind you.'

They walked in procession back to the terrace and Harry responded with a wave as people called out, 'Good luck, Harry.' Some of them came over to meet Jeannie, or rather, she thought, to take a look at her.

'Thish is my wife.' Harry grinned. 'Ain't she a bonny lass?'

And they nodded and looked her up and down and agreed that she was.

When they arrived back at the house and crowded into the small kitchen Nan immediately swung the kettle over the fire.

'Can't we have a fire in 'front room, Nan?' Rosie moaned. 'There's too many of us for in here.'

'Aye, if you fetch a bucket o' coal and mek it,' Nan snapped. 'I'm not made o' brass, you know!'

'It's supposed to be a special day,' Rosie retaliated, and then, glancing at Jeannie, said, 'Have you got money for coal, Harry?'

'No, I haven't.' He pulled out his empty trouser pockets. 'Nowt.'

Rosie ran her tongue over her teeth and looked again at Jeannie. 'Nobody else got any?'

Jeannie said nothing. She had a little money, which her mother had given her, but she would use that for necessities and not for warming the toes of someone she didn't know who had been barely civil to her.

'Do you live here?' she asked Rosie. She was conscious that she knew nothing about Harry's relations, for he had never mentioned them.

Rosie stared at her. 'No. I live wi' me Auntie Dot. Didn't you see her at 'church?'

Jeannie shrugged. 'I might have done, but I wouldn't have known who she was.'

'She's me daughter, Harry's da's sister,' Nan broke in as she took cups and saucers out of a wall cupboard. 'She took Rosie in and I took Harry when their ma left 'em an' jiggered off wi' a foreigner when Harry was ten. She took 'two youngest bairns wi' her.'

'Oh!' Jeannie said. 'I didn't know.'

'Did you tell her nowt?' Nan asked Harry, who had taken the easy chair and lay sprawled in front of the fire.

He shook his head. 'Not much.' He grinned. 'There weren't any time for history. I had a train to catch.'

Jeannie blushed to her hair roots and felt that everyone was looking at her. Billy, who was standing by the window, snorted a laugh which he turned into a cough.

'Get 'milk jug out of 'scullery,' Nan said to Rosie. 'Don't stand there doing nowt. And there's some sweet biscuits in 'cupboard. Fetch 'em out – and put 'em on a plate,' she bellowed after her. 'Don't want folk thinking we've no manners,' she muttered, and Jeannie realized that, in spite of everything, Nan Carr was trying to do her best in a situation not of her choosing.

'Can I do anything?' she offered. 'Shall I make the tea?'

'Aye, you can. 'Kettle's steaming.'

'Where do you keep the tea?' she asked, and picked up a teapot from the side of the range.

'Don't use that,' Nan said. 'Use 'bigger one that's in 'scullery. Rosie'll show you. Tea's in yon caddy.' She nodded towards the shelf over the range. 'Be sparin' wi' it.'

The tea leaves were like dust, Jeannie thought. It was the cheapest tea possible, and she surmised that life and money were probably a struggle for the old lady.

'I don't want tea,' Harry said. 'Fetch us a jug o' ale, Rosie.' He crossed his legs, taking up all the space in front of the fire.

'You can go 'n' jump up,' she retaliated. 'I'm going to have a cup o' tea. Fetch it yoursen – or send your wife,' she added.

'Nay, she can't go. They don't know her.'

'Well, I'm not going. Anyway, you said you'd no money.'

'I'll put it on 'slate.' He yawned, and turned to Connie. 'You'll go, won't you, Con?'

Connie's mouth opened as she pondered. She looked at Rosie, who turned her head away, then at Jeannie, who was concentrating on pouring the tea, and lastly at Billy, who just grinned and asked her to make it a large jug.

Connie slipped her wet shawl round her shoulders and, glancing at Harry with her limpid brown eyes, went out again, through the scullery into the yard, which Jeannie surmised was the everyday exit and entrance.

'What about Connie's tea?' Jeannie asked. 'Will she be long? Shall I pour it?'

No one answered her, so she poured it anyway, draining the teapot and then half filling it with more hot water.

A little later some of the neighbours called round, all of them using the back door which they accessed from the terrace by a narrow passageway, and all agreeing to 'tek a drop' from the jug of ale which Connie had brought back, to drink the health of the newly-weds. None of them were offered tea, which was just as well, Jeannie thought, for there was barely enough to make another pot. She resolved that the first thing she would do on Monday would be to go out and buy more, and keep it hidden just for her and Nan.

As the evening wore on, Rosie and Connie left, and Nan told Billy it was time he was making a move.

'*He'll* not be going anywhere tonight,' she said, indicating Harry, who was snoring in the easy chair. 'He's had his fill, so you might as well hop it.'

'Aye, all right then,' Billy said compliantly, and Jeannie was astonished how everyone seemed to do Nan's bidding, no matter how she spoke to them.

After Billy had left, Nan cleared away the crockery and the tankards from the table and took them into the scullery, then came back for the kettle of hot water.

'Shall – shall I make up the bed, Mrs Carr?' Jeannie

126

said diffidently, wondering what had happened to her bag of belongings. Her mother had given it to Billy, who had said he would run back to the house with it before joining them at the wedding breakfast.

'It's done,' Nan said. 'And your things are up there as well. I took 'em up. You needn't think anybody else has had their hands on 'em.'

'Thank you,' Jeannie said. 'I'll go up and unpack.' She gave a nervous laugh. 'It'll not take a minute. I hadn't a lot to bring.'

'Nobody has,' Nan muttered. 'Not folks like us, though I thought at first you might be a cut above.' She looked directly at her. 'But I see now that you're not. You're just 'same even though you're a Scarborough girl. We'll talk in 'morning about how we'll manage.' She paused for a minute. 'You can call me Nan.'

Later, in the narrow bed, Jeannie shuffled for space beside Harry, who not only took up most of it but tried to lie on top of her.

'No,' she whispered, conscious of his grandmother in the next room. 'You'll hurt the bairn.'

'You'll have to come on top then,' he grumbled, and she could smell his beery breath. 'You're my wife. I want what's mine.'

'I'm not objecting,' she said. 'It's just uncomfortable.' She hadn't realized that it would be like this; she had assumed that they would kiss and cuddle up for their first night, and just be happy that they were wed. After that . . . well, in truth she hadn't thought any further than that, nor guessed that they would have to share this narrow bed.

Harry had one foot on the floor, but she couldn't lie on top of him either for she kept rolling off and after a few frustrating minutes he turned over and urged her to move up because he was dead beat, and going to sleep. Jeannie realized that he had had far too much to drink to attempt any lovemaking, and that he didn't want to kiss her or hold her tight, but only to sleep. With her nose pressed up against the wall and Harry's arm across her neck and his snores in her ear, her paramount emotion was disappointment, coupled with the sensation that she had just made the most enormous mistake.

She shoved his arm away from her and crawled over the top of him and he was too far gone to even notice. She threw the thin blanket over him, pulled her shift over her knees and padded across the cold floor out of the bedroom and into Nan's room. The old lady was fast asleep on one side of the bed, both hands under her cheek and a gentle *phut phut* quivering from her parted lips. Jeannie shivered; then, hesitating no more, she carefully turned back the covers and climbed in beside her.

CHAPTER FOURTEEN

Nan was up first the next morning and made no comment on Jeannie's presence in her bed. As soon as she had gone down the narrow stairs, Harry came through the door from the other bedroom.

'What you doin' in here?' he said in a loud whisper. 'I thought I was onny dreaming that we'd wed.' He climbed in beside her and drew her close.

'The bed was too narrow,' she whispered back, putting her arm round him. 'We'll have to get a bigger bed.'

'No money for that.' He rolled on top of her and covered her mouth with his hand as she began to warn him again about the child within her. 'It'll be all right,' he muttered. 'Come on, Jeannie, mek some effort. We're married now.'

But she didn't need to make an effort. Although she wanted him too, he was in too much of a hurry to be gentle and tender or considerate; he gasped and rolled over on to his back without giving her as much as a kiss or a loving squeeze, and as she looked at him with his mouth open and his eyes closed she felt bruised and sore, frustrated and disillusioned.

She dressed in the small bedroom and went downstairs, leaving Harry still in Nan's bed. She found Nan in the scullery.

'I need to wash,' she said hesitantly. 'Can I – is it all right to . . .'

Nan pointed to a tin bowl. 'If you fill that you can tek it upstairs. There's some hot water in 'kettle, but fill it again before you go up and you can mek 'tea when you come down.'

'Yes,' Jeannie murmured, and wondered how long it would take her to get into the new routine. The kettle was in the kitchen, the tap in the scullery, but, she thought as she refilled the kettle, this was comparative luxury. At home they didn't have an inside tap, only the pump over the sink which they sometimes had to prime and which froze if it was a very cold winter.

She went back upstairs to find Harry fast asleep. She had a warm wash and dried herself on the towel she had brought with her, dressed again and brushed her hair, made the small bed, and went downstairs with the bowl of water.

Nan looked up at her. 'Keep yourself clean, don't you?' she said.

Jeannie gazed at her in astonishment. 'Yes,' she said. 'Always.'

'Good,' was the terse answer. 'I can't be doin' wi' slovenliness. Cleanliness is next to godliness. Were you taught that?'

'Erm, yes, something like that,' Jeannie said, as she made the tea. 'Ma always kept us as clean as she could. My brother Tom never liked getting washed when he was little.' She smiled. 'His toes were always full of sand.'

130

Nan nodded. 'He looks like a fine lad. Works hard, does he?'

Jeannie was pleased to hear Tom praised. 'Yes, he does. He's doing a boat-building apprenticeship. He decided against being a fisherman like our father was. He was always sick when he went to sea.'

'And what about you?' Nan asked soberly, adding, 'You can pour 'tea. No use waiting for Harry; he won't be up till dinner.'

'Until dinner time!' Jeannie was astounded. Her mother would never have allowed that.

'Aye.' Nan sat down at the table and waited for Jeannie to pour. 'And what about you?' she asked again. 'What do you do?'

'I mend nets,' she said. 'Same as my ma. She's Scottish, used to be a herring girl. I can gut and pack herring as well – I've done it every season since I was fourteen. Ma and my grandmother showed me how.'

Jeannie didn't know if it was her imagination or whether she saw a visible sign of relief on Nan's face.

'I'll be able to do it here until my time,' she said. 'And then, well, I was thinking that if Harry could fix up a frame outside, I could work on the nets here and look after the bairn.'

Nan nibbled on her fingers, and then took a sip of tea. 'Not Harry,' she said. 'He'd never manage that, but Billy Norman could. He's a ship's carpenter. It'll be no trouble to him.' She heaved a sigh and took another drink. 'I'll ask him when I see him. Good,' she murmured. 'Mebbe things won't be so bad after all.'

'I hope not,' Jeannie said. 'I'll pull my weight. I shan't expect you to keep me. Is there much work for women? On the nets, I mean.'

'For them as are good, yes,' Nan said, adding, 'You can work wi' me. That'll be for 'best, then 'other women will know you belong. Everybody knows everybody else on Hessle Road. Fisher folk are like one big family.'

Jeannie nodded. 'Just like at Scarborough then. And Harry,' she said hesitantly, not wanting to be disloyal, but wanting the truth. 'Has he got work?'

Nan pursed her mouth. 'Not at 'minute, he hasn't. But he'll have to find some, especially wi' a bairn coming.'

'Yes,' Jeannie murmured. 'It'll be an incentive, won't it?'

Nan glanced at her. 'Let's hope so.'

It was Sunday and Nan put on her grey bonnet and the same black skirt and coat as she wore for the wedding, and went off to chapel. She asked Jeannie if she'd like to go with her, but she said she'd wait for Harry to get up and maybe they'd take a walk. It was a bright sunny day and she felt that she'd like to have some fresh air and have a look round the area which was now her home.

But at almost midday he was still in bed, so she climbed the stairs and went to waken him. He woke with a start and for a second he looked at her as if he didn't know her. Then he reached out and grabbed her, pulling her into bed with him. She didn't object, for he looked tousled and endearing, and he smothered her with kisses and lifted her skirt just as she heard the scullery door open.

'Nan's back,' she said in an urgent whisper. 'She'll be coming up to get changed.'

'Still got time,' he grunted. 'Come on, be quick.'

And so once more she felt downhearted and dissatisfied and as she smoothed down her clothes and turned away she asked him, 'Why did you marry me, Harry?'

He gave a grin and stretched. 'Why d'ya think? It's great bein' married.'

She hesitated and looked down at him as she heard Nan's feet on the stairs. He doesn't love me as I love him, she thought. He was charming and persistent and I was willing. Would we be married now if I'd refused him back in March? Somehow she doubted it. I'll make him love me, she thought. He must. Maybe once the baby is born things will be different.

She gave a little shrug at Nan as she came up on to the top step. 'He's a slug-a-bed,' she told her. 'I think we're going to have to tip him out.'

'Aye, I reckon so. Get a bowl o' cold water. That'll fetch him out.'

Harry yelled and sprang out of bed, his nightshirt flapping, and dashed into the other bedroom, and for the first time Jeannie saw an indulgent half-smile on Nan's face.

Before she had left for chapel Nan had put mutton chops and onions in the side oven, and when she opened the oven door to check on them the aroma filled the house. She asked Jeannie to scrub some potatoes and carrots whilst she beat up a bowl of batter for Yorkshire pudding, and in under an hour they were sitting down to eat.

'Go down 'dockside and show your wife 'fishing fleet,' Nan told Harry. 'And look for Billy Norman. We want a frame putting up in 'yard.'

Harry took a mouthful of food and chewed before asking, 'What sort o' frame?'

'For hanging nets on, o' course, what do you think?' Nan glared at him. 'Somebody's got to work to pay 'rent.'

'Yeh, righto,' he said, quite unperturbed by the jibe intended for him. 'He'll be sailing tomorrow, though. Mightn't be able to do it straight away.'

'Ask him,' she said tersely. 'Don't forget. Go and ask his ma where he is, and if he's in 'pub then turf him out.'

Jeannie glanced at her. She looked very fierce, but Harry seemed not in the least concerned. Was she all shout and yet as soft as butter with Harry?

She put on her shawl when they left the house, as much to hide her pregnancy as because she was cold. Harry put his arm round her waist and kissed her cheek once they were out of the terrace and she smiled at him. Maybe things were going to be all right.

They went to another terrace and down a side passage where Harry lifted the sneck of a yard gate and then knocked on a scullery door. A small woman with grey hair under a bonnet answered.

'Is Billy in, Mrs Norman?' Harry asked politely. 'I need to ask him summat.'

'That's a daft question; course he's not. He's sailing tomorrow, isn't he?'

Harry nodded. 'Where is he? 'Criterion? 'Wassand Arms?'

'How would I know? Try 'Wassand, that's his usual.' She looked hard at Harry. 'Got any work yet?'

'Not yet,' he said, and then added confidently, 'Got a few contacts though. Lookin' good.'

She twisted her mouth wryly. 'Oh aye. This your new missis?'

'Yeh.' Harry drew Jeannie near. 'This is Jeannie. She's from Scarborough.'

Mrs Norman nodded. 'I heard. How do,' she said to Jeannie. 'Hope it works out all right for you. When are you due?'

Jeannie took a breath. How quickly word gets around. 'Not for a bit,' she said weakly.

'Right. Well if you need me for owt, let me know. Nan Carr knows me. I do midwifery.'

'Thank you,' Jeannie murmured, suddenly realizing that she hadn't given a thought to the actual birth. Suddenly she wanted her mother. She had only been married a day and she was missing her already. But she's not here, she thought as they walked back down the terrace. It's just me and Harry, and Nan.

They trawled several pubs on Hessle Road before they found Billy, and each time Harry asked her to wait outside whilst he went in and each time, when he came back out, she knew he had had a drink. At the last location, Jeannie stood outside waiting until finally an older man touched his cap to her as he was about to go inside and she plucked up courage to speak.

'Excuse me,' she began. 'Do you know Harry Carr or Billy Norman?'

'I do,' he said. 'I know 'em both.'

'Then could you ask Harry to come outside, please?' she said nervously. 'I'm his wife.'

'Ah!' The man gazed at her and a beaming smile lit his weathered face. 'I heard as he'd married a Scarborough lass. Nice to meet you. I'll get him right away.' He tipped his cap again and went inside and within five minutes both Harry and Billy came out.

Harry's face was flushed. 'I've just been doin' a

135

bit o' business, Jeannie. Work, you know.' He gave a wink. 'Summat might come of it.'

'Oh, good,' Jeannie said on a breath. 'I do hope so. Hello, Billy. Did Harry ask you about fixing up a frame? For net mending?'

Billy looked at Harry. 'No,' he said. 'When? I'm sailing tomorrow.'

'Today?'

'It's Sunday,' he said. 'Nan won't allow it, will she?'

Jeannie thought about Nan going off to chapel early this morning and took a chance. 'Yes, I think so. Can you make it somewhere and just come and fix it in place tonight?'

'Aye, I reckon so.' He glanced at Harry, who shrugged.

'How much will it cost?' Jeannie asked cautiously.

'Well, nowt for mekking,' he said. 'And I might be able to scrounge a bit o' wood. Where do you want it?' Again he looked at Harry. 'In 'yard?'

'Yes,' Jeannie said emphatically. 'In 'yard.'

They left Billy and continued along the road, stopping from time to time as Harry spoke to people and introduced Jeannie, and then crossed over and cut down another which brought them out close by the Albert Dock.

'We'll start here,' he said. 'This was 'first dock on Hessle Road, though not 'first in Hull. First one in Hull was 'New Dock, though now it's called Queen's Dock after 'queen, then there's 'Humber Dock and Princes Dock, Railway Dock and Victoria Dock.'

'Heavens!' Jeannie exclaimed. 'I didn't realize that Hull was so big, though Ethan once said—' She stopped, suddenly confused, and Harry immediately picked her up on it.

'Is he the chap we met that day?'

'Yes. He's a friend. He's a fisherman too. He used to come down to Hull sometimes with the herring.'

'Mm,' Harry said. 'Has he got his own boat?'

'Part shares, I think.' She was reluctant to talk about Ethan, but Harry probed.

'How come? He's onny about my age, if not younger.'

'His father part-owned a smack, but they didn't go out together. In case of accidents, you know. Ethan was nearly drowned in a storm eight years ago. His brother was lost overboard.'

She mused on that day; she could remember it so clearly. Both she and Tom had been badly shocked by it.

'Still don't explain how he comes to own shares,' Harry persisted.

'I don't know,' she said, though she knew that Ethan had worked hard towards it. 'He never told me. It's a smack,' she added, 'nothing big,' as if that explained it.

'They're about finished,' Harry muttered. 'Steam trawling is tekkin' over. Anyway, this is Albert. It was named after 'Prince of Wales.' They came to the Albert Dock, built alongside the Humber foreshore, and then walked along towards the William Wright Dock adjacent to it; she was overwhelmed by the sheer size of the waterway and the amount of shipping in both docks.

'This is nowt compared to St Andrew's,' he said. 'Wait till you see that.'

Jeannie was beginning to tire by the time they reached St Andrew's Dock, which Harry said had only been completed five years before. 'This dock'll tek over five hundred ships. Biggest in 'country, I reckon.'

'I'll have to stop for a minute,' she said, and went to rest on a bollard whilst she got her breath back.

'You said to me once, Harry, that there was always work for a fisherman in Hull.'

He glanced warily at her. 'Did I?'

'Yes, you did.' She had to know, and he would only tell her if she asked why he wasn't working. 'This is so huge,' she said, looking about her. 'But will there be work for me on the nets? I can't mend the trawl nets, they're far too big.'

'There are still some smaller craft,' he acknowledged. 'And there's still line fishing.'

'Ah,' she said. 'So that's all right. But what about you, Harry?' She looked up at him. 'Why is it that you don't have any work?'

His expression set and she couldn't tell if her question had angered him or not.

'I'm your wife, Harry.' She reached up to touch his arm, but he pulled away from her. 'I need to know,' she pleaded. 'I need to know what's in front of us.'

'I'll tell you what's in front of us,' he said bitterly. 'Penury. I can't get work because I've been blackballed. That's what. Nobody will tek me on.'

CHAPTER FIFTEEN

'Blackballed! Why?' Jeannie was horrified. Whatever had he done to have been given such a punishment?

'Don't want to talk about it,' he muttered.

'But we must,' Jeannie said. 'For how long?'

Harry stared straight ahead across the dock. 'Since ages ago.'

'No, I mean, when will it be lifted? How are you expected to earn a living?'

He shrugged but said nothing.

'Harry!' she said. 'Please. We have to talk about it. Does Nan know?'

'Course she knows! Everybody knows.'

'Everybody but me!' Jeannie said. 'Why didn't you tell me?'

He turned and looked at her. 'I didn't need to tell you,' he said sharply. 'I'd hardly tell a lass I'd just met that I hadn't got a job, now would I? Why else would I have 'time to be gallivanting round Scarborough?'

'But Billy was with you, and another friend.' She searched his face for the truth. 'How was it that they had time off?'

'Because they were waiting on a ship, like I told you I was – except I wasn't.' His face took on a petulant look. 'I didn't have a ship to go back to;

and you needn't look at me like that. I didn't think that it mattered at 'time.'

She let the remark slowly sink in. 'And the next time you came? Did that not matter either?'

He hesitated for a moment. 'Well, I was on me own. All my pals had gone off and I was at a loose end; and I got to thinking about you.'

Jeannie took a deep breath and then swallowed hard. Had she been a complete fool? 'And?'

'Well,' he said, 'I wondered if you'd still be there by 'harbour and that it'd be nice to see you again, so I borrowed some money from Nan. Told her I had a job in 'offing and jumped on 'first train.' He put his arm round her shoulder. 'I wanted to see you again, Jeannie. I mean that. I hadn't met anybody else that I was tekken with as much as you.'

She nodded. He had seemed fond of her, it was true; but was it because he was frustrated because he had no work? Maybe none of the Hull girls he knew would have anything to do with him because he hadn't any prospects.

'So why were you blackballed?' she asked. 'You have to tell me now.'

'Let's walk then, and I'll tell you.'

He took her arm and she felt oddly comforted. 'My da was a skipper and he got me apprenticed,' he began. 'And I was all right with him. Some of 'skippers treated 'apprentices like scum. We lived wi' Nan, me da and me, after Ma left and our Rosie went to live wi' Auntie Dot. Then, five years ago, we'd just got back from a trip when Da was asked to skipper a smack. Money was a bit scarce so he went. He went to 'Dogger Bank wi' a fleet and a gale sprang up.'

Harry pressed his lips together and his voice was choked when he went on. 'Twenty-six smacks were lost, including 'one that my da was on. I was gutted. We were such pals, me and him, an' I didn't think I wanted to go on wi' fishing. I was scared, for one thing. I didn't want to die, an' if anybody tells you that they're not scared o' goin' overboard then they're liars, cos everybody is. Especially 'young lads that get 'rough end of everybody.'

Jeannie squeezed his hand, remembering the tragic storm of eight years before and how affected everyone in Scarborough had been, especially Ethan.

'It's a hard trade,' she murmured. 'I know only too well.'

'But I started drinking,' he went on. 'I was six-teen when me da was took and somebody took me to an alehouse to give me some Dutch courage to sail again. Da never drank afore he went on a trip. He allus said you needed your wits about you, not have them addled by ale. Not that it did him any good. He'd have been as sober as a monk but he still went down wi' his ship.'

'I'm so sorry,' Jeannie said. 'So – is that why . . .'

He took a deep breath. 'I finished my indentures last year when I turned twenty-one. My da's pal Bob had tekken me on to finish 'em and he turned a blind eye to my drinking. He was a bit of a drinker himself was Bob. Not like my da.'

They stopped again to allow Jeannie to rest. She couldn't tell whether it was the long walk that was making her queasy and tired or Harry's melancholy tale.

'I thought I'd be well fixed up wi' him,' he went on. 'But then he had an accident just after and had

141

to give up fishing, so I applied to other companies.' He kicked at a stone and sent it skittering over the cobblestones. 'They can have their pick o' men, these big companies,' he said. 'An' word had got out that I was a drinker. You wouldn't think that it'd matter, would you? Most fishermen tek a drink.'

Jeannie considered. Ethan didn't drink when he was sailing, and neither did Josh.

'So is that why?' she asked.

Again he shook his head. 'No. I still got work, brought in plenty o' money most of 'time, until autumn afore last when my pal Joe and me had had a skinful of ale 'night afore we were due to sail. Next morning we were still hungover and we were late going on board; nearly missed 'tide so we were in 'skipper's black books to start with and he logged us. And somehow we could do nowt right for him. We were allus in 'wrong place and it was a really hard trip.'

I don't feel well, Jeannie thought. Her heart was pounding and she could barely take a breath, yet she felt it wasn't anything physical, it was the fear of what Harry was going to tell her and most of all of how they would manage without a man's wage coming in. Fishing would be all that he knew.

'I'll have to stop for a minute,' she said breathlessly.

He gazed down at her. 'You'll have to shape up,' he said. 'Most women keep on workin' when they're expecting.'

'I know that,' she answered sharply. 'But give me a chance. I've only just got here. I gave up a job to marry you, don't forget!'

Harry lifted his shoulders but made no answer

142

and she rested again before saying, 'So what happened?'

'We were part of a boxing fleet and I never liked fleeting. I'd rather do single boating any day, cos wi' fleeting you're too long away from home for one thing and for another it's much harder work.'

He paused and Jeannie saw a shadow pass over his face.

'Were they using steam cutters?' she asked. 'To ferry the boxed fish?'

'Aye,' he said. 'I forgot you'd know about fleeting.'

She nodded. In Scarborough there were still many single smacks fishing independently, but these smaller craft couldn't travel to distant waters as trawlers and larger vessels could. Some owners spent hard-earned money stripping out their smacks, cutting them in half and fitting a new keel to take a larger-beam trawl; steel warps enabled them to fish in deeper water and the new steam capstans made trawling the nets less hazardous to the crew.

Some years before, a group of Scarborough smack owners had got together to form their own fleeting company, after seeing the success of others in Hull and Grimsby. The fleet of smacks was accompanied by fast steam cutters which took delivery of boxes of fish ferried to them via rowing boat from the smacks and then conveyed them swiftly to the London market, ensuring fresher fish than if carried by the railway. But the fishermen didn't like it.

'If they haven't done it,' Harry was saying, 'nobody knows just how hard it is to tek boxes of fish and load 'em from 'smack into an open boat an' then on to 'deck of a cutter. None of 'crew like doing it. All 'boats rush at 'cutter as soon as they see it coming just so they can be first to load on board. Me and Joe were working as part of a team an' when we reached 'cutter there was a heavy sea running and all these other boats were pushing and shoving up against us. I was steadying Joe so that when we were carried up on 'next wave I'd push him up on to 'ship.'

He stopped speaking, as if he didn't want to go on; as if some unwanted memory had rushed back at him.

'So – did he miss it?' Jeannie asked softly. 'Did he miss the deck?'

'Yeh,' he muttered. 'He'd reached it an' I shoved, but he couldn't hold his balance; he had one hand on 'bulwark an' as he struggled to get on deck our boat dipped again an' he was left wi' his legs dangling an' he fell into 'sea.'

Jeannie swallowed. She hardly dared ask the question, but as she knew well, fishing was a hazardous and dangerous occupation.

'We lost him,' Harry said quietly. 'By 'time we saw him again he was way out o' reach, an' though everybody, even crews from 'other boats, tried to reach him we couldn't cos 'sea was running that high.'

He turned to look at her. "Skipper blamed me. He said that I wasn't watching out for him, which wasn't true. He was my best mate, course I was watching out for him,' he said bitterly. 'But I couldn't go in 'open boat again on that trip, an' 'skipper said I'd have to or he'd not tek me on again.' He shook his head. 'But I didn't. I said I'd pack 'fish or cook or do owt else but I'd not go out in an open boat.'

He shook his head. 'It was an unlucky trip. 'Next day we were nearly run down by a steamer, and 'following week a storm blew up and two of 'fleet were missing. Then we lost sight of 'Admiral of 'fleet an' some of 'crew were all for packing up an' going home but 'skipper would have none of it, so we went single boating to make up for 'loss of fish.'

He shrugged. 'And then when we got home, I started drinking again, and I went to some meetings; some of 'fishermen wanted to strike against winter fleeting an' I spoke up an' that's when I got blackballed. They said I was a troublemaker.'

They turned without speaking to make their way back from the vast dock towards Hessle Road; then Jeannie took his hand and squeezed it. 'I'm sorry,' she said. 'Really sorry about your friend; we'll try to think of what to do. I'm sure there'll be a company that'll take you on. We'll explain how you were affected by Joe's death, and then maybe—'

He dropped her hand. 'What do you mean *we'll* think on what to do? There'll be no *we* about it. I'm not having anybody thinking I can't fight me own battles; that I'm hiding behind a woman's skirts.' He shook a finger at her. 'Don't you start interfering wi' what I do or you'll be sorry for it.'

Jeannie stared at him. That wasn't what she'd intended. She hadn't thought of interfering; but surely they could discuss their livelihood if it concerned them both? She would work, of course, that was why she had asked Billy to put up a rig for her, but until word got around that she was a good neat worker what would they live on?

She paused at the junction of Hessle Road and looked west. Here and there between the streets and beyond were patches of land which looked marshy, but some were being built on.

'Come on,' Harry said. 'Look sharp.'

'Where does the road lead to?' she asked.

'Hessle.' His tone was begrudging. 'That's why it's called Hessle Road! It's where 'ship owners an' 'company directors go to live once they've made their money. Build themselves big houses out of 'likes of such as us.'

'But they've taken a chance, haven't they? Some of them have worked their way up from being fishermen, I expect. You can't blame people for trying to better themselves.'

He grunted and began to walk on in the direction of home. Jeannie followed more slowly. This was the first day of her marriage and it wasn't turning out in the way she had hoped for. They were almost at their street end and outside a tavern when Harry turned to look back at her.

'You go on home,' he said. 'I'm going for a drink. Tell Nan I'll be in for supper.'

'Tell her yourself,' she muttered under her breath. 'I'm not your servant.'

'Did you say summat?' He paused for a second with his hand on the tavern door, but she ignored him and walked on without even glancing in his direction, and said not a word in reply.

CHAPTER SIXTEEN

When Jeannie pushed open the scullery door all was quiet, and when she entered the kitchen it seemed warm and cosy. Nan was asleep in the chair by the range but she roused herself, instantly alert, when Jeannie came in.

'You can mek 'tea,' she said. 'I'm ready for a cup.'

'There's not much left,' Jeannie said.

'Try that one.' Nan pointed to a corner wall cupboard. 'I keep a supply in there.'

Jeannie reached up and brought down a brass tea caddy. 'My gran has one just like this,' she said. 'She keeps it locked in a cupboard too, but she brings it out when my ma calls.'

'Is that your da's mother?'

Jeannie swung the kettle back over the fire and it soon began to steam. 'Yes,' she said. 'Ma goes up quite a lot to make sure she's all right. Gran can't get down the hill now because of her legs.'

'Mm. Not all daughters-in-law care one way or another. Mine didn't, and sons-in-law aren't much better either. I hardly ever see mine, nor my daughters either for that matter.'

Jeannie made the tea. 'How many daughters have you got?'

147

'Three,' she said. 'One of 'em's married to a drunk, one's gone to live in Lowestoft where his family live and 'other one's done so well for herself that she hasn't 'time or inclination to come and see her ma. There was onny Harry's da who ever bothered and now he's gone.'

'Was your husband a seaman?' Jeannie asked, taking two tin mugs out of another cupboard.

'Aye, he was. You ask a lot o' questions, don't you?' Nan said abruptly.

Jeannie sat down at the table to pour the tea. 'It seems as if it's the only way I'll get to know who's who. Harry's told me nothing about anybody. I didn't know he had a sister. I didn't know his mother had left home.'

'Aye, well,' Nan sipped her tea. 'He wasn't encouraged to talk about her. She was a trollop and no mistake. I'm not even sure if all 'bairns belonged to Fred.'

'Your son?'

'Aye. Harry did, and Rosie. Harry's spitting image of his da.' She sighed. 'Hasn't got his backbone, though.'

'How will we manage if Harry doesn't get a ship?' Jeannie asked. She felt this to be an opportune time to speak of it as Harry wasn't there, and Nan hadn't asked where he was; no doubt she knew or guessed. 'I know I'm asking questions, but I need to know; I'll have a bairn to think of before long. I've to feed and clothe it and I can't do that on just mending nets.' She paused for a second and then said, 'I don't want to go crawling back to Scarborough with my tail between my legs. I've got some pride.'

'Huh! Pride, is it?' Nan sneered. 'There'll be none

148

o' that left if we don't mek ends meet. You should've thought o' that some months back.'

Jeannie wanted to cry. Her dreams were shattered. A few moments of blissful ecstasy was all she and Harry had shared. Not love at all on Harry's part, but simply lustful hunger, and on hers a youthful, yearning desire.

'I should,' she agreed. 'I hadn't thought of the consequences.'

Nan looked at her with something like pity, or it could have been scorn. 'So are you going to leg it back to Scarborough to cry on your ma's shoulder or are you stopping to face up to 'misfortune of your own mekkin' and give your bairn a father?' She stared hard at Jeannie, not helping her out at all, not making any suggestions or giving her advice, simply waiting for her decision.

Jeannie drank her tea before answering. It was strong – she'd put an extra spoonful of tea leaves in the pot and it was making her feel nauseous, yet she felt she couldn't waste it.

She put the mug on the table and it rattled from the tremble in her fingers. Dared she go home and say she had left her husband? Dared she face up to all those who knew her; all the women and girls who worked at the harbourside? The fishermen who always had a word for her and her mother? Her mother! The shame wouldn't be Jeannie's alone. It was her ma's and it was Tom's and even Granny Marshall's. And then there was Ethan. Could she ever face him again?

She shook her head and was conscious of Nan's intent expression.

'No,' she said. 'Like it or not, I'm stopping.'

*   *   *

Nan stood up and looked at her. 'It'll not be easy,' she said brusquely. 'Life's very hard here, but folk help each other out. I don't know of anywhere else but Hessle Road where they do.'

Jeannie nodded. It was no different from Scarborough, or at least Sandside, where the community stuck together, but she wasn't going to spoil Nan's illusion if that was what she believed. She also knew that she could expect no favours from her. Just because she was married to her grandson didn't mean that Nan would warm to her or support her. Jeannie had heard her tart words to her granddaughter Rosie, and to Billy Norman, though not to Connie. She had barely spoken to Connie; it was as if she hadn't even noticed that she was there.

Nan continued to gaze at her for a few seconds; she blinked a few times, pressed her lips together, and then said, 'Right then. Let's go up and swap 'bedrooms.'

Jeannie put her head on one side. 'What?'

Nan gave a deep sigh. 'I've slept in that bed for nigh on forty years. Nivver thought I'd have to give it up.'

'But . . .' Jeannie rose to her feet. 'There's no need. We'll buy a bed as soon as . . .'

'Aye, as soon as your ship comes in. I've heard that afore. In 'meantime you can have mine and I'll have Harry's.'

Jeannie noticed that it was still Harry's bed and not hers and Harry's.

Nan made her way to the stairs. 'You'll need a bigger bed when 'bairn comes, and,' she added

150

prosaically, 'afore that too if you're to mek summat of this marriage.'

Jeannie followed her up the narrow stairs and together they emptied a rickety chest of drawers of Nan's hairbrush and other personal things, of which there were only a few, and moved them into the small bedroom. Then they moved Jeannie's bag, which contained her everyday clothing, her apron and her boots, and Harry's clothes, including his heavy boots, thick trousers and warm coat.

Jeannie picked them up and buried her nose in the coat; she thought she could smell the sea, or maybe it was fish.

'Will he ever fish again?' she murmured, more to herself than to Nan.

'He'll have to,' came Nan's terse reply. 'Or we'll all sink.'

When Harry arrived home it was well after supper time. Jeannie and Nan had had bread and cheese and a mug of cocoa. Nan had said that cocoa was good for pregnant women, that it helped to make strong bones for the growing child, and though Jeannie didn't know that she was happy to drink it, for it was what she and Tom had always had when they were little.

'Why didn't you wait?' Harry's words were slurred. 'I'm not late.' He grinned. *'I'm not late, why didn't you wait? Hey. I've made poetry!'*

Jeannie lifted her eyes from her knitting. Her mother had bought her some white wool and knitting needles and put them in her bag without telling her. She'd also put in instructions on how to knit a baby coat. Nan too was knitting a navy blue jumper, and Jeannie surmised it was a gansey for Harry.

'Not exactly Wordsworth,' she murmured, remembering her old teacher's love of the poet and her efforts to drum up enthusiasm for poetry in the uninterested children, and recalling her own favourite.

With ships the sea was sprinkled far and nigh,
Like stars in heaven, and joyously it showed;
Some lying fast at anchor in the road,
Some veering up and down.
One knew not why.

'But not a bad try,' she conceded and began another row of stitches.

Harry stood over her. 'Are you mocking me?' His tone was belligerent.

'No. Why would I do that?'

'Sit down,' Nan said, putting down her knitting and getting up from the chair. 'I'll mek you some supper.'

'No,' he said. 'You sit down! Jeannie can do that. That's her job from now on. Time you took it easy for a change.'

Jeannie put the knitting back into a paper bag and stood up. Harry moved into her chair. 'Will you have the same as we've had?' she asked. 'Bread and cheese and cocoa?'

'Aye, if there's nowt else.' He stretched his feet towards the hearth. 'Haven't you got a bit o' beef?'

'No,' she said. 'We had mutton for dinner, if you remember, but there's none left.'

'I'll have cheese then. You'd best get off shopping down 'road tomorrow. Nan'll show you 'best places to go, won't you, Nan? Get some beef – or ham, I don't mind a bit o' ham.'

'All right,' she said amiably. 'I'll do that.' No sense in bringing up the subject of money at this stage, she thought. Not in the irritable mood she sensed he was in. 'Cocoa?'

'No, an' I don't want tea either,' he said, 'so you can put 'teapot away.'

'There's nowt else,' Nan broke in. 'You've had plenty of ale by 'look of you.'

'What is this?' He got to his feet. 'Are you two ganging up on me in me own house?'

'You what!' Nan stood up and faced him, putting her fists on her thin hips. 'Whose house exactly? Who's been paying 'rent all these months?'

He had the grace to look sheepish. 'Aw, sorry, Nan, it's just—'

'There's a surprise for you upstairs, Harry.' Jeannie tried her best to smile and look happy. 'Nan's given up her bed for us. We've swapped round.'

'Have you, Nan?' To Jeannie's astonishment, he took a step towards his grandmother and planted a kiss on her leathery cheek.

'Give over,' Nan said, making a show of rubbing her hand across her face. 'Daft beggar!'

I don't understand him, Jeannie thought as she sawed the bread for Harry's supper. One minute I could hate him, he's so boorish, and the next he's so sweet and lovable. Is it the drink that makes him so moody, or the fact that he's out of work and feels worthless?

She looked up and smiled at him, and after scrutinizing her for a second with a small frown above his nose he smiled back. Perhaps it will be all right, she thought for the umpteenth time. We'll both have to try harder.

In the larger bed that night he held her close and was more loving than he had been the night before. 'I'm sorry, Jeannie; my lovely Jeannie. My sweet and bonny lass. I'm glad I married you, an' I'll get work, I promise. I'll keep off 'drink and first thing tomorrow I'll be off to 'docks.'

'Yes,' she whispered back. 'We'll be all right, won't we, Harry? Together we'll manage. We just have to trust each other and work together to make a home for us and our bairn.'

'Aye.' He yawned, and kissed her cheek. 'That's it. We will.'

CHAPTER SEVENTEEN

But Harry's 'first thing' and Jeannie's didn't tally. At eight o'clock she and Nan were ready to go out *on 'road* as Nan put it and Harry was still in bed. Jeannie went up to wake him.

'Are you going to get up, Harry?' she asked anxiously. 'It's gone eight.'

He turned over in bed. 'In a minute,' he muttered, and sighed deeply. 'I used to sleep in here when I was a bairn.' He didn't even open his eyes as he spoke and she knew he would go back to sleep as soon as she left the room.

As she and Nan left the house they saw that Billy had put up the frame in the yard. Nan muttered about folk working on a Sunday, but then added that Billy was a good lad. She led Jeannie out of the terrace and up Walcott Street and on to Hessle Road itself, which even at this early hour was teeming with people, with horses and carts, men pushing wheelbarrows, and packed horse trams.

'We'll go to 'butcher's first,' Nan said, 'and let him know who you are.' She clutched a small black cloth purse in one hand and in the other a cotton shopping bag. 'And then to 'baker's for some flour and yeast.'

'It must be good to bake your own bread,' Jeannie said. 'We don't have a range with an oven like yours; we just have a fire grate with bars in our cottage.'

'What? Do you have to buy bread?' Nan tutted.

'No, Ma makes it once a week and the baker bakes it for us.' Jeannie smiled as she recalled the mouth-watering smell when she fetched the warm bread from the baker.

'Ah, well, some folk do that round here, but I wonder how they know they're getting their own.'

'Ma used to put our initial on it,' Jeannie explained, but Nan shook her head as if she didn't credit that.

They joined a queue of other women at the butcher's shop and Nan spoke briefly to some of them, but Jeannie got the impression that Nan Carr wasn't one for social chit-chat or gossip.

When they reached the counter, Nan told the butcher, 'I'll have a pound o' scrag end o' beef.'

'No scrag end today, Mrs Carr,' the butcher said. 'I've none left. Nice bit o' salt brisket, or how about some belly pork? Very nourishing, very cheap.' He winked at Jeannie as he spoke. 'Pigs' trotters, neck o' lamb, sheep's eyes?'

Nan tutted and glared at his humour. 'I'll have a rabbit,' she said. 'Skin it for me, will you?' It wasn't so much a request as a command. 'This is my grand-son's wife. You'll have heard he'd got wed.' She turned her head to the waiting queue of women to include them. 'She's from Scarborough. She'll be doing 'shopping from time to time.'

'How do, miss – missus,' the butcher corrected himself. 'Look forward to doing business wi' you.'

Jeannie began to speak but Nan interrupted. 'An'

we'll expect 'same consideration. She's one of us now.'

'Oh aye.' The butcher finished skinning the rabbit and wrapped it in a newspaper. 'I allus look after 'locals, you know that, Mrs Carr.'

She paid sixpence for the rabbit and asked for a lump of beef suet, which the butcher gave her; then they went on to the grocer where she bought a stone of flour, two ounces of yeast, and a few slices of boiled ham. After that they called in at the greengrocer for a bunch of carrots and half a stone of potatoes.

'What you've to remember,' she told Jeannie as they walked back up the road with Jeannie carrying the parcel from the butcher, 'is that it's still possible to eat well even if you've not much money.'

Well, I know that already, Jeannie thought. We've hardly been living a life of luxury in Scarborough; I don't really know what the word means. But we always ate a lot of fish; there was always plenty of that.

'Don't you get fish, Mrs— Nan?' She found it difficult to call her Nan; maybe it would be easier after the baby was born. 'We generally had it given, or at least bought it cheap.'

'Aye, I did, but Harry's not working, is he, to bring any home. So what groceries I've bought today will have to last all week. I've onny got my relief money to live on till Harry gets work.'

Jeannie knew how hard that must be. Nan was too old for regular work, although apparently she still mended nets when she could. The relief money, which Jeannie's mother also received, was handed out to widows and orphans through a fishermen's benevolent society. She resolved to start asking around for work immediately.

'Do you know any fishermen who'd bring their nets to me?' she asked Nan. 'I'd like to get started right away and work for as long as I can.'

'I'll put 'word about,' Nan said. 'There's still a few men work for themselves and not for a company, though they're few and far between.'

And she was as good as her word. She stopped several times to speak to wives and mothers of fishermen; she told Jeannie that not all of them were able to mend nets, or even expected to earn, as their menfolk didn't agree with women working, but preferred them to be at home looking after the family.

'Which is all very well if your man is in work,' she muttered. 'Some of us can't be that choosy.'

Jeannie's spirits sank lower the nearer they got to the terrace. Would Harry be up? Might he even have gone out as he promised?

But no, neither of those things had happened, she discovered when they entered the house. Harry was still in bed. She went upstairs.

'Harry, get up,' she urged. 'I want you to take me down to the dock. I want you to tell the people you know that I'm available for work. I'm a good net mender. There must be somebody who'll employ me.'

Harry sat up and swung his bare legs to the floor. He stood up. 'Are you trying to shame me?' His voice was loud and angry.

'No, of course not. I'm good at what I do,' she retaliated. 'And somebody has to earn money until you get a ship. Nan can't keep the three of us and another one to come.'

'Clear off downstairs whilst I get dressed,' he shouted. 'And get me some breakfast.'

She turned away and headed down the stairs. She was shaking; she could almost have imagined that he was angry enough to hit her. This wasn't how she thought marriage would be.

When Harry had sullenly eaten his breakfast and drunk a mug of tea, and Jeannie had picked at a slice of boiled ham and a piece of bread, he told her to get her shawl and they'd go out.

'An' if I meet anybody,' he warned, 'don't speak until I say so. I'll not have any of my mates thinking I'm under your thumb as soon as we're wed.'

'No, Harry,' she said meekly, though inwardly seething. 'You do the talking, but don't forget to tell them how good I am. One of the best braiders in Scarborough, I was.'

'Mebbe so,' he muttered. 'But you're not in Scarborough now.'

They retraced their steps from the day before, along Hessle Road and back to St Andrew's Dock, and Harry walked by her side not speaking. They took the route alongside the dock and Jeannie observed the women and girls on the fish quay and thought that after the baby was born she might be able to get a job there; they seemed a friendly lot who waved and shouted to them. Some of them seemed to know Harry and he called back in a familiar manner.

Many of the ships they had seen on the previous day had sailed on the morning tide, but there were still hundreds of various types: the steam trawlers which were replacing smacks; paddle tugs which had been adapted for fishing; steam cutters making ready to accompany the fleet on the following day's tide. Some of the ships were taking ice on board, for other industries had been spawned by this new dock and ice-making companies had sprung up in the area, as had smoke houses and roperies. Other ships were loading up with crew provisions and empty fish boxes ready for sailing.

Hundreds of people allied to the fishing trade worked on or near this dock: carpenters and coopers, sailmakers and rope-workers. All depended on this industry for their living.

Harry nodded and greeted various acquaintances. He stopped once or twice and told the men that he was showing his wife the fishing craft of Hull.

'She's from Scarborough,' he explained. 'Doesn't know Hull.'

They tipped their caps or touched their foreheads and she smiled back, but Harry didn't introduce her, or mention the net mending. When she reminded him, he told her gruffly that they were mostly dock labourers and not fishermen and that he knew what he was doing.

'But they might know somebody,' she pleaded. 'That's how word gets around.'

'Be quiet, will you,' he said. 'I've told you I know what I'm about!'

And so she kept quiet, not wishing to antagonize him further and risk his turning back for home.

They came eventually to an area where some vessels were laid up for repairs and Harry hailed one of the men who was watching work being done on a smack. He straightened up and Jeannie saw that he was considerably older than Harry, with a wiry grey beard and keen blue eyes. He wore a navy fisherman's gansey under his wool jacket and heavy cord breeches.

'How do, Harry! Haven't seen you about for a bit.'

Harry nodded towards the vessel. 'This one o' yours, Mike?'

'Aye.' The man grinned. 'Mortgaged up to 'neck I am. But she's a grand lady. We've had her modified and fitted her with a ten-horse-power engine. She's just about ready and we'll be off 'day after tomorrow.'

'Have you still got *Daisy Belle?*'

'Aye, but onny a quarter share; I'm not made o' brass! She's been refitted as well but wi' a twenty horse power. We're trying her out off Flamborough at 'minute.' He glanced at Jeannie and touched his cap. 'This your missis? I heard as you'd got wed.'

Harry reached out and drew Jeannie close, keeping his arm round her shoulder. 'This is Jeannie, Mike. We've onny been married a couple o' days.'

'How do, Jeannie.' Mike took off his cap, revealing thick grey hair. 'Pleased to meet you. Glad to see that Harry's settling down. How you getting on wi' Nan? Leading you a dance, is she?'

Jeannie smiled. 'I'm watching my p's and q's,' she said.

'Aye, you do that.' He grinned. 'She was allus a bit of a tartar but she's all right when you get to know her.'

'Mike was a pal o' my da,' Harry explained to Jeannie. 'Mike Gardiner. They were apprenticed at 'same time.'

'Oh, I see,' she said. 'It's nice to meet you.' Then on impulse she added, 'My father was a fisherman. He used to sail out from Scarborough.'

'Did he?' Mike folded his arms across his chest again, and then he frowned. 'Was, you said? Lost was he?'

161

'Yes. I don't really remember him. It was ten years ago. A storm off the Dogger Bank.'

He nodded. 'We've lost a few brave lads in those waters,' he said. 'Including Harry's da.' He sighed. 'He was a good mate o' mine. What you doing now, Harry? Are you wi' one o' bigger companies?'

'Not at 'minute I'm not,' Harry said. 'I've refused a couple o' jobs wi' them and word got round that I was work-shy, which I'm not. But I'd rather be wi' one of 'smaller owners like yourself, Mike.'

Jeannie was unsure whether what he said was true or not, but Mike was listening sympathetically and nodding his head.

'If you're owt like your da, you'll not be work-shy,' he said. 'So what 'you doing for money?'

Harry shrugged. 'On 'slate,' he said. 'Folks know me so they know I'll pay 'em back.'

Mike grunted and shook his head. 'Hard though, specially when you're just wed. I reckon you trusted him enough to tek a chance, eh, Jeannie?'

'Oh, yes,' she said eagerly. 'And I'm looking for work too,' she added. 'Just to tide us over. I'm a net mender; one of the best' – she smiled – 'though that sounds like boasting.'

'Ah! I might be able to put some work your way then,' he said. 'And Harry, I need a third hand for this smack. It's a bit lowly for you, I know, but if you're willing to tek it on for this trip, there might be 'chance o' summat better later on.'

Jeannie held her breath as Harry appeared to consider. It was a lower position than he was qualified for, but at least it would bring in some much needed money and put food on the table.

'Well,' Harry said slowly, 'I could. I'm doing nowt

right now – so, aye, I will! Thanks very much, Mike.'

They took their leave after Harry had been given instructions on times and terms of employment and walked back along the dock. Harry said nothing but kept his arm on her shoulder, until, out of listening distance of Mike Gardiner, he blew out a long breath and gave her a huge squeeze.

'Phew! Thank God for that.' He glanced down at her. 'Telled you, didn't I, that I knew what I was about?'

'You did, Harry.' She smiled, and thought how lucky it was that after a good deal of persuasion he had at last agreed to come down to the dock. 'You did really well. How lucky that we should see your father's old friend.'

'Aye, he's done well has Mike. If my da had lived, well who knows but he might have been a partner wi' him. He allus dreamed of having his own ship, or at least shares in one.' He paused and considered; then, drawing himself up tall, he said, 'And I'd probably be skipper by now. He'd have seen me right would Da.'

Jeannie squeezed his hand. 'That he would,' she said, thinking of Josh Wharton and Ethan and his stepbrother Mark. 'You'd have worked together. Does Mike Gardiner have any sons?'

'Aye, he does.' He gave a laugh. 'One's a butcher; the other's a skipper. Not much older than me.' Then his mouth turned down. 'He's allus had his da there to give him a helping hand.'

'You'll be all right, Harry,' she said reassuringly. 'Your da would be proud.'

'Do you think so, Jeannie?' A frown wrinkled his forehead. 'Do you reckon he's watching?'

Jeannie swallowed. If Harry's da was watching him, then her own father would be watching over her and Tom too. That was what her Scarborough grandmother had taught her, but was it what she believed?

'I hope so, Harry,' she said. 'I really hope so.'

They walked on and turned on to Hessle Road, heading for home. There were still crowds of people about and the long row of shops was thronged with shoppers.

'Your nan will be pleased to hear about the job with Mike Gardiner,' Jeannie said. 'She'll know him, of course?'

He nodded. 'Oh yeh. Known him all his life.' He looked about him as if assessing something. 'Erm, tell you what, Jeannie. You go on home and tell Nan about Mike. I'm just going to have a jar of ale and meet up wi' some of 'lads, them that's about, and tell 'em 'good news. I'll not be long. Save me some rabbit stew.'

I should have known, she thought despondently as she watched Harry enter the nearest hostelry and then walked slowly on alone. I really should have known.

164

CHAPTER EIGHTEEN

When Harry sailed two days later Jeannie heaved a sigh of rather guilty relief. The last few days had been very draining. The experience of being married and finding it wasn't quite what she expected, living with Nan who, even when in the best of humour, was inclined to be acerbic and blunt, and the effort of encouraging Harry to make a real thrust at finding work, had left her feeling tense and on edge. She hoped now that after spending a few weeks apart they would be able to make a fresh start under better circumstances and rekindle the emotion she still wanted to believe they had both felt on their first meeting.

The day hadn't started well. Jeannie had woken very early, but when she nudged Harry to awaken him, he'd turned over, grumbling that there was plenty of time.

'But there isn't,' she'd urged. 'Come on, I'll go down and make your breakfast whilst you get dressed.'

She'd gone downstairs in her nightshift and shawl, riddled the fire and put on more coal, and swung the kettle over. There was gruel in the oven which had been simmering all night and she cut two slices of bread and brought out a pot of jam which she had bought from the grocer as a special treat. But she could hear no sound of activity from upstairs and she crept back up to find he was still in bed.

'Harry,' she'd whispered urgently. 'It's half past five.' It was a lie, but a justified one, she thought; the night before she had moved the hands of the clock forward ten minutes in case of just such an emergency. It had the desired effect, for he sat up with a start and scrambled out of bed and into his trousers and navy blue gansey.

'For God's sake, Jeannie, why didn't you wake me? You know I've to catch 'tide.'

She hadn't answered, but went downstairs again to make and pour his tea and dish up the gruel.

He'd glanced at the clock on the wall as he sat down at the table. 'Onny twenty past.' He frowned. 'You said half past.'

'I think the clock is slow,' she replied calmly. 'I noticed just the other day. Anyway, don't you have to be on board and out of the dock before the tide turns?'

He paused in the act of taking a gulp of tea. 'Don't be telling me what I already know,' he muttered. 'There's nowt *you* can tell me about ships and tides.' He pressed his lips together with his fingers. 'So button up!'

She sat down opposite him. 'I'm sorry,' she said. 'It's just that I'm nervous. I want this to be a really good trip for you, Harry.'

He'd pushed aside the empty gruel dish and picked up a slice of bread which she'd spread with jam. 'It will be. But I'm tekkin' a lowly position, you know, just to be in work. I should be skipper by rights.'

'Yes,' Jeannie murmured. 'I realize that.' She turned her head at the sound of footsteps on the stairs. 'Here's Nan coming down to see you off.'

Nan came into the kitchen dressed in a long flannel nightgown with a shawl over her shoulders and her grey hair in a long plait. She looked tired and old, Jeannie thought, with her back bent and her thin face pale and wrinkled.

'No need for you to be up yet, Nan,' Harry had told her. He pushed his chair back from the table. 'You get off back to bed.'

'I just wanted to tell you that 'clock's a bit slow,' she croaked. 'Don't want you to miss 'tide.'

'For heaven's sake, both of you,' he exclaimed, but he said it with good humour and Jeannie had felt the tension easing. He picked up the heavy bag containing his oilskins and boots which was by the door. 'Cheerio, then. I'm off. Give us a kiss, both of you.'

He put his cheek towards Nan who gave him a peck, but Jeannie said, 'I'll come to the door with you.' She wanted to give him a proper kiss, a loving, come home soon kind of kiss. One that he could think about whilst he was away.

'Right then.' He turned to the door leading to the scullery. 'But don't come out,' he said. 'I don't want folks lookin' at you in your bedgown. And don't whatever you do come down to 'dock when we sail.'

'I won't,' she said.

'Nor down to 'river!' he warned.

'No,' she said. 'Of course not. There won't be time.'

'I'm not talkin' about time,' he said sharply, opening the back door. 'I'm talkin' about bad luck if you do.' He frowned. 'You know about that, don't you? Being a harbour girl?'

167

'I know about it, yes,' she agreed. 'I won't come. Give me a kiss, Harry. I'll see you on your return.'

He'd kissed her lips. 'Yeh. About three weeks, that's all. We'll have a good fish supper then!'

When she returned to the kitchen Nan was pouring a cup of tea. She looked up at Jeannie. 'You wouldn't think about going down to see him off, would you? We don't do that here; 'fishermen don't like it.'

Jeannie had sat many times by the Scarborough harbour and waved goodbye to the fishermen, but she knew that many were superstitious about such things and wouldn't allow their wives to see them off. She didn't believe in such old wives' tales herself, but she showed respect to those who did.

'I won't go,' she said. 'Not if Harry doesn't want me to.'

'He doesn't,' Nan said firmly. 'So don't forget. And,' she added, 'yon clock is fast. I put it on ten minutes to mek sure he wasn't late.'

Jeannie laughed. 'So did I! It's only just gone half past five; why don't you go back to bed for an hour? There's no need for you to be up so early.'

To her surprise, Nan agreed. 'I will,' she said, slurping her tea. 'I feel a bit tired,' and pushing away her half-finished drink, she went back upstairs.

Jeannie ate her breakfast, glad of the chance to be alone with her thoughts without Nan sitting across from her. She was still quite nervous of her and wondered how she would cope with just the two of them in the house – Nan's house, not hers. She suddenly thought of her mother and Tom and pondered on whether they were missing her at home. Her mother would be, she was sure, but maybe not

Tom, for he was probably considering his own life, and the new one he would make with Sarah, and not thinking about her at all.

I'll write to Ma soon, she thought. She'll want to know how I am and what we're doing. I can tell her the good news that Harry has gone to sea and that I'm hoping to do some braiding fairly soon when word gets round.

Later in the day she took a walk along the road to get to know the area. Nan didn't want to go out, she said, but would stay home by the fire. 'I'll enjoy me own company for a change,' she muttered. 'Sit and do a bit o' knitting without interruption.'

I suppose that remark was meant for me, Jeannie considered as she turned out of the terrace. I enjoyed my breakfast alone; maybe Nan wants to do the same. It can't be easy having a stranger living in your house, even if she is married to your grandson.

She hadn't been out more than ten minutes when she heard someone calling. 'Mrs Carr!' The name didn't register at first, but then she heard 'Jeannie!' and looked about her in astonishment. Who knew her here in Hull?

A man on the opposite side of the road was waving at her as he walked alongside a youth pushing a handcart. A horse and waggon went by, obscuring her view, but when it passed she recognized Mike Gardiner.

'I was just coming to see you, Mrs Carr. Or is it all right to call you Jeannie? You don't seem old enough to be married.' He grinned.

'Please do,' she said. 'I didn't recognize myself as Mrs Carr! But I am old enough.' She smiled,

169

thinking how nice it was to see a friendly face. 'I'm nearer seventeen than sixteen.'

'Practically an old lady then,' he teased. 'And just married and already your husband has left you to go to fishing.'

'Yes, but that's what I expected,' she said. 'It's what we do, isn't it?'

He nodded. 'Quite right, Jeannie. Quite right. I see you've a sensible head on your shoulders.' He turned and pointed across the road to where the youth was waiting by the handcart. 'I've got a net there needing some expert work on it. I've brought 'lad myself to show him where you and Harry live and then he'll know for another time. Are you off somewhere or can you come back to have a look at it?'

'Oh, I'll come back,' she said eagerly, buoyed up by the thought that there would be more jobs after this, if he was pleased with her work.

Mike whistled to the boy to follow them and Jeannie turned round to go back home.

'I've had a frame put up in the yard,' she told him, 'but somebody will have to help me drape the net, just for the present.' She blushed, but was reassured when he nodded and murmured that he and the lad would do that and that it had already been dipped to remove the salt and seaweed.

She examined the net when they had stretched it over the frame so that it didn't fold on to itself. There were several large holes and rips and snagging, and she knew there was a good deal of work to be done on it.

'Some of these holes will take a deal of mending,' she said. 'It looks as if the fish have been forced through. Unless,' she murmured, 'you've had a shark in them.'

'No shark,' he said grimly. 'But there was a lad on board on 'last trip that I hadn't hired before. I saw he was riving at 'nets. He's 'son of someone I know and I took him on as a favour. Shan't use him again. That's why I asked Harry to crew this time.' He looked over her shoulder at the net. 'Can you do it or shall I ask somebody else?'

'Oh, I can do it all right,' she was quick to assert. 'But it's not a day's job. It will take two or maybe three days.'

'That's all right,' he replied. 'As long as it's ready for next week when 'other ship goes out.'

She fingered the net. 'Where's the best place to buy hemp and twine?' she asked. 'I don't know anywhere in Hull.'

'I'll tek you.' Nan had come out into the yard. 'There's a warehouse just off 'road. They've everything that's needed for net mending. How do, Mike.' She nodded in his direction. 'Still mekkin' money, are you?'

'Not much.' He grinned. 'But spendin' it anyway. Acquired a second ship; did Harry tell you?'

'Aye, he did. Hope it's seaworthy wi' my lad on it.'

Jeannie listened as they bantered. Harry is still her lad, doubtless always will be; I shall have to get used to that. I'll probably never have him to myself.

After Mike had left, Nan told Jeannie that she had some mending thread if Jeannie wanted to use it, but didn't seem offended when she said that she would rather buy her own.

'I prefer to have a look at the quality,' she said.

171

'Scarborough fishermen are always particular about their nets; I expect the Hull men are the same.'

'Aye, they are,' Nan agreed and fetched her shawl so that they could go out immediately.

On the road, Jeannie saw Connie walking towards them and wondered why she wasn't working. As the girl came nearer, she saw that she had her left hand held in a makeshift sling. She stopped to speak, but Nan without any acknowledgement of Connie walked on.

'Have you had an accident, Connie?'

Connie nodded. 'I fell down some steps,' she said. 'I think I might have broken a bone. My wrist is swollen anyway so I can't work.' Her face twisted in a grimace. 'I just hope they'll keep my job open for me.'

'Where do you work?'

'On 'fish quay. You need two hands for gutting and filleting.'

'Course you do. I hope it doesn't take too long. Have you tried putting your hand in ice to take the swelling down?'

The girl shook her head. 'No. Haven't done owt but put 'sling round it.'

'Why don't you go to work and ask for some ice? Then at least they'll know you're not skiving off.'

Connie looked pale and drawn. 'Yeh,' she said. 'Mebbe I'll do that.'

Nan called Jeannie to hurry up. 'We haven't got all day to stand yammering,' she said. 'There's work to be done for some of us.'

When Jeannie caught up with her, she explained what Connie had done. 'She fell down some steps; she thinks she might have broken a bone.'

'Huh! Pushed more like,' she grunted with not an ounce of sympathy in her voice. 'They're not a good family. You'll be as well to keep away from her.'

Jeannie looked at her in astonishment. 'But – she's Rosie's friend, isn't she? She came to our wedding.'

'Dare say she did,' Nan grouched. 'But not at my invitation. And what Rosie does is nowt to do wi' me. She's not under my care and she's old enough to do as she likes.'

There was nothing more to be said on the subject and they continued walking in silence until they came to the warehouse, which was stacked to the ceiling with every type of net, including trawl and seine nets, lines and rods for single boating and anglers too, various reels of hemp and sisal thread, and net needles.

Jeannie had brought her own needle with her from Scarborough but decided to buy another as a spare. Her mother had always had two in case one broke or got lost, though the latter was hardly likely, for net needles were precious items to the net menders.

Nan stood back whilst Jeannie examined the goods on offer and then made her purchases, but she nodded approvingly as they went out, muttering, 'So you know what you're doing after all, in spite of being so young!'

Jeannie smiled. That was as good a compliment from Nan as she was ever going to get.

CHAPTER NINETEEN

As soon as Jeannie and Nan had finished their mid-day meal of chops cooked with onions, potatoes and carrots, Nan told her she would clear away.

'You get on wi' net,' she said. 'It's a fine day and you might as well mek 'most of it.'

Jeannie agreed. It wasn't pleasant working in the rain or the cold, although she had done both, and she didn't know if Nan would allow her to bring the smaller nets into the house as sometimes she and her mother had done to mend on their knees.

Today was fine and sunny and she couldn't help but think of the times when they and the other women had mended nets by the Scarborough harbour, looking at the sea and the sands and the ships and talking to the visitors who stopped to watch them work. Here she was confined to the small yard and she grimaced a little as the odour from the fish meal factory and the smoke houses wafted through the air. Instead of the shrill cry of herring gulls, she could hear the shunt of railway trains from the Dairycoates locomotive sheds close by St Andrew's Dock, where boxed fish began the journey to the inland markets.

Come on, Jeannie, she told herself. This is the life

you've chosen. She stretched out the net again and with her scissors carefully cut off the loose and torn fibres. Then she checked the other knots to make sure they were strong and secure and loaded her flat net needle with hemp. With a clove hitch to catch the top strand of the net she began to work the knots slowly and methodically from left to right, matching them to the original knots so that they were of even size and gradually closing the gaping holes and rents.

She became totally absorbed in her task for over an hour, until Nan opened the back door and handed her a mug of sweetened tea.

'Best tek a break,' she said. 'Rest your legs for a bit.'

Jeannie gratefully took a sip. 'I'm all right,' she said. 'I'm enjoying doing it, although it's a challenge. It's an old net and it's been mended several times before. It's difficult to see where the original knots are.'

'Aye, but I'm thinking on 'bairn you're carrying,' Nan said. 'Best sit down an' rest yoursen.'

Jeannie sat down on the stool which Nan had brought outside. She might have known that it wasn't her welfare Nan cared about but that of Harry's child.

'Hasn't Mike Gardiner got a wife who can mend nets?' She sat drinking the tea whilst Nan examined her work.

'No.' Nan turned to go back in the house. 'Dead. He's a widower.'

Jeannie was curious to know who had mended Mike's nets previously. Somebody must have worked on them, unless he did them himself as many fishermen did, but she hoped that she wasn't depriving some other woman of a job. No use asking Nan. She would probably know, but was unlikely to impart any information. I'll ask him when I see him, she thought.

Which was at the end of the following day, when he knocked on the back gate that Nan had locked 'just in case', she had said. Jeannie didn't know what she meant, because surely no one would come in and steal a net. This was a fishing community and everyone would respect other people's livelihood.

She smiled on seeing Mike when she unlocked the gate to let him in. 'Imprisoned, are you?' he whispered. 'Nan your jailer?'

'I don't know why she locked it,' she said. 'Habit perhaps from when Harry was away and she was alone. Ma and I never locked our door.' She saw him glance towards the net. 'It's not quite finished. I'll have it ready by dinner time tomorrow.'

'You're doing a grand job, Jeannie,' he said enthusiastically. 'It's my lucky net. I didn't want to get rid of it.'

Ah, she thought. So you were trying me out on an old one after all. 'I was hoping I wasn't taking another woman's work,' she said. 'Who normally mends your nets? A daughter? Nan told me you are a widower.'

'No. I've two sons. My wife died a few years ago when my boys were young. It was hard bringing them up on my own.'

'I'm sorry,' she said. 'We – my family in Scarborough, I mean – have a fisherman friend whose wife died. She left him with several children to bring

176

up so it was very hard for him. His eldest daughter was eleven when her mother died and she became the mother to them all, even the baby.'

'Difficult for her,' he murmured. 'No life of her own?'

Jeannie shook her head, and thought of Susan Wharton, a busy housewife with all the eligible young men already spoken for, and then she thought of Ethan and a shadow settled on her.

'Do you miss everybody?' he asked quietly. 'Your family? Your friends?'

Jeannie felt a hard lump in her throat and she swallowed. 'Yes,' she murmured. 'I do.'

He patted her arm and then looked up as Nan appeared at the scullery door.

'Oh, it's you,' she said. 'I wondered who was 'caller.'

'I was passing,' Mike said, 'so thought I'd tek a look at 'young seamstress's work.' He smiled at Jeannie. 'She's got a good hand.'

'Aye, she has,' Nan said grudgingly. 'What happened to Annie Croft? Has she given up mending?'

'It's given her up,' he said. 'She's crippled with rheumatics. Can't hold a knitting pin let alone a net needle. Don't know what she'll do for money.'

'Same as all of us, I expect.' Nan's reply was sour. 'She'll have to learn thrift.'

Mike nodded. 'Yeh. Well, better get going. I'll send 'lad over tomorrow tea time, shall I?'

'Yes,' Jeannie said. 'It'll be ready for sure by then.'

She reflected that they hadn't discussed payment, but he hadn't forgotten for in the next breath he added, 'Usual rate? If I give you 'same as I was paying Annie Croft just to start with? You can do all of my nets if you're able to.'

177

She beamed at him. At last things were looking up. 'Thank you. I'll be glad to.'

After supper, when they were settled with their knitting by the kitchen range, Nan commented, 'It's remarkable what a pretty young face can do.'

Jeannie looked up from counting her stitches. 'What do you mean?'

'All this time – I didn't let on I knew, but it's been weeks since Annie Croft gave up on her mending, and he never once thought of sending any work to me.'

Jeannie didn't know what to say. In Scarborough word went round if a woman couldn't work on the nets, and others would fill in for her until she could.

'Perhaps he didn't think,' she said lamely. 'Or maybe somebody else offered. It was Harry who asked him to consider me,' she added, knowing that wasn't strictly true.

'Hmph,' Nan muttered. 'Well, fine chap that he is, he's a single man.' She looked at Jeannie from beneath frowning eyebrows. 'So don't forget that tongues wag. Mek sure that 'lad allus fetches and carries 'nets for him, especially when Harry's away.'

Jeannie put her knitting down on her lap and ran her fingers over her forehead; she felt the beginning of a headache. What was it that her mother had said about not being browbeaten by anybody? To stand up for what she believed in. She believed that Mike Gardiner was a sincere friendly man, who had not only helped Harry by taking him on as crew but had also given her the chance to show she could earn a living. She didn't want to upset Nan or be disrespectful to her, but she felt she should be honest and open with her.

'I'm sorry, Nan, but I'll do no such thing,' she said with a calmness that she didn't feel. 'Mr Gardiner has shown me nothing but respect and I'm very grateful for the opportunity to work for him. There's no reason why anyone should suspect any ulterior motive. I doubt that he'll bring the nets himself, being such a busy man; but if he should and you're not here, I wouldn't dream of being anything other than polite.' She took a deep breath. 'It's the way I've been brought up and the way I'll continue. And,' she added, 'I'm quite sure that Harry would approve.'

Which was telling Nan, she thought as she gathered up her knitting needles and wool, that she needn't try to get Harry on her side or give him the impression that Mike Gardiner had his eye on his wife.

'I'm going to bed,' she said. 'It's been a long day. Good night.'

Jeannie was up first the next morning and had raked the fire and made the tea by the time Nan came down.

'I'll do all o' that of a morning,' Nan told her. 'There's no need for you to do it when you've 'nets to work on.' She got out the dishes for the gruel and took the bread out of the crock. 'An' I'll clear up after. We have to work together.'

It was hardly an apology for her words the night before, but it was a kind of acknowledgement that she had been wrong to utter them.

'I don't want to interfere with what you've always done,' Jeannie said. 'It's your home, but if there's something you'd like me to do I hope you'll ask me. If I can get work on the nets then that's my contribution, and with Harry's wages we should be able to manage fairly comfortably.'

'I hope so.' Nan took the gruel from the oven. 'We're a bit behind wi' rent but 'landlord's allus been understanding. Mebbe we can pay off some of 'arrears when Harry gets home.'

This was the first indication she had given that things might be difficult, but then why should she tell me, Jeannie thought. She's known me less than a week and I'm another mouth to feed so no wonder that she's grumpy.

Jeannie finished the mending by dinner time and carefully checked it over to make sure she hadn't missed any rips and that the last row of stitches was secured. Then, on impulse, she opened the back door and called to Nan.

'Would you just check it over with me?' she asked. 'Two pairs of eyes are better than one.'

She could tell that Nan was pleased as she hurriedly wiped her hands on her apron and came scurrying out. 'Well, my eyes aren't as sharp as they used to be but I'll tek a look.' She peered over the net and examined it with her fingers, and then said, 'I can't tell which you've done, 'knots match up that well. I reckon he'll be pleased.'

'Good.' Jeannie was relieved. 'Let's hope you're right.'

And she was. Rather than send the lad, Mike Gardiner came to collect the net himself. He carefully looked it over again, nodded and then smiled. 'Well done,' he said. 'I've another in 'handcart if you can tackle it.'

He paid her the offered rate, unhooked the net from the frame and took it out of the yard. His lad brought the other one in and draped it over the frame, telling her that he would collect it towards the middle of the following week.

She jiggled the coins in her hand, and suppressing a sense of elation went inside and handed it all over to Nan. Nan curled her gnarled hand over it and then said, 'Nay, I can't tek it all,' and handed back sixpence. 'Put summat by for 'bairn.'

It was after supper when they were sitting by the range that Nan suddenly asked, 'Are you prepared for 'coming event?'

Jeannie, who had been daydreaming into the coals of the fire, blinked and sat up; then, realizing what had been said, she lifted up her knitting. 'Yes,' she said. 'And my mother is sewing a layette. She's got a very neat hand.'

'I didn't mean that,' Nan said gruffly. 'I meant 'birth itself. Do you know what happens?'

'Oh,' Jeannie said and found she was blushing. 'Erm, yes, sort of, but nobody talks about it.'

Nan shook her head and sighed. 'If they talked about it it'd never happen again. I'll ask Mrs Norman to come and see you, shall I?'

That night after Nan had gone to her bedroom and firmly shut the door, Jeannie sat in bed and by the light from a candle stub began a letter to her mother.

Dearest Ma,

After a shaky start things are beginning to look up. During the first few difficult days I felt like running away and coming home, but Harry has sailed as third hand on a ship owned by a shipmate of his father's; it's a chance to earn some money and get him back into working again as he's been off for a while. I've started on net mending and have had a promise of plenty of work. But the best thing is that although Harry's grandmother seemed to resent me at first, I think she's now accepted that I'm Harry's wife and I'm here to stay. She's rather grumpy and I've yet to see her smile, but she makes sure that I rest and put my feet up, for the bairn's sake if not for mine.

She went on to tell her of the enormous docks and the fish quay and the people she had met, and finished by saying that she was sure that everything would turn out for the best once she and Harry had settled into their new life together.

I'm lonely sometimes, and I miss you such a lot, and Tom too and everybody I was fond of – even Granny Marshall. Her tongue isn't as sharp as Nan's. Please give my love to everyone I know, and keep lots for yourself.

Your ever loving daughter,
Jeannie.

CHAPTER TWENTY

Mary found the letter from Jeannie waiting for her on the doormat when she arrived home from the harbour. It had been cold and wet for most of the day and at four o'clock she had decided to go home. Next week the herring girls were due. The work would be hard but there'd be money to be made.

She dished up some soup which had been simmering on the low fire and sat down to eat. Tom had told her that he was having supper at Sarah's house and not to wait for him. She scanned Jeannie's letter as she ate and then with a frown read it again.

During the first few difficult days, she read. Why were they difficult? I wonder.

Mary had had some doubts about the marriage on meeting Harry and his family for the first time, but then decided that probably everyone was on edge, including Harry's grandmother, and reminded herself that they too were meeting strangers for the first time. Jeannie doesn't mention Harry's sister, she thought, and I'd hoped that she might make a friend of her, but then it's early days yet; perhaps she's waiting to let Jeannie settle in.

She finished her soup and turned her chair towards the fire, which was now blazing with the extra shovelful of coal she had tipped on to the embers. It seems that things started to improve after Harry left to go to sea, which is rather odd, she thought. She gave a pensive smile as she recalled how the days used to drag whilst she waited for Jack to come home from a voyage. But then I wasn't pregnant and rushed into a hasty marriage. Perhaps it was a mistake, she thought. Jeannie needn't have gone. We would have managed somehow, even though folks would have talked; I wouldn't have been bothered by that. And then the notion struck her that perhaps Jeannie had gone ahead with the marriage because of her and Tom. She didn't want to shame us, she decided; that's why she married him.

She had closed her eyes wearily, relishing the comforting warmth of the fire, when there came a familiar knock on the door. 'Come in, Josh,' she called. 'The door's open.'

She saw Josh quite often down by the harbour and he called frequently at the end of the day, sometimes bringing her a parcel of fish or other times just calling for a chat. She had told him long ago that he could come whenever he wanted to and didn't need an excuse or reason to visit. He'd grinned and said that he wouldn't want to deter any possible suitor by coming too regularly, but she'd assured him that she didn't want a suitor anyway and that his presence would be welcome to keep away anyone with that intention.

They had an easy friendship and he often asked her advice about his family, particularly regarding Susan, his eldest daughter, who he felt had ruined her chance of marriage by looking after her siblings. For Mary's part she rarely asked him for anything, being a woman able to do most things for herself. She lived a simple life, grateful, she told herself, that she could get from one week to the next without too much difficulty.

'Sit down,' she said. 'Would you like a cup of tea?'

He shook his head. 'No thanks. Susan will have supper ready.' He hesitated for a moment. 'It's about Susan that I've come. I think she might have a friend.'

Mary raised her eyebrows. 'She'll have plenty of friends, won't she? Or do you mean a new friend? A man friend?'

'Mm.' He nodded. 'Well, not new exactly. He's a Scarborough lad; works for a butcher in Eastborough.'

'And do you have a worry over that? It's a respectable trade.'

'No. No, I don't. It's just that he's been married before. His wife died of influenza about three or four years ago. He was left with two children.'

'And you think he's looking for a wife to take care of them?'

Josh looked anxious. 'Yes. Susan has spent her childhood looking after Stephen and the others. If she's going to look after any bairns they should be her own.'

'How old is he? This butcher's lad?'

Josh shrugged. 'Twenty-six or so. Don't misunderstand me. I've nothing against him. He seems like a decent type. I've asked around already.'

Mary smiled. 'Of course you have. But if he'd wanted someone to look after his bairns he would've done that already. Who's been looking after them in the meantime?'

'His mother and his sister, but his sister's getting married and his mother's not well, and that's why I'm worried.'

'You've made some enquiries,' Mary commented. 'And now you'd like me to dig a little deeper?'

'Please!' Relief showed in his face. 'If you would, Mary. I'll trust your judgement.'

Mary nodded and remembered the time when Granny Marshall had warned her that Josh would be looking for a wife to take care of his children after his wife had died. But he hadn't. He'd managed, with the help of Susan.

'I'll ask around,' she promised. 'Susan deserves someone nice, even if he already has children.'

Josh looked at her for a second, and then he smiled. 'Yes, she does.'

'I've had a letter from Jeannie,' she told him. 'I can't make out whether she's happy or not. It seems that Harry has gone to sea as a third hand.'

'I assumed he had his skipper's ticket,' Josh said. 'He's old enough, isn't he?'

'Yes, but I gathered from conversation at the wedding that he didn't have a ship.' She pressed her lips together anxiously. 'Maybe he's taken on any job that was offered.'

'Well that's good, isn't it?' he said. 'It shows the lad isn't work-shy. They'll need all the money they can get, especially as there's a bairn due.' He glanced at her. 'I am supposed to know that, aren't I?'

She gave a wry laugh. 'I think everybody does.'

The next day, instead of taking her usual walk along the harbour at midday, she walked up the hill to Josh's cottage and knocked on the door. Susan opened it and Mary could tell immediately that there was something different about her. She seemed livelier and brighter.

'It's my dinner break,' Mary said. 'I thought I'd pop up and ask how you are.'

'Come in,' Susan said. 'I thought you might call.'

'Did you? Why's that?'

'Da! He's found out about me seeing Robin. I knew he'd ask you to come and find out if it's serious.' The brightness on her round face faded. 'Well, you can tell him it's not. He needn't worry. I'll not leave him in the lurch.'

Mary frowned. 'Him?'

Susan sighed and nodded. 'Da. I'll not leave him to cope on his own, even if Robin asked for me. Which he hasn't,' she added. 'I've given him enough reasons not to.'

'Oh, Susan!' Mary said. 'That's not what your father is worried about. He's anxious that – Robin – just needs a wife to look after his wee bairns. He wants you to have the chance of a proper marriage and your own children.'

Susan sat down and motioned Mary to do the same. 'Does he? But how can I leave him to manage on his own? Stephen's not nine for another couple of weeks.'

'And you're only twenty,' Mary said softly. 'It's time you had a life of your own, Susan.'

Susan shook her head. 'I think that Ethan and I will both finish up unwed, living here with Da to the end of our days. Ethan is devastated about Jeannie. He'll not look at anybody else.' She glanced across at Mary. 'After Ma died, I used to wish that Da would marry you and we could all live together. And that Ethan and Jeannie would get married, and then

Tom and Ida would, and that would just leave me and Nancy and Stephen with you and Da; and as it is' – she gave a deep sigh – 'Tom's going to marry Sarah and Ida is courting and Nancy is already eyeing up the lads.'

Mary smiled. It was time for Susan to enjoy her remaining youth. 'Which means that you'll soon be free. How long have you known Robin? Are you fond of him?'

'He runs a butcher's shop in Eastborough. I started going there about four or five years ago after our old butcher gave up his business. Then just after that, Robin's wife died and I told him that if ever he was stuck for somebody to mind his bairns for an hour or two, I'd do it. He never asked me cos his mother and sister looked after them, but I think he was grateful that I'd offered. I haven't walked out with him, but we've met from time to time and not accidentally,' she finished, blushing slightly.

'So why does your father think it's serious?'

'He saw us one evening. I'd gone out for a walk along the sands and Da remembered he needed something from the chandler's and he saw Robin walking with me, and then only last week he saw us together again.' She laughed. 'He put two and two together and made six. He needn't bother himself,' she repeated. 'I'll not leave home.'

'But you like him, do you?' Mary persisted.

Susan turned her face away. 'Yes,' she said softly. 'I do.'

Mary made it her business to call at the butcher's shop the next morning. She bought two mutton chops and a pork pie. She assumed it was Robin who served her. He was a tall thickset man with sandy-coloured hair and an easy manner.

'Thank you, madam,' he said when she paid him. 'Haven't I seen you down at the harbour?'

'More than likely.' She smiled. 'I don't know why I don't put my bed down there.'

'You're a braider,' he said.

'Yes, and a herring girl.'

'Ah! Hence the Scottish accent.'

She nodded. 'It never leaves me, even though I've lived in Scarborough for over twenty years.'

There was no one else in the shop and he seemed happy to talk. 'The herring fleet's late this year.'

'It is. I hear they've had good fishing in Shetland. The curers are up there and the Dutch have had their noses put out of joint. They'll be here next week, I hope.'

'I hope so too. They bring business to the town, though I'll not sell much meat.' He grinned.

'Is Mr Robson not here any more?' she asked, speaking of the butcher whose shop it was.

'He pops in now and again; he's not been well. He's happy for me to run it until he comes back. I've been here since I was a lad.'

A few more pleasantries and she left, hurrying down the hill with her purchases and knowing she was behind with her work. Nothing to worry about there, she mused. Nice young man. I'd be happy to have him in my family, bairns or not, and this was what she told Josh when she saw him next.

'Tell her she's free to go courting,' she said. 'It's you she's bothered about. She thinks you can't manage without her.'

'Course I can,' he spluttered. 'And besides, our Ida

189

can do her share of housework for a change, until she weds, which won't be yet. She's far too young.'

It was Ida who altered the state of the Wharton household. She announced one evening about a week later that she was no longer going out with the young man on whom she had pinned her hopes of marriage because she had seen him hand in hand with someone else.

'That's just as well,' Josh told her, 'because you're too young to be married anyway. You can help our Susan and learn what it's like to run a household and mebbe then you won't be in so much of a hurry to be wed.'

'But I go to work, Da!' Ida was aghast. 'Susan doesn't!'

'Susan does work,' her father said. 'All the week and without a day off. But things are going to change.'

His three daughters stared at him. Stephen was out playing on the sands with his school mates.

'Susan is going to have a day off every week. You can choose which day, Susan, and it doesn't have to be always the same one. Both of you' – he pointed to Ida and Nancy – 'will help with the ironing and cleaning the brasses and you'll strip the beds ready for washday. And Stephen will clean all the boots and shoes, shake the rugs and sweep the yard every morning before he goes to school.'

Susan began to cry and after a moment Ida put her hand on her shoulder. 'I'm sorry, Susan,' she said. 'It's only now that Da has spelt it out that I realize what a lot you do for us.' She bent and kissed her sister's cheek. 'I've been a selfish pig, but I'll help from now on and mebbe you and me can take a walk together sometimes like we used to when we were little.'

'I will as well,' Nancy piped up. 'I quite like cleaning the brass and making it shine. I can just remember Ma doing it and letting me help her.' Her eyes filled with tears. 'I can't remember much about her, but I can remember that.'

Josh turned away, full of emotion. He still felt the loss of his wife and stepson keenly, but thought how lucky he was to still have such a loving family. They had made another life for themselves, but he was determined, now that his eyes had been opened, that each of his daughters should also have a life of her own. As for his sons, Stephen was just a schoolboy, full of mischief as he had once been himself, whereas Ethan . . . He gave a small sigh. He couldn't help Ethan, who was steeped in misery, who hardly spoke of anything except fishing or his boat. Ethan had had plans of his own but he hadn't shared them, not even with Jeannie, who had been included in them. Well, she was lost to him now with a husband and a child on the way. Ethan too would have to make another life.

CHAPTER TWENTY-ONE

Charlie, a young man of about Harry's age who knew Mike Gardiner, brought a trawl net for Jeannie to mend. It was badly rent and full of holes and he said he needed it back urgently.

'I was told it wasn't worth mending,' he said. 'But I can't afford to buy another.'

He told her he had inherited his father's half share in a smack. His father had had to give up fishing as he was infirm and unable to leave the house. Charlie was now the only wage earner.

She asked him to hoist it on to the frame for her to examine. It was an old net and heavy to handle. Some of the outer mesh was badly damaged, as was the cod end, the narrow tapering cone of the net, as if it had been snagged among rocks. It had been roughly mended, probably by fishermen in a hurry to use it again; repairs which would need undoing and starting again. 'I'll do what I can,' she said. 'But it'll take some time; maybe four or five days working on this alone.'

He nodded. 'Can you finish it for when I get back from 'next trip? I'm off in 'morning to 'Dogger. I expect to be away just over a week. If you can mend this for when I get back I'll bring you another, then I'll have three good 'uns.'

Jeannie agreed, though she told him she would have to charge him extra for this one. 'I might have to get some help with it.' She thought she would ask Nan to give her a hand.

'It'll still be cheaper than buying another,' he said. 'And I've been told that you're good.'

It seemed that word was spreading and it was a relief to her that she was earning money, though she knew it might not be regular work. Most fishermen or their wives mended their own nets; it was single men like Mike Gardiner or Charlie who needed the work doing.

She asked Nan to help her and the older woman seemed pleased and flattered by the request. 'Aye,' she said. 'I've mended many a net for my husband, and my father too. We'll get started in 'morning.'

Jeannie shook her head. This was her work. She would decide when they started. 'Today, after dinner,' she said. 'Otherwise I'll have all on to get it finished in time. But tomorrow's fine for you, Nan. Whenever you can, when you've finished whatever else you have to do.' She gave a little laugh and added, 'And you're in charge of the house and the cooking so you have less time than I have,' and was pleased to see that Nan, who had started to bridle, relaxed at that, mollified.

Nan joined her with the mending the following day; she had in the meantime been to the butcher's for some beef which was stewing in the oven with onions and potatoes, ready to make a pie for when Harry came back.

'It won't be long afore he's home,' she said. 'And I allus liked to have some food ready for him when he'd been on a trip. Nowt like 'smell of home cooking to tempt a man to stop at home.'

Jeannie looked up with a half-smile. Well of course Harry would be glad to stay at home after being at sea. Where else would he want to be but at his own fireside with his family?

It began to rain heavily whilst they were in the yard and Jeannie went indoors to put on her rubber boots, another woolly jumper and the sou'wester which had once been Tom's. She didn't want to catch a chill and risk losing the baby. When she came out again, Nan said she would make them a hot drink.

Jeannie's fingers were cold and she thought that she must buy some wool to knit fingerless gloves now that the weather was turning colder. Another few weeks and winter fogs would be here. She turned her head as she heard the sneck lift on the back gate. If it was Mike Gardiner with another net, she would have to tell him that she was busy for the whole of the week.

It wasn't Mike, but Harry, standing there with a puzzled expression. Jeannie opened her arms wide, and then quickly hooked her needle into the net.

'Harry! Oh, you're back!'

'Jeannie! Is it you? I didn't recognize you with that gear on. Let me look at you.'

Jeannie took off her waterproof hat and her hair fell about her face. 'It's me! I'm net mending. I've got work!'

She put her arms round him, but he took a step back, and then leaned forward and kissed her cold cheek. 'You're wetter than I've been at sea,' he said. 'Come on inside and let me tek a look at you.'

Jeannie gazed at him. Was she mistaken or had she smelled ale on him as he'd bent to kiss her? Surely he would have come straight home from the ship?

Nan was making cocoa when they went inside. She looked up, and although Jeannie saw a gleam of relief in her eyes she merely said, 'Oh, you're back then. Had a good trip?'

'Yes, thanks, Nan.' Harry dropped his bag and bent to kiss her cheek, and as usual she dashed it away with the back of her hand.

'Daft beggar,' she muttered. 'How was it?'

Jeannie had taken off her wet coat and he put his arm round her and squeezed her. 'It were all right. By heck, Jeannie. You've put some more weight on.'

She smiled as she looked up at him. He was joking, wasn't he? 'Well, that's good, isn't it?' she said. 'Maybe it's going to be a big strong lad like his da.'

Harry put his head back as he considered. 'Oh, yeh, mebbe it is. Give us a cuppa tea, Nan, and then I'll be off to see 'lads. I won't be long.' He glanced at Jeannie. 'Just going to see if owt's happened down on 'road while I've been away.'

'Nowt much has happened,' Nan told him. 'You've not been gone five minutes.' But she made a pot of tea anyway and poured it into a large mug and put a spoonful of sugar into it.

He didn't sit down but drank standing up, casting a glance first at one and then the other. 'By, that were good,' he said, draining the last dregs. 'I'll fetch a parcel o' fish back wi' me.'

'Nan's making a meat pie,' Jeannie said. 'The meat's cooked. Don't be too late or it'll spoil.'

His eyes flashed and she thought she saw anger, but then he said, 'No. I just said: I'm off to see 'lads an' I won't be long. There's some wet gear in me bag. It'll be stinking if it's not hung out.' He headed towards the door. 'Shan't be long.'

Jeannie picked up her cocoa and sat down by the fire. She didn't say anything. What was there to say?

Nan sat opposite her. 'It's 'way it is,' she said. 'I've nivver known owt different. Just be thankful that he's safe home.'

'I am,' Jeannie murmured. 'But I didn't think he'd be going out again as soon as his feet were inside the door.'

Nan shrugged. 'Like I said . . .'

They sat drinking their cocoa and saying nothing until there was a knock on the back door; they heard it open and someone come into the scullery.

'Are you there, Nan?' It was a man's voice and Nan called back for him to come in. Billy Norman put his head round the door.

'Has Harry got home?' he asked. 'I heard his ship had come in.'

Nan nodded. 'You've just missed him. Not five minutes since.'

Billy nodded at Jeannie. 'You all right, Jeannie?'

'Yes, thank you, Billy,' she said and thought that at least he had asked about her well-being, unlike Harry, who hadn't. 'If you see Harry, will you remind him there's a meat pie waiting for his dinner?'

'Oh, aye. I certainly will. My ma's cooking fish. Brought a nice parcel of haddock and turbot home. Not enough turbot to sell so I said I'd have it.'

Jeannie smiled at him. 'By the way, Billy, thank you for making the frame. It's been really useful. I'm mending nets already.'

He flushed slightly. 'Oh, you're all right, Jeannie. It didn't tek any time at all. I'll be off then.' He seemed to hesitate.

'Did you have a good trip?' Nan asked. 'Who were you with?'

'Usual crew.' He half stepped into the kitchen.

'Like some cocoa?' Jeannie asked. 'The kettle's still hot.'

He glanced at her and then Nan. 'If it's no bother,' he said. 'It'll warm me up, then I'll be off, catch up with 'lads.'

'I'll mek it,' Nan said. 'Sit down and warm thysen,' she told him. 'So who did you say you were with?'

She seemed persistent, Jeannie thought, and Billy's comment about catching up with the lads echoed Harry's remarks. It must be tradition, she thought. Perhaps they check up on each other, making sure they're all safe home after a trip.

'Jock Hall, Bill Clark, Tony Swift, all 'usual lads,' he said in answer to Nan's question. 'Mark Fowler . . . Des Turnby.'

He paused before uttering the last name and Nan grunted at it. Billy gave a slight shrug in Jeannie's direction and lifted his eyebrows, but she didn't understand what it was supposed to mean.

'He still gets work then?' Nan muttered.

'Aye, he's a strong chap. Good pair of hands.'

'Troublemaker.' Nan handed him the steaming drink. 'You'd be as well to keep away from him, and his family.'

'He's no trouble to me, Nan.' Billy blew on the

197

cocoa and took a sip. 'Never has been.'

Jeannie pondered the conversation after Billy had hurriedly finished his drink and left. There were many things she couldn't possibly know about, but she idly wondered why Nan was so set against the Turnby family. Nan seemed to have quite fierce likes and dislikes, and she thought about meeting Connie on the road that day, when Nan had all but ignored her.

The meat pie was cooked and the crust turning brown and crisp when Harry arrived home. He was quite drunk but amiable and sat down immediately at the table and picked up his knife and fork, holding them in his fists.

'Right then, where is it? Fetch it to 'table. Billy said it were ready. I'm starving; been looking forward to some good grub.'

Jeannie held her tongue. Meal times had been important in her old home. Her mother had always said that if she took the effort to cook it then Jeannie and Tom should be there to eat it when it was ready. Harry, it seemed, didn't abide by those rules and she wondered if he would have been here at all if Billy hadn't reminded him.

They were halfway through the meal when Jeannie broke the silence. 'So did you get a good catch? Was it a strong sea?'

Harry licked his lips. 'Aye. We got plenty o' cod and haddock. Hard, though. I was at 'beck and call of everybody cos I was third hand. Fourth was just a lad, fourteen or fifteen. I was packing boxes as well as trawling 'nets and helping him cook. He'd not been at sea afore. 'Skipper – Aaron, Mike's lad – said they'd be fleeting next time rather than single boating. He said there was more money in it and they could stay out longer.' He took another mouthful of pie. 'Not sure if I'll do that even if I'm asked.'

Jeannie took in a breath, but Nan said, 'That's 'way that things are going from what I hear. Single boating'll soon be finished. Fleeting is going to be 'onny thing to do unless you go on 'trawlers.'

Harry gave a belch. 'Beg pardon. Well, I'll see.'

'Did – did you get a bonus this time?' Jeannie ventured. 'If you got a good catch?'

Harry turned to look at her. He blinked and it was as if he wondered who was asking.

'I was hoping that you would – for the bairn, you know?' she added quietly.

He opened his mouth and then closed it again.

'She's asking if you brought some money home,' Nan said sharply. 'We need to pay 'rent.'

'I'm not home five minutes and you're asking me to turn me pockets out!'

Jeannie said nothing but held his gaze.

He stood up, crashing back his chair. 'Well, as a matter of fact . . .' He put both hands in his pockets and drew out a cache of coins which he threw on the table. He grinned. 'There you are! Plenty o' money there.' But he gathered up several coins again and put them back in his pocket before patting the side of his nose. 'Need them to pay off 'slate at 'Wassand.'

'Aye, do that,' Nan agreed, rather sourly. 'You don't want to be turned away from there, do you?'

'By heck I don't,' Harry said. 'I'll slip along now and settle up.' He burped again. 'I've left a parcel o' fish in 'bucket at 'back door. Shan't be long.'

He didn't come back until late and Jeannie was in bed and almost asleep when he crashed into the

199

house. She heard the back door open and then his grunts as he took off his boots before climbing the creaking stairs. Nan called out to him from her bedroom.

'Did you lock 'back door?'

'Aye. I did.' He stumbled into the bedroom. 'Like I allus do.'

Jeannie held her breath. She wondered whether to feign sleep but she wanted to talk to him; ask him how the voyage really went and if next time he might get a skipper's post, but as she heard him struggling to take off his belt and his trousers and unbutton his shirt, she realized that her questions would have to wait until the morning when he was sober.

He fell into bed next to her and put his stubbly cheek next to hers. 'It's good to be home,' he slurred. 'I missed you, Jeannie. I thought about you all 'time I was away.'

'Did you, Harry?' She snuggled up close to him and wondered if it was the drink talking; but even if it is, she thought, it's what I want to hear.

'Aye.' He yawned. 'I'm glad we got married. It was what Nan wanted as well. She was allus on at me to find somebody else. Somebody who'd be strong for me.'

'What do you mean, Harry?' She leaned on her elbow to look at him.

He gave a deep sigh. 'I'm dead beat, Jeannie. Come here, give us a kiss. We'll talk in 'morning. We don't have to be up early. No early rising, thank God.' He turned over with his back to her. 'Night!'

Jeannie lay back on the pillow and stared up at the ceiling. 'Good night, Harry.'

CHAPTER TWENTY-TWO

Harry didn't get up until midday the following day. Jeannie excused him, for he must have been tired after the trip. But she was disappointed when, after eating bacon and sausage and two eggs and swilling down two mugs of tea, he put on his coat and said he was going out.

'Going to fix up another trip?' she said hopefully. 'Is there one in the offing?'

He gazed at her. 'Might be,' he said. 'I'll see what 'news is out on 'road.'

At the Wassand, you mean, she thought resentfully; when do I get to talk to you? And she considered, for the first time, how lonely her life would have been if Nan hadn't been there. Though she wasn't much of a conversationalist, at least she was another presence in the house.

'Nan,' she said as they worked on Charlie's net. 'Harry said last night that you'd wanted him to get married. Why was that? He doesn't spend much time at home.'

Nan concentrated on her braiding and joined up the knot she was making. 'Aye, I did. I thought he'd settle down and not get into bad company.'

'Was there a chance of that?' Jeannie asked. 'And

he said you wanted him to marry someone strong.'

'Did he?' Nan said caustically. 'That'd be 'drink talking.' She paused, and then said, 'Well, there was a – were some local lasses who had their eyes on him – undesirable types. I was a bit worried about that.' She paused again and then said, 'That day when you came to 'house – I was angry wi' pair of you, but then I realized that for you to come all 'way from Scarborough to search him out took some courage.' She gave what might have passed for a wry smile but was merely a sideways shifting of her thin lips. 'And you weren't scared o' me, not like some folks are, so I reckoned you'd be able to handle Harry.'

Jeannie was flabbergasted. Not only was this the longest speech she had ever heard Nan utter, she was also admitting, to some extent, that she approved of her. She hid a smile. 'I hope you're right, Nan,' she murmured. 'I really do.'

She finished the net for Charlie in time and he brought another, equally old and tattered. 'Sorry,' he said. 'Seas were rough. I lost a lot o' fish and had all on to get home. As soon as I mek a profit I'll buy some new.'

'Do you need any extra crew?' she asked him. Harry hadn't yet got the promise of another ship in spite of going out every day and *asking around*, as he put it.

'I need a mate,' he said. 'It's an old smack, lug rigged, and teks some handling. I want somebody wi' experience if they'll tek lower role and money.'

'Harry might,' she said. 'But you'd have to ask him.' She dared not suggest it and be accused of interfering. The offer would have to come from Charlie.

'He's got a skipper ticket, hasn't he?' Charlie said. 'He won't want to come on my old tub.'

'Ask him,' she said. 'You'll find him at the Wassand Arms.'

When Harry came home that evening he announced that he'd be sailing in three days' time. 'I'm to be mate, and part-time skipper,' he said, a slight note of conceit in his voice. 'Charlie Hodge has been looking for somebody like me with all-round experience.'

'Oh, I'm so pleased, Harry,' Jeannie said, and she was. He seemed to have grown a couple of inches and taken on more confidence. 'I knew there'd be somebody who'd see your worth.'

Harry preened. 'It was lucky I happened to bump into him. He's tekken on his da's smack – well, it were half owned by his da. 'Other owner doesn't sail now; they're both past it from what I hear. You never know, I could end up wi' shares in it.' He sat down by the fire and stretched his legs. 'Charlie said you'd mended some nets for him.'

'Oh, *that* Charlie! Yes, I did. I'm mending another for him as well. Three days?' she said, smiling. 'I'd better try to finish it before you sail, then you can take it with you; don't want you losing any fish.'

He took two more trips with Charlie. They were equally qualified, which meant that Charlie could rely on him, but Harry was less of a seaman than the skipper; though he knew his sails and rigging, the running gear and pumps, knew the tides, buoys and beacons, he was less proficient than Charlie in the keeping of charts and judging the nature of the fishing grounds. Nevertheless, they worked well together.

The weather was getting bad. Winter was drawing in fast and the last trip they made was fraught with danger. They'd sailed to the Dogger Bank, which was as far as Charlie said he wanted to sail in the old smack; they'd come across stormy weather and the craft had taken in water.

"Young lad did well,' Harry told Jeannie, speaking of the apprentice on his return home. 'But he was dead scared. He was kept bailing for hours and then he was hit by 'boom and all but went overboard. I fastened him to 'mast in 'finish. Don't know if he'll come back, but in any case Charlie's got to have some work done afore he can tek 'ship out again. Pity. There was loads of fish. You can tell by 'colour of 'water if shoals are about and herring were practically flying into 'nets.' He gave a little grunt. 'And yet to hear some folks talk they say we're fishing 'seas dry.'

Jeannie was only half listening. She thought of Ethan being tied to the mast all those years ago; and then thought of her mother and the herring girls. She'd had a reply to her letter in which Mary had told her that Susan Wharton was courting a butcher, a widower, and that there might be wedding bells. She'd also said that the herring fleet had been and she'd caught up with news from her old friends.

I wish I could see her, she thought, but there's no chance now. I can't risk going, and besides I have to make as much money as possible. Maybe after the bairn is born I could go on the train. Ma will want to see it.

She was beginning to feel tired, and standing on her feet all day mending the nets was taking its toll.

Nan suggested that as Harry was at home he could bring the nets inside where she could sit down.

'Don't you mind?' Jeannie asked her. 'I didn't think you'd want that.'

'Can't turn work away,' Nan said. 'I'll tek 'rugs up and move 'table back and then there's nowt to harm.'

So Jeannie put on her rubber apron and sat by the fire and Harry brought in the nets for her to repair on her knee.

'You sure you're all right doing 'em, Jeannie?' Harry asked one morning. He seemed quite solicitous and Jeannie thought that perhaps Nan had had a quiet word and told him that her time was almost due. 'Don't want you mekking yourself badly.'

'I'm all right.' She smiled. 'And we need the money, don't we? Another mouth to feed.'

He nodded, and went out shortly afterwards. He didn't come in until well after dinner time and Nan had put his meal in the oven to keep warm.

'Got a ship,' he announced. 'I'm going out with Mike Gardiner's lad again.'

'Fleeting?' Jeannie asked. 'I thought you didn't want to. What position?'

'Onny third,' he said. 'But I told him I was willing to do it if he'd have me. Telled him I had a bairn on 'way and needed 'money.'

'Oh, Harry!' Jeannie was overcome with emotion. 'Thank you.'

He grinned. 'Can't have you losing 'bairn, can we, and it means you don't have to tek on so much work.'

There wasn't much anyway, she thought. She'd finished Charlie's nets and now his ship was laid up there wouldn't be any more for a while. She had one more to do for Mike and he hadn't promised any others. 'I'll be glad of the rest,' she told Harry, and that night in bed he was tender and considerate and she felt happier than she had in a long time. 'Come safe home,' she whispered, and thought that when he did come home there might well be another person in the house.

Harry had said that he'd be home for Christmas, and in the weeks running up to it Jeannie and Nan had prepared a plum pudding, mixed mincemeat for pies, and ordered a piece of beef, sausage meat and a pork pie from the butcher for Christmas Day.

'Hope I'll be able to eat it,' she told Nan. 'I've a feeling I might be otherwise engaged.'

'I'll ask Mrs Norman to call again,' she said. 'She'll know.'

Billy's mother had called to see her once before and told Jeannie that she seemed very fit and there were no apparent problems. This time when she came she said that she thought the baby was due very soon. 'Call me in if you need me,' she said. 'Any time, don't matter when. Unless you want 'doctor to come?'

Jeannie didn't. They hadn't the money to pay for him, for one thing, and for another, she had never to her knowledge ever seen a doctor. Her mother always had a host of remedies for any childhood ailments, of which there had been few. She and Tom had had a healthy childhood, spending most of their time out in the sea air. She began to take short walks in the mornings and then after the midday meal sat in a chair and rested. She felt heavy and sluggish, but thought that the walks did her good even though the weather was sharp and cold. The sky was often bright but then low cloud would descend and she felt that snow was on its way.

On Sunday morning after Nan had gone to chapel, Jeannie wrapped up warmly and went out of the terrace and on to the road; she too was beginning to refer to Hessle Road just as *the road*, as the locals did. Ahead of her she saw Connie trudging along with her head down, and called her name.

There was no response, though Jeannie thought there was a slight stiffening of the girl's shoulders. 'Connie!' she called again. This time Connie turned round.

'Oh!' She looked relieved and her tense body relaxed. 'It's you, Jeannie. I didn't hear you . . .'

'Are you all right, Connie? How's your hand? Are you back at work?'

Connie nodded. 'I did what you said and went to show them my hand. Somebody strapped it up for me, and 'foreman said he'd keep my job open. I'm back now, though it still hurts.' She held out her hand and Jeannie saw it was still puffy and bruised. 'Has Harry gone to sea? I've – I've not seen him about much.'

'Yes,' Jeannie said. 'He's gone fleeting. He'll be home for Christmas.' She smiled. 'Babby's due any time, so it'll be a Christmas present for him.'

'Oh, that'll be nice.' Connie's voice was low and without enthusiasm. 'You're lucky, aren't you? I wish – I wish . . .'

'What? What do you wish, Connie?'

Connie shrugged. 'I wish I was you. Looking forward to havin' a bairn and havin' somebody like Harry to look after me.'

Jeannie reflected that Harry hadn't done much

looking after her, not until the week he'd gone away when he had suddenly become considerate. But then, she thought, if Nan were to be believed, in Connie's eyes even what she had must seem perfect.

'Don't you have a young man, Connie?' she asked. Connie was older than her, maybe about twenty.

'Who'd have me?' Connie's voice was bitter. 'I'm not pretty like you. No man'd look at me.'

'Oh, that's not true,' Jeannie said quickly, unable to suppress the thought that it was true Connie was not in the front row when beauty was given out. 'You have lovely eyes. Such long lashes.'

'But nowt else,' Connie muttered.

'Looks aren't everything,' Jeannie said feebly. 'Men want a wife to talk to and bear their children, someone to be comfortable with. They don't want to be looking at a beautiful face for the whole of their lives, and if they did, they'd be disappointed. Anyway,' she added, 'there are very few handsome men about, so why should women care?'

Connie looked at her and Jeannie thought she saw a fleeting glimpse of jealousy in those brown eyes. 'It's all right for you,' she muttered. 'You've got Harry.'

'I know,' Jeannie said softly. 'But Harry and I knew at our first meeting – we just – well, there was something special between us. It wasn't as if I knew anything about him; I didn't know his family or if he had another girl. *Did* he have another girl? Was there ever anybody else?'

Connie dropped her gaze. 'Dunno. None that I knew of.'

But you wanted him, didn't you? Jeannie thought. And you'd have every reason to stop and chat to him without it being obvious that you were totally besotted, because he was your friend's brother. But he didn't want you. Poor Connie. But it wouldn't have worked anyway, because Nan wouldn't have accepted you. She considers your family as the enemy – and then she recalled what Nan had said when she had asked why she had wanted Harry to be married: there had been some undesirable types of women, she'd replied. Not *some*, Jeannie thought. She meant Connie; she had seen that Connie wanted Harry and was determined to put a stop to it.

CHAPTER TWENTY-THREE

Jeannie tucked her arm into Connie's. 'Do you mind if I walk with you?' she said. 'I don't often get the chance to talk to somebody of my own age.'

She felt Connie tense and look about her; then she said lamely, as they walked on, 'I'm older than you. I'm 'same age as Harry. We went to school together.'

'Oh, did you?' Jeannie said, adding chattily, 'Do you see much of Rosie? I haven't seen her since our wedding day.'

'No,' Connie muttered. 'Except at work. She's not bothered about me any more. She onny went about wi' me to annoy her nan.'

'Did she?'

Connie fell silent and Jeannie glanced at her; she seemed to be chewing something over, and as they walked, her eyes skimmed the street as if she was expecting somebody.

'Why would Rosie want to annoy Nan?' Jeannie asked.

Connie shrugged. 'Dunno.'

'Is it your father who's a fisherman?' Jeannie said conversationally.

Connie gasped and stopped, pulling away from Jeannie's arm. 'Why 'you asking that?'

Jeannie was astonished by her response. 'No reason,' she said. 'I just heard the name Turnby crop up. Billy Norman happened to say they'd been in the same crew on the last trip.'

Connie put her hand to her mouth, her expression scared as she glanced about her. 'No,' she muttered from beneath her fingers. 'Not my da. My uncle. Des. He's my da's brother. He was on 'same trip as Billy.'

'I'm so sorry. I just thought . . .' Jeannie bit her lip. 'Have you – was your father lost at sea? Like mine?'

Connie gaped at her; there was fear in her eyes. She shook her head. 'No,' she whispered. 'I'm not supposed to talk about him. I'd get a good hiding if they heard me.'

Jeannie too glanced about her. They? Who were *they*? There were a few people about, but not many; most were just strolling, some of the women wearing hats as if they'd been to church or chapel. That made her think of Nan and wonder if she ought to be turning back.

'Maybe I ought to be going home,' she told Connie. 'Nan will be back from chapel soon, and I don't want to get you into trouble.'

It was Connie's turn to be contrite. 'I can't – I haven't to mention his name, my ma says, and Uncle Des says 'same.'

'I see,' Jeannie murmured, although she didn't. 'He isn't dead then? I'm glad about that, Connie. My father was lost at sea when I was six and I hardly remember him; not what he looked like or anything, although my ma always talked about him to me and Tom. Tom's my brother,' she added.

211

Connie nodded. 'Yeh, I remember him at 'wedding.' She seemed to consider and she turned and walked back with Jeannie. 'You're lucky to have a brother.'

Jeannie gave a small wry smile. Lucky again. Connie seemed to think that she was the only one who didn't have any luck. 'Don't you have any brothers or sisters?'

There was a slight hesitation. 'I might have,' she muttered.

'What do you mean?'

'My da went off. He left home when I was ten. I haven't seen him since. Well . . .' She seemed uncertain. 'I thought I saw him once, coming out of our house; onny Ma said it wasn't. She gave me a good slapping cos I said I wanted to see him.'

'I'm really sorry, Connie,' Jeannie said. 'I didn't mean to pry.'

'It's all right,' Connie said in a strangled kind of voice and blew her nose on a piece of rag. 'It's quite good to talk about it really, seeing as I can't at home. Uncle Des and his wife and their two lads live with us. They moved in just after 'time I thought I saw my da. Des said it was to mek sure my da didn't come back and bother us.'

Jeannie knitted her meandering thoughts together. 'Was that about the time that Harry's mother left? She went off with a foreigner apparently and took her youngest children with her.'

Connie turned to stare at her. 'He weren't a foreigner,' she whispered. 'It was my da. Harry's ma and my da went off together.'

'Oh! But – Nan definitely told me she'd gone off with a foreigner.'

Connie gave a choking sob. 'He were from Brixham,' she said. 'And that's where they ran off to.'

'Brixham?' Jeannie said.

'Yeh,' Connie said. 'That's where he came from. He was a trawler man and fetched up in Hull. There was a lot of controversy over trawling, so Uncle Des said, cos he came at 'same time. They both decided to stop here cos 'fishing was good. An' then my da met my ma and they had me. I don't know what happened after. I onny remember they were forever shouting at each other. I was 'onny bairn and I think Da would have liked a son. Ma allus blamed him an' he said as it were her fault. I once heard him say that she was frigid. I didn't know what it meant then but I allus remembered 'word.'

Jeannie nodded. So that was why Nan was so set against Connie's family. And that's so unfair, she thought; when it was nothing to do with Connie but only to do with the adults.

'I'm sorry I asked, Connie,' she said again. 'I'd no idea. Does Rosie know? Or Harry?'

'Yeh. I think Rosie's Auntie Dot told her and she told Harry. That's why Rosie made friends wi' me.'

'I don't understand,' Jeannie said. 'Why would she do that?'

'Because Nan never had a good word to say about Rosie's ma, and she was allus mekking out that she'd gone off wi' a foreigner and didn't want Rosie but onny 'younger bairns. Then she made Rosie go and live with her Auntie Dot. She said that Rosie was flighty and needed a firm hand, but Rosie said that Nan onny wanted Harry cos one day he'd be a fisherman and'd be able to keep her. So when Rosie found out that it were my da that her ma had gone off wi' and not a foreigner at all, I think she became my friend just to torment Nan; to keep reminding her of what had happened.'

She paused for a moment as if considering something; her eyes narrowed and she put her chin in the air. 'Rosie knew that I liked Harry and she tried to push us together, just to rub salt into 'wound; Nan would have been right mad if she'd thought that me and Harry – if we'd . . .' She pouted. 'But we didn't – at least he didn't, cos like I said, who'd look at me? Not somebody like Harry, anyway.'

Connie turned her limpid gaze on Jeannie; her eyes were damp and soulful and she chewed on her lip. 'Rosie was furious when Harry said he was going to wed a Scarborough lass, and after we'd met you at 'wedding she kept saying horrible things about you, trying to make me jealous and to hate you.' Tears trickled down her cheeks. 'But I don't, Jeannie,' she pleaded. 'Honest to God I don't.'

Jeannie was stunned. She didn't blame Connie. She was a pawn in a game that Rosie was playing. But what? Why should Rosie take against someone she didn't know?

'Here's Nan coming up 'road,' Connie gasped. 'I'd better go.'

'No,' Jeannie said. 'Walk with me. If you will,' she added. 'I'll choose for myself who my friends are, Connie.' She smiled at her. 'I don't have to ask Nan.'

Connie blinked. 'I wish I was as brave as you. I'm scared o' my own shadow.'

Jeannie tucked her arm into Connie's again. 'Come on then,' she said firmly. 'Let's brave the shadows together.'

It was as they were walking towards Nan that Jeannie felt a sharp pain in her lower back. She grimaced and clutched Connie's arm. Then she felt another. Was this it? she thought. Is this how it happens?

'I need to get home, Connie,' she murmured. 'I think I'm starting in labour.'

Connie stared at her. Her mouth opened and she breathed heavily. 'What shall we do?'

'Just walk slowly,' Jeannie said. 'Don't let me rush.'

Connie held her arm steadily and then, to Jeannie's astonishment, she signalled to Nan, who had almost reached the top of Walcott Street, that she should come to them. Nan hesitated, her back held ramrod straight, and then she hurried towards them.

'What?' She looked at Connie and then at Jeannie.

'We have to get Jeannie home, Mrs Carr,' Connie said nervously. 'She thinks she's starting wi' babby.'

'I don't think there's any hurry,' Jeannie said tremulously. 'But the pain is spreading. And I need the privy,' she whispered.

Nan took her other arm and slowly they walked towards Walcott Street.

'Are you all right, Jeannie?' Connie asked softly when they reached the house.

Jeannie pressed her lips together. 'Yes,' she breathed. 'I think so.'

'We can manage now,' Nan said curtly and put a key in the rarely used front door. 'Thank you,' she added.

'No. Wait, Connie,' Jeannie said. 'Help me to the privy. I don't think I can make it on my own. I'd love a cup of tea, Nan.' Her voice sounded weak, even to her.

Nan looked at them both but said nothing, and as Jeannie and Connie went through the house towards the scullery door she swung the kettle over the fire. When they came back, she had made the tea and put three cups on the table.

'Shall I fetch Mrs Norman?' Connie asked.

'Drink your tea first,' Nan commanded. 'Jeannie, you'd better sit down.'

Jeannie swallowed. 'I'm not sure if I can,' she said. 'I feel very strange.'

'Help her upstairs,' Nan told Connie, who hastily put her cup back on the table. 'She might be better lying down.' Her voice, though crisp, was shaky.

Connie put her hand on the small of Jeannie's back as she went up the stairs behind her. 'Stop a minute,' she said halfway up. 'Tek a rest. 'Stairs are steep, just like ours.'

'Yes,' Jeannie said breathlessly. 'We didn't have – stairs in my ma's house.'

When they reached the bedroom, Jeannie perched on the edge of the bed whilst Connie knelt down to unbutton her boots.

'Will you unfasten my skirt, Connie?' Jeannie whispered. 'And then fetch Mrs Norman. Tell her it's urgent.'

'Yeh! I'll run.' She exhaled, as if she'd been holding her breath. 'It'll onny take me five minutes. Had you better lie down like Nan said?'

Jeannie shook her head. 'No, not yet. Don't be long, will you, Connie?'

Connie sped down the stairs. Nan was sitting by the table with her hands clasped tightly together. 'I'm going to fetch Mrs Norman,' Connie told her. 'Jeannie asked me to.'

216

'You know where she lives?' Nan asked. 'Stricky Street,' and at Connie's nod she said, 'Be quick.'

It did only take her five minutes to reach Strickland Street, and Mrs Norman was at home. Connie hurried back and the midwife came on more slowly. 'There'll be no hurry,' she called after Connie's retreating back. 'First babbies tek their time.'

Connie knew nothing about babies, but her instincts seemed to tell her that Mrs Norman might be wrong.

She knocked briefly on the scullery door and went in. 'She's coming,' she called upstairs as Nan was no longer in the kitchen. She heard Jeannie's faint voice but couldn't catch what she was saying. She stayed at the bottom of the stairs until Mrs Norman knocked and came in, and then she moved aside to let her pass.

'These stairs'll be 'death o' me,' the midwife puffed. 'Why they have to build 'em so steep I don't know. Now then, Nan,' Connie heard her say. 'Why don't you go down an' mek us all a nice cuppa tea, an' then put 'kettle on again for some hot water. Have you got plenty o' clean towels an' some old sheets?'

When Nan came downstairs she sat down abruptly. Connie saw that she was trembling. 'Is there owt I can do, Mrs Carr?' she asked.

'No. Yes. Fill 'kettle again. Mrs Norman wants a cup o' tea, but don't mek it till she comes down and onny mek a small pot. We're about drowning in tea – an' price of it . . .' Her voice trailed away.

'I'm sure Jeannie will be all right,' Connie ventured in a small voice, guessing that the old lady was anxious.

'How do you know?' Nan snapped. 'You know nowt about it.'

Oddly Connie wasn't upset by her manner; rather she was pleased that Mrs Carr was actually talking to her. Generally she ignored her as if she were invisible.

'I lost two babbies at birth,' Nan muttered. 'You never forget it. It's a dangerous business is birthing, 'specially for us that's poor.' She glanced at Connie as they heard Mrs Norman's footsteps on the stairs. 'You can mek 'tea now. I don't want a cup,' she said, 'but Jeannie might.'

Mrs Norman breezed in. 'It's not going to be long,' she said cheerfully. 'Her waters have broken already and 'babby's well on its way. Oh, thanks, love,' she said to Connie as she poured a weak cup of tea. She looked into the cup. 'Did you put any leaves in 'pot? I'll not be able to tell my fortune wi' this.'

'I don't like mekkin' it too strong,' Connie said nervously. 'Specially when it's somebody else's tea.'

'Quite right.' Mrs Norman blew on the hot liquid. 'Jeannie said for you to go up if you were still here.'

Connie glanced at Nan for her approval but Nan didn't look at her, so she escaped and ran upstairs. Jeannie was still on her feet and pacing about.

'Mrs Norman said I should stay in bed,' she whispered. 'But I can't. I don't want to. I wish Ma was here.'

'Shall I walk about wi' you?' Connie asked her. 'Mebbe if you've somebody to lean on?'

'Yes, please,' she breathed. 'If you would.' She grasped Connie's arm. 'That's better. Thank you, Connie. I'm so pleased that you're here.'

To Jeannie's astonishment, tears welled up in

Connie's dark eyes and ran down her face. Connie gulped. 'Nobody's ever said that to me afore,' she said huskily. 'I'm allus a nuisance, allus in 'way of everybody. I wonder sometimes why I'm here at all, cos I'm not of any use to anybody.'

'Don't say that,' Jeannie begged. 'Of *course* you are. I'm glad you're here anyway, and I think that probably Nan is too, though she'd never admit it. She wouldn't have been able to fetch Mrs Norman so fast, for one thing.'

Connie wiped her streaming eyes on her sleeve. 'No, she couldn't run as fast as me to Stricky an' that's a fact.' She gave a weeping laugh and then glanced anxiously at Jeannie as she stopped in their perambulations and bent double.

Jeannie groaned. 'Fetch Mrs Norman back, Connie – please!'

Mrs Norman was regaling Nan with some tale when Connie went into the kitchen but Nan wasn't really paying any attention and she looked up sharply when Connie said, 'Jeannie needs you, Mrs Norman. She wants you back upstairs.'

'Sit down,' Nan said to Connie when the midwife left to climb the stairs again. 'How does she seem?'

'A bit uncomfortable but not bad considering,' Connie said, careful not to make any wrong judgement. 'Women are brave, aren't they? I don't know if I would be.'

Nan gazed into the fire. 'Have to be, haven't we? We just have to get on wi' it. It's worse seeing somebody else go through it than it is for yourself. Some onny have one, though. Like your ma.' She was silent for a moment and then pronounced, 'Mebbe if she'd had more bairns her man might have stopped at home an' not run off wi' somebody else's wife.'

Connie didn't know how to answer, or even if an answer was required, so she kept quiet and gazed down at her lap.

'Still,' Nan went on. 'That's 'way it is an' it wasn't your fault. You were onny a bairn when he went.'

'I was ten,' Connie whispered.

Nan heaved a sigh. 'Aye, you would be; 'same as our Harry.'

There was a sudden shout from upstairs and Connie leapt to her feet. Then a squalling sound and Nan covered her mouth with her hand. 'That's it,' she quavered. 'That's it. Please God they're both all right.'

Connie looked at her. She would have liked to hold her hand or touch her, but did not dare in case of a rebuff. 'Is it over, do you think?' she whispered. 'It were quick!'

Nan swallowed. 'Aye. It was.'

Mrs Norman yelled from the top of the stairs. 'All over,' she exclaimed. 'Mother an' babby are fine. It's a boy! Better put 'kettle on again.'

CHAPTER TWENTY-FOUR

The baby was small but perfect. Everyone agreed on that as they gathered round the bed.

'That's why he was an easy birth,' Mrs Norman pronounced. 'Think yourself lucky, girl,' she told Jeannie. 'I've delivered some whoppers in my time and they're never easy.'

'He'll soon grow.' Nan looked down at him in the crook of Jeannie's arm. 'He's got a look of Harry already,' she said. 'All that dark hair.'

Jeannie smiled. She was dark-haired too. 'Would you like to hold him, Nan? Your great-grandson!'

'My word.' Nan's voice was husky. 'I hadn't thought o' that.' She took him from Jeannie and put a finger under the baby's chin. 'Now then, young Harry.'

'I'm going to call him Jack after my father,' Jeannie said firmly. 'He'll be Jack Foster Carr. Foster's a Hull name,' she told Mrs Norman. 'My da's family came from Hull.' She gave the information quickly, before Nan could make any objection to her choice of name.

'Aye? There's still a few Fosters scattered about,' Mrs Norman told her.

Connie was allowed to hold the infant and then Mrs Norman took him, wrapped him tightly in another sheet and placed him in a drawer that she had commandeered and softened with a thin pillow and blanket.

'Let him rest now,' she said. 'He's had a difficult journey coming into this world, and his ma needs a rest too. A cup o' cocoa is called for.' She addressed Connie as if she was in charge of the refreshments. 'Nowt like it for building up new mothers an' getting 'em ready to feed a hungry bairn.'

Jeannie felt herself blushing. There was so much she didn't know about babies. She suddenly felt vulnerable and anxious. She was not yet seventeen and was in charge of another human being. What a responsibility. She felt tears gathering in her eyes. If only Ma were here, she thought for the umpteenth time. She'd know what to do. And I wish Harry would come home; it was almost Christmas and she wanted him to share the joy of their first Christmas together.

She was advised to stay in bed, and when Connie had left she asked Nan if she would like Connie to come in and run errands for her. 'She'd be more than willing, I know,' she said. 'And I don't like to think of you having to climb up and downstairs.'

Nan said that she could manage, that she didn't need any help from anybody, but the next day, when Connie timidly knocked on the door and asked if there was anything she could do, Nan unexpectedly told her to come in and asked her if she'd take a drink upstairs to Jeannie.

'And mebbe you could slip to 'butcher's afore he sells out,' she said. 'See if he's a bit o' beef left and I'll mek some broth. Finest thing for building you up.' She sat down in the chair by the fire and gave a deep sigh. 'I might have some myself. Buck me up, it would.'

'I can't believe she's talking to me,' Connie whispered to Jeannie. 'She never looked 'side I was on afore an' now I'm running errands for her.' She sat on the bed and looked down at Jeannie and the baby. 'Isn't he beautiful?' she said. 'I could run away wi' him.'

Jeannie changed Jack over to her other breast. 'I'd find you.' She smiled. 'Maybe you'll have a bairn of your own one day, Connie. And don't say nobody will have you, because it isn't true.'

Connie shrugged. She seemed different. Not quite as bowed down as she had been. She'd seen Rosie, she said, and told her about the baby.

'She asked me how I knew an' when I told her I'd been here at 'birth, she was flabbergasted. Said at first she didn't believe me, that Nan wouldn't have me in 'house. But when I told her that I'd run to fetch Mrs Norman and that I'd made tea *and* cocoa, she shut up tight as a clam.'

'I wonder if she'll come and see her nephew,' Jeannie murmured. 'Does she have a grievance against Harry?'

Connie hesitated, and then said, 'Rosie has a grievance with everybody.' She rose from the bed. 'I'll have to go. I've to catch 'butcher.' She bent to stroke the baby's cheek and gave a sudden grin which lit up her plain features. 'See you tomorrow, Jack.'

She delivered the meat to Nan, and also some marrow bones which the butcher had given her when he heard who it was for. But she didn't come the next day, or the day after, and the following afternoon Jeannie decided she would get up and sit downstairs and make the child a crib in a shopping basket.

'I'm not an invalid, Nan,' she said when the old lady said she would rue being up too early. 'I feel fit and I don't like being upstairs on my own. Nor do I want you to be running about after me. And besides, I want to be downstairs for Christmas. I wonder why Connie hasn't been?'

Nan hmphed. 'Can't be trusted,' she grumbled. 'It's just as I thought. Bad blood.'

Jeannie let out a sigh. 'I don't think so. She meant to come to see Jack. She told him she would.'

Nan looked at her. 'Telled him? An' what did he say?' she said, her voice harsh with sarcasm.

They heard the back door open, but Jeannie knew it wasn't Connie. Connie would have knocked. It was Rosie.

'I heard you'd been delivered,' she said, standing with her arms crossed in front of her. 'News gets round.'

'Yes,' Jeannie said, wondering whether Rosie's delay in coming to visit was deliberate. 'It'd be Connie who told you, I expect?'

Rosie lifted her shoulders nonchalantly. 'Might have been. Can't remember.' She looked down at the baby and her face softened. 'He looks like our Harry.'

'That's because he is Harry's,' Jeannie said pointedly. 'Has Connie been at work?'

'Not for a couple o' days, no. Why?' Her eyebrows lifted. 'Is she your best friend?'

'She might be,' Jeannie said. 'She was here when she was most needed.'

Rosie looked uncomfortable. 'Yeh, well – I know when I'm not wanted.'

Nan gazed at her quizzically. 'You allus disappeared when you were asked to do summat, even when you were a little bairn,' she said. 'So don't come over all hard done by.'

'I'm not,' Rosie muttered sullenly. 'Anyway, I'm here now, aren't I? What 'you going to call him?'

Jeannie was sure she was only feigning interest. 'Jack,' she said. 'Jack Foster.'

Rosie looked at her. 'Jack Foster?'

Jeannie nodded and picked up the baby. 'Jack Foster Carr is his name. Would you like to hold him?'

Rosie shook her head. 'No thanks. I'd be scared o' dropping him. Anyway, I've got to be going. Auntie Dot's waiting for me to fetch 'fish in for supper.' She turned to leave. 'I expect Harry'll be pleased it's a lad.'

'I hope so.' Jeannie smiled. 'I can't send him back!'

Rosie glanced at her. She didn't smile in return; she obviously didn't think the remark funny.

'You shouldn't be having visitors,' Nan said after Rosie had gone. 'And you mustn't go out.'

'I wasn't going to,' Jeannie asked. 'I don't want to; it's too cold and wet for the bairn, and besides, I want Harry to see Jack before anybody else does.'

'It's supposed to be unlucky to go out,' Nan muttered. 'You should be churched first.'

Jeannie swallowed. She'd heard of it. Churching: originally a religious ritual of purification for those who believed that women who had given birth were unclean and sinful. We were sinful, I suppose, she thought, Harry and me, conceiving a child before marriage. But we married in church so our child

225

isn't illegitimate. And anyway, why is the mother sinful and not the father?

'When Jack's baptized, I'll ask the parson to bless me,' she said in what she thought was a kind of compromise.

To her surprise, Nan, after chewing this over, said, 'I'm never sure whether I believe in all that. And I don't think it's done in chapel. But it might be unlucky if you don't,' she added.

I'll chance that, Jeannie thought.

'If you go out on the road, will you ask about Connie?' she said. 'Ask if anybody's seen her.'

'No I won't!' Nan's voice was scandalized. 'Whatever will folks think if I start asking about that family?'

'It's not other folk or her family I'm bothered about,' Jeannie said quietly. 'It's Connie.'

The following day was Christmas Eve, and when Nan came back from shopping, armed with everything they had ordered, she was full of renewed energy. 'Harry's ship's coming up 'Humber,' she puffed. 'I've just seen Billy Norman. He says it'll dock at dinner time. Praise be,' she murmured. 'I hope they've had a good trip an' earned some money.'

Jeannie felt huge relief washing over her, but she glanced at Nan and wondered how she'd paid for the shopping. Since finishing Charlie's nets she hadn't earned anything; she knew that Nan's money pot would be low. To give the old lady her due she didn't grumble about the lack of money, but now Jeannie was anxious.

'Did you have enough money to pay for the Christmas food?' she ventured. 'For the extras, I mean? The pork pie and everything.'

Nan sighed. 'I got a smaller pork pie than we'd

ordered. I don't like it as much as I used to,' she added.

'You did right, Nan,' Jeannie told her, 'and I shan't want much, it's too rich, so there'll be enough for Harry.'

Nan nodded. 'He'll bring money home; course he will.' Her voice dropped to a mutter. 'He'll not let us go short won't Fred. He's a good lad.'

Jeannie smiled. 'Harry, you mean,' she said.

Nan blinked. 'That's what I said,' she snapped. 'Harry. He'll be home soon and looking forward to seeing his son.'

'Do you think anybody's told him?' Jeannie said, and out of the blue she recalled Josh Wharton and how she'd been sent to tell him to hurry home. Poor man; the birth of an infant and the loss of his wife a few days later. The perception of those consequences was more powerful now than when she had been a child. But that's not going to happen to me, she thought determinedly. Harry and I will have lots more children and a long life together.

But thinking of Josh Wharton, she couldn't help but dwell on Ethan. How would he react when he heard, as inevitably he would, that she was the mother of a child? Would he, after all, look round for a wife he could love and forget Jeannie, even though he had vowed that he never would? And if he did, what would she feel? Regret? Remorse for having hurt him? Or relief that he could love someone else and live a life without her? Jealousy, she thought; her emotions, heightened after the birth of Jack, tingled at the mere thought of it. That is what she would feel. For she knew in her heart that whilst he was a single man a part of him would always belong to her.

'They mebbe have,' Nan answered and Jeannie looked up, having forgotten her question. 'Mrs Norman will have spread 'news. He'll be rushing home any time now.'

But two o'clock came and then three, and conviction grew upon Jeannie that Harry had gone straight to the Wassand Arms and was spending his hard-earned wages. At half past three the back door crashed open and Harry staggered in.

'Let's have a look at him,' he bellowed, coming into the kitchen. 'Let's see my son.'

His face was weathered and his dark hair curled on his neck. He wasn't drunk but he was very merry, and Jeannie thought she couldn't blame him for that. On hearing the news that he was a father his mates would no doubt have carried him off to celebrate the birth.

She lifted the baby out of his basket, loosened his swaddling sheet and held him up to Harry, but Harry stepped back as if astonished. 'He's onny little, isn't he? Will he grow?'

'Come and sit down, Harry,' Jeannie said, feeling slightly put out that he hadn't even looked at her, 'and then you can hold him.'

'I don't think I want to.' He frowned, but bent closer. 'Look at his little fingers.' Tentatively he put a finger towards him and Jack curled his tiny hand over it. 'Look at that,' he breathed. 'How strong he is. Do you think he knows who I am, Jeannie?'

'Yes,' she said, feeling a rush of tenderness for the father of her child. 'I think he knows that you're his da.'

CHAPTER TWENTY-FIVE

Harry had brought home a parcel of fish, which Nan set about cooking straight away.

'Not sure if I want any, Nan,' Harry said. 'Have you nowt else?'

'No,' she said firmly. 'We haven't. But tomorrow we'll have a joint o' beef an' Yorkshire pudding an' savoury sausage meat, *and*,' she said, turning to look at him, 'Christmas pudding. And if you've any money left over mebbe we could run to a drop o' brandy for 'sauce.'

Harry grinned, and putting his hand in his pocket brought out a small bottle. 'You see! You thought I'd forget, didn't you?'

Nan took it from him. 'Yes, I did,' she said, and Jeannie, not part of this tradition, looked on at Nan's softened expression and Harry's satisfied smirk, and felt like a stranger.

Harry tipped out the money in his pocket and threw it on the table. 'There you are. There's me wages. Well – most of it.'

Jeannie and Nan both looked at the small amount and although Jeannie said nothing, meaning to have a discussion later, Nan asked, 'Is that all there is? It don't seem much for 'time you've been away.'

Harry shrugged. 'I was onny third hand, so no bonus is there? And 'word is that smacks are finished; there's no profit any more.' He paused for a second and then said, 'So I'm applying to go wi' one of 'bigger companies. Trawling.'

'Trawling?' Jeannie and Nan said as one. 'You'll be away longer,' Jeannie added, 'but there'll be more security, won't there?'

Nan gazed solidly at Harry. 'They'll have you, will they?'

'Aye, they will. That other business is forgotten. I wasn't 'onny one who was blackballed,' he said sharply.

'Which company?' Nan asked, unperturbed by his manner.

'Humber Steam,' he said. 'It's well established. Plenty o' capital.'

Nan's mouth shaped into a round O. 'That it is,' she said. 'Wish I'd had some money for a share in it.' She turned to Jeannie. 'Humber Steam 'n' Fishing,' she told her. 'He'll be all right wi' them if he can get took on. They've got new steam trawlers as well as adapted ones. And ice,' she added.

She was well informed, Jeannie thought. The fishermen's wives and mothers, and grandmothers too, it seemed, always were. They had the best interests of their men at heart and were always supportive, often vehemently so. But, she thought, working for such a large company Harry could never aspire to being more than a skipper. If smacks were finished, as he said, there would be no opportunity for a fisherman like Harry to become master of his own vessel. Men like Josh Wharton and Ethan who had bought shares in their ships would become a dying breed.

*　　*　　*

This Christmas Day was going to be very special, Jeannie thought. Jack was nine days old, Harry was confident of getting a ship and life seemed much rosier than it had previously. She wrote to her mother and Tom and told them of Jack's safe arrival and that she would try to come to Scarborough in the spring and bring Jack to see them.

'You'll adore him, Ma,' she wrote. 'He's an angel. Nan says he looks like Harry, but I'm sure you'll say that he looks like me. I haven't been out yet, and am waiting until he's been baptized, which will probably be in the New Year.'

She had felt very homesick as she gave Harry the letter to put in the post box when he went out on Christmas morning to meet his mates at the Wassand Arms. She didn't begrudge him this pleasure; she and Nan were preparing food and he had promised to be home by midday. Nan had warned him that if he wasn't home as agreed then they would start without him; she wouldn't overcook the beef and let it spoil, she told him.

She and Jeannie had decided between them that they would have the meal ready by half past twelve in case he was late, and at precisely that time the yard door opened and Harry came in. 'I'm not late, am I?'

Jeannie was in the scullery and had started to smile at his sheepish demeanour when she realized that he seemed agitated. 'What is it, Harry?'

He put his finger to his lips. 'Trouble, I think,' he whispered. 'Don't know what to do.'

Jeannie's brows creased. 'Is something wrong?'

Harry nodded, and putting his hand on the

231

door sneck said, 'It's Connie. She's outside.'

'What's happened? Bring her in.'

He shook his head. 'Nan!'

Harry didn't know that Connie had been there when Jack was born, that Nan had, grudgingly at first, allowed her inside the house. Or that she had been useful to her.

Jeannie put her hand over his. 'Let her in,' she said. 'It'll be all right.'

He bit on his lip. 'You sure?'

'Yes,' she said, and he opened the door.

Connie was out of sight, crouching by the wall. Harry went out and pulled her to her feet and she turned towards Jeannie.

'I didn't want to come,' she said thickly. 'But Harry said I should.'

Jeannie was appalled at the sight of her. Connie's mouth was swollen, her lips twice their size; her cheeks and nose were puffy and one eye was completely closed. She was dressed inappropriately for the time of year, with just a thin shawl over her cotton skirt and bodice.

'Who did this to you, Connie?' Jeannie drew her into the scullery.

Connie shook her head. 'Can't say,' she mumbled, 'or I'll get more of 'same.'

'Her uncle,' Harry blurted out. 'That's who! Bastard! He'll know about this, just see if he doesn't.'

'No,' Connie moaned. 'Don't! You'll mek it worse.'

'What's going on? 'Dinner's spoiling in here—' Nan came through from the kitchen but stopped when she saw Connie and ran her tongue over her lips. 'You'd better bring her in,' she said. 'She'll need a cold compress on that eye.'

Harry stared at his grandmother. He clearly wasn't expecting such a comment. He ushered Connie in and turned to Jeannie with a questioning glance.

'I'll explain later,' she breathed. 'Connie was here when the bairn was born.'

Nan sat Connie down by the fire, and fetched a bowl of cold water and a cloth. 'Here,' she said to Jeannie. 'You bathe her eye while I dish up. Yorkshires are done. They'll be ruined if we don't eat 'em now.'

As Jeannie drew up a chair in front of Connie and applied the wet cloth to her face, she saw Nan take another plate from the shelf, to make four. She gave an inward sigh of relief. The animosity appeared to be over. Connie was going to eat with them.

The meal was eaten in silence, apart from Harry's attempts to be jolly and exclamations that this was the best meal he had had in weeks. It was true the beef was tender and the puddings risen and golden. Connie ate very little, and Jeannie guessed that it wasn't because she wasn't hungry, but because her face ached. She put her hand over her mouth at one point and mumbled that she had lost a tooth.

Whilst Nan dished up the Christmas pudding, Connie cleared away the dirty dishes and put them in the scullery sink. Jeannie followed her in.

'When did this happen, Connie?' she asked in a low voice.

Connie's eyes filled with tears. 'Day after I'd been here. Somebody had seen me coming out and told my ma. She slapped me about an' said I hadn't to come again, but then when Uncle Des came in he asked why I was crying an' she told him.' She took a choking breath. 'An' he said he'd give me summat to cry about. He gave me a good hiding an' when I tried to get away from him I fell over and hit my face on 'table.' Tears ran down her cheeks. 'He pushed me out of 'door an' told me not to come back till I'd bucked my ideas up or he'd give me summat else to remember.'

'So where have you been since then?' Jeannie whispered.

Connie shook her head. 'Nowhere. Just wandering about. I couldn't go to work looking like this, could I?' She sniffled. 'I've probably lost my job anyway. 'Foreman won't have kept it; there's plenty o' lasses looking for work.'

'Come on; stop that nattering in there.' Nan's voice called them back to the table, and as Jeannie was finishing her pudding Jack woke up and bawled with such intensity that Harry cringed and Jeannie had to put down her spoon and feed the hungry baby straight away.

'By, he's got some lungs on him, hasn't he,' Harry said in amazement. 'You wouldn't think that such a little bairn could mek a row like that.'

'He's got to shout to mek himself heard,' Nan said, 'otherwise we'd never know.'

Connie got up from the table and began clearing away. 'Can I wash 'dishes, Mrs Carr? Then I'll get off out of your road.'

Nan pursed her lips and nodded. 'Aye, you can.' She paused, not looking at Connie. Then she lifted her head and stared straight at her. 'An' then where'll you go?'

'Dunno.' Connie shook her head. 'Not home, anyway. I daren't go back. I'm too scared o' *him*. I think he'll kill me.'

Jeannie drew in a breath and the baby hiccuped. 'You can't live on the street, Connie. You'll be arrested as a vagrant.'

'I'd get a roof over my head then, wouldn't I?' Connie said miserably. 'It's that or 'workhouse.' She put her head down and muttered, 'It's cold out on 'street – and dark – and I kept getting accosted by drunks.'

'All right!' Nan seemed to have come to a decision. She sat up straight and folded her stick-like arms in front of her. 'It's Christmas and I wouldn't like to think I was found wanting in Christian charity. I'll not pretend that I want you here, cos I don't, not after what has gone on afore wi' your family an' mine; but I'd not let a dog roam 'street at this time o' year, let alone a fellow human being. You can stop here till you find somewhere else; a room or lodgings. There isn't a bed, but you can sleep on 'rug in front o' fire.'

Connie stared at her, her lips parted. She seemed to be having trouble breathing, but Jeannie thought that was because of her swollen nose.

'I'll have to find work afore I can afford a room, Mrs Carr, an' I've no money for my keep. I gave my wages to my ma.'

Nan pondered, and both Jeannie and Harry sat looking at her, waiting for her decision.

'As soon as you're earning then,' she said at last. 'You'll give me your first shilling an' after that you can look for a room.'

'Oh, thank you.' The relief in Connie's voice was plain. 'Thank you. I'll not be a bother, an' I'll clean for you or do any jobs that you ask.'

Nan nodded. 'You can start tomorrow an' donkey-stone 'doorstep. I like to see it white. And when you've done that you can go back to 'dock an' see if your old job's still open. Never mind about your black eye. Let 'shame of Des Turnby's fist be clear for everybody to see.'

Connie managed a smile but it was evident that she wasn't too happy about that command. 'I usually lie about me bruises,' she said.

'And your damaged hand?' Jeannie asked.

Miserably she nodded. 'Yes,' she said. 'Though I expect everybody knows. They all know what he's like. He used to beat up his lads but now they're bigger than him an' fight back.'

'What about them?' Harry asked. 'Have they ever hit you?'

'No,' she said. 'An' Des doesn't hit me when they're there. They'd stop him, I think. They're nice lads.'

Harry knew Des Turnby's two sons, and told Jeannie later, when they were alone in the kitchen whilst Connie and Nan cleared up in the scullery, that although they were tough lads when they were in drink, they would never hit a woman.

'I suppose Connie would be too frightened of her uncle to tell them,' she said.

'She's frightened of her own shadow,' Harry said. 'Always was, even when she was a bairn; an' I expect she tells 'em 'same tale as she tells everybody else, that she's fallen or bashed her head on summat.'

'It's a pity no one else has told them,' Jeannie said. 'They might warn their father off.'

Harry lifted his chin as he contemplated. 'Aye,' he said. 'Mebbe they would.'

He went out later that evening after they'd eaten a Christmas tea of cold sausages, pork pie and pickles, followed by fruit cake and cheese. 'Don't wait up,' he told Jeannie. 'I'm meeting some of 'lads.'

This was not what I expected, she thought. We've had no time together, no time to talk; on Christmas Eve he'd fallen into bed and was instantly asleep and didn't wake even when the baby cried during the night to be fed, and he was still asleep when she'd got up on Christmas morning.

'Our Fred allus sleeps in after a trip,' Nan had said when Jeannie went downstairs. 'He gets worn out.'

Jeannie had busied herself with Jack and this time hadn't contradicted her, not over the use of her dead son's name, nor when she had chucked the child under the chin and said fondly, 'Now then, young Harry.'

Now Harry had gone out, leaving the three women together: Nan knitting by the low light of the oil lamp, Connie lost in thought as she perched on a hard chair as if ready for flight, staring into the fire; and Jeannie, nursing Jack, thought that her first Christmas as a married woman was almost over. Another week would bring in a new year and a year after that a new decade.

She looked down at the sleeping, satiated Jack, his milk-dribbled mouth still gently sucking, though he had abandoned her superfluous breast. What will those years bring us? she thought. Not riches, that's for sure, and never having had them I'd not wish for them; but security, food in our bellies, a roof over our heads – that's what's important. She smiled and gently touched her baby's soft cheek. Your da to stay at home sometimes would be nice, and a brother or sister for you.

The baby gave a sudden cry of wind and she picked him up and patted his back. Nan looked up from her knitting and gazed from Jeannie and the baby to Connie.

'Better put 'kettle on,' she said. 'Fred'll be home soon.'

CHAPTER TWENTY-SIX

When Harry came home, jubilant, three days later to say he had been taken on by the Humber Steam and Fishing Company and hoped for a ship the following week, Jeannie didn't mention her concern about Nan; she didn't want him to worry whilst he was away. Connie had come in on Boxing Day and told them the foreman had taken her back in her old job at the fish quay, although he had warned her that any more time off and she would be out.

'Did he ask how you came to be bruised?' Jeannie asked and Connie shook her head.

'No, but I think he knew. He asked if I was still living at home and I told him I'd found temporary lodgings.'

Harry heard some of the conversation. 'I just happened to mention to Billy Norman that I'd seen you, and that Des Turnby had given you a beating. He knows Des and his lads so it'll get back to 'em that folks know about it.'

Connie looked at him with frightened eyes. 'I hope he doesn't come lookin' for me,' she said in a small voice.

'He won't come here,' Harry assured her. 'I'm bigger than him.'

But when you're away he might, Jeannie thought, and wondered if Des Turnby would come and warn her and Nan off befriending Connie.

'I'll leave as soon as I can,' Connie said. 'I'll give your nan 'first shilling like I promised and look for somewhere else to live.' She bit on a fingernail. 'But everybody knows everybody else on Hessle Road; he'd soon find me.'

'Then you'd better stay here for a bit longer,' Harry said. 'Nan won't mind an' while I'm away you can sleep wi' Jeannie and 'babby.'

Jeannie looked sharply at him, and Connie must have seen the protest in her face for she quickly said, 'I'm fine down here in front of 'fire.'

'Better there than being woken up during the night,' Jeannie said firmly.

Nan made no objection; in fact she appeared to have forgotten her original bidding that Connie should look for lodgings after paying her the shilling. After the New Year, Harry left on his voyage and Nan bought the same amount of food for the three of them and seemed to accept Connie's presence.

'What'll I do, Jeannie?' Connie whispered. 'Shall I pay Nan for my keep at 'end of 'week?'

'Give it to me,' Jeannie said. 'Then she won't be reminded that she asked you to leave. I'll put the money in her purse when she's not looking.'

But when she did that, at the end of the following week, worryingly she saw that Nan's purse was almost empty, apart from a few coppers. Yet she had gathered up the money that Harry had brought home from his last voyage.

It wasn't much, I know, Jeannie thought. But if it's all spent, then we must be living on credit. She attempted to ask Nan if she was managing all right, but was brushed off with the rejoinder that she had always looked after the household purse and didn't need any advice from Jeannie.

'Stay a little longer, Connie,' she said one evening. Nan had gone outside to the privy. 'There's no hurry for you to leave,' and once again, Connie gave her the money for her board and lodgings, keeping only a few pence for herself.

'I don't need much,' Connie said. 'There's nowt I want to buy, and besides I feel safe here.'

'I wish I could go out,' Jeannie said. 'When Harry comes home I'm going to ask him to make the arrangements for the christening and my churching, and I'm going to ask my ma if she can come. The weather's not bad, although it's wet, but she's used to that so I think she will. I want her to see Jack.'

She glanced towards the scullery door and heard Nan come in from outside. 'Will you stand as Jack's godmother, Connie?' She knew no one else she could ask, and knew that Connie was fond of the child.

'Oh!' Connie's face was wreathed in smiles. 'Do you mean it? Honest? Oh, yes, I will. Nobody's ever asked me such a thing afore. I'd be, I'd be – what's 'word I'm lookin' for?'

Jeannie smiled at her exuberance. 'Erm – honoured? Privileged?'

'Yeh,' Connie agreed. 'But – *special*. I'd feel special if I was asked to be a bairn's godmother, cos I don't think I'll ever be anybody's real mother.'

'You shouldn't think so poorly of yourself, Connie,' Jeannie chided her, but then surreptitiously put her finger to her lips as Nan came into the room. Twice that day Nan had referred to the baby as Harry, and chucking him under his chin had told him that his da would soon be home.

Mid-morning the next day, as Jeannie was changing Jack, someone knocked on the front door. 'Nan,' she called. 'Are you there? There's somebody at the door. The front, not the back,' she added, as she heard Nan lift the back door sneck.

'Who's this?' Nan grumbled as she came through from the scullery. 'Trouble, I'll be bound. Nobody ever comes to 'front.'

I did, Jeannie thought, though I suppose I was trouble. It's somebody who doesn't know us, anyway.

But it was someone who knew her. She heard Nan muttering that they'd better come through; when she looked up she felt a sudden rush of joy as she saw her mother standing in the doorway.

'Oh, Ma! Oh, I'm so glad to see you.' Jeannie burst into tears. 'I was going to write and ask you to come!'

Mary took Jack from her and gently kissed his warm cheek. 'I couldn't wait,' she said softly, and then kissed Jeannie. 'I couldn't wait a minute longer to see you and my grandson.' She turned to Nan, who was hesitating as if not knowing where to go or what to do. 'Isn't he a fine boy, Mrs Carr? And Jeannie looks so well; you're obviously taking great care of her.'

Nan wore a puzzled frown until Jeannie said softly, 'I think this calls for a cup of tea, don't you?' and then Nan turned to the range, lifted the kettle and shook it, then put it on the hook.

'Is there enough water in the kettle?' Jeannie asked her, knowing that she had used most of the water for bathing Jack. 'Does it need filling again?'

'Oh, aye, reckon it does,' the old lady muttered, taking it off the hook again. 'I'll just . . .'

'I think she's failing,' Jeannie said in a low voice as Nan went into the scullery. 'And she's getting very forgetful. She keeps calling Jack Harry.'

'Don't correct her,' her mother said. 'You know who she means. It'll embarrass her if you tell her.' She smiled down at the child on her knee. 'He's beautiful, Jeannie. He looks just like you did when you were a bairn. Now, I want you to tell me every-thing. How are you getting on in this fine town?'

'I don't know it, Ma,' Jeannie confessed. 'I only know Hessle Road. I've not had the chance yet of looking at any of the other places. There's a huge dock in the centre of Hull, and several others, but I've only seen St Andrew's and the Humber Dock. The town's much bigger than Scarborough. And there's a fair,' she added. 'Only I didn't know about it until it was too late. It was on the week after we got married. Nan says it always comes in October.'

Mary hummed a refrain of the old ballad 'Scar-borough Fair' to Jack, and Jeannie smiled.

'Hull Fair stays for a week. Mebbe I'll be able to go this year,' she said. 'But tell me about Tom and Sarah, Granny Marshall and Granny Anderson, and Susan Wharton and – everybody.' She didn't want to ask about Ethan, but she wanted to know.

'Well, Granny Marshall's tongue is as sharp as ever, but my ma didn't come with the herring this year. She didn't want to leave Andrew.' Her mother laughed. 'That's my guess, anyway. Susan Wharton is going to marry her butcher, and Tom . . .' – she hesitated – 'our Tom and Sarah are going to be wed at the beginning of next year. He's doing really well at the yard, Jeannie, and he's got the promise of a regular job there.'

'So you'll be alone, Ma.' Jeannie gazed at her mother with wide eyes. 'And I'm too far away to see you very often.'

'Ah, don't worry about me, bairn,' her mother said. 'I might be alone but I'll not be lonely. I've plenty of company by the harbour and—'

'Plenty of work?' Jeannie interrupted. 'Harry says that smack fishing is about finished.'

'So I've heard,' her mother agreed. 'But there are still plenty of nets to mend. Josh keeps me busy with them and so does Ethan.' She glanced at Jeannie as she mentioned Ethan's name. 'You haven't asked about Ethan,' she said.

'Oh!' Jeannie said vigorously. 'Yes, how is Ethan? Has he still got his smack?' He called it after me, she thought, but perhaps he's sold it now and bought another with a different name.

Mary nodded. 'He's still got it, and half shares in another. He's doing well is Ethan. Do you recall Pamela Osborn? She's a year or so older than you.'

'Vaguely,' Jeannie said. 'She was a chandler's daughter. What about her?'

'Oh, I heard that she and Ethan are walking out together. Don't know if it's true or not.'

Jeannie felt an icy chill touch her. But he said there would be no one else for him, she remembered. It hasn't taken him long to change his mind.

'Where's that tea?' Mary whispered. 'I'm fair gasping. I've had nothing to drink since first thing this morning.'

'I'll go and see what she's doing,' Jeannie said. 'She doesn't usually take so long.'

Nan was standing in the yard with the empty kettle in her hand. She looked at Jeannie in an uncertain manner. 'I don't know what I'm doing with this,' she said. 'What's it for? I've got a headache.'

Jeannie took it from her. 'Let me fill it for you, Nan,' she said softly. 'Come inside and see if the bairn is all right.'

'Yes,' Nan said vaguely. 'I will. He shouldn't be left on his own.'

When Jeannie had boiled the kettle and made the tea, her mother said quietly, 'Will you be able to manage with this one' – she glanced towards Nan who was staring into the fire – 'and the bairn as well?'

'Yes, I think so.' Jeannie told her mother that a friend had been staying with them, but not about Connie's family or her bruises. 'I'll ask her to stay on. I know she'll be glad to. She'll help me and bring in some money until I can earn again. I'm fit enough to start mending but I can't do that until after the christening and my churching.'

Her mother clicked her tongue in a disapproving *tsk* sound. 'The sooner the better then, Jeannie.'

As she spoke, someone hammered on the back door. 'Shall I go?' Mary said, for Nan had not moved on hearing the knock.

Jeannie had just sat down and picked up the child to feed him. 'Please, Ma. If you will.'

When Mary came back, she said there was a man asking for Connie Turnby. 'I told him there was no one here of that name, but then he asked to speak to Nan Carr.'

Jeannie swallowed. 'I'd better go,' she said, handing Jack to her mother and buttoning up her

245

blouse. 'Connie's the friend I was telling you about.'

At the door with his foot over the threshold was a thickset man, not tall but very broad across the shoulders. His face was weather-beaten, with purple thread veins around his nose, and his ears protruded from beneath his thinning hair.

'Yes?' Jeannie said. 'Mrs Carr isn't well. Can I do anything for you?'

'Not well, isn't she?' he sneered. 'Well tell her from me that she'll feel more than sick if she doesn't send that bitch of a girl back home to her ma afore 'day is out.'

'Who are you?' Jeannie asked, though she could guess and quaked at his words. 'I don't know who you are or what you're talking about.'

'Connie Turnby is who I'm talking about and we want her back home.'

'So that you can beat her up again, Mr Turnby? Is that what you want? And you're not even her father.'

'I've never laid a finger on her,' Des Turnby blustered. 'Never in my life.'

'That isn't what I heard,' Jeannie said bravely. 'I heard from a reliable source that you often beat her.'

Jeannie felt her mother's presence behind her shoulder and then she heard her speak. Mary had a good vibrant voice when she was roused.

'Did I hear you threatening my daughter?' she said in her strongest Scottish accent. 'Do I have to bring my brothers and my sons and all the fishermen of Scarborough to discuss your grievance? Who ever you are?'

Des Turnby took a step back as if alarmed by this tall red-haired Scotswoman. 'I'm – I'm not threatening her,' he stammered. 'I'm onny telling her that

Connie's mother wants her lass back home where she belongs.'

'Then you'd better ask Connie's mother to come here herself,' Mary declared, 'and tell her not to send any jug-eared errand lad with her messages.'

Des Turnby backed away. 'Didn't mean to frighten you, missis,' he began, 'I just—'

'Frighten us!' Mary said in a sinister whisper. 'It'll take more than a sprat like you to frighten the Marshall clan. Now be off with you!'

Jeannie's heart was pounding when they went inside, but then she began to giggle. 'You were magnificent, Ma. But what whoppers you told. Da wasn't a Scotsman; there's no Marshall clan. And you were an Anderson!'

'There *is* a Marshall clan,' her mother said. 'A famous one that's been around for hundreds of years. The first known one was reputedly a gypsy – a boxer and a bandit – so if that ruffian starts asking about the Marshalls he'll soon find himself bogged down in clan warfare. And,' she grinned, 'a white lie now and again is quite acceptable. So, Jeannie, don't give the wee bairn hiccups, but you'd better tell me what all that was about.'

CHAPTER TWENTY-SEVEN

Over another pot of tea and a slice of bread and potted meat, Jeannie told her mother about Connie. She'd poured Nan a cup but she seemed to be having trouble drinking it, lifting the cup awkwardly and not quite hitting the target of her mouth. She mumbled something and Jeannie asked her to repeat what she'd said as she hadn't quite caught it, but Nan seemed not to hear her.

Jeannie bit on her lip anxiously. 'I don't think she's well, Ma. She's acting very strangely, and she told me earlier that she had a headache.'

'Is she usually fit?' Mary asked. 'I noticed she was walking with difficulty.' She bent towards Nan. 'Mrs Carr! Are you feeling unwell?'

Nan gazed at her, and it was as if she couldn't form any words, but Jeannie thought she was trying to say *Fred*. Or perhaps it was bed.

'I think she's had some sort of apoplexy,' Mary said in a low voice.

Jeannie gasped. 'I don't know what that is. What can I do?'

'Make her comfortable.' Mary looked round the room. 'A pillow, if you've got one, and a blanket . . . and have you got a stool she can put her feet on?'

Jeannie scurried to do her mother's bidding, and then took a spoon and gently dribbled some tea into Nan's mouth. Nan put out her tongue and licked her lips and Jeannie gave her a drop more. 'That's better, isn't it, Nan?' she said. 'Nothing like a cup of tea.' But her words were shaky as she considered what might happen next.

'There'll be no money for a doctor, I suppose?' her mother asked, and when Jeannie shook her head said hesitantly, 'If you can't manage . . . I expect there'll be a workhouse infirmary?'

'I don't know,' Jeannie said. 'Harry wouldn't like that.' She wondered whom she could turn to for help. 'I'll ask Connie if she knows who I can ask.' She suddenly thought of Mrs Norman, who had delivered Jack; she seemed to be a person who would know about such places.

'When Connie comes back from work I'll ask her to fetch somebody. Oh, this is no good!' she exclaimed. 'I feel so helpless not being able to go out.'

Her mother nodded. 'But you must be careful not to overtire yourself, Jeannie. I know you're young and fit, but . . .' Mary had gone back to work at the harbour within two weeks of having Tom. She had wrapped the baby warmly in blankets and placed him by her side in a basket. Money had been short and her husband was away, just as Harry was now. 'Be careful,' she repeated, 'but make arrangements for the baptism and churching straight away. No use waiting for Harry. He'll understand, I'm sure.'

He'll be more concerned about Nan than about missing the christening, Jeannie thought. And Ma's right – I can't wait for him for I don't know how long he'll be away.

Mary stayed as late as she dared, but she was fearful of missing her train. 'I've to be at work in the morning,' she said. 'I've taken time off today and what a good thing I did, but I'll have to catch up with the nets tomorrow.'

When she stood up to leave she pressed a shilling into Jeannie's hand and a silver threepenny bit into Jack's tiny fist. She kissed his cheek and whispered, 'I wish it were a silver florin, bonny bairn, but those are hard to come by.'

'It'll bring him luck, Ma. I'll keep it safe,' Jeannie said, swallowing a lump in her throat at her mother's departure, but also knowing that the welcome shilling would buy them some supper.

Connie was late coming in but she brought with her a parcel of fish. 'I worked late to get in 'foreman's good books,' she said, 'and he gave me all this cod. Shall I peel some taties to go with it?' She looked at Nan sitting wrapped in the blanket. 'What's up?' she asked in a lowered voice. 'Is she badly?'

'Badly? She's not well, if that's what you mean. My ma's been today and she thinks she's had some kind of apoplexy.'

'Your ma's been! From Scarborough?' Connie's mouth opened in astonishment. 'Oh! Were you glad to see her? What's an apoplexy?'

'I'm not sure,' Jeannie confessed. 'A sort of fit, or something that goes wrong with your heart or brain, I think. She can't talk, anyway. Connie – could you fetch Mrs Norman to take a look at her? Maybe she'll know what's wrong.'

'Yeh.' Connie gathered up her shawl from where she'd dropped it on the back of a chair. 'I'll go now. I thought she was acting funny 'other day and she seemed to be walking lopsided.'

'We'll soon have you put right, Nan,' Jeannie said more cheerfully than she felt. 'Mrs Norman will know what's happened.' But Nan just sat and stared into the fire and didn't answer.

Mrs Norman didn't know, but agreed with what Jeannie's mother had said, that Nan might have suffered an apoplexy. 'They used to bleed people for that,' she told her. 'I think some doctors still do. Can you afford a doctor?'

'What would they charge?' Jeannie asked her. 'I've only got about a shilling.'

'More'n that,' Mrs Norman said wryly. 'If I were you I'd wait till 'morning and see how she is. I've got some aspirin you can give her. Finest medicine you can tek, I allus say, 'cept for laudanum, but I don't suppose you've got any of that, have you?'

'I don't think so,' Jeannie admitted. She felt like a stranger in the house. She didn't know where Nan kept items like aspirin or bandages, or whether indeed she did. Jeannie's mother had always kept a box with medication and scissors, liniment for chesty coughs and ointment for sore elbows and knees when she and Tom were children; every spring she mixed up a concoction of flowers of sulphur and treacle which they had to submit to.

'We'll try the aspirin, Mrs Norman,' she said. 'Thank you. If she's no better in a few days, is there a hospital that would take her?'

Mrs Norman took a deep breath. 'Oh, I don't know. Not without a doctor's say-so. Don't worry about her now. She'll be all right, I expect. She's a tough old lass. Aren't you, Nan?' She bent down and shouted in Nan's ear. 'Nowt much wrong wi' you, is there?'

Nan gazed at her from blank eyes and lolled to one side of the chair. 'Mm.' Mrs Norman screwed up her mouth. 'I'll come again in 'morning, and if she's no better you'll have to send for 'doctor an' scrape up as much money as you can.'

After she had left, Jeannie and Connie debated how they'd get the old lady upstairs to bed. 'We'll never manage her up those stairs,' Connie said. 'I think she should sleep down here in 'chair. I'll keep an eye on her during 'night.'

'Will you, Connie?' Jeannie said gratefully. 'It would be for the best, I think, and if we got her up we'd never get her down again. She'll rest easy enough in the chair by the fire.'

It was late by the time Jeannie had cooked the fish and potatoes, and although she tried to persuade Nan to eat she wouldn't open her mouth except for sips of water. Jeannie made her as comfortable as possible and Connie built up the fire, and when at last Jeannie climbed the stairs holding Jack in her arms she felt quite exhausted and rather tearful.

'I wish your da were here,' she whispered to the nuzzling baby as she sat in bed and he searched for her breast. 'He wouldn't be able to do any more than we've done, but he'd take the responsibility.' A tear trickled down her cheek. 'I'm not ready for being grown up yet, even though I love you. I don't want to run a household, which is what I'll have to do if Nan is ill. I want my ma.'

Mrs Norman didn't come until after eleven o'clock the next day and Jeannie pottered about the house as she waited for her. Nan was lying quite still and again would only take a sip of water, which Jeannie dribbled into her mouth.

'I'll pop to 'doctor's on 'way home,' Mrs Norman said. 'There's nowt more we can do.'

'Mrs Norman,' Jeannie said desperately. 'I can't go out because I haven't been churched and Jack hasn't been christened; do you think that the parson would call here?'

'Aye, he might.' The midwife pondered. 'Some folk are very particular about it. Tell you what. Why don't you pop out to church now and I'll keep an eye on Nan and on 'bairn? Put a shawl over your head and nobody'll know you. You'll be back in ten minutes and nobody any 'wiser. You can have 'bairn christened at some other time, cos you'll have to arrange for godparents.'

'I've asked Connie.'

'You'll need a man for him as well.'

Jeannie was glad to escape the house and she knew that Jack would be safe in Mrs Norman's care. She wrapped her shawl over the top of her head and kept it low, and relished the freedom of being outdoors again.

As Mrs Norman said, it didn't take ten minutes for the blessing. The parson insisted that she should bring the child to be baptized the following Sunday; she explained that there was some difficulty at home but said she would try. She heaved a sigh, but at least she could walk back to Walcott Street with her head up without risking offence.

Someone called her name and she looked round, surprised as always that anyone should know her. It was Mike Gardiner, smiling and waving, and she felt a surge of friendship towards him.

'Hello,' she called back. 'Happy New Year.'

'And to you, Jeannie.' He took her hand and shook

253

it. 'And congratulations. I heard that you've a son. Are you well?'

'Yes, I'm very well, thank you, but Nan isn't. Harry's away, and I don't know whether I should send for a doctor. Nan's not talking or eating and just sitting in a chair. Mrs Norman is with her now and looking after the bairn. I've been to be churched,' she added, 'so that I can go out and do the shopping and – and everything.'

He frowned, a crease appearing above his nose. 'Is no one else at home with you?'

'Connie Turnby's been staying,' she began, and saw his eyebrows shoot up. 'She – she needed a refuge,' she faltered, dropping her voice.

'Ah!' Mike nodded. "Word out on 'road is that Des Turnby has been warned to stay away from her.'

Jeannie put her hand to her mouth. Had Des Turnby exaggerated her mother's warning?

'What?' Mike said.

Jeannie shook her head and tried not to smile. 'Nothing. But I must tell Connie that she can stop looking over her shoulder.'

Mike surveyed her for a moment. 'Is Mrs Norman there now, did you say?' Jeannie said she was. 'Then shall I come back with you? I might be able to help. Fetch 'doctor or do summat anyway. It'll not be easy for you trailing about wi' a new bairn. And you must be careful of yourself.'

'Oh, thank you,' she said in relief. She was sure he'd be able to make the right decision over Nan; he'd known her for a long time. A lot longer than she had.

He walked by her side towards Walcott Street, and it was a comfort to have a conversation with someone.

He knew that Harry had gone on the trawlers and thought it good for him to be with a bigger company than his and his son's.

'Harry will be fine once he's settled down into regular work,' he told her. 'And especially now he's got a son. It'll give him 'incentive to do well.'

Jeannie thought that everybody knew more about Harry than she did. He'd been part of this community all his life. Mike had known his father and probably his mother too, as he would have known Connie's and all of her family. She felt like an outsider. I'm the stranger here and it's going to take years and years before I'm one of them. Is this what it was like for people coming to Scarborough? she wondered. Did we make them welcome?

What's the matter with me? she chastised herself. I'm already part of the community because I'm Harry's wife. Nan has accepted me, so have Connie and Mrs Norman, and Mike Gardiner is walking beside me to find out if he can help. She suddenly felt lighter in spirit and smiled up at Mike.

'I think you're right about Harry,' she said. 'He just needed some encouragement and the offer of work, and you did that for him.'

But Mike didn't answer. They'd turned into Walcott Street and he was looking towards the house, where Mrs Norman was standing with a bundle in her arms. He quickened his steps. 'I'll hurry on,' he said. 'Don't you rush.'

But Jeannie caught her breath. Jack! It was Jack in Mrs Norman's arms. Was he ill? What had happened? She saw Mike reach Mrs Norman and their glance towards her. 'Oh, God,' she moaned. 'My baby.'

She hurried down the terrace and Mike came to

meet her. 'There's no hurry,' he said softly. 'Not now, and your babby's all right.'

'It's Nan,' Mrs Norman said quietly. 'I'm sorry, lass, that sorrow has come so fast after joy. Nan died, not ten minutes since, just after you'd gone out.'

CHAPTER TWENTY-EIGHT

Jeannie wondered afterwards how she would have managed without Mike Gardiner and Mrs Norman. Mike went immediately to fetch a doctor and Mrs Norman ushered Jeannie and the baby upstairs and told her to get into bed and wait there until everything was seen to. Presently she brought her a cup of cocoa and said that Mike was back, the doctor was on his way and that all would be taken care of.

She clutched the cup with trembling fingers and looked down at Jack as he slept beside her, and felt sad that he would never know his great-grandmother. 'She was all right, was Nan,' she murmured. 'Though I didn't like her at first. She was so fierce, not just with me but with everybody; but she had a softer side and she would have spoiled you, Jack, I know that for sure. I don't know what I'm going to say to Harry.' Tears blurred her vision. 'He'll be devastated.'

She thought later that Mrs Norman must have dosed the cocoa with something for she fell asleep and didn't wake until dark and saw Connie leaning over her.

'Are you all right, Jeannie?' Connie whispered. 'You can come downstairs now if you want.'

Jeannie sat up. 'Nan?' she said. 'Where . . .' She couldn't bear the thought of coming down and seeing Nan still sitting in the chair.

'She's in 'front room.' Connie kept her voice low. 'Mrs Norman's done her up real nice. She looks ever so bonny. Better'n she ever did afore. There's been a few folk in to see her already. And Rosie's been as well. She didn't say much, though.'

'I'll get up.' Jeannie threw back the blanket. 'We'd better have something to eat.' Her legs trembled as her feet touched the floor.

'I've warmed up 'fish an' taties,' Connie said. 'I'm not much good at cooking but Mrs Norman showed me what to do an' Mike Gardiner has brought in a box o' groceries. Bread 'n' eggs, a string o' sausages an' bacon an' things.'

'Oh, how good of him.' Jeannie was overcome. She draped her shawl around her. She'd got into bed in her day clothes, not guessing that she would spend almost the whole of the day there. 'Are they still here? Mrs Norman and Mike?'

Connie shook her head. 'No, they've gone, but Mike said he'd come back in 'morning and Mrs Norman will send one of her bairns to see if there's owt you want.'

The kitchen had been tidied, and the chair where Nan had sat had been moved and another put there. Two places had been set at the table and the door into the front room was firmly closed.

'I'll go in and see her tomorrow,' Jeannie murmured, as Connie dished up their supper. 'Not tonight. I can hardly believe what's happened. It's all so unreal. You know what Harry said about you sleeping in my bed when he was away? Well, if you like, tonight you can; and then tomorrow, if you decide to stay that is, you could have Nan's room. I'll change the sheets and—'

'Mrs Norman's already tekken 'sheets and blanket off her bed an' says she'll wash 'em,' Connie interrupted. 'And yes, please, I'd like to come upstairs. I don't fancy sleeping down here on 'rug – not tonight I don't.'

When Mike Gardiner came the next day, he told Jeannie that he'd enquired about Harry's ship and the word was that it had been seen off the Faroe Banks and wouldn't be home for at least three weeks.

''Funeral will have to go ahead without him. It's not possible to wait that long. You won't be expected to be there,' he told her. 'I'll mek 'arrangements and Mrs Norman will put on a funeral tea. It's what's done round here,' he added. 'Folks will want to come and pay their respects.'

'I – I don't know about paying for it,' Jeannie stammered. 'I don't know if she paid in for anything like that.' She knew that Granny Marshall paid into what she called her funeral club, but she had no idea if Nan had done the same. How little I know, she thought.

'I'll pay, and when Harry comes home we'll sort something out,' Mike said. 'I expect there'll be a whip-round if there's no money. Folk are usually very generous towards their own.' He looked at her and then said quietly, 'Have you been in to see Nan yet?'

Jeannie shook her head. 'No,' she whispered. 'I haven't.'

He reached for her hand. 'Neither have I. Let's go in together and then you can tell Harry about her.'

Jeannie was astonished at the benevolence that surrounded her over the following week. She found a parcel of fish on the back doorstep, and people she didn't even know appeared with a meat pie or a fruit cake. Mrs Norman told her how many neighbours had come to the funeral tea at her house.

'Everyone's been really kind,' Jeannie said. 'I don't know what to say or how I can possibly repay them.'

'They don't expect to be repaid,' Mrs Norman said. 'It's what we do.'

But not everyone was touched by the hand of human kindness, as Jeannie was to discover a few days later when she answered a knock on the back door and found a shabby-looking man wearing a bowler, carrying a worn leather bag and clutching a thick black notebook in his hand.

'I understand that Mrs Carr is deceased,' he said without preamble. 'I represent 'landlord o' this property and I'm here to inform you that 'rent is overdue and has been for 'last six weeks.' He gazed at her bleakly. 'Are you a relative, and will you be tekkin' over 'arrears?'

Jeannie stared. Six weeks! That meant that Nan had been behind for over a month before she died. Why hadn't she paid? Did she not have the money? And why didn't she say?

'Are you sure?' she said hoarsely. 'I thought she always paid promptly.'

The man nodded. 'She allus used to. Then she started coming up wi' excuses why she couldn't pay. Are you tekkin' over 'rent book?' he asked again.

'She was ill,' she said vaguely. 'That must have been why she forgot to pay.'

260

He said nothing but just stood looking at her.

'Erm, my husband is away at sea.' Jeannie licked her lips. 'Could you give us time? He'll be home soon. We – we've only just had Mrs Carr's funeral,' she said, knowing even as she explained that he wasn't in the least interested.

He opened up his notebook and wrote something in it. 'I'll call again next week.' He snapped it closed. 'I've got plenty o' folk wanting a nice house like this,' he said sharply. 'If you can't manage 'rent I can offer you summat smaller for less.'

He fingered his bowler and turned away, crossed the yard and was gone, leaving her shaking.

I must start work on the nets again, she thought. Dare I ask Mike if he has any? I hate to be a nuisance when he's been so helpful, but what else am I to do? The only money that was coming in was from Connie and that had been used to buy coal, milk and bread.

When she told Connie about it that evening, Connie thought for a moment and then said, 'We could do a moonlight – a flit,' she explained when Jeannie looked at her blankly. 'We don't need a big house like this, not even when Harry's at home. You don't ever use 'front room.'

It was true, they didn't. Jeannie pondered. It had only been used the once whilst she had been living here and that was for Nan. She was heartened too that Connie had said *we*, which meant that she wanted to continue living with them.

'It's not your responsibility to pay 'arrears,' Connie went on. ''Rent book was in Nan's name, so if we did a flit nobody'd come after us.'

'But what about Harry?' Jeannie exclaimed. 'He

wouldn't know where we'd gone. He'd come home and there'd be nobody here!'

'Oh.' Connie pooh-poohed her concern. 'He'd soon find us. We'd not be moving far. Just further along 'road.'

'I don't know.' Jeannie hesitated. 'I'll have to think about it. It seems dishonest somehow.'

Connie shook her head. 'Folks keep movin' all 'time. It's what 'landlord expects. 'Agent won't bank on finding you here when he comes knockin' next week.'

She was still unsure about it, but when she tentatively mentioned to Mrs Norman that she was thinking of moving because she couldn't afford the rent, Mrs Norman agreed with Connie that the present house was too big for her and Harry anyway.

'When you've a few more bairns then mebbe you could look at summat as big, but I've heard of a smaller place that's just come empty. It'd be just right, especially when Harry's away. I'll put in a word for you, if you like?'

And Jeannie found herself saying, 'Yes please.'

Mike Gardiner offered the loan of his horse and cart and on the third evening after that Jeannie, with Jack strapped to her chest, Connie and all the furniture were in the back of the cart being driven to the other house. There wasn't much furniture to be moved: chairs and table, the rickety chest of drawers, two beds and an old wooden chest which held spare bedding. It was when Jeannie took up the rug at the side of Nan's bed that she discovered a small cache of coins that had been laid in a circle beneath it. It didn't add up to very much, but it would have been enough to pay two weeks' rent. She gathered it up and put it in her pocket, relieved that there would be sufficient to visit the butcher as well as paying the first week's rent at the new house.

'All old folk hide money,' Connie said when she told her. 'They think they're saving it for a rainy day, but then when it rains they forget where they've put it.'

Jeannie looked about her. They had driven further down Hessle Road towards the town before turning into Wassand Street and then on to a long road which Mike said was English Street and ran parallel with the docks; then he had taken several other turns until he reached a narrow terrace of houses surrounded by factories, a steam mill and a foundry.

Mike began to unload the cart. He glanced at the terraced house. 'It's mebbe not what you're used to, Jeannie,' he murmured. 'But you'll manage till Harry comes home.'

'We only had a small cottage,' she said. 'In Scarborough, I mean.' She felt a sudden choking in her throat as she thought of it. 'Ma never had much money.' She pressed her lips together, hard, to stop herself from crying. 'But we managed. At least she did.'

Mike nodded. 'I wasn't thinking of 'size of 'place, more of where it is. This used to be all right – it's just that it's overcrowded. Folks round here haven't any money or prospects of mekking any.'

Jeannie glanced around. The area looked poor. There were small front gardens, not much more than dirt plots where once there might have been grass, which were now filled with debris. Some of the houses had no curtains, but only cardboard covering broken windows.

'Not their fault,' he said, heaving the table off the cart. 'They do what they can to survive. Putting bread into their bairns' mouths is 'priority. Have you got 'key?'

Connie had it and she opened the door. A stale odour greeted them as they entered the house. Jeannie held Jack tight to her. Was the house clean? No, it wasn't. It looked as if it had been abandoned. Somebody, in Connie's words, had done a moonlight. Why, she wondered, would Mrs Norman think she would want to live here?

'We'll soon get it cleaned up.' Connie peered about her, and then, going from the room they had entered from the street into the scullery, she called out, 'There's a tap and a sink, but nowt else.'

Jeannie just stood there; she heard Connie open the scullery door and then shout again. 'And a yard wi' a privy, so we don't have to share wi' anybody.'

But no cooking range such as Nan had, which I'd got used to, Jeannie thought, just a dog grate in the hearth like Ma has at home. I'll have to boil the kettle and pan on there. She felt her shoulders drooping, but she turned and put on a bright face when Mike came in and said, 'I'll tek beds up first and get them out of 'way. Just watch 'cart, will you, Jeannie? I don't want anybody running off wi' my hoss.'

Or the furniture, she thought. But surely nobody would be desperate enough to do that? She stood in the doorway; it had started to sleet and she realized that they couldn't make a fire for they had no wood or coal.

'Did you look in the coal house before we left, Connie?' she called out when she heard her pottering about inside. 'Was there any coal?'

Connie grinned as she came through. 'What would you do wi'out me?' she said. 'While you were upstairs stripping 'bed, I was shovelling coal. I got a good bucketful, and some firewood. It's in 'back of 'cart.'

Jeannie clenched her eyes tight shut and then heaved a deep breath. She put Jack in a chair and tucked a blanket at each side of him so that he couldn't roll out, turned up her sleeves, and said, 'Good. Well done, Connie: so first things first. I'll light a fire and boil a kettle and we'll get this place looking like home.'

CHAPTER TWENTY-NINE

It was as Mike was preparing to leave that Jeannie remembered that they'd left behind the frame that Billy Norman had made for her.

'I'm so sorry to be a nuisance,' she said to him. 'But I must have it. How can I work without it?'

He sighed and shook his head. 'Can't resist a plea from a pretty girl,' he said wryly. 'I'll go and fetch it now afore anybody goes nosing about and sees that you've done a flit.'

Connie screwed up her mouth after he'd left. 'I'd nivver be able to get any man to do owt for me. That's a knack I haven't got.' She sounded like the old downtrodden Connie she had previously been.

'If Harry had been here – but he's not, so who else could I ask to fetch it? I have to have it, Connie, or I can't work. I can do the smaller nets on my knee, but what about when Jack starts crawling?'

'That won't be yet for a bit!' Connie exclaimed. ''Bairn's onny a month old.'

Jeannie knelt by the hearth and blew on the firewood to stir the flame. 'I've still got to look ahead. Harry might not be home for a couple of weeks.' She looked up at Connie. 'How am I supposed to live in the meantime unless I do the mending?'

'There's my money,' Connie said, suddenly pouty and sullen.

'I know, and I'm grateful. I don't know how I'd have managed without you, but I need to earn some money of my own. It's not fair that you should have to provide for me.'

Connie sat down and looked down at her hands. 'Nobody's ever needed me afore,' she muttered. 'I was quite enjoying that. My da didn't want me with him and my ma couldn't have cared less. I've felt useful for these last few weeks, but I should have known it wouldn't last.'

Jeannie rocked back on her heels. 'Connie! You've been a godsend. All I'm saying is that whilst Harry's away I need to earn some money. You're a friend. I'm not asking for your friendship because of the wages you're bringing in!'

Connie gazed at her and then looked away. 'Do you mean that if I lost my job and didn't have any money, we'd still be friends?'

Jeannie put her hands to her head. 'Of course we would! What sort of person do you take me for?'

Connie gave a shrug. 'Dunno.'

Mike not only brought the stand but also erected it in the yard so that it was in place as soon as Jeannie was ready to use it. She didn't ask him if he had any nets for her as she didn't want to stretch their friendship too far or presume any favouritism; but a week later he brought a trawl net which was badly damaged and needed almost a week's work to repair it.

It was bitterly cold out in the yard and although she was wearing most of her outdoor clothes, her rubber boots, thick socks and a shawl wrapped

267

around her head, she couldn't work for more than an hour without coming in to warm herself by the fire. She also wanted to keep checking on Jack, who was wrapped in a blanket in a basket which she placed in the middle of the table away from any draughts.

She and Connie practically lived on fish, boiled potatoes and cabbage, but the cabbage produced colicky wind in Jack and he kicked his little legs and screamed, so she had to stop eating it. She bought milk from a dairy two streets away and boiled it thoroughly before making semolina puddings. She had seen the thin and unhealthy-looking cows paddling about in their undrained stalls and the cowman with his unwashed hands and wasn't prepared to take any chances. When Connie brought home her wages and Mike paid her for the mending, they shopped at the butcher's for marrow bones for making broth, and, feeling relatively well off, bought a pound of scrag end of beef for a stew.

There were a great many shops springing up, fronting the road and in the side streets which housed the mass of people who worked in the fishing industry, on the docks or on the railway; most of them, Connie told her, had come during the period when St Andrew's Dock was being built. There were also new churches, banks and pawnbrokers to serve every need of the community. But this end of the road, as Mike Gardiner had said, was an area of great poverty, and Jeannie saw many barefoot and bedraggled children sitting at the edge of the footpath, hoping, she assumed, to beg a penny or a crust from a passer-by.

'Saturday night is 'night to stop at home,' Connie told her. 'Especially when you've got a young bairn. 'Road is packed wi' folks and all 'pubs and hostelries are full. Some of 'shops are open till midnight and you can hardly get through 'crowds.'

They had been living in the house for nearly five weeks, and Jeannie was beginning to worry about Harry. She was also worried about paying the rent. She had kept back some money from the net mending, but hadn't worked on any more since the one that Mike had brought.

'Wives and mothers do them,' Connie said, when Jeannie told her about her fears. 'There're not many fishermen who are looking to put 'em elsewhere. Course, you could allus get work on 'fish quay.' She shrugged. 'I dunno what other women do. Tek their bairns to a child minder, mebbe, if there isn't a gran to look after them.'

'No!' Jeannie hugged Jack closer. 'Never.'

A few days later, Connie was about to leave to go to work and Jeannie was sitting feeding Jack when there was a hammering on the door. Connie froze. It seemed that she never got over the fear that her uncle would come looking for her.

'I daren't go,' she whispered. 'It might be Uncle Des.'

'He doesn't know where we are,' Jeannie whispered back.

'He does.' Connie stared at her. 'He'd mek it his business to find out.'

The hammering got louder. Jeannie got up and handed the baby to Connie. She wrapped her shawl closer over her night shift. 'I'll go,' she said. 'He'll get a piece of my mind if it is him.'

She opened the door a crack and peeped out. It was still dark and there was no light outside; but a smile crept over her mouth as she recognized the size and shape of the man at the door.

'*Harry!* Oh, Harry. At last!' She opened the door wide to let him in, but drew back as she saw the anger on his face.

'What the devil are you doing here?' His voice was loud and furious. 'I've been home and somebody else is living in our house! I've had 'devil's own job to find you.'

He stepped inside and saw Connie holding Jack. 'What's going on? Why's she holding 'bairn? And where's Nan?'

Jeannie took Jack from Connie. 'You get off,' she murmured. 'Don't be late for work. Come and sit down, Harry. The fire will soon be ablaze.'

He glared at her. 'Don't try and soft-soap me! What a fool I must've looked, not knowing where me own house was.'

'We – we didn't know when you'd be home. Mike Gardiner was going to try to catch you when your ship docked – to tell you.'

'Mike Gardiner!' he bellowed. 'What's he bin doing sniffing around while I'm away?'

'Helping,' she said weakly, knowing how pathetic that would sound when he didn't know the circumstances.

'Where's Nan? I can't understand her allowing you to move. She's lived in that house for years; brought me up there. What happened?'

He seemed a little calmer. Taking off his coat, he sat abruptly in the chair nearest the fire. She took the one opposite him.

'I'm sorry, Harry. I've got some really bad news and you're going to be upset, but I have to tell you.'

Harry stared at her. 'What?'

'Nan was taken ill. She died, Harry.' Tears trickled down her face when she saw how shocked he was. 'It was very sudden. I asked Mrs Norman to come in and look at her because she seemed unwell. I thought she might know what was wrong, and Nan died whilst she was there. We had to have the funeral. We couldn't wait. Everybody said how nice it was and – and there were a lot of people there. I couldn't go because of the bairn, and . . .' Her words trailed away. There really wasn't any more she could say.

Harry put his head in his hands. 'No. I don't believe it. Not Nan. Nan's allus bin there for us.' He fished in his pocket for a handkerchief and brought out a grey rag. He blew his nose. 'Did you fetch 'doctor?'

Jeannie shook her head. 'There wasn't time,' she said softly. 'It was too sudden. Mrs Norman had come to see how she was, and she stayed with Nan whilst I went to be churched.' Harry looked at her with a question in his eyes and a frown on his forehead, and she hurried on. 'I had to do it, Harry, otherwise it meant that I couldn't go out to do the shopping or anything if Nan wasn't well, and when I got back – I was only ten minutes – Nan had died and Mrs Norman was waiting to tell me.'

She wiped away her tears and decided that she wouldn't tell him how helpful Mike Gardiner had been, in case he took offence. But she told him that Mrs Norman had put on a funeral tea and that people she didn't even know had come round with parcels of food for her.

Harry sniffed. 'I still don't see why you had to move,' he said. 'Specially to a place like this. You shouldn't have made that decision yourself. You should've waited for me to come home.'

'It was because of the rent,' she explained. 'It was in arrears and I had no money to pay. Connie had been paying her board, but that wasn't enough for the rent as well. Then there was the chance of this house,' she rushed on. 'And it's less rent and quite big enough; we don't really need a front room.'

He sat silently, just looking into the fire. 'You mean that Nan hadn't been paying 'rent?'

She nodded, and then said, 'I think she'd been struggling, but she never said. She'd always managed before, I suppose, and didn't like anybody else interfering with her affairs.' Especially somebody like me, she thought.

'All right,' he muttered grudgingly. 'I expect you did what you could. Who paid for 'funeral?'

She swallowed. 'Mike Gardiner. He said he would sort it out with you when you came home. I didn't know if Nan paid into a subscription club.' She saw the fury in his face when she mentioned Mike's name. 'And I knew you wouldn't want her to have a pauper's funeral.'

His mouth dropped open as the possibility dawned on him. 'No I wouldn't,' he said hoarsely. 'I'd onny ever want 'best for her.'

'That's what she had, Harry, and it was because of your friends being there when they were needed. Mrs Norman, Mike Gardiner and Connie. I don't know how I would have managed without them.'

He got up from the chair. 'I'll go and see them,' he said. 'So Connie's still living here, is she?'

'Yes. Is that all right, Harry?' she asked in a small pleading voice. 'It'd be very lonely for me on my own when you're away.'

'Aye.' He appeared to consider for a moment. 'I expect it would. An' she'll be glad to stop, I expect.' He glanced round the room and saw the familiar furniture, though it was cramped in the smaller room. 'This'll do for 'time being, till we get on our feet, but then *I'll* decide whether we flit or not. Now then. Give us hod of 'bairn and you can cook me breakfast.'

'There's nothing to cook,' she said. 'No bacon or eggs, I mean. I can make you some porridge; that's what we've had.'

He stared at her, holding the child awkwardly on his knee. 'No grub? You mean I've come home after being at sea all these weeks and there's nowt to eat?'

She shook her head. 'There's no money left. Not until Connie gets paid. If . . .' She hardly dared ask. 'If you've got your wages I'll slip out and buy some food.'

He stood up and handed Jack to her, then fished in his pocket and threw some money on the table.

'Don't bother,' he muttered. 'I'll go and get myself a steak pie from 'Wassand.'

'It's no bother,' she insisted. 'I can go to the corner shop and get bacon and bread. It'll be good to have a proper meal.'

But he just looked at her and put his coat back on.

'Harry,' she begged. 'Please don't go out. I want to talk to you. I want to know how you've been, what sort of voyage you've had. And to tell you about Jack.'

'What about him?'

'Well, how he's thriving, and—'

'That's women's stuff,' he said abruptly. 'Not mine.' He pulled up his coat collar. 'I'll see you later.'

CHAPTER THIRTY

It was very cold on the Scarborough fish wharves and someone had lit a brazier for the women to warm themselves by. Most of them wore fingerless gloves as they braided but even so their finger ends became blue with cold.

Mary was barely recognizable beneath her shawls and Josh Wharton laughed when he eventually found her.

'I've peered into every braider's eyes,' he said, his mouth creased with good humour, 'and been given a tongue-lashing for it.'

She smiled back. 'They wouldn't mean it, Josh. Not with you. They all know which side their bread is buttered.'

Josh was instrumental in bringing the women nets to mend, but that apart he was still an attractive man and many a single or widowed woman had him in their sights as a possible husband. Mary didn't know whether or not he was aware of it, for he never showed interest in any of them, even though there was every opportunity.

'You flatter me, Mary,' he said. 'Which is unlike you. Come on, come and take a walk. Stretch your legs and get the blood coursing through your veins.'

She nodded. 'I will. Just give me five minutes and I'll meet you along the harbour side.' Not only did she want to tie off what she was doing, but she did not want it to be too obvious that she was meeting Josh. Though she always said she was satisfied with her single life some of the women would read more into it than there was.

She saw him standing by a soup stall which a former seaman had set up when he could no longer go out to sea. His wife made the soup and he sold it at a small profit mainly to the women braiders or the men who had just landed their catch and were ready for sustenance.

'Here, Mary. This'll warm you up.' Josh handed her a bowl of vegetable soup, thick with potatoes and carrot.

'Want some bread, missis?' The stallholder handed her a thick slice to dip into the soup.

They sat on the harbour wall as they ate and Mary's nose began to run as the heat percolated through her.

'Oh, that's good.' She sniffed. 'It's bitter cold this morning. But I'm glad to see you – I was meaning to catch you. I've had a letter from Jeannie.' She pressed her gloved hand to her nose. 'Harry's grandmother has died and Jeannie's had to move house. She said she couldn't afford the rent and has gone to something smaller.'

'She's got a good head on her shoulders has Jeannie,' Josh remarked. 'She'll manage all right, even though I know you worry about her.'

'She has, but I do,' Mary agreed. 'She's had a friend staying with her for company while Harry's been away, though she says he's home now. He's working with a trawler company so the work is more regular. But it'll mean he's away for much longer at a time, won't it?'

'Yes.' Josh looked thoughtful. 'The steam trawlers are the ones which, in my opinion – and the owners can deny it all they like – are depleting the North Sea stocks. But they can go further afield now – they've got massive hauling gear and high pressure boilers, unlike the smacks. And it's just as well, because they've been banned from some areas, like the Moray Firth.'

'Which means what?' Mary asked. 'Where will they fish?'

'Faroes. Ireland. Norway. As far as Iceland.'

'Like the old whaling ships used to,' she murmured.

'Yes, but they relied only on sail,' he said. 'Now they don't need to. And they can stay away for weeks on end.'

He took the empty bowls back to the stallholder. 'Shall we walk for five minutes before you go back?' He teased his beard as he spoke, and Mary thought there was something he wanted to discuss. They walked towards the lighthouse and then turned before he said, 'Ethan is thinking of buying shares in a paddle steamer.'

She turned to look at him. 'But some of the Scarborough companies have failed. Why would he do that?'

Josh sighed. He was clearly uncertain about it. 'He thinks it's the only way to progress from a smack, and he can pick one up at a reasonable price because of the companies that have folded. He's done quite well up to now. He had his smack converted to auxiliary power, as you know; if he buys a paddle steamer, then in a few years he says he'll move on to a bigger horsepower.'

'I thought the paddles were being accused of exhausting the local fishing?'

He nodded. 'So they are. But Ethan says that he'll fish away from home waters.' He shrugged. 'He's a single man. There's no reason for him to stay around Scarborough. He can go to the Irish Sea and drop his catch at Milford Haven. He doesn't have to come back here.' He sighed again. 'What a business to be in, eh! You lose one son to the sea, and then—'

'You won't lose him. And you've still got Stephen,' Mary interrupted.

'For how long?' Josh muttered. 'Stephen's nine. Already he's saying he wants to be a fisherman like Ethan, and Ethan says he'll teach him; take him on as an apprentice, just as I did with him and Mark.'

Gently she put her hand on his arm. 'It's what we have to do, Josh,' she said softly. 'It's our way of life, and it isn't as if you won't see Ethan ever again. He'll still come back to Scarborough.' She frowned a little. 'What happened to the girl he was walking out with – Pamela . . .'

'Nothing.' His lips turned down. 'I think she gave up on him. She obviously realized that there'd be no wedding bells.'

They continued walking back towards the fish wharves. The breeze was freshening; dark clouds scudded across the sky. Mary shivered. 'I hope they've kept the fire alight.'

'I'll fetch some wood,' he said. 'But going back to Ethan – he told me that he wouldn't be selling his first smack, but only the half share in the other one.'

'Sentimental, is he?' Mary smiled. 'So where will he get the money for the paddle shares? A loan?'

'He's having a meeting with some of the other smack owners to find out if they're interested in setting up a company. Then they'd all put in a share. And he asked me if I'd like to be involved.'

Mary took in a breath. 'Not to go to sea, Josh? Surely not!'

He grinned. 'I'm not too old.'

'No. No, you're not. But you said—' She swallowed. 'You said he'd fish away from home.'

He grinned again, but kept his eyes on her face. 'And would you miss me if I weren't here?'

She tilted her head and returned his gaze. 'I might,' she bantered. 'But I was thinking more of Stephen and your daughters, and the fact that Susan is going to be married soon. Could you go away and leave them?'

He smiled. 'It won't happen yet; and you know that I couldn't. Scarborough is where I belong.' He took her cold hand in his and gently pressed it. 'Everyone I care about is here.'

Mary lowered her eyes and eased her hand from his. 'You still make a living, don't you?'

'Of sorts,' he said. 'And if Ethan kept the *Scarborough Girl* here then I'd use her and do some local fishing; enough to keep the wolf from the door. There'll be fewer mouths to feed by then anyway.' He continued to gaze down at her, his lips slightly parted as if considering, or waiting for her to make a comment or observation.

'Yes,' she said softly. 'Soon we shall have only ourselves to think about – freedom!' She gave a shaky laugh as she thought of Tom leaving when he married. 'If that's what it is! I must go,' she said hurriedly. 'I must get finished. It gets dark so early.'

What? she wondered. Something else? Some unspoken question? A small frown appeared above her nose. Usually she could read Josh, but not this time. There was a hesitancy about him, an uncertainty, when he was usually so positive. Was he worried about Ethan and his possible departure? But no, this hadn't seemed like worry over his son; it was something to do with her. It was as if he was trying to gauge her opinion, her reaction to something he wanted to tell her. Some secret, perhaps? But no, she was fairly certain she knew all there was to know about Josh; he was so open and sincere. He wasn't taciturn, not with her. There was no mystery, of that she was certain; so what was it?

A sudden excited shout and squeal from the women braiders made her look up. Some of the younger women were dancing around another, whirling her about in their midst. Mary smiled. Alice! She had been walking out with a fisherman. He must have asked for her hand and the others had found out.

Asked for. Not tell. Josh was not trying to tell her anything. He was plucking up courage to ask her something. Surely not! She slowed her steps as she considered. He wouldn't. Why now? Because their children had flown the nest? But he knew how she valued her independence, her ability to cope with life on her own – and she would be completely alone when Tom married. She walked back to her stand and asked her neighbour, 'What's happening?'

'Alice's beau has asked for her at last,' Lou said. 'They're to be married in the spring, God bless 'em.'

She sighed. 'I wish them luck, for they'll need it in these hard times.'

'Time and life, they're always hard,' Mary answered. 'No matter when.' She lapsed into her own thoughts, while her fingers continued knotting and mending. She had done this work for so long that it was second nature to her and her mind could wander, but several times she had to undo what she had worked and redo it as she considered the implications of what she might do if her reasoning was correct.

She watched Alice, flushed and trying to hide her delight. Mary smiled and waved at her, nodding her approval. Young bliss, she thought. There's nothing to beat it, but is it the same a second time around? She gave herself a mental shake. It couldn't possibly be. Yet it must be comforting to have someone sharing your fire, sitting across from you at table and – she paused in her thinking – to feel the contentment of a warm and loving body next to yours.

Was that what her mother had missed after the death of Mary's father? Was that why she chose to marry Andrew, to spend what was left of her life in companionship rather than alone? And do I miss that companionship too, and am I unwilling to admit it, even to myself?

'I'm packing in now,' she said after another hour. 'I'm frozen. I'm going home to light my fire and thaw out my old bones.'

'Not so old,' Lou said. 'Not as old as me.' She looked up as Mary stood over her. 'You're a fine-looking woman, Mary. You should find a good man to warm your bones, never mind lighting a coal fire.'

Mary laughed. 'Find one for me then, Lou,' she jested. 'And make him rich and handsome.'

'Aye, I'll try.' Lou grinned. 'But if I do I'll keep him for myself.'

Mary walked towards home, but then on impulse continued walking, past her cottage, past her mother-in-law's house and up towards the castle. She was warmer now and slightly out of breath when she reached the top of Castle Road, but she didn't go through the castle entrance. Instead she leaned against the churchyard wall and looked down over the graveyard of the ancient St Mary's church: the church where she and Jack were married.

This would always be her favourite view of Scarborough. Beyond the church, the town and harbour and ships turning into it spread out before her; the sea, silent from up here, dashed frolicking waves against the harbour walls, whilst the dome-topped lighthouse stood out white and stark and reassuring as darkness descended, obliterating the last faint streaks of day. Yellow lamps glowed in house windows, and along the harbour side stallholders lit up their counters to catch any late customers before closing for the night.

'What should I do, Jack?' she breathed. 'Just supposing I should be asked? I might be barking up the wrong tree, of course, but in case I'm not, what should I do?'

She leaned her elbows on the wall, and propping her chin in her hands peered into the night. I've had a good marriage, she thought, even though a short one. I've got two bonny bairns and don't need more, though I'm not too old to have another. She sighed. I think I'd say no. Faithful to you for ever.

CHAPTER THIRTY-ONE

Jeannie put money aside for the rent and then, wrapping up as warm as she could, she tucked Jack under her shawl and went out shopping. It was raining hard and she became very wet; she bought a cheap cut of beef, begged a lump of suet from the butcher, and bought onions, potatoes and carrots. I'll make a stew and dumplings, she thought. It's nourishing and will smell good when Harry opens the door.

He didn't arrive home until after six o'clock and was well oiled by drink. Connie came in a few minutes later. She glanced at Harry and then at Jeannie as if assessing their mood, but didn't speak. She looked down at Jack sleeping soundly in his drawer, and bent to pick him up.

'Oh, Connie,' Jeannie complained. 'He's only just gone off to sleep!'

'He's still asleep,' Connie murmured, kissing his warm cheek. 'Isn't he 'best bairn ever, Harry?' Her voice was deferential, yet possessive.

Harry sat down and stretched his legs, making it awkward for Jeannie to reach the pan from the fire. 'Dunno,' he muttered. 'Don't know any others.'

'Mebbe we could get him christened now that Harry's home, Jeannie,' Connie suggested.

'Yes,' Jeannie replied vaguely, wondering about the *we*. 'Could you put him down, Connie? I want to dish up and there's barely any room.'

Harry shifted his legs. 'Shouldn't have moved house then, should you?'

Connie put Jack back, tucked him up, and then drawing in a breath said sulkily, 'Well, if you want me to move out . . .'

The remark, Jeannie thought, was aimed at her. She turned from the fire with a cloth in her hand. 'I never said that. I never meant that.'

'There's no need for you to move, Connie,' Harry grunted. 'You're fine here with us, never mind what anybody else says.'

Jeannie stared, first at Harry and then at Connie. 'I never said you should move! I've told you how much I appreciate your being here.'

Connie shrugged and sat down at the table. 'Well, let me know if you change your mind.'

Jeannie shook her head in disbelief. Why were they taking things the wrong way? Had she ever implied that she didn't want Connie here once Harry was at home? Surely she hadn't. In fact she preferred her being here, in the hope that Harry would be more agreeable with other company in the house.

They ate mostly in silence and Harry obviously had difficulty in keeping awake. His eyes were constantly closing and once or twice he swayed, abruptly rousing himself before crashing on to the table.

He hiccuped when he'd finished. 'I'm beat,' he slurred. 'Where's 'bedroom?'

'Upstairs,' Jeannie declared flatly. 'Usual place.'

'How many beds have we got?' He stood unsteadily, holding on to the chair.

'Two,' Jeannie told him. 'They're not as big as at the other house. Connie's room is very small. We could hardly get the bed in.'

He frowned. 'How did you get 'beds upstairs?'

'Oh, we managed,' Connie interrupted. 'We're quite strong, aren't we, Jeannie? And we borrowed a hoss and cart to get 'furniture here.'

Harry slowly nodded his head. 'Right. All right. I'm off up. Don't be long, Jeannie.'

Jeannie bit on her lip. 'No. I won't be. G'night.'

'Phew,' Connie whispered as they heard him stumbling up the stairs. 'I thought he was going to ask who'd helped you with 'move. It wouldn't do to tell him it was Mike Gardiner.'

Jeannie pondered. What had brought that on? Harry had grumbled about Mike earlier and yet he'd given Harry his first chance of work; he'd proved to be a good friend. Why was he suddenly an undesirable person? It worried her, for Mike was the chief supplier of nets for her to work on.

She turned to Connie. 'Why did you think that I didn't want you here, Connie? I've never said that you should move out when Harry came home.'

Connie made a moue and shrugged. 'Just thought you'd want Harry to yourself.' She lowered her eyes. 'You might not have wanted another woman in 'house.'

'There's no reason for you to think that. I'm happy for you to be here.'

Connie nodded and gazed into the fire. 'That's all right then.'

Jeannie cleared away the dishes. She felt as if there was a leaden lump in her chest. The food she had eaten tasted sour in her mouth and she wanted to cry. This should be a happy time, she thought. Harry was home from the sea, they had a young baby, they were a proper family at last. But something was wrong. No, she reflected, not so much wrong as not quite right.

Harry was home for a week before his ship was due to sail again. He generally spent the mornings in bed, awoke at midday, snatched whatever food Jeannie rustled up for him, and then went out, not returning until the evening in time for his next meal, after which he fell asleep in front of the fire. Bedtime was difficult for Jeannie for he was demanding sometimes, and uninterested in her at others. His tenderness had disappeared and she didn't understand why.

Billy Norman called round after work early one evening to ask if Harry was in and was he coming out for a drink. 'I've not seen him since he came home,' he said. 'Where's he hiding himself?'

Jeannie invited him in; it was sleeting down, icy sharp needles which bounced off the ground, and he was very wet. She shook her head. 'Hasn't he been at the Wassand?' she asked. 'I thought that was his favourite place.'

'I've not seen him there, though I don't go in as much now that I've got a shore job. Don't feel 'need.' He must have seen something in her expression, for he enquired, 'Nowt wrong, is there?'

When she didn't answer but put her fingers to her mouth, he looked down at his boots and murmured, 'You know, when you've been at sea, it's a relief to have a drink wi' your mates. You can talk to 'em about what's happened on board, about what might have happened if such and such hadn't done this or that, or have a jaw about 'weather an' how many fish boxes an' whether 'skipper would get a bonus an' that . . .' His voice tailed away as Jeannie opened her mouth to speak.

'I know that, Billy. But he could tell *me* all of that. I'm a fisher girl after all. I do understand. I was brought up with fishing.'

'Aye, an' so are many of 'other wives on Hessle Road,' he said. 'An' that's one reason why I nivver settled down wi' anybody. It didn't seem fair somehow, when women are virtual widows when their men are at sea, for them not to have their company when they get home. Not all men are like that though,' he added hastily. 'Some of 'em don't move from their fireside till they go back to sea again. They just want to stop wi' their wives an' bairns.'

Jeannie blinked away the tears that had started to form. How different Billy seemed now that she knew him better. When she'd first met him on that fateful day in Scarborough, he'd grinned at her and she'd thought he was assuming she was like the loose women who were seeing the men off at the station. Now she realized that he was a decent and considerate man.

'An' being married is new to Harry,' he added. 'He just had Nan before.' He laughed. 'An' Nan wouldn't have wanted him under her feet all day.' His laugh was so infectious that she smiled back.

Poor Harry, she thought as she waved goodbye to Billy. He wasn't ready for marriage, any more than I was. And now he has the responsibility of a wife and child when previously he was single and carefree. But as she closed the door, she also thought that Harry probably hadn't been all that satisfied with his life before he met her. He hadn't any work; Nan was keeping him with her pittance; and coming to Scarborough and meeting her was a bright interlude in his life. He hadn't intended it to continue, she thought. He was just imagining how it would be to have a different life.

She looked down at Jack, who was wide awake and contemplating her from his sea blue eyes. She gently touched his cheek and he opened his mouth and sought her fingers. 'But I have you,' she murmured. 'And that makes up for everything else.'

'This is your last day at home, Harry,' she said to him the next morning. It was ten o'clock and she'd brought him a cup of tea in bed. 'Shall we go out for a walk? It's cold but not wet. I haven't been into the town yet. I thought you could show me round.'

He grunted. 'What d'ya want to do that for? There's everything you want on 'road.'

'I – I know,' she stammered. 'But it'd be nice to see other parts of the town.'

He took the cup from her and had a drink. 'No. I don't think so. There's nowt much to see. Onny shops and – well, 'pier's all right, I suppose.' He finished the tea in one huge slurp, and handing the cup back to her he slid back down into bed.

She turned away, disappointed, but looked back when he said, 'You can come back to bed though.' He leaned on one elbow. 'Like you said. It's my last day.'

That was a big mistake, she reflected two months later as she retched into the privy. On that particular day she had thought it would give them a fresh start. A chance to put things right between them.

They had had little time together since they were married, first because of living with Nan, then the birth of Jack, and now living in the small house with Connie as a constant companion.

Harry had done another long trip, but on returning home had once more slipped into the habit of spending most of his shore days at the Wassand Arms, arriving home for supper and then bed. Connie had started to go out after work, meeting some of her work mates, she'd said. 'It'll give you and Harry some time to yourselves,' she'd added.

But it hadn't worked out like that and increasingly Jeannie found herself spending her evenings alone. Now he was away again and not due back for several weeks, and she felt obliged to tell Connie about her pregnancy.

Connie stared at her, her mouth dropping open. 'I didn't think—'

'What?' Jeannie said. 'Didn't think what?'

'Erm – that you could get caught so quickly after 'first bairn.' Connie seemed baffled, peeved almost, as the frown on her forehead showed. 'Bet Harry won't be pleased. It'll be more expense wi' another bairn.'

He should have thought about that at the time, Jeannie considered, but she too was perplexed and went to see Mrs Norman. 'I thought you couldn't get pregnant if you were still breastfeeding,' she confessed. 'It's going to be hard with two young bairns.'

Mrs Norman nodded sagely. 'A fair number of mothers get caught out wi' that old wives' tale. But you'll manage, I expect. You'll have to, anyway. There's no way round it, unless . . . You wouldn't want—'

'Oh, no!' Jeannie said hastily. 'I wouldn't.'

'That's what I thought,' Mrs Norman agreed. 'They're a gift when all's said an' done.'

A gift, Jeannie thought as she walked back. A gift that will surely cost us.

Jack wriggled in her arms. He was thriving and getting heavier to carry. How would she manage in seven months' time? Jack would be crawling by then and how would she carry him when she was pregnant? A perambulator, or bassinet as she had sometimes heard them called, would be all right, like those that nursemaids used when they pushed their charges along Westborough or by the Scarborough sands.

She sighed. No chance of that, not for the likes of us. A box on wheels, more like. A box on wheels! A fish box. I could scrub one out – where could I get some wheels, and how would I fix them? What did Ma use for me and Tom? She kept on working: she must have put us in something.

The next day she sought out Mrs Norman again. She always seemed pleased to see her, and was never too busy for a word. Jeannie was grateful for that. Since Nan's death she missed having someone to talk to.

'Mrs Norman,' she said, having found her washing her front windows, 'I don't want to be a nuisance, but could I ask you something?'

'Ask away, m'dear.' Mrs Norman gazed at her. 'Summat bothering you?'

'Yes. I was wondering how I'll manage as time goes on and Jack gets heavier, carrying him, you know. I've never noticed what other mothers do.' If only Ma were here, she thought. She'd know.

'Ah, you poor bairn.' Mrs Norman shook her cloth. 'Come on in and tek 'weight off your feet and we'll have a little chat.'

Jeannie burst into tears. 'I'm so s-sorry,' she wept. 'I don't know who to talk to about things and I can't keep writing to my ma cos I don't want to worry her.'

'I don't suppose she'd mind,' Mrs Norman said practically, leading the way inside her house. 'But don't you worry your head about it. I'll get our Billy to make you a pushcart. He's done 'em afore. It's quite handy having a son who's a carpenter. He'll mek you one out of a fish box or an orange box. If it's fish, bairn'll grow up sick of 'smell of fish and if it's orange he'll want to travel to exotic countries to recapture 'smell. So what do you think? Which shall it be?'

CHAPTER THIRTY-TWO

Harry arrived home on the same day as Billy brought the pushcart. 'What's this?' he said when he saw his friend trundling it up the terrace.

'It's for your bairn,' Billy said. 'He's getting too heavy for Jeannie to carry.' He stopped abruptly, almost as if he was about to say more but had thought better of it.

Harry frowned. 'How much?' he demanded.

'What? Aw, come on, mate.' Billy looked astonished. 'I don't charge a pal for a bit o' wood and a few nails, now do I? You can buy me a drink if you like.'

'Right,' Harry muttered. 'Have you seen her? How d'ya know she needs one?'

Billy stared at him. 'What's up wi' you? My ma told me. It was her that suggested it.'

'Ah! Sorry, mate. I've had a rough trip. Not in 'best o' tempers.'

'Well don't tek it out on me,' Billy admonished him. 'And don't tek it out on your missis either. She's got enough on her plate.'

'What d'ya mean?'

'Nowt.' Billy stopped at Harry's gateway. 'Here.' He thrust the cart towards Harry. 'You tek it in.' He turned about and walked away.

'See you in 'Wassand then?' Harry called after him.

Billy lifted a hand but didn't answer.

Jeannie was sitting by a low fire feeding Jack when Harry opened the door. She looked up and a smile lit her face.

'Harry. Oh, Harry! I didn't expect you. What time did you dock?' She slipped her shawl over her breast and lifted her face for a kiss.

'You don't have to cover yourself in front o' me, do you?' he said brusquely, bending to drop a kiss on her forehead.

'Habit,' she said. 'In case the door opens.'

'Why? Who else comes in?' He took off his coat and hung it on the back of his chair before sitting down.

Jeannie gazed at him. Then, lifting Jack to her shoulder, she gently patted his back. 'Nobody,' she said. 'I don't see anybody from Connie going out to her coming home, unless I go out on the road; and if the weather's bad I don't go out. But it's getting better,' she said, trying hard to be cheerful. 'The weather, I mean. I think spring is on its way. Cup of tea?'

He nodded. 'Not a good fire. It's freezing in here.'

'There's not much coal left,' she said. 'You've come home just in time.'

'Run out o' money already?' He sat down opposite her and she felt as if she was entertaining a stranger. 'What 'you spent it on?'

Jeannie licked her lips; then she rose from the chair and put Jack in his makeshift crib. 'Food and coal,' she said. 'And the rent, of course. No luxuries.'

'I've got summat for you outside.'

'Have you?' she said eagerly. 'A present? Fish, I bet. I'll make a fish pie for supper.'

'Not fish. An' I'm sick o' sight o' fish. Haven't you got some beef?'

She shook her head. 'No, but I'll go and get some – if you've got your wages.'

He heaved a sigh. 'Aye, but we're a bit short. 'Skipper decided to try 'Moray Firth, but he set up within 'three-mile limit and we were sent off wi' our tails between our legs wi' Scottish fishermen after us. That lost us time and no fish, so then we sailed for Norway.'

Jeannie was animated. This was the first time he had ever discussed any of his trips. 'And was the fishing good there? Lots of halibut, I should think.'

'Aye, but then we snagged our nets and lost half of 'catch.' He stood up. 'I'll just get this cart from 'front door,' he said.

Cart? She'd put to the back of her mind Mrs Norman's promise that Billy would make one for her and she gave a small gasp as Harry brought it in.

'Oh, it's just what I want! Harry, I've something to tell you.'

'I haven't finished,' he said bluntly. 'An' then we had trouble wi' boiler and were stuck for three days wi'out power an' Norwegian Sea was packed wi' British trawlers so 'skipper decided to come home. That's why we're short. So what's all this about?' He indicated the pushcart. 'How come Billy Norman made it for you?'

Jeannie swallowed. 'Jack's getting quite heavy.' She gave a nervous laugh. 'He's putting on weight – and I asked Mrs Norman what other mothers did when their bairns got too big to carry; she said she'd ask Billy to make Jack a little pushcart. He's made them before, she said – and Harry, I'm pregnant.'

'You what?' Harry breathed heavily. 'Pregnant! Again?' He let out a gasp of exasperation. 'We haven't got on our feet yet! How can you be pregnant again? What'll we do for money?' His tone was accusatory.

'I don't know,' she said miserably. If he had shown any joy at all at the news, she would have been prepared to put away her fears and be happy. But it seemed that it was her fault. Which it must be, she thought. I must be very fertile.

'So Mrs Norman knows,' he said. 'And I suppose she told Billy?'

'I shouldn't think so,' she said. 'She's not a gossip. And what does it matter if she did? Everybody will know anyway in a few weeks' time.'

'Mek us that cuppa tea,' he said flatly, 'an' then I'm off out. I'm onny home for three days.'

She filled a pan with water and placed it on the fire basket. There was no luxury of accoutrements, no ironwork on which to swing a kettle. She'd brought Nan's kettle with her, but the pan was quicker when the fire was low.

'Will you leave some money?' she said in a small voice. 'I'll slip out and get some meat for supper.'

'What would you have done for food if I hadn't come home today?'

'Waited for Connie,' she said. 'She generally brings some fish home. Then we have fish and potatoes or fish broth. I've had to economise on food, Harry. I do my best, but paying the rent is the most important.'

He nodded, but didn't speak. Then he got up and put his coat back on. 'I'll not bother wi' that tea,' he said. 'That pan'll tek for ever to boil.' He fished in his pocket for some money and brought out a handful of coins which he handed to her. 'There's enough there for 'rent.'

Jeannie looked down at the money. 'And – what about our supper? And for the rest of the week?'

'Haven't you any work on 'nets?'

'No,' she breathed. 'Not since we moved. I haven't been able to ask anybody. Can you ask about when you're out?' she pleaded. 'Maybe Charlie or Mike Gardiner—' She saw his face set.

'I'll see what I can do,' he muttered and gave her some more coins. 'I'll be home 'bout seven.'

I have to talk to him, she thought as she walked home from the butcher's. We have to have some kind of conversation, discuss how we're to manage with another bairn.

She made the supper, enough for three, and there was a good smell of stewing beef and onions when Connie came in.

'I'm going out,' she said, after taking off her head shawl, brushing her hair and washing her hands and face. 'I'm meeting some of 'other lasses.'

'Don't you want any supper?' Jeannie asked. 'Harry's home.'

'Yeh, I heard his ship was in. No, I – oh, go on then. I'll just have a bit if there's plenty.'

'Of course there's plenty,' Jeannie said. 'I did enough for all of us.'

'Thanks,' Connie said. 'Do you mind if I don't wait for Harry? He might be ages.'

Jeannie didn't answer, but spooned some meat and thin broth into a dish and put it on the table.

'Is there any bread?' Connie asked.

Jeannie took the fresh loaf that she'd just bought and cut a slice without a word.

'Summat up?' Connie asked. 'You don't mind me going out? I shan't be late.'

'I'm not your mother,' Jeannie snapped. 'You can go out whenever you please.'

'Yeh, I can.' Connie didn't look at her but concentrated on her food. 'I've nivver had 'chance afore. Allus stuck at home.'

Jeannie nodded. She couldn't blame Connie. She was single and free to do whatever she wanted. But, she thought grudgingly, I think I had something to do with that. Without my encouragement you would never have broken free from your family's iron grip.

She sat with a blanket over her and Jack after Connie had gone out. I'll order some coal tomorrow, she thought, but I'll have to be careful with the money. If I can make the coal last we can have more stews and broths – they're economical and nourishing. I must keep up my strength. I'll be feeding three of us and not just two.

She fell asleep and woke when Harry came in at about eight o'clock. She'd put the pan to one side of the fire so that it didn't boil dry, and now she slipped it back on to the grate.

'Won't take long to warm up,' she said in a low voice. 'Do you want to have a hold of Jack?'

'No. Put him back in his crib,' he said. 'I want to talk to you.'

He seemed quite sober and that made her nervous. 'What about?' she asked, tucking the baby up so that he was warm.

'About us,' he said, sitting down in the chair and staring into the fire. 'We seem to be at cross purposes most of 'time, and now you tell me that you're pregnant again.'

'It takes two, Harry,' she said softly. 'I didn't get pregnant on my own.'

'I know. There should be summat to stop it happening.'

There is, she thought, but that's up to the man, not the woman. She shrugged. 'It's happened, Harry. We have to make the best of it.'

She gazed at him, at his dark brown hair curling about his forehead and his neck, and knew why she had instantly fallen for him. He had a wistful expression, but he didn't smile any more, not like he used to, not like when he'd first met her at Scarborough harbour side. Then he seemed merry, exciting and full of promise.

'Why did you want to marry me, Harry?' she asked. 'When we were at Scarborough? Why did you say we would be married?'

'I was besotted by you,' he said softly. 'That day I first saw you, you looked fresh and rosy and you had such a smile; I was sure that you were 'right girl for me. I thought you'd bring me luck. I'm sorry, Jeannie.' He looked across at her. 'I'm really sorry. It was when I got home again 'second time and into 'usual routine that I realized it wouldn't work. You were lovely, but too good for 'likes o' me.'

Jeannie shook her head. 'We were the same,' she whispered. 'And I loved you.' But it seemed that he didn't hear her or wasn't listening.

'And so I forgot about you, or at least I tried to.' He looked down at his hands clasped in his lap. 'An' then when you turned up on 'doorstep that day an' Nan saw you first, I reckon she saw summat in you; she saw that you were strong and'd be able to sort me out. And having a bairn as well, I think she thought that would mek me settle down. It were Nan who said we should be married. If it had been left to me . . .' He pressed his lips together, and then heaved a great sigh. 'I wouldn't have.'

CHAPTER THIRTY-THREE

Jeannie was stunned. What else was he telling her? Was he leaving her to manage alone with a child and no income?

'What are you going to do?' she said in a husky cracked voice that sounded nothing like her own. 'Are you leaving me? Abandoning me?'

'No!' He seemed shocked. 'Don't think that. What sort o' man d'ya think I am?'

Her lips were dry. 'I don't know,' she whispered. 'I don't think I've ever known.'

'I'll allus support you, Jeannie. As best I can.' He frowned as he considered. 'To 'best o' my ability, anyway.'

Jeannie gave a short laugh. 'I don't know what that means. Tell me what it means, Harry. You'll support me! Does that mean that you'll come home between trips and pay the rent? But we—' Something occurred to her. 'Will we be man and wife?'

He couldn't meet her eyes. 'I don't want you to get upset if I don't allus come home. I want us to still be friends.'

'But you don't want to share my bed?' she said bluntly. 'So whose bed will you share? You're a man

300

with an appetite, especially when you're drunk,' she couldn't help adding, her voice bitter.

Harry shook his head. 'I wanted us to talk about it, so as you'd know how I felt. I wanted to be honest wi' you, Jeannie.'

'And what about how I feel?' She felt hot tears gathering. 'Don't you think I have feelings too? I'm seventeen, Harry. I loved you, and because of that I shall have two children to look after and no husband – no proper husband – to share them with.'

'I didn't say I wouldn't support 'em; didn't say I didn't want to see 'em!' His tone now turned from apologetic to aggrieved and misunderstood. 'I'll still bring my wages home, although mebbe we could look for summat a bit smaller. Less rent.'

Great fat tears ran down her face. Look for something smaller? He was so angry when she'd moved from Nan's house. And how could they live in something smaller than this when they had two bairns instead of one? Unless Connie moved out, but she couldn't ask her to do that: she was settled here and was company when Harry was away. And besides, they needed her money until she, Jeannie, could obtain work.

She said nothing but dished up Harry's stew into a bowl, sliced some bread and put it on the table. She waved a vague hand for him to sit and eat, but she couldn't face food herself, even though she knew she should eat.

Harry ate all that was in his bowl and then said, 'I'll have a drop more o' that. Very nice.'

The way to a man's heart is through his stomach, she thought sourly as she gave him her portion.

Poppycock! That's another old wives' tale we can disregard.

She picked Jack up. 'I'm going to bed,' she said. 'I'll clear up in the morning.'

He rubbed his hand across his nose. 'Right,' he muttered. 'I'll lock up.'

'Nothing worth stealing,' she remarked, loudly enough for him to hear, as she put her foot on the first tread of the stair. 'I've got everything that's precious upstairs with me.'

Harry sailed again three days later. He hadn't shared her bed again but slept downstairs in the chair, but after spending the morning with his mates he'd gone upstairs and fallen asleep on the bed; Jeannie had heard him snoring. She barely spoke to him until the evening before he sailed, and then she said, 'Harry, I think we should try to work something out between us. I think the shock of my being pregnant so soon has brought all this uncertainty on. It's worrying, I agree, but we'll manage.' She reached for his hand, but he pulled away. 'Other people do,' she pleaded. 'And it makes their marriages stronger. It's not the end of the world. We should try to get some of that loving back into our lives again.'

He shook his head. 'It's too late, Jeannie. It were my mistake in 'first place. I should nivver have tekken advantage of you – cos that's what I did.'

'I wanted you,' she interrupted. 'Just as much as you wanted me.'

'Aye, but you believed me when I said I wanted to marry you.' He paused as if considering. 'I shouldn't have said that. Cos it weren't true.'

She gave up then, for what else could she say? But

302

she was given some hope the next morning when she got up to make his breakfast; he was sailing on the eight o'clock tide and his bag was packed by the door. Before he left he leaned forward and kissed the top of her head.

'See you when I get back, Jeannie. Tek care o' yourself and 'bairn.'

'You too,' she murmured, and then turned as Connie came downstairs. She wasn't yet dressed but wore a shawl over her night shift.

'Cheerio, Harry,' Connie said. She seemed cheerful, not her usual glum morning self. 'Have a good trip.'

Harry glanced at her and nodded. 'Aye. Hope so,' and was gone.

Connie yawned and stretched and helped herself to porridge. She glanced up as Jeannie said, 'Connie, have you forgotten – you haven't given me any board this week.'

'Ah, no I haven't, have I? Can I give you half now and 'rest later?' She pulled a face. 'I've been a bit of a spendthrift. Going out with 'other lasses.'

Jeannie gave a tight smile. 'I'm glad you've been getting out, Connie,' she said. 'It's just that Harry's wages were short this trip, and I need to buy some more coal. I've got enough for the rent money, but . . .'

'Do you think you should look for another house?' Connie said. 'Less rent?'

Her words almost echoed Harry's and Jeannie sat down opposite her at the table. 'Where?' she asked. 'Where would I look? *Is* there anywhere cheaper than this place?'

She hated the area. She still hadn't got used to

303

the smell of fish meal which permeated the whole road, though Connie said she couldn't smell it, she'd become so used to it. She hated walking along the run-down terrace, conscious always of curious faces peering out of the broken windows. There was no community spirit here, unlike where they had lived before, in Nan's street. Here, the residents were engaged in keeping body and soul together and a roof over their heads, too engrossed in the business of staying alive to show any concern for anyone else. Not one person she had seen or heard from the neighbouring houses had ever passed the time of day.

'I'll ask about if you like?' Connie volunteered. 'There might be somewhere.'

'No,' Jeannie said. 'I won't bother just now. Maybe when the weather perks up and I can go out and look for myself.'

Connie spooned a mouthful of porridge, swallowed and muttered, 'Suit yourself.'

The weather was improving steadily and Jeannie began to go out more now that she had the push-cart for Jack. She padded it well with a blanket and dressed him in the warm coats that her mother and grandmothers had knitted for him and wrapped a warm shawl over him. She walked along the Hessle Road, familiarizing herself with the area and wondering, though not too seriously, where else they could live at a price they could afford.

One day she ventured into the town. The day was sunny and promised to be so all day. She packed up a slice of bread and cheese for her midday meal and decided that she might as well stay out for most of the day. There was no reason to rush back. Connie would be at work until tea time and there was no one else for her to visit or talk to, except for Mrs Norman, and she didn't want to bother her too often.

She had some kind of freedom now that she had the pushcart and Jack seemed to be happy in it. She'd padded beneath his head so that he was slightly elevated and he looked around as if noticing his surroundings, chortling and kicking his legs.

Jeannie stopped at the end of Hessle Road, wondering which way to go. Twice before, when she had come to Hull, she had come on the train, so this was the way she went now, heading for the railway station to get her bearings.

The Paragon railway station itself was a most imposing and grandiose terminal and linked to a splendid hotel, something she had failed to notice on her previous visits, so nervous had she been. The town was much larger and more prosperous than she had anticipated; there were numerous grand buildings holding banks and building societies, theatres, hotels and rooming houses on practically every street she walked down. It was also busier and noisier than she had expected, full of people, horse trams, waggonettes and drays, and children, some of them barefoot and ragged.

The town had been built on the proceeds of whaling, fishing and commerce. This she was told by a woman whom she had asked for directions as she walked towards the town docks. The woman was a mine of information, having lived in Hull the whole of her life, she said.

'Finest town in 'country,' she vowed. 'Though if you're poor, it's no better than any other, I suspect. It was founded on whaling in case you don't know, and more recently on fish. Folks come from all over 'country to fish from our waters and to use our dock.'

Jeannie nodded, but the woman seemed determined to continue. She had a confident, unabashed manner. 'They've got a grand fish dock at 'top of Hessle Road; St Andrew's. Fishing has really took off since that was built, and it's freed up 'rest of town docks for other commerce.'

She cast an eye over Jeannie. 'You might wonder how I know all this. Well, I'll tell you.'

Jeannie was beginning to wish she had never asked for directions and found her own way, but the woman continued.

'My family used to live on Hessle Road; my da was a fisherman, but now he sells it, rather than catches it. He's opened a fish shop!' Her voice rose with pride. 'He and my ma cook it and sell it hot with 'taties. 'Finest food you can buy, and 'cheapest. He sleeps in his own bed at night and meks enough money not to worry about his future.'

'I'm so pleased,' Jeannie said, edging away. 'It's good to hear a success story.'

The woman followed her. 'Aye, it is.' She shook her head. 'But I miss being on 'road and so does my ma. It were a special place. Everybody looked out for everybody else. Still do, I expect,' she said wistfully.

As Jeannie finally managed to get away at last, the woman called to her, 'Nice little babby cart you've got there. Did somebody mek it for you?'

'Yes,' Jeannie said. 'A friend.'

After visiting the vast town dock to see the commercial shipping moored there, she walked over a swing bridge and alongside the Junction Dock, bearing towards the estuary. At last she stepped on to the wooden boards of the Victoria Pier and went to the rail to look over the Humber to Lincolnshire on the other side. The estuary was packed with shipping, with sail and with steam: a steam trawler alongside a trawling smack, a yawl with a coble on board; coal barges and ocean-going vessels were steaming towards the mouth of the estuary. Many of the vessels were trawlers laden with their catches of fish and there were some, though not many, sailing smacks, which were heading towards St Andrew's Dock.

Jeannie narrowed her eyes as she observed them. These vessels were the ones she had grown up with, like the one her brother had sailed in when he was so sick and decided against going to sea; like the one Ethan had sailed on as a boy, whose mast he had been tied to during the dreadful storm; and – she leaned forward the better to see – and yes, one of them was very similar to the *Scarborough Girl*; could almost be the same, except of course it wouldn't be. To her knowledge, Ethan never came to Hull. There were two figures on board and one was sheeting in a sail.

It *was* her! The *Scarborough Girl*. She could see the name quite plainly now. She felt a flutter of excitement, which quickly died; so he'd sold it after all. Well, that was men for you, full of promises which came to nothing. She felt sick when she thought that just as Harry had moved on from her, Ethan would have no use for the smack any more. They were both becoming outdated.

She sat on a wooden bench to eat her bread and cheese and then nursed Jack. She wrapped herself carefully in her shawl as he nuzzled into her breast and pondered yet again on her circumstances.

I could go home, she thought. Ma wouldn't mind. I am after all a respectable married woman; but how would I explain being there without my husband? And what about the newborn? Will Harry want to see it? He said he'll support us. Why did he have to say anything? I'd rather have been left in ignorance over his feelings for me than hear him say what he did.

Jack gave a little cry and she lifted him to her shoulder, patting him gently. He burped and she said softly, 'I'm sorry, Jack. Are my angry thoughts giving you wind, my poor bairn?'

She put him to her other breast and watched the muddy brown water of the Humber, deep and strong, moving inexorably on its journey.

The sun was still warm, the sky bright with slow-moving wisps of cloud, but Jeannie felt cold and shivered in the cool breeze that was carried along the estuary. She stood, wrapped Jack up and placed him back in his cart, and went for one last look at the shipping. She took a deep breath. I just have to get on with life as best I can, she thought. I'll try to get some work, at least until my time. And after that . . . well, I'll think about that later.

She took another breath, deeper this time, to give her energy for the walk back; a cormorant flew over, followed by a flock of herring gulls, screeching as they flew, and she smiled, though wistfully.

'Listen to them, Jack,' she said to the infant, who gazed up at her from his darkening eyes, eyes which would be like Harry's and so a constant reminder of him. 'Those are the sounds from the sea: of fishing, of deep briny water which gives us our

308

living and sometimes takes it from us. And smell that!' She closed her eyes and breathed in. Above the oily odour of fish meal came the essence of the sea, cleansing her nostrils, sharp, pungent and salty. The smell of home.

CHAPTER THIRTY-FOUR

It was a much longer walk back than when she came into town. She thought she could walk alongside the Humber bank towards Hessle Road; from Nelson Street, where the pier was situated, she cut to Wellington Street and found herself between a dock and a dock basin and on the wrong side of a railway line; she took another turning and became completely lost. The pushcart trundled and jerked over rough paving and Jack was jiggled about no matter how careful she was, and her back ached with trying to keep it on an even keel. If only the cart had springs, like perambulators, she thought, but I suppose that's why they are so expensive.

There were many people about, all going about their regular business, men with handcarts, women dressed in aprons and wearing clogs, and once more she asked for directions. She turned back along the dock, turned again to avoid another railway line, and became quite disoriented.

She wanted to weep. She was tired and Jack was grizzling, but there was nothing for it but to try to find her way back to where she had started and begin again. She asked a dock worker for further directions and reached a street called Blanket Row on the corner of Sewer Lane before she faltered again. Which way now? She was hesitating when she heard the rattle of wheels, the clip-clop of hooves and someone calling out, 'Can I give a damsel in distress a ride home?'

Jeannie could hardly speak, such was her relief. 'Mike! Rescue!'

'What 'you doing down here, Jeannie?' Mike jumped from his waggon. 'Come on. Are you going home?'

'I was.' Her voice broke. 'I was being too clever by half and thought I could walk home along the Humber bank.'

'You can if you know 'way and if you're not pushing a bairn in a cart. Come on, young feller.' Lifting Jack out of his cart, he handed him to Jeannie, then picked up the cart and put it in the back of the waggon. 'Where've you been?'

'Exploring,' she admitted. 'I walked into town. I hadn't been before and wanted to take a look to see what it was like. But it was a long way in, and' – she gave a rueful grimace – 'even longer coming back.' She heaved a sigh and climbed into the front of the waggon, tucking the baby under her shawl. 'I can't believe that you've come to my rescue yet again.'

'We shall get talked about.' He grinned.

Jeannie laughed. 'That's what Nan said.'

Mike turned to look at her, then shook the reins and the horse responded. 'You're joking, of course?'

'No. I'm not. I can tell you now that she's no longer here.' She hugged Jack closer as they trotted through the busy streets. 'She said I hadn't to let you into the house when I was on my own. She said that folk would talk.'

Mike grinned. 'I'm flattered that 'old girl thought I still had a breath o' life left in me. She'd forgotten that I'm old enough to be your father. Harry's da and I were mates.'

'It was because you are a widower, I think,' Jeannie said.

He shook his head and sighed. 'I don't think she ever forgave me for being alive when Fred wasn't,' he said quietly. 'She never quite got over that.'

'Maybe not,' Jeannie agreed. 'During the last few weeks before she died she sometimes referred to Harry as Fred, as if she'd forgotten that he'd gone.'

'Are you settling in at 'new house?' he said after a while. 'Are you managing all right? What did Harry think?'

'He wasn't pleased,' she told him. 'In fact he was quite angry; he said Nan had lived in the other house for a long time, it was where he was brought up.'

'It was, but he was forgetting that there'd been no money going in for some time either. Nan must have been scrimping and saving to even pay 'rent.'

'Yes, I think she was.' Jeannie gave a deep sigh and on a sudden whim went on, 'Harry wishes he'd never got married. He told me so. He says he'll support me and he wants us to be friends – though we'll not be – but he doesn't want to be married.'

Mike turned and stared. 'Never! He couldn't wish for such a thing.'

Jeannie's shoulders drooped. Perhaps she shouldn't have said anything, but she felt the need to talk to someone and Mike had always been kind.

'That's what he told me,' she said again in a quiet voice. 'He said he wouldn't have married me if it

312

hadn't been for Nan insisting; and she *did*. The first time I came to Hull looking for him and talked to Nan, she said he would have to marry me; she didn't want the shame of it, and told him he should – *would* – honour his commitments.'

Mike nodded. 'That sounds like Nan,' he said. 'It's a pity there aren't more like her.'

'Yes,' Jeannie conceded. 'But she's not here now, so Harry can say and do whatever he likes.' She gave an even deeper sigh; she felt as if she couldn't get enough air and every breath she took might choke her with the stench of fish meal and the pungent odour from the smoke houses. 'And what he did say was that he didn't mean it when he said he wanted to marry me.'

Mike was silent, but as they turned on to Hessle Road he said, 'If he'd been my lad I'd have said he'd made his bed so he'd have to lie on it. So what are you going to do? What's Harry going to do? He'll surely not leave you? He's got to support you and 'bairn. If he doesn't his reputation'll be torn to shreds.'

'Two bairns, Mike,' she whispered. 'I'm pregnant with another. And I don't know what I'll do. I'll have to find work; I can't rely on Harry's promises to support us. I think he's full of good intentions, but . . .' Her words tailed away. Sooner or later Harry would resent having to support her, and whenever he came home from a trip he would call in at the nearest hostelry to drown his sorrows.

Mike asked if he could drop her off near the end of the terrace as he was going back to St Andrew's Dock for a meeting. He had said little after she'd confessed she was pregnant, but had just listened; it was as if he was shocked by what she had told him and she hoped she hadn't embarrassed him. Where will his loyalties lie? she thought. He's known Harry since he was a boy, the son of his best friend. I'm just a newcomer.

The house was cold when she entered, the fine grey ash in the grate burned through. There would be no dinner unless she built a fire so that was the first thing to do. She wrapped another blanket round Jack but he kicked them off, gurgling at her and clapping his hands, which delighted her. How fast he was growing and developing.

The bundle of twigs and small pieces of coal took ages to light no matter how she coaxed and blew on the flickering flame, but eventually it caught, drying out the damp wood and licking round the wet coal, issuing a spasmodic smoky blaze. Jeannie rocked back on her heels. It would take hours to heat a pan of soup or cook potatoes. She looked in her purse. Connie would be hungry when she came in after work; would she bring fish to cook, or maybe a pair of kippers? The last time Jeannie had eaten kippers she had had indigestion all night, and they hadn't agreed with Jack either.

She put her shawl back on and tucking Jack under it went out again, heading back towards the shops on Hessle Road to spend her precious money on a ready cooked meat and potato pie.

'Mm.' Connie wiped a slice of bread round her plate to soak up the gravy when she had finished. 'That made a nice change.' She licked her lips. 'You must get fed up o' cooking, don't you?'

'I don't mind,' Jeannie answered. 'But it's not easy knowing what to have when there's not much money. I couldn't really afford to buy a pie, but the

314

fire wouldn't burn and I knew we'd be eating at midnight unless I bought some ready food. I'll be pleased when Harry comes home. I don't know how much longer I can manage.'

It wasn't meant as a hint that Connie had been lax with her board money again, but Connie took offence at the innocent remark and went upstairs, returning a few minutes later with her purse.

'*I'm* not earning a fortune, you know! *And* I've to buy my dinner every day. I don't pack up like some of 'lasses do.'

'Well, you could,' Jeannie told her. 'There's usually enough bread.' But the reason Connie didn't pack up was because she was essentially lazy and would rather spend another quarter of an hour in bed than get up to prepare food for her midday break.

Connie handed over her money. It wasn't enough, she surely knew that, but she didn't look at Jeannie as she announced, 'Anyway, I'm going to mek it easier for you to manage. I've got another room. A bob a week including coal for a fire. I've just to find my own food.'

Jeannie felt as if she'd been struck. 'Why?' she asked hoarsely. 'That's what you pay to live here and I provide the food, except when you bring fish.'

Connie shrugged. 'I fetch 'fish in. I can cook it m'self so I'll eat for free.'

There seemed to be no logic to that. 'But why?' Jeannie asked again. 'I thought we were company for each other.'

Connie stretched and then sat down. 'We were. But I'm going out more now. I'm getting on better wi' lasses at work, and anyway once you've got another

315

bairn to look after you'll not have 'time to talk. And I don't really like this part of 'road either.'

Jeannie thought for a moment. She'd felt that Connie had been behaving oddly for some time. She'd been unsettled, more like the person she'd been when Jeannie had first met her.

'Is it me?' she asked. 'Is it something I've said or done that's made you want to move? Or Harry! Has Harry said something to upset you?'

Connie did look at her now, lifting her head and speaking sharply. 'Harry? No. Why'd you think it was Harry? No. It's nowt to do wi' him.'

But Jeannie noticed a slow blush on her cheeks and thought that perhaps she wasn't being truthful. Connie had had a soft spot for Harry. Maybe she was finding it difficult living in close proximity. 'When will you be leaving?'

'End o' week. Sorry.' Again she looked away. 'It's nowt personal. But I've got on me feet and I can manage on me own now. About time, isn't it?' She gave a forced laugh. 'I'm not scared like I used to be. I've grown up.' She dropped her eyes to Jack sleeping in his makeshift cot. 'I'll miss 'bairn, though.'

'Come and see him then. When you've the time.' Jeannie could hardly speak. Another slap in the face. Unwanted. There's only Jack who really needs me. She heard her voice mouthing words. 'Don't think that you can't call, Connie. I understand that you feel the need to have your own place.'

'Yeh, I will.' Connie got up again. 'I'm off out now. I need to buy some cups and plates an' stuff – an' sheets. I don't suppose—'

'No,' Jeannie said firmly. 'I'll need all the crockery

316

and bedding, especially when I've two bairns. I might have to take in a lodger,' she said, as the thought suddenly occurred to her. 'To make ends meet.'

'Oh, yeh!' Connie nodded. 'Course. Mebbe you could get somebody down on their luck who'd look after 'bairn while you get a job.'

'And teach them how to stand on their own two feet?' Jeannie couldn't help the sarcasm, but it was wasted on Connie. 'I don't think so.' Her eyes began to stream. 'I'm very particular about who looks after my child. Harry's child.'

'Well, you would be.' Connie stared at her for a moment and then ran her tongue round her lips. 'He'll be precious to you. And you'll bring him up right, won't you, Jeannie? No matter what.'

'What do you mean?'

Connie shrugged. 'Nowt really. It's just – well – we don't know how life's going to turn out, do we? It's a struggle, I know that better'n anybody. Abandoned by my da, and unwanted by my ma.' She seemed to be searching for words but couldn't find the right ones. 'But you're strong, aren't you? If somebody knocked you down you'd get up again.'

'I don't know what you're talking about, Connie.' She was beginning a headache and wished Connie would go out and leave her to her thoughts.

'What I'm trying to say is that I allus need somebody to pick me up and point me in 'right direction. But you, you allus know which way to go or what to do; you don't need anybody else to tell you.'

What I wouldn't give right now to have someone tell me what to do for the best, Jeannie thought. But there's no one. Only my mother, and I won't ask her. Why would I worry her?

317

She shook her head. 'It's not true, Connie,' she said. 'Everybody needs somebody to lean on.'

'Yeh!' Connie agreed eagerly. 'That's what I'm trying to say.'

CHAPTER THIRTY-FIVE

Mike Gardiner had to lift his head considerably to look his new acquaintance in the eye. He held out his hand. 'Glad to meet you, Ethan. They mek big lads in Scarborough, don't they?'

Ethan laughed, his grin wide between his fair moustache and thick beard. 'Not all as tall as me,' he bantered. 'This is my brother Stephen. He's nine and promising to be bigger than everybody.'

The tall thin boy beside him looked down at his feet.

'Say how de do to Mr Gardiner, Stephen.' Ethan gave a nudge, and Stephen put out his hand to Mike.

'Good to meet you, Stephen,' Mike said. 'Are you planning to be a fisherman like your brother?'

Stephen nodded. 'I think so. Ethan said he'd try me out. Fishing runs in the family.'

'Yes, it usually does. I've one son who's a fisher-man, and 'other's a butcher, so we're never short of food!' He looked towards the dock. 'So, you've travelled here by smack rather than train?'

'Yep,' Ethan said. 'I don't often get the chance to come out in her, thought it would be good to sail; we've not used the engine at all, have we, Stephen? He's learning the ropes. I think it's important.'

'But you don't fish in her?'

'Onny sometimes. At night. She's an indulgence.' He smiled, but Mike thought he looked wistful.

'So about this other business. You're keen to set up a company?' Mike gazed shrewdly at him.

'Yes. Can we sit down somewhere? There's a fair bit to discuss if you're interested.'

Mike led them to a lean-to shed which he said was his office, where they sat down on a wooden bench. 'You met my lad Aaron, didn't you?' he said. 'Where was that?'

'No, that wasn't me. That was Len, another Scarborough skipper. Len and I and a couple of others were thinking of converting a paddle steamer, but there were a few disagreements and so it came to nothing. Perhaps it's just as well. Some of the paddle steamer companies that were set up are failing, but I'm still keen to upgrade and so is Len, and my father said he might come in, and then Len met Aaron somewhere, I'm not sure where, Flamborough maybe, and they hit it off and started discussing expanding. We've got to do it, Mike, or else we're finished. Smacks are at their limit now; even with bigger engines we can go no further than the Shetlands. A purpose-built screw steam trawler wouldn't be dependent on home waters.'

'It's true,' Mike agreed. 'Grimsby trawlers are doing well off Iceland and 'Faroes, though they're taking some stick from 'local fishermen.'

'That's always going to happen,' Ethan said. 'It's happened in Scotland too when some trawlers didn't stick by the three-mile limit; the Danes have set four miles, but with a bigger ship we wouldn't even need to stay in northern waters. We could go much further.'

'You say your father might come in?' Mike asked. 'Only might?'

'I think he'll be persuaded. He's got shares in another smack which he'd be willing to sell, and if I keep this one he can use it for onshore fishing.'

Mike raised his eyebrows. 'You'll not sell yours?'

'Not this one I won't. As I say, she's an indulgence. I've shares in another which I'll sell if I can, though the smack market is dropping.'

'The Scandinavians would buy,' Mike said. 'All right. Let's have your proposal and I'll have a think about it.' He winked at Stephen. 'We've this lad's future to think about.'

They talked for an hour or so and agreed to meet again. Mike said he'd talk to Aaron and Ethan said he'd go to his father and Len with the proposals. They'd both agreed they would need to raise some capital, as even with the sale of shares and smacks there wouldn't be enough. But they had a good basis for going ahead and Mike was not only interested in the scheme but struck by this young man's enthusiasm, and said he would look into what vessels were available. There were many ship-building companies in the Humber district of Brough, Hessle and Beverley; they wouldn't be able to afford to buy new but Ethan said he knew someone in the boat-building business who could also advise them.

As he said this, he wondered if Tom Marshall, Jeannie's brother, would be interested in the venture, but he instantly dismissed the idea. Tom was getting married soon and wouldn't want to risk the money he earned.

The two men shook hands and Mike walked back

with them to where the smack was tied up. It was a smart vessel, he saw, well trimmed and spotless. Obviously didn't do much fishing now, and he wondered how Ethan could afford to keep such a luxury. Few fishermen sailed for pleasure only. It wasn't a pastime but a means of earning a living.

He stood with his arms folded as Stephen unhooked the painter and Ethan prepared to cast off, instructing Stephen, telling him to watch and learn. He heard him tell his young brother that once they were out of the Humber, beyond Spurn and in sea water, then he could take the helm. Good lad, he thought. The sandbanks in the Humber were treacherous and not for a beginner.

As Ethan got under way, Mike called to him. 'I know a Scarborough girl. She lives on Hessle Road.'

'Oh, yes?' Ethan called back. 'What's she like?'

'Lovely!' Mike said. 'Rich brown hair, beautiful smile. Married, though, with a bairn.'

He saw Ethan take in a breath of air before saying, 'Lucky man!'

Mike nodded. 'You'd think so, wouldn't you?' and lifted his hand in farewell.

Stephen watched and learned but kept quiet as his brother followed the pilot boat and rounded the Spurn Head sandbanks into the wide reaches of the North Sea – which their father often referred to as the German Ocean – and headed for home.

'Ethan!' he called. 'You know what Mr Gardiner said about that Scarborough girl?'

'Er – yep?'

'Well, do you think it might have been Jeannie Marshall he was talking about?'

'Don't know. Here – we've a fair wind. Come for'ard and you can sail for home.'

'Can I?' Stephen moved for'ard eagerly. 'But do you think it could have been? Jeannie, I mean?'

'No idea. Might have been.'

'Well, she went to live in Hull.' Stephen fixed his position. 'She got married, and her ma said she'd had a babby.'

'Did she? Watch what you're doing, helmsman. Concentrate. These are tricky waters just outside the Humber.'

'I know,' Stephen said. 'I'm onny asking. It'd be good if it was her, wouldn't it? I'd like to see her again. I liked Jeannie. I like her ma as well. I wish Da would marry her.'

'Don't be ridiculous, Stephen. Keep your eyes keen. Keep her running.' But even as he chastised his young brother he knew he was talking to a born seaman. Stephen had a natural affinity with the ship and the sea.

'You know what I think, Ethan?' Stephen said, his eye and his hands steady. 'I think you were sweet on Jeannie and that's why you don't want to talk about her. Cos she left you and married somebody else.'

'Is that what you think? What a wise man you are.' Ethan stood behind him. 'Well, I can tell *you* that you're sailing close to the wind; so trim your sails, sailor, and get us safe home.'

CHAPTER THIRTY-SIX

Jeannie didn't feel well with this pregnancy, unlike when she was carrying Jack. She put it down to not having such nourishing food. Nan had always cooked and made sure that Jeannie ate well. Now she didn't always feel like cooking just for herself once Connie had left. She felt tired most of the time and it was an effort for her to make a fire in the morning; it hardly ever stayed on all night no matter how she packed it with slack before going to bed.

The days were longer and brighter, but the sun's warmth seemed to intensify the odours of fish and its by-products, making her feel more nauseous day by day. And she was constantly anxious about the lack of money. Mike and Charlie occasionally brought her nets to work on, which she eagerly accepted. Charlie's were often torn to shreds and difficult to mend, and she knew she did not charge him as much as she should; but she knew too that he was short of money as well – he must have been or he would have bought new nets.

Mike confided to her that he and Aaron were joining in with some other fishermen to form a company. 'It'll be make or break,' he told her.

She wondered if Harry knew about it and if there

would be any work for him, but when she asked, Mike said not.

'I'd appreciate it if you didn't mention it, Jeannie,' he said, and she wondered why he had told her if it was such a secret. 'And Harry's better off with 'Humber Steam Company. It's very stable and there's no knowing if ours will be. We're all tekkin' a chance.'

'How many of you?' she asked.

'Six so far, unless we can get a couple more.'

Jeannie smiled. 'I'd join you if I had some capital, Mike, but I've barely enough even for the essentials.'

He put his head to one side. 'Harry's in regular work, isn't he? Still bringing his wages home?'

'Oh, yes,' she lied, 'but it doesn't seem to go far.'

In truth Harry always seemed to be short when he came home. He tipped out his pockets but always gathered some of it back and went off to meet his mates. There were occasions when he didn't return until the following day, and he never said where he'd been.

She had confronted him, telling him she'd been worried and had hardly slept, knowing that the door was open. He'd got over that issue by having another key cut, telling her that she could now lock the door and go to bed without being anxious that someone would break in.

'That's not the point, Harry,' she said imploringly. 'Why don't you come home?'

'I told you afore,' he blustered. 'I don't want you to get upset if I don't allus come home of a night.'

'But I am upset!' she wept. 'Where do you go when you don't come home?'

He shook his head, and then said, 'Don't cry. I

don't want you to cry, Jeannie. It's my fault, I know, but that's 'way it is.'

She held back a sob. 'You can't leave me alone, Harry. How will I live? How will I know when you'll be here and when you won't? What if I hear that your ship is in and you haven't been home?'

He leaned on the table, putting his head in his hands. 'I'd come home, Jeannie,' he said in a muffled voice. 'Except that it isn't home any more. Home was where Nan was. She allus looked out for me.'

She put her hand on his shoulder. 'I'll look out for you, Harry. Give me a chance and we'll have a good life together. But I can't do it alone,' she whispered, 'and I'm alone most of the time now that Connie's gone.'

He sniffled and rubbed his nose. 'You've got 'bairn for company,' he said.

'He can't talk, Harry. There's no conversation!' She was suddenly struck by an idea. 'You don't like this house, do you? Well, neither do I. Shall I look for somewhere else? Perhaps a room in a shared house. It would be less rent and I'd have company when you were away. Would you agree to that?'

He breathed heavily as if he'd been running. 'Aye, mebbe. You mean summat like Connie's got?'

Jeannie paused and swallowed. She hadn't seen Connie's room. Harry, as if he was suddenly aware of what he had said, added, 'I met her out on 'road. She said she'd got a nice room.'

'Yes,' she said softly. 'One like that. But how would you find me if I moved?'

He considered. 'Tell Mrs Norman,' he said, 'and she can tell Billy. I'll see him at 'Wassand.'

After he'd sailed she made it her priority to look

for somewhere else to live. She would be glad to get away from this run-down street and derelict housing. On her wanderings one day she called on Mrs Norman, who invited her in. Over a cup of tea, Jeannie told her about her search.

'I don't like the area, Mrs Norman,' she said. 'I never see anybody. People round there don't seem to go out much. I'd like to be among people, so I can get to know them.'

Mrs Norman nodded. 'Well, I did wonder,' she said. 'But I knew you wanted summat smaller and less rent so I thought it would fit 'bill. And then, Connie was stopping wi' you.' She eyed Jeannie. 'But not your sort o' place, is it?'

'No.' Jeannie had a catch in her voice. 'Mrs Norman, if I found somewhere, could I ask you a favour?'

'Aye, you can ask.'

'It's just that I need to work. There doesn't seem to be a need for braiders. The fishermen and their wives do it. Mike Gardiner and Charlie bring me their nets sometimes, but it's not enough, so I'd get a job at a smoke house, or filleting fish, if I didn't have Jack. I wonder, would you consider looking after him if I got a part-time job? I'd pay, of course.'

Mrs Norman considered, playing her fingers against her lips as she did so. 'What about 'babby you're carrying? You shouldn't be heaving fish boxes about when you're pregnant.'

'I know.' Jeannie bent her head. 'But I don't know what else to do. There just isn't enough money to make ends meet.'

Mrs Norman sighed. 'There nivver is. I'll think about it,' she said. 'But I've to think about my other

327

work – my young mothers, you know, they rely on me.'

'I know,' Jeannie said. 'As I will when it's my time.'

'What about Harry?' Mrs Norman asked abruptly. 'What does he think about you working when you've got a babby and another one expected?'

'Harry!' Jeannie gave a shrug. 'I don't think he cares one way or another.'

Mrs Norman found her a room in Strickland Street only a few doors from her own house. An elderly widow, Mrs Herbert, lived in it and didn't use her front room. She said that Jeannie could have it with the use of the scullery for one shilling and sixpence a week.

It was clean but fusty from the lack of use, but Mrs Norman said that once fires were lit it would soon air and warm up. Jeannie was delighted, and very grateful to her for such a quick response.

'She'll be glad of 'company, I expect,' Mrs Norman said. 'Owd lass gets a bit dowly living on her own.'

Billy helped Jeannie move; Mrs Norman offered his services, for he had left the sea and taken a job as a carpenter on the docks. He came on a Sunday with a handcart, making several trips to move her furniture and the braiding frame, although she was doubtful if she would ever get the use from it.

Mrs Herbert was deaf, very thin and under-nourished, and Jeannie guessed that her rent money was a blessing to her. She told Jeannie that she hadn't thought she was allowed to sublet but that Mrs Norman had assured her it would be all right to do so. She told Jeannie that her husband

and son had been lost at sea and she was wholly dependent on money from a seamen's charity fund. Just as Nan had been.

'I don't want to finish up in 'workhouse with folk I don't know,' she said. 'I've lived on 'road all my life and I'd like to die here.'

Jeannie fervently hoped that she wouldn't die yet. She seemed quite a sweet old lady, and besides, it would mean looking for somewhere else to live yet again.

Harry came home three weeks later, having been directed by Billy to Mrs Herbert's house. He stepped inside from the front door and looked round. 'Not a bad place, Jeannie. I reckon you'll be comfortable here.'

Jeannie looked at him. '*We*, you mean, Harry. You and me. *We'll* be comfortable here.'

He looked anywhere but at her. 'How much 'you paying?'

'One and six for the room and use of the scullery,' she muttered. 'And then there's coal to buy. Mrs Herbert uses the coal house so I can only buy it by the bag, which costs more.'

He put his hand in his pocket and held out a handful of silver. 'Here's ten bob. That's 'rent for five weeks and a bit over for 'coal.'

Jeannie took it from him and kept her hand out. 'And the rest, Harry. I need to eat. Jack needs to be fed.'

He looked blank. 'Jack?'

'Yes,' she said. 'Your son Jack! I've started him on soft food, pobs and mashed potatoes and such.'

'He won't eat much, does he?'

'No. But I have to. I'm still feeding him and

expecting another. What's the matter with you, Harry?' She suddenly lost her temper. 'There's food to buy, I have to put money in the gas meter, there's oil for the lamp . . . candles. My boots need mending and there's never enough money to take them to the cobblers.'

'I've to buy new gear as well, you know. I need another gansey—'

'Then give me the money for wool and I'll knit you one,' she shouted. 'That's what fisher wives do; they knit and cook and bake and keep their homes nice for their man's return, but you're not giving me a chance to be a proper wife!'

'There's no need to shout,' he blustered. 'I'm doing me best.'

'Your best isn't good enough,' she said, utterly deflated. She picked up Jack, who had started to cry. 'We've to do this together or else we're both the poorer.'

'Tek it then.' He threw more money on the table. 'Tek it all. I'm not on shares, you know. My wages are fifteen bob a week less expenses. I shan't be able to afford to buy a round at 'Wassand now.'

'Then don't go,' she pleaded. 'Stay at home; get to know your son. He hardly knows you, Harry. Is he to grow up wondering who his father is?'

Harry shrugged and picked up his jacket. 'He's too young to know owt yet. Anyway, I'm off out.'

She stared at him. 'Will you be back?'

He shrugged again. 'Don't know. Might be. Don't wait up.'

She gave a bitter laugh. 'In case you hadn't noticed, the bed is right there.' She pointed over her shoulder to where the double bed was pushed up against the wall. Mrs Herbert had left a sideboard and two wooden chairs in the room, saying that she didn't want to get rid of them in case she should need them at some time. And whereas Jeannie found the sideboard useful for storing food, the room was now crowded with her bed, table and chairs; she'd sold the single bed and chest of drawers but kept the old chest for storage.

'Was that Nan's bed?'

'Yes, and the table and chairs.'

'Where's 'other bed?'

'There wasn't room for it,' she said. 'I had to sell it.'

'That were mine. It were a good bed. How much did you get for it?'

'Not much. Not enough for the first week's rent.' She stared at him, daring him to question her further.

He nodded. 'Right.' He turned for the door. 'You should be all right for a bit, then?'

Jeannie didn't answer. What was there to say? It seemed they had run out of anything to say to each other. A chasm as wide as the estuary was between them and she had no hopes of the gap ever closing. How had this happened? What was the cause? Was it her? Were they so very different that their relationship was doomed to failure before it even began?

Harry it seemed had the answer to that and she was as hurt as if he'd delivered a physical blow. He stood with the door open and chewed on his lip before saying, 'Thing is, Jeannie – well, trouble is, you know . . . you're not one of us.'

CHAPTER THIRTY-SEVEN

Jeannie applied for work at one of the smoke houses, having left Jack with Mrs Norman. They hadn't any vacancies at present, she was told, but in a way she was relieved for whilst waiting she had seen Connie, who when she saw her had turned her back. She tried another company but was given the same answer. From there she went to the fish quay to enquire if there were any vacancies for fish filleters.

The foreman had looked at her and said, 'Well, there might be, but are you carrying a bairn?'

When she hadn't answered, he said. 'Why don't you come after you've had it, eh? Get somebody to mind it while you're at work. Is it your first?'

She shook her head. 'No.'

'Well then! Is your husband not in work?'

'Yes,' she said. 'He's a trawler man.'

'You shouldn't need to be doing this then, should you? Not wi' another bairn on 'way.'

'No.' She heaved a breath as she turned away. 'I shouldn't.'

There was no other work option open to her, and to fill the days and empty weeks, when she didn't walk into town to continue her exploration of it, she took to walking westward along Hessle Road, past

332

St Andrew's Dock and the Dairycoates locomotive sheds, and along the banks of the estuary in the direction of the town of Hessle. She never did manage to walk as far as Hessle, as Jack was getting much heavier and the ground was too rough to push his cart.

Some days she felt very alone and extremely depressed; she had sold her wedding dress that her mother had struggled to buy, but there was barely anything left of that money and the coal bucket was almost empty. She lived on porridge and fed Jack with the milky pobs of bread and milk. On one particular Sunday, whilst walking, when Jack was grizzling and she felt very tired, she wondered what the point of her life was. The brown waters of the estuary looked deep and comforting and a heavy swell seemed to be beckoning her, but she looked down at Jack in her arms and he stopped his crying and gave her a wide toothless smile which lifted her heart, and she knew she had to find the strength and stamina to carry on.

'There has to be more to life than this, Jack,' she told him, and he patted her face in response. 'But I couldn't leave you behind or take you with me on such an unknown journey; that would be too cruel.' She turned her back on the drowning undertow of a watery grave and set off back home.

There was little left of the once rural countryside, where the village of Dairycoates was now a distant memory, replaced by the clang and whistle of the railway, but here and there were the remains of an open field which had yet to be built on, and it was on one of these that she saw Billy crouched on the ground, examining something.

'Hello, Billy,' she called. 'What are you doing?'

'I'm digging for worms.' He grinned. 'I thought I might go fishing.'

She smiled and walked towards him. 'Do you miss it?'

He shook his head. 'I miss seeing my mates, but I don't miss being out on a rough sea on a cold wet Sunday with a tide running high and no chance of getting warm and dry.' He held up a can of worms. 'This kind of fishing suits me better.' He scrutinized her. 'Where've you been?'

'Just walking,' she said. 'Passing the time.'

He blinked a little and looked away and then said awkwardly, 'It's a nice day for walking, or fishing.'

She cast around for any reason why he should be embarrassed, but could think of none, so said, 'Well, I'd better be off. This young fellow will be wanting some food. He's got a goodly appetite. I've started him on fish.'

'Good,' he said. 'Let him get a taste for it. I'm going that way. Shall I tek him?'

'Oh, yes, please!' She handed Jack over to him. 'Are you not going fishing today?'

'No, I'm going to feed these worms and fatten 'em up and mebbe go out one night.' He hitched Jack on to one arm and held the can with the other hand.

They walked in silence for a while, and then Jeannie said, 'Haven't you got a sweetheart to see on a Sunday, Billy?'

He gave a shy grin. 'I did have, but she fell out wi' me.'

'Did she? Why was that?' The more Jeannie got to know Billy the more she liked his openness and genuine friendly manner.

'I blotted my copybook,' he said. 'You remember when we came to Scarborough that day and you met Harry?'

How could I ever forget, she thought, recalling that sunny day when Harry had stood in front of her as she mended the nets, but she just nodded and gave a murmur of assent.

'Well, she took umbrage at that, said we'd gone looking for girls.' He pulled a wry expression. 'We had, but onny larkin' about really. Nowt happened, but she didn't believe me. She hasn't spoken to me since.'

'I'm sorry. Do you still care for her?'

'Aye, but there are other difficulties as well. Her – erm – family don't think I'm good enough for her.'

'Oh dear,' Jeannie sympathized. 'Life isn't always easy, is it? Billy,' she said on a sudden whim. 'I'd like to ask you something.'

He nodded. 'Ask away.'

She swallowed. 'When Harry came home a few weeks ago, just after I'd moved to Strickland Street, we had a quarrel, and he said – he said that – well, what he meant was that I didn't belong here. He said, "The trouble is, you're not one of us." Those were the words he used and I wondered if they were true. When I first came he used to tell people that I was a Scarborough girl, which I am, but I thought that now I was the same as everybody else. I'm from a fishing family, just the same as he is.'

Billy whistled through his teeth. 'I can't believe he said that. What made him say that? What's 'matter wi' him? He's talking rubbish.' He glanced down at her. 'Everybody who lives on Hessle Road migrated from somewhere else at one time, or at least their families did, and not only from Hull. My grand-parents came from Ramsgate and my ma's family from Whitby. That must have been one heck of a row you had,' he added. 'What was it about, or shouldn't I ask?'

'Money, of course. Or at least not enough of it.'

'But he's in regular work; he'll be getting a decent wage. What is he? Mate? Third hand? He'll get a share of 'settling either way.'

Jeannie hesitated. Harry had told her he wasn't on shares. Was he lying or had he taken whatever position he was offered? He had enough experience under his belt to be second hand, but he'd told her that he earned less than fifteen shillings. Did that mean he was fourth and hadn't told her?

'I don't know,' she admitted. 'I'll ask him when he gets home. His ship is due in any day.'

It was the non reply, the sudden silence that descended as she spoke, that made her turn to face Billy.

'What?' she said. 'Have you heard? Are they coming upriver already?'

Billy didn't answer, but only pressed his lips together and shook his head as if in disbelief. Jack grabbed a handful of his hair and pulled.

'Billy!' she said. 'What? Have they docked already?'

'Ow! Yes,' he said reluctantly. 'Yesterday.'

She hurried back, wanting to be at home when he eventually arrived. Billy carried Jack all the way, seeing her right to her door and silently handing Jack over to her. Harry hadn't got a key; she'd told him she would have another one cut, which she had, and she'd left it on the mantelpiece. Mrs Herbert would have let him in, she thought, or at least I hope she would; he'll have something to say if he can't get in. But where's he been? Had he docked too late for him to come home last night? She knew in her heart that wasn't true and hadn't questioned Billy any further. If Harry had arrived late why hadn't he come home this morning? She was simply clutching at straws, hoping that her worst fears would not be realized.

She built up the fire, made onion soup, put potatoes under the coals to bake for dinner, fed Jack and straightened the bedcover, then gazed round the room and thought it looked as welcoming as she could possibly make it. By five o'clock she was still waiting and wrung out with anxiety.

Perhaps Billy was wrong. Perhaps Harry's ship hadn't docked. Billy didn't say that he'd seen Harry. Maybe only part of the fleet had arrived and the rest was on its way upriver now. He'd be home soon and they'd sort out their problems. But seven o'clock came and she knew it was too late; already the tide would have turned and there would be no ships docking until the morning.

Jeannie began to feel a slow-burning anger. Short of a disaster, which she would have heard about, she was convinced that Billy was telling the truth; he wouldn't have any reason to lie to her. Now, when she thought about his obvious discomfort, she realized that he was as shocked as she was.

She dampened down the fire, lifted the sleeping Jack from his drawer and wrapped him in another blanket, draped her shawl over them both and went out.

It was Sunday evening and the numerous churches and chapels had emptied of their congregations; the most pious had gone home to their supper or to a coffee house, and the rest of the population seemed to be visiting inns, beer houses, hostelries and public houses, of which there were many.

As Jeannie stepped out of Strickland Street on to Hessle Road she was greeted by an oncoming crowd who swarmed along the footpaths and in the middle of the thoroughfare, dodging the horse trams and waggonettes that careered along the road. She stopped to watch. A ship must have come in earlier, or maybe two or three, for she could see that many of the men were fishermen; not by their mode of dress – for these men had changed out of their heavy seagoing gear and were wearing their best jackets and trousers, waistcoats and bowlers – but by their jaunty air, carefree manner and, above all, comradeship as they walked with arms about each other's shoulders, intent on making the most of their short time ashore.

There were some women there too, though Jeannie hazarded a guess that few of them were wives. These women were like the scavenging herring gulls, she thought, meeting every ship so that they might have a share in the feast, their partiality being gin or port.

As she watched, something, some instinct, made her turn her head. In the middle of a crowd on the opposite side of the road was Harry, and clinging to his arm was Connie. He was laughing at some remark that another man had made, and she froze. How could he laugh? How could he be with Connie when she, his wife, had been waiting at home with his son?

She crossed over at an angle so that she would be ahead of him, and hardly thinking what she was doing she stood in the road, facing the oncoming crowd, and put out her hand.

'Help me, sir,' she begged. 'I'm waiting for my husband's ship to come in. Help me, please. I've no money to buy food for my bairn or coal for a fire.'

A young man stopped. He'd be no more than sixteen, she thought, and was already merry with drink. 'What'll you do for a penny?' he slurred. He stepped towards her and she flinched. 'Come on, darling,' he continued, 'what'll you do?'

'Give over, Isaac,' another man shouted at him. 'Leave 'lass be.' He came towards her. 'What ship is your man on? Or are you on 'game?'

Jeannie felt sick with shame; what had she done? 'No game,' she said, her voice breaking. 'I've got a bairn here and another on the way. I thought he'd be home, but his ship's not come in. Harry,' she said. 'Harry Carr. Do you know him?'

The man stared at her. 'Harry Carr? Yes, I know him. We're on 'same ship.' He looked about him. 'Has anybody seen Harry Carr? This is his wife, or says she is!'

A woman pushed forward. She was older than some of the other women and was with an older man who might have been her husband.

'Yeh, she is. You're from Scarborough, aren't you? I saw you wi' Nan a couple of times.' She turned round, searching the crowd. 'I've seen Harry not five minutes since.'

A murmur swept through the crowd, the numbers of which seemed to be increasing – a murmuring question of *'Where's Harry Carr?'*

And then there he was with a silly grin on his face which was wiped off when he saw Jeannie confronting him.

'Jeannie! Ah, I was just on me way.' He looked down at Connie, unsure it seemed how to explain her presence, but Connie had no such qualms as she clung to Harry's arm.

'Hiya, Jeannie.' She chewed on her lip. 'I heard you'd flitted again.'

Jeannie didn't even look at her, but kept her gaze on Harry. 'I'm sorry you had to catch me like this, Harry,' she said witheringly. 'But I haven't any money for food or coal. You remember you left me the rent. I've tried to get work but nobody will take me on with a bairn and pregnant with another.'

There were mutterings in the crowd and Harry began to bluster. 'I was just coming. I've onny just docked.'

'*Liar!*' A voice shouted above the hubbub. 'You docked last night. Where've you been since then?' It was Billy who came from out of the crowd. Billy, Harry's best friend, his former shipmate, coming forward to tell the truth about him.

'He's been wi' his fancy piece,' a woman shouted. 'I've seen 'em together. Can't get your own man, can you, Connie Turnby, so you pinch somebody else's?'

Jeannie thought for a moment that the incident was going to turn nasty as both Harry and Connie were berated by the crowd, but in a moment a man thrust his bowler at her. 'Here, missis,' he said. 'We've just had a whip-round. There'll be enough to buy a bucket o' coal and some bread for 'morning.' He nodded sagely. 'I think you'll find that Harry turns his pockets out when he gets home.'

She started to weep. 'Thank you,' she cried. 'Thank you so much.' She held out a corner of her shawl and he tipped the contents of the bowler into it.

Billy appeared at her side. 'I'll tek you home, Jeannie,' he said, 'and wait till Harry comes, just in case—'

'He'd not hurt me, Billy.' She put the coins in her skirt pocket and wiped her eyes on the shawl. 'He's never been violent.'

'No, an' he's nivver bin shamed in front of his shipmates afore. An' as for Connie – well, what are 'lasses at 'fish house going to think when they hear? So I'll wait, if that's all right wi' you.'

CHAPTER THIRTY-EIGHT

Harry hadn't come by nine o'clock and Billy stood up to leave.

'I'm sorry, Jeannie, but I'll have to go. I don't want anybody chinwagging that I stayed all night. Will Mrs Herbert still be up?'

'Yes, I think so,' Jeannie said wearily. 'She generally looks in before she goes to bed.'

'In that case I'll go in and say goodnight.' He put on his coat and knocked on the kitchen door.

'You'll have to knock louder than that. She's deaf,' Jeannie told him, so he gave a sharp rat-a-tat with his knuckles.

'I'm going, Mrs Herbert,' he called. 'I've bin waiting for Harry, but he's not turned up. Will you lock up after me? Jeannie's feeling badly; I think she's worried about Harry.'

Mrs Herbert shuffled through in her slippers. 'He'll surely not come now. You'd best get to bed,' she said to Jeannie, who sat in the chair by the fire, her face pale and drawn.

'Thank you, Billy,' Jeannie said. 'I appreciate your staying and your support. I – I really don't want to come between your friendship with Harry. It isn't fair – you've known each other so long.'

'Aye, we have; doesn't mean to say it's allus been plain sailing, though.' He looked anxiously at her. 'You sure you're all right? Shall I ask Ma to drop in to see you in 'morning?'

Jeannie shook her head. 'I'll be fine, thank you, Billy.' She smiled, though she wanted to weep. 'Good night.'

How thoughtful he was, she thought as she climbed into her lonely bed. She gave a deep sigh. I'm so tired, and I don't feel all that well. I never thought that Harry and Connie— How long has that been going on? Since she moved out, or before then? I suspect she's always been sweet on Harry, but I thought she'd become my friend.

She spent a restless night and woke the following morning feeling more tired and nauseous than the night before and with an aching back. Jack was grizzling and whiny and fisting his wet mouth.

'Poor bairn,' she soothed. 'Have you got sore gums?' She ran her fingers inside his mouth, feeling for the emerging sharp new teeth, and he bit and gnawed on them. 'When your da comes I'll buy some oil of cloves to rub on them,' she murmured. 'He'll surely come today and bring us some money.'

She gave a grimace as she was struck with a sudden grip of pain in her back and abdomen. She put Jack back into the middle of the bed and folded a blanket at his back to raise him. Then she took a breath as another pain assailed her.

'Ah!' She gave a gasp. What's this? I shouldn't have lifted the coal bucket. Or maybe it's because of carrying Jack last night. He's getting so heavy, though with what I can't think. I'm sure he's not feeding as well as he should be. Her milk was drying

343

up and she was supplementing the child's food with oatmeal porridge and sometimes giving him a carrot to gnaw on.

'Ow! Oh! Something's not right.' Tears welled into her eyes as yet another pain tore through her. I'm starting in – no I can't be, it's too soon, I'm going to lose the child! 'Mrs Herbert! Mrs Herbert!' She leaned over the bed. She can't hear me!

She waited a moment for the pain to subside and then, holding on to the chair, the table, the sideboard, she eased her way to the kitchen door, but stopped as Jack began to wail.

'Wait, Jack, wait for a minute. I'm coming.' She half turned to pacify him and almost fell as an attack of dizziness struck her, making her reel.

'Mrs Herbert!' she called again, staggering to the door. 'Help me!'

But as she opened the door into Mrs Herbert's kitchen she saw that there was a guard against the damped down fire and remembered that it was Monday, the day when Mrs Herbert went out early, hoping to buy cheap bread and meat that the baker and butcher might have left over from the previous week.

What am I to do? I'd better lie down; keep still and maybe I won't lose the baby. 'Jack! *Please* stop crying!' She got back into bed, hugging him to her and putting him to her breast to console him, pulling the blanket over both of them.

The pain lessened and Jack dropped off to sleep and cautiously she eased herself out of bed and to the front door, unlocking it in case Harry came home. She didn't want him to arrive and find the door closed against him.

She went slowly through Mrs Herbert's room into the small scullery beyond and reached into the cupboard for the oats to make porridge for her and Jack. As she reached up, she felt a razor-sharp pain in the pit of her belly, so cutting that she retched. She turned and leaned on the small table, her fists clenched and her eyes screwed up as she fought to control the pain.

As it subsided, she half filled a pan with water, picked up the bag of oats and staggered back into her own room, only to feel wetness on her thighs and trickling down her legs to her bare feet. She lifted her shift and looked down and, with a rising sense of distress and disbelief, saw the blood.

How long Jeannie had been lying in the middle of the floor she had no idea. It could have been hours or only a few minutes, but when she opened her bleary eyes she saw a figure kneeling beside her and heard Jack crying; as her vision cleared she saw a fair head and blue eyes gazing anxiously at her.

'Lie still. I've been round to Mrs Norman's,' Rosie said softly. 'She's on her way. It's lucky I came. I'm on my dinner break.'

'What . . .' Jeannie tried to sit up. 'What happened?'

'Don't know,' Rosie said, gently pushing her back to the floor, and Jeannie realized she was gripping Rosie's hand. 'I'd heard what went on last night wi' Harry and Connie and thought I'd come and see if you were all right.' She let out a breath. 'I found you all of a heap. At first, when I saw all 'blood, I thought somebody had attacked you. I rushed round to fetch Mrs Norman.'

'Thank you,' Jeannie whispered. 'Thank you. Have I miscarried?'

'Can't say,' Rosie said. 'I don't know about these things. There's a lot o' blood.'

Mrs Norman bustled in through the front door. 'What's happened? Billy said you looked peaky when he came in last night. I'd have been here earlier but I've had two births and a death already this morning.' She knelt at the side of Rosie. 'Looks like a miscarry here.'

Rosie got to her feet. 'Well, if you don't need me any more I'll be off.'

'Do you have to go?' Jeannie said. 'Oh – of course. You've to get back to work.'

'Help me first, will you?' Mrs Norman said. 'Put 'bairn in his cot an' then help me lift Jeannie into bed, then I'll clean this lot up.' She shifted Jeannie into a sitting position. 'You've lost 'babby, I'm sorry to say.'

Jeannie felt as weak and limp as a wet rag and allowed herself to be hoisted up into the bed, where Mrs Norman, who must have come prepared, had draped an old sheet over the blanket.

She saw Mrs Norman glance at Rosie and heard her mutter, 'You don't have to leave on my account, you know.'

'I'm not,' Rosie said. 'I don't want to be in 'way, that's all.'

'You're not in my way,' Mrs Norman answered sharply. 'And if you hadn't turned up when you did, this lass might've died. Now how about putting 'kettle on and mekking her some cocoa if there is any, and for heaven's sake give that bairn summat to eat an' stop him bawlin'.'

'I think he's teething,' Jeannie murmured, and in her weakened state, tears and sorrow succumbed to Mrs Norman's administrations whilst Rosie made cocoa and comforted and fed Jack, who finally gave her a chuckle and a smile, showing her his pink gums and two tips of white enamel.

Rosie left to go back to work but promised to return at the end of the day. 'I have to go,' she said. 'I'll lose 'wages if I'm late, but I'll be back after six. Can I fetch anything in?' she asked Mrs Norman.

'Eggs,' the midwife replied, 'and milk.'

'I – I don't have any money for eggs,' Jeannie said lamely, feeling inadequate and exhausted.

'It's all right. I'll lend you it,' Rosie said, surprisingly. 'You can pay me back when you've got it.'

'I don't know when that'll be,' Jeannie said hoarsely after Rosie had gone. 'Do you know if anybody's seen Harry?'

'Don't let's worry about Harry right now,' Mrs Norman said grimly. 'He'll get his comeuppance if he doesn't watch out. Billy's on 'warpath an' so are some of his other mates. Now then, I'm going to tek this bairn home wi' me so you can have an hour or two's rest. I'll leave a note for Mrs Herbert that you're in bed and to keep an eye on you, and to fetch me if she thinks you're badly. Are you quite comfortable?'

'Yes, thank you. I just feel very tired.'

'Aye, well no wonder. But you'll soon be right as rain. You're made of strong stuff an' there'll be plenty more babbies to come, don't worry about that.'

Jeannie closed her eyes and heard the door close. She gave a deep sigh. But not Harry's babies, she thought. That's over, but I don't want to think about that right now.

She must have slept for several hours, for she awoke only when she heard the rattle of coals as Mrs Herbert mended the fire and tiptoed out again. The next time she awoke, Rosie was standing over her with Jack in her arms.

'How you feelin' now?' Rosie asked. Jack put out his arms to Jeannie to come into bed with her.

Jeannie kissed the top of his head. 'Better,' she said. 'Thank you very much, Rosie. I don't – I can't bear to think what would have happened if you hadn't come in.'

'Ah, well!' Rosie shrugged. 'I'm sorry you lost 'bairn.'

Jeannie looked pensive. 'Not meant to be, was it? That's what my ma would've said.' She began to cry. 'Who knows what kind of life it would have had – any of us will have. Harry doesn't want me, Rosie,' she sobbed. 'He said he didn't. He only married me because Nan said he should.'

Rosie sighed. She drew up a chair next to the bed and sat down. 'I know,' she said. 'I knew it wouldn't last. Harry's not 'marrying kind.' She gave a shake of her head. 'That's why – that's why I never got close to you. I knew it'd be a flash in 'pan wi' Harry and – well, I thought that you'd finish up going back to Scarborough.'

'I thought it was because you didn't like me, because . . .' She tried to recall what Connie had told her. 'Connie said . . .'

Rosie gave a wry grimace. 'Don't tek any notice of what Connie says. She lies most of 'time. She meks up all sorts o' things. She has such a miserable life she has to invent a different one.'

Jeannie pulled herself up to a sitting position and tucked Jack close to her. 'Isn't it true about her father and your mother, then? And about her uncle beating her?'

'Oh, yes.' Rosie nodded. 'Both those things are true. But she could have left and got a room or lodgings, except she never had 'backbone to strike out on her own. Connie's only aim in life has been to have Harry. But she knew Nan wouldn't allow him anywhere near her. She was devastated when she heard he was going to marry somebody else.'

She pondered for a moment. 'Harry's my brother and I care for him; but I know he's weak. He's just like our da. I can say that now that Nan's gone cos she thought 'sun shone out of his backside. Onny it didn't, and that's why my ma went off wi' Connie's father. They're all right together. Ma writes to me at Auntie Dot's. They're a proper family.'

'Wouldn't you like to live with them?' Jeannie thought of what both Connie and Nan had said about Rosie's mother.

Rosie smiled. 'No. Auntie Dot never had any children, but she's allus treated me as if I was a daughter. When my mother first went she said that she'd send for me as soon as she was settled, but by 'time she was I wanted to stay wi' Auntie Dot. You should come and meet her. She's nice; you'd like her. She's nothing like Nan. Nan was very hard on her when she was young and jealous when she married into money. They live on 'Boulevard. They've got a lovely house.'

The Boulevard didn't mean anything to Jeannie although she had passed the end of it on her walks and always meant to turn down the tree-lined avenue one day. 'I'd like to come and meet her,' she said. 'If she wouldn't mind.'

'She wouldn't,' Rosie told her. 'She keeps asking, but . . .' She hesitated. 'You and Connie were as thick as thieves so I never asked.'

'I was sorry for her,' Jeannie murmured. 'Everybody seemed against her.'

'They weren't.' Rosie shook her head. 'Onny Nan was, but Connie has a chip on her shoulder an' thought everybody was. But they are now! All 'lasses at work are dead set against her after what happened wi' you and her and Harry. All of 'road is talking about it.'

'I see,' Jeannie said softly. 'It was awful. I felt so humiliated. If it hadn't been for Billy . . .' She saw a sudden inexplicable tightening of Rosie's expression. 'He was really kind and helped me home. He asked me if he should get his mother to call but I said no. I was wrong; I should have said yes. False pride, I suppose.'

'Oh!' Rosie muttered. 'Is that what Mrs Norman meant? About Billy saying you looked peaky?'

'Yes.' Enlightenment flooded through Jeannie. So it was Rosie who had been Billy's sweetheart and had been angry with him about his visit to Scarborough. 'He's such a good man, isn't he? Some lass is going to be lucky to catch him one day.' She lowered her voice confidentially. 'He told me that he'd been sweet on a girl but she'd given him the brush-off because she thought he'd been chasing other women, except he hadn't. I expect it was only Harry who had done that, cos that was the time when Harry and I met.'

'Oh,' Rosie murmured. 'So he isn't seeing anybody else, then? I mean – I haven't heard that he is and usually everybody knows what's going on along 'road.'

Before Jeannie could answer someone knocked on the front door and Jeannie slid down into the bed. 'Do you think that's Harry?' she whispered. 'If it is, will you stay, Rosie? I don't want to see him by myself.'

Rosie nodded and went to the door. Jeannie heard low voices, and then Rosie came back in.

'It's not Harry. It's Billy, and he's brought a message from Harry – and some money.'

CHAPTER THIRTY-NINE

'Tell him to come in, Rosie.' Jeannie covered her shoulders with her shawl. 'I think I'm respectable.'

'Course you are,' Rosie said, and going back to the door she invited Billy in.

'I, erm . . .' Billy shuffled his feet. 'Sorry you're not well, Jeannie.' His cheeks were red and he chewed on his lips. 'I've, erm, I've just had a set-to wi' Harry. Found him at 'Dairycoates Inn; he's not going in 'Wassand at 'minute cos nobody'll talk to him. He's sailing in 'morning so I made him empty his pockets.' He fished in his own pocket and put a pile of coins on the table. 'That's all he had left, but it's better than nowt.'

'So – he won't be coming to see me before he leaves?' Jeannie asked. 'Does he know I've miscarried?'

'He knows now if he didn't before, but he's still not coming. He said would I tell you he'll come when he gets back from this trip. I don't think he dares come now.'

'I'm hardly in a fit state to scare him.' Jeannie's voice cracked. 'He might at least have come to say he was sorry. Was Connie with him?' she asked abruptly.

Billy looked down. 'Yeh, she was. I don't think he

can go anywhere without her now. Besides, they've nobody else to talk to.'

'It's a pity you can't divorce him,' Rosie chipped in. 'Like 'toffs do.'

'We promised till death us do part,' Jeannie said softly. 'But it doesn't seem to mean much. At least not to Harry.'

Rosie and Billy left at the same time, with Billy saying he'd walk along Hessle Road with Rosie, making what Jeannie was sure was an excuse that he was going that way anyway. She got up after they had gone and pottered about slowly, making tea and preparing food for Jack, and after he'd gone to sleep she sat by the fire and pondered on what was in store for her.

I must make more effort to find work, she thought. It's not going to come to me. The small amount of money that Harry had sent wouldn't last any time at all, not once she'd paid the rent. The Fishermen's Mission provided family assistance in times of bereavement if a fisherman was lost at sea, but Jeannie mused that she'd hardly qualify for consideration just because her husband had decided not to support her and their child.

There was one option, she thought, cringing at the very idea, and that was to try for assistance from the Poor Law Union which was there to provide a relief fund for those at rock bottom. I can't! I can't! The humiliation! I couldn't bear it. I'd only apply if there was a danger that I couldn't feed Jack.

Going out the next day, she shivered. There was a nip in the air, and the screeching of gulls over-head warned of rough weather out on the coast. She bought the cheapest cut of meat and asked the butcher for a bag of marrow bones to make soup. He glanced questioningly at her but made no comment, used, she supposed, to requests like hers. From there she went to the greengrocer for potatoes and carrots and with a sigh of satisfaction knew she had enough food for her and Jack for a week, providing she had enough coal to keep the fire going.

Later that evening Billy called round with a sackful of wood from the joinery yard and said with a wink that as he brought plenty of wood home most days, his mother wouldn't miss this. Jeannie was overjoyed and soon had a blaze going; she prepared a large saucepan of beef broth to which she would add a carrot and a potato each day and supplement with the addition of suet dumplings so that they wouldn't go hungry.

She spent the next three weeks staying mainly at home to conserve her energy and her money. But then she ran out of coal and wood and potatoes and knew she would have to go out on the road and spend the last of her small cache of coins. Rosie had been to see her twice and seemed more cheerful than usual, and had also brought her a parcel of fish for which she was very thankful. Rosie also repeated that her Auntie Dot was looking forward to seeing her.

But Jeannie was wary of going just yet. She felt tired after the miscarriage, and shabby, and knew she looked thin and undernourished, which she was sure Rosie's affluent aunt would notice. Not knowing her, she felt she would either be condescending towards her, or alternatively offer her money which Jeannie was far too proud to accept.

Her mother had written saying that she was

worried that she hadn't received a letter or postcard from her recently and hoped that everything was all right. Tom had been disappointed that she hadn't been able to attend his wedding and Jeannie too had been saddened, but she knew that the train fare to Scarborough was out of her reach. I'll write, she thought, and tell her that everything is fine, especially since we moved in with Mrs Herbert. No need to bother her by saying that I moved without Harry and that he's not living with me; Ma would say come home for sure. But I can't do that, she thought tearfully. I can't admit that my marriage is a failure.

Eventually she was persuaded by Rosie to visit her aunt and one Sunday morning she dressed Jack in his warmest clothes and wrapped him in her shawl, which he immediately pulled off. He was already crawling and attempting to walk, and delighting her with his babbling words. Another few weeks and it would be his first birthday and she hoped that Harry would remember it. He was due home at any time and she made a mental note to remind him when he came, as he'd promised.

Rosie met her out on the road and they took it in turns to carry Jack. He'd grown out of his cart and Jeannie had burned it on the fire one day when she'd run out of wood. I'll not need it now, she'd thought regretfully. Not now I've lost a bairn. There'll be no more children for me.

Rosie's Auntie Dot lived in a large house on the Boulevard. Her husband had founded a successful chandler's shop at the beginning of the upturn of the fishing industry. The proceeds from this bought him a half share in a smack and then a little later several shares in a smoke house before he sank more cash in a coffee house and a beer shop. He was a man with many interests and irons in several fires. The culmination was the purchase of the house on the Boulevard. He and his wife had no children, and because he was a prudent man they lived, not lavishly, but well.

It's a very grand house, Jeannie thought as she followed Rosie up the front steps. The Boulevard was a wide avenue with tall trees which had now shed their leaves but whose bare branches, crowned by black shaggy crows' nests, stood out majestically against the grey sky. All the houses were substantial and respectable, many of them three-storeyed and elegant.

A maid held open the front door as they entered the wide hall. Rosie took off her coat and handed it to her, but Jeannie shyly shook her head when asked if she'd like to leave her shawl. She didn't want the maid or Rosie's aunt to see her worn blouse beneath it.

Dorothy Greenwood, plump and dark-haired, was dressed neatly and simply in a dark skirt and a crisp white blouse with leg o' mutton sleeves. She received Jeannie warmly. 'Call me Auntie Dot,' she said. 'We're practically related, aren't we, seeing as you're married to my nephew? Although, as I understand it' – she waved Jeannie to a comfy chair – 'he's being rather a naughty boy. And as for that minx Connie! Oh yes,' she said, seeing the disquiet on Jeannie's face. 'I don't miss much and I don't need Rosie to tell me any gossip. I'm out on 'road most days and I hear what's going on. And I must say that my opinion of Connie is 'only thing that my ma and me ever agreed on.

'Course,' she went on, sitting in a chair across from Jeannie next to a blazing fire, 'in a way, 'poor lass never stood a chance wi' a mother like she's got, but that's no excuse for pinching somebody else's husband.' She pressed a bell on the wall. 'We'll have a cup o' coffee. And cake?' She leaned forward to Jack, who was sitting on Jeannie's knee staring at her. 'I bet you'd like cake, wouldn't you? Can he eat cake?' she asked Jeannie.

'I've never given it to him,' Jeannie confessed, thinking how nice it would be to be able to afford cake. 'But I expect he can, as long as he doesn't choke.'

'Bread and jam then,' Dot suggested. 'That might be safer; we don't want 'little mite choking. Are you coming to Auntie Dot?' She put out her arms to Jack, who to Jeannie's astonishment slid down from her knee and staggered towards her. Dot picked him up and jiggled him on her wide lap and allowed him to play with the string of beads round her neck.

'Never wanted any bairns of our own,' she said cheerfully. 'And fortunately they never happened, but I quite like other people's as long as I can hand them back if they become unsavoury or troublesome.' She patted Jack's cheek. 'I could tek to you, though,' she said softly. 'And you look just like your da did when he was your age.'

Jeannie felt her eyes fill with tears. He might look like Harry, but she hoped with all her heart he wouldn't grow up to be weak and unreliable like him.

'Go find Minnie, Rosie,' Dot said. 'Tell her to hurry up wi' coffee. It's going to be dinner time by

357

'time she brings it. And bring bread and jam and some milk for 'bairn!'

Rosie got up and went to the door. She raised her eyebrows at Jeannie, who smiled back, both knowing that Dot hadn't yet asked for the coffee but only rung the bell.

'Now then,' Dot said to Jeannie when they were alone. 'How are you managing, or mebbe you're not but onny just surviving?' She tilted her head to one side and surveyed Jeannie. 'I don't want to pry, but you're family and if I can help I will. Rosie told me that Harry didn't leave you much money before he went back to sea. She also told me about you losing 'bairn you were carrying.'

'Yes,' Jeannie said. 'Both those things are true. And you're very kind to offer help, but I have to manage as best I can. Harry will be home again soon; I shall talk to him then and explain that until I can find work on the nets he'll have to support me and Jack.'

'Well, you can explain all you like,' Dot said, playing pat-a-cake with Jack, 'but it doesn't alter 'fact that no matter how sorry he is or how many promises he makes, he'll still let you down.'

'How do you know?' Jeannie whispered, not wanting to believe it. 'He might change.'

'He won't,' Dot said matter-of-factly. 'He's just like my brother – his da. *He* was full of promises that he never kept. But I'm not going to press you. Come to me if and when you need to. I'll be here.'

'Thank you,' Jeannie said, just as they heard the peal of the doorbell.

'That'll be Sam – forgotten his keys again,' Dot commented. 'He allus seems to know when 'kettle's on. No, don't get up,' for Jeannie had started to rise from the chair. 'I want you to stop for a bit; you're not in a hurry, are you? Besides,' she went on, 'he'll not stop long. He's supposed to be meeting somebody today. A bit o' business, you know; he can't seem to give it up,' she added indulgently.

A large man came through the door and started when he saw Jeannie. 'Sorry,' he said in a boom-ing voice which started Jack crying and holding out his arms to Jeannie. 'Sorry,' he said again. 'I didn't know we'd company.'

'We haven't,' his wife said. 'She's family. This is Harry's wife.'

'How do?' he said. 'Samuel Greenwood. Call me Sam. Hope you don't mind, Dot, but I've brought somebody back wi' me. We've a bit o' business to dis-cuss. We'll go in my office.'

'Bring 'em in first,' Dot commanded, handing Jack over to Jeannie. 'We're allus glad to meet folks.'

'Well, you know Mike Gardiner,' he said. 'And this young fellow-me-lad's come wi' him. Come in. Come in,' he said to someone in the hall. 'Here's the wife,' he added as Mike came into the room, 'and this bonny lass here is . . .'

'How do, Dot.' Mike grinned. 'And I know who this is. Hello, Jeannie. Are you all right?'

'And this young chap is from Scarborough, so you might know him.' He turned to the door and Jeannie's eyes followed him. 'Ethan Wharton,' he said. 'We're hoping to go into 'trawling business together.'

CHAPTER FORTY

They were both lost for words. Jeannie searched for a greeting but could find none, whilst Ethan stood as if struck dumb.

'Have you met, then? Or not?' Mike asked in a puzzled voice. 'Scarborough's not that big a place.'

Ethan cleared his throat. 'Yes – yes, we have. It's, erm, nice to see you again, Jeannie.'

Jeannie managed a smile. 'Yes, you too. It's been a while. How – how's everybody?'

Ethan nodded, his eyes on her face, and it seemed to Jeannie that the two of them were displaced, trapped in an uninhabited void, whilst around them Mike, Dot and Sam were speaking words without sound or form.

She blinked. 'Did you go to Tom's wedding?' she asked huskily. 'I couldn't – I couldn't go. The journey, you know, with Jack. Too difficult.'

Ethan looked down at Jack as if seeing him for the first time. 'He's a fine boy.' He smiled down at the child. 'Looks like you. I was Tom's best man. It was a great day – almost.'

'Almost?' she faltered.

He nodded again. 'You weren't there,' he said softly. 'Your ma missed you.'

Jeannie's mouth trembled. 'It's been difficult,' she whispered. 'I . . .'

'Right then,' Sam Greenwood boomed. 'Let's leave 'ladies to their gossip and we'll go in my room and have a chat about business.'

He ushered the men out and Minnie carried a tray into the room.

'Will you stay for dinner?' Dot asked Jeannie as she poured the coffee. 'There's plenty – you needn't be bothered that there won't be enough to go round. We allus eat well. Sam's got a good appetite. We're having roast beef today.'

Jeannie licked her lips, salivating at the thought of roast beef. 'If you're sure it's no bother,' she said, putting Jack down on the floor to eat the bread and jam Rosie had brought for him.

'No bother at all.' Dot passed her a cup. 'Rosie, go and ask Mike and that young chap if they'd like to stop for dinner and if they say yes, go and tell Minnie.'

Rosie took a sip of her coffee before putting down her cup and going off to do her aunt's bidding.

'You knew that young fellow, didn't you?' Dot asked. 'What was he? A sweetheart?'

'We lived nearby,' Jeannie prevaricated. 'All the fisher families know each other, just like here.'

'Ah, I see. I thought he seemed a bit sweet on you, that's all.'

'Oh, no.' Jeannie forced a laugh. 'Nothing like that. He's courting a girl, I think. A chandler's daughter.'

'Really? Well, there's some money there, and I should know.'

'Ethan wouldn't be bothered about that. He works very hard,' Jeannie said quietly. 'He's been a fisherman since he was twelve. He worked on his father's smack.'

'Mm.' Dot sipped her coffee. 'And now he wants to go into trawling?'

'I don't know. He's ambitious. He had his own smack and fishing is all he knows, so he'll be willing to try anything to make a living – I should think,' she finished lamely, thinking that she had said more than she should about a mere neighbour.

Auntie Dot looked at her over the top of her cup. 'Yes, I dare say he would. He looks 'positive type of man. Sam'll like him, I'd say, and especially if Mike recommends him.'

'I didn't know Mike knew him.' Jeannie shook her head. 'It's such a coincidence, isn't it?'

'Aye, it is.' Dot raised her brows. 'Funny old life, isn't it?'

Ethan couldn't stay for the midday meal. There was a crewman waiting on the smack and he told Rosie they wanted to catch the afternoon tide to get back to Scarborough. Mike also declined, as he'd been invited to his son's house for Sunday dinner. But Ethan came back into the sitting room to say goodbye.

'Is there any message to carry home?' he asked Jeannie. 'To – your ma?'

Jeannie's eyes prickled. 'Yes, please, and to Tom and Sarah. Tell Ma – tell them – that I miss them all.'

'And that you're well and happy?' His voice dropped. 'Are you happy, Jeannie?'

Jeannie pressed her lips together. What should

she say? 'I've been unhappy,' she whispered, conscious of other people in the room, Mike chatting to Dot, Rosie gazing into the fire. 'I've been ill. I've just lost a bairn – but I'm all right now,' she added quickly, seeing his face tense. 'The people round here are very supportive. They help one another. Tell Ma everything's fine.'

'Goodbye, then.' He took her hand and she felt the warmth, the strength, the comfort of it.

'Maybe we'll bump into each other again,' she murmured. 'If things go to plan?'

'Mebbe,' he said, his expression set. 'Mebbe not.'

She released her hand from his. 'No, perhaps not.'

Ethan strode with his long stride alongside Mike down the Boulevard and towards Hessle Road. 'Nice area,' he commented. 'Is this where folk come when they've done well?'

'Aye,' Mike said. 'When they've made their pile. Greenwood's done well. He's got a good head on his shoulders. Did you tek to him? It's important if we're to work together.'

'Well, the way I see it, he'll look after the money side, Len – who you'll meet when we get to the harbour – and I will organize a crew and the fishing, and you'll look after everything in between. I gather you won't want to come out on a trip?'

'No, I've done wi' all that,' Mike said. 'I've had enough of stormy voyages, being cold and wet through. It's a young man's game and I like my own bed of a night.'

Ethan nodded. 'My father said the same, although I think he might come on the first trip. Greenwood will do everything right, won't he?' he asked anxiously. 'Insurance and so on?'

'Oh aye, you can count on it,' Mike said. 'He's very canny and won't want to risk his money. He'll want to tek a look at 'ship, too, even though he knows little about sailing in 'em.'

They crossed the Hessle Road and continued on towards St Andrew's Dock.

'How long do you think before he'll make up his mind?'

'Oh I reckon he's already made it up,' Mike said cheerfully. 'Tomorrow mornin' he'll be talking to his lawyer, then in 'afternoon to his bank. I think within a fortnight we'll strike a deal and be able to tell 'shipwright to start mekkin' modifications.'

Ethan eased out a breath and grinned. 'I can't wait to get home to tell my da. He'll be pleased as punch.'

'Will you mek your base here? It'd mek sense.'

'Yes, I'll have to. I'll look for lodgings once everything's agreed.'

'You can stop wi' me if you've a mind to. I've plenty o' room in my house. There's onny me, so you can come and go as you want. Just till you're established, you know. No commitment.'

'That would be grand. Thanks.' Ethan nodded. He liked Mike and thought they'd get on well together. 'I'll probably be bringing my brother Stephen, if Da agrees; would that be all right?'

'Fine. Like I say I've plenty of room. You'd need to do your own cookin' when you're ashore, though. I'm no great shakes at that.' Mike grinned. 'I get meat 'n' tatie pies brought in from time to time, from womenfolk, you know, who want to get on 'best

364

side of me.' His grin became wider. 'I expect there'll be even more when you move in and they find you're single! Mebbe you'll have to put it about that you've got a lass waitin' in Scarborough.'

Ethan laughed, rather cynically Mike thought. 'Mebbe I will, except that I haven't. Not any more.'

It was dark and wet when Ethan and Len sailed into Scarborough harbour and headed towards the West Pier. Len was inclined to be taciturn, and although Ethan had wanted him in on the meeting with Greenwood he'd declined, telling Ethan he trusted him to do what was best as he'd no head for figures.

The sea had had a rolling heavy swell; they'd heard the odd crack of thunder and a strong wind had whistled through the canvas and the rigging, but Ethan knew his ship and Len had no fear of what he called a pocket of wind and they came into harbour without difficulty. They secured the smack and climbed the iron steps on to the quay side. A figure detached itself from a small group of men and came towards them.

'Now then, lad,' Josh said. 'Everything all right?'

'Yes. What's going on?' Ethan looked towards the gathering; there was something about their stance, the way they shuffled their feet, the manner in which they rubbed their noses and pulled their collars up around their ears as if they had been standing in the cold too long, that alerted him that something was not quite right.

His father looked out beyond the harbour. 'The *Sweet Flower* is late. She should have been in two or three hours ago. What's it like out there?'

'Calm enough,' Ethan said. 'But there's a heavy undertow. Who's on it?'

'Clarkson brothers and two others. They know what they're doing.'

'She's a refitted smack,' Len put in. 'They've only got ten horsepower. Mebbe it's broken down and they're having to sail back.'

'That's what I said,' Josh agreed. 'Or mebbe they've gone too far; or mebbe they've found a good shoal.' He pulled his woollen hat over his ears. 'Who knows?'

'We'll know the worst by the morning,' Ethan said. 'Let's hope there's good news before then.'

Whenever a ship was missing or late, it brought back a small stab of fear as he recalled the loss of his brother all those years ago. But it didn't deter him from depending on the sea for his livelihood. Rather, it made him more careful, more aware of what could happen out on the watery wastes. His feeling was that if he were to die young, it would be the sea that took him and not any accident or illness on land.

Len left them and joined the waiting group of men.

'How did you get on?' Josh asked Ethan. 'Are we on?'

'I think so. It's looking good. I met Greenwood, who'll be putting up the bulk of the money. He seems very keen and Mike Gardiner seems to think we'll know for sure in a couple of weeks.'

'Good,' his father said. 'It's just what we need. We can't go on as we are or we'll be bankrupt like so many others.'

'Will you want to come on the first trip?' Ethan asked. 'And what about Stephen?'

'Not Stephen,' Josh said emphatically. 'He's too young, even though he's keen.' He drew back his shoulders and put his head up. 'But yes, I'll come. I'd like to try my hand at trawling even though I said I was against it. But I seem to be in the minority and I've decided that I'm not ready for retirement. I'm not that old and I've no wife at home waiting for me.'

Ethan glanced at his father; was there a tinge of regret in his voice? 'What about Stephen? Will he go to Susan?'

There was a slight hesitation before Josh said, 'Yes, course he will. She's practically brought him up, hasn't she? I want him to go to school in any case.'

Ethan murmured agreement. 'I saw Jeannie when I was in Hull,' he said.

'Ah! How was she? Mary will be glad to know.'

Ethan hunched into his coat and said, 'She looked ill, if I'm honest. She has a young bairn – a son – and she told me she's just lost a child. I don't know if her mother knows or if I should tell her.'

'Tell her you've seen her,' Josh advised, 'but don't say she looks ill or Mary will worry. If Jeannie's just lost a bairn she's bound to be out of sorts, but she'll soon pick up. She's a strong healthy lass.'

I don't think she is, Ethan thought as they strode the last few yards towards home. I don't think she's strong at all; she's lost weight, she's thin and the colour's gone from her cheeks and I hate to see her looking so sad and unhappy. Something's wrong!

CHAPTER FORTY-ONE

The word that a Scarborough smack was missing filtered through to Hull. Jeannie heard it as she waited in line at the greengrocer's two days after she had seen Ethan. She felt sick and faint and almost staggered.

'You all right, missis?' A woman next to her took hold of her arm. 'Shall I tek 'babby?'

Jeannie clung tightly to Jack. 'I'm – thank you, I'm all right. I just heard . . .' She felt as if she could hardly breathe. 'I just heard somebody say there was a Scarborough smack missing.'

The woman's eyes creased sympathetically. 'Know somebody on it, do you? There's allus sorrow for somebody.'

'Do you know the name? I'm from Scarborough, you see. I might know them.'

'You're Harry Carr's wife, aren't you?' Enlightenment lit the woman's expression. 'My husband was a shipmate of his da years ago. He didn't go on that last trip, thank God.'

'But do you know the name of the Scarborough smack?' Jeannie desperately tried to get the woman back on track. 'Where were they sailing?'

'Somewhere near Shetland, I heard,' the woman

said. 'They've been missing all weekend.'

Relief flooded through Jeannie. She wanted to weep. To cry as she had done when she returned home on Sunday afternoon after finishing her dinner of roast beef, mashed potatoes, carrots and turnip and thick onion gravy which, hungry though she was, she had to force down, so edgy and overwrought was she after seeing Ethan again.

Jack had been asleep in her arms, and although Rosie had walked part of the way back with her they had spoken little, both lost in their own thoughts. The fire had gone out in her room and it was very cold; Jeannie had put Jack into bed and then taken off her boots, slipped out of her skirt and shawl and climbed in beside him and wept and wept.

How, she sobbed, how could I have not seen how kind and loving he would have been? How could I have been so stupid as to have been taken in by Harry's show of charm and superficial words of love which meant nothing, as he's admitted?

Her sobs racked her body but they didn't wake Jack, who, tired out by the attentions of Dot and Rosie and a full stomach of beef gravy and mash, slept on oblivious of her anguish. Eventually she fell asleep to a restless night of dreams, waking early the next morning feeling washed out and exhausted.

Now, after hearing the dreadful news of the missing Scarborough smack and then nearly being overwhelmed by the relief that it wasn't Ethan's, she left the shop and walked along the road, intent on taking her small purchases back to her room, after which she would take Jack out for a walk. The weather was cold and dreary but she would walk simply to pass the time and shorten the day, which stretched as empty and lonely as all the others.

She thought that Harry might be home soon, but felt so apathetic towards him, knowing she could rely on him for nothing, that she hardly dared let him enter her thoughts in case her anger swamped her. Her main aim was to get through each day with enough left from her dwindling money to buy food for Jack and coal to heat the room. She herself ate little, taking only a few mouthfuls of soup. Her milk was dwindling, and she put Jack to her breast purely for comfort and not nourishment.

'Jeannie! Jeannie!'

She turned slowly. Dot Greenwood was on the other side of the road, waving frantically.

Jeannie crossed over, her legs feeling heavy, as if they didn't belong to her. 'Hello,' she murmured, and Dot looked at her questioningly.

'Are you all right? You don't look well.'

'I've had rather a shock.' Her voice was low, barely a whisper. 'I heard a Scarborough smack had gone missing over the weekend, and' – she swallowed – 'I wondered if anyone I knew was on it.'

'Ah!' Dot's manner was perceptive. 'And was there?'

Jeannie shook her head. 'I don't know.'

'I see. Poor souls,' Dot said. 'And you thought it might be that young fellow's ship?'

'Just at first I did,' Jeannie admitted. 'But it wasn't, because he left here on Sunday and the missing ship had been up to Shetland.'

'A blessing for you but sorrow for somebody,' Dot said softly. 'Listen, Jeannie. I was just coming to see you. I've had an idea. I had to talk to Sam first but I knew he wouldn't mind. He's not at home much anyway. Will you come back home wi' me for a bit o' dinner?'

Jeannie gazed at her. More food! She licked her lips; she could save the soup she had made for another day. And what was Dot's idea? She nodded. 'Yes, thank you. If you're sure.'

'I wouldn't have asked you if I hadn't wanted you to come, would I? There'll just be us – Rosie's at work and Sam's gone to see 'bank manager and won't be in till later. Shall I tek Jack for a minute?' Dot lifted Jack from her without waiting for a reply. 'You're a fat lump, aren't you?' she told the child. 'I'll not be carrying you far. I know somebody who's got a perambulator. They've no use for it now. I'm going to ask if they'll sell it.'

'Oh!' Jeannie was alarmed. People like her didn't have perambulators. 'I couldn't possibly afford—'

'I wasn't thinking of you buying it,' Dot said brisk-ly. 'I thought I'd buy it. If I'm going to look after him I can't be expected to carry him about and he's not yet ready for walking.'

'I don't understand.' Jeannie fell into step beside her, walking back towards the Boulevard. 'What do you mean, look after him?'

'It came to me after you'd left on Sunday. I took Rosie in when she was a bairn, you know, after her ma left home. She could have gone to Nan but I knew she'd end up being 'drudge, not like Harry who could do nowt wrong in Nan's eyes.'

Jeannie nodded. She'd already heard this from Rosie.

'Well, I enjoyed having her; she wasn't a bad little lass, but she doesn't need me now, and I think she's courting though she's keeping quiet about it.'

Billy, Jeannie thought. At least I hope so.

'So what I thought was,' Dot went on, 'as you need to get a job to keep 'wolf from 'door, seeing as Harry's so unreliable, you could get a part-time job at 'smoke house or fish house or mending nets or whatever you can find, and I'd look after Jack.'

Jeannie felt her spirits lift. She sensed she could trust Dot with Jack as she'd trust no one else except her own mother.

'And don't ask me if I'm sure,' Dot continued, 'cos I wouldn't—'

'Say it if you didn't mean it,' Jeannie finished for her. 'I can't believe how kind you are to offer. It would mean that I didn't have to rely on Harry for money.'

'But you're not to refuse it if he brings any,' Dot warned. 'He's got to support you and Jack, and if he's not careful he'll be ostracized on 'road even more than he is now.'

'Oh, thank you!' Once more Jeannie began to weep. She was so full of tears; it was as if there was a hidden spring buried deep inside her. But now she had hope. She could buy food with the money she earned and that would make her feel well again and Jack would benefit from being with someone else instead of only her and her sorrow.

Dot disregarded her tears. 'If I can get that pram,' she said, using the popular name of the perambulator, 'we can tek a walk with him, me and Minnie. 'Girl who helps me, you know,' she added. 'She's from a big family; she knows about bairns. Here.' She handed Jack back. 'You can tek him for a bit.'

*   *   *

372

A week later, Jeannie started work on the fish quay for three days a week. Three days, she reckoned, was probably as much as Dot could manage, for Jack needed watching constantly. Another week and he would be a year old, and Dot was planning a party for him with cake and blancmange. She had also bought him two new smocks to replace the ones that Jeannie had made out of one of her own cotton shifts. These new ones were of a warmer material and fastened with tiny buttons down the front rather than ties at the back. She had also bought him a new bonnet to protect his head if he should fall.

'You can pay me back when you're earning if you've a mind to,' she told Jeannie, when she saw her hesitation over accepting the gifts. 'Or you can regard them as birthday presents.'

Jeannie had smiled. Dot, she was sure, was gaining as much pleasure from buying Jack presents of much needed clothing as she was from accepting them.

She was at home with Jack in their room on one of her days off when there was a sharp rap on the door. Jack was in his old clothing, for Jeannie kept his new for when they went out on the road or when she was taking him to Dot's. He was sitting on the floor next to her, grizzling with the pain of his raw gums; the damp coal in the grate wouldn't burn but would only emit black smoke, no matter how she blew on it or wafted it with her apron.

'Come in,' she called from her kneeling position, and brushing her hair out of her eyes she looked up, wondering who it might be so early. 'The door's open.'

Harry. He had his sea bag over his shoulder and

he stepped inside, carefully wiping his boots on the mat. 'How do, Jeannie!' he muttered.

Jack started to wail on seeing him and lifted his arms to his mother. Jeannie picked him up and shushed him, murmuring reassuring words, and he hid his face on her shoulder.

'I reckon he doesn't know me,' Harry observed.

'That's hardly surprising, is it,' she said sharply. 'Seeing as you're never here.'

'Can't help that, can I?' he retaliated. 'I have to earn a living.'

'Everybody does,' she agreed, getting to her feet 'But he never sees you on your trips—' She was going to say home, but changed it to 'ashore'.

Harry shrugged. 'Any chance of a cuppa tea?'

She hardened towards him. 'Only if you've brought money for me to buy some. You must have realized that what you sent last time is long spent.'

'So how've you been managing, then, if you say I didn't give you enough?'

'Managing? I haven't. I've been surviving. Living on potato soup and beef broth from bones I begged from the butcher!'

Harry gazed at her. 'You've changed, Jeannie,' he said. 'You're not 'girl I once knew. You seem to have grown bitter.'

Jeannie's mouth dropped. 'You've not the slightest idea, have you?' she said incredulously. 'You haven't given any thought to how I'd cope without money for rent or food, let alone clothes for Jack or boots for my feet. Would you have let us starve? Did you know that I miscarried our child? *Our* child, Harry. I might have died but for Rosie coming and finding me and fetching help.'

'Oh, *Rosie*,' he sneered. 'She's your best friend now, is she?'

'Well, it was Connie,' she answered quietly. 'But not any more.'

He blew out his lips. 'I thought I was doing right by coming, but it seems that I'm not so I'll go.'

He half turned towards the door and Jeannie was seized by panic that he'd leave without giving her any money. Should she beg for her rightful dues? But he must have had second thoughts for he turned back, digging in his pocket to put money on the table.

'Did you remember that it's Jack's birthday this week?' she asked quietly. 'His first.'

'Oh aye,' he muttered. 'Course it is.' He put his hand back in his pocket and brought out more coins. 'Better tek a bit more then, although I don't suppose he knows it's his birthday.'

'No,' she sighed. 'He doesn't. But I do.'

He nodded and turned for the door again. 'This is onny a forty-two-hour trip home, then another short trip away. I'll be back afore Christmas.'

'Would you like that cup of tea?' she asked, relenting.

Harry paused as if weighing up his options. 'Mm, mebbe not, thanks. I'd better get off.'

Jeannie didn't ask him where he was getting off to for she knew very well in which direction he would be going; but he hesitated with his hand on the sneck.

'I'll come by next time, Jeannie. I'll fetch more money. I'll not leave you short again.' He looked her straight in the eye. 'I'll try and sort my life out. I'm sorry. Sorry that it's turned out like this. I never meant this to happen.'

She swallowed hard. She felt such sorrow, such misery, yet knew that there was no turning back for either of them. There was no love between them, nor would there ever be, not now, and although she retained some affection for the appealing, artless side of his nature, she knew they could never have a life together. And they were tied together for life.

CHAPTER FORTY-TWO

The snow came down thick and fast and as Jeannie trudged towards the Boulevard with Jack in her arms she was glad that he would soon be safe and warm in Dot's house. She would be very cold as she gutted and filleted on the fish quay, even though she was wrapped in all the clothes and shawls she possessed; she wore thick woollen socks inside her rubber boots and fingerless multicoloured gloves she had knitted from scraps of wool. On her head she wore the hooded woollen shawl like the ones the Scottish herring girls wore that her mother had knitted for her when she first started work on Scarborough quay.

For Jack's birthday, Dot, as she'd promised, bought him the second-hand perambulator. He loved it, and jiggled and rocked it with squeals of delight.

Jeannie had proved herself fast and slick at gutting and boxing up and was given a slight rise in wages; the foreman asked if she would come in for the other three days a week. She had to refuse; she dare not infringe on Dot's generosity too much, knowing how much of a handful Jack was now that he had started walking, taking his first proper steps on his birthday. She was managing reasonably well, and paid Mrs Herbert her rent before spending any money on food or coal, and although there was little left at the end of the week she felt a sense of satisfaction that she was coping.

'You'll come to us at Christmas, won't you?' Dot asked her one evening when she had gone to collect Jack after work. 'Sam likes a house full of folk for Christmas dinner. We have a tree as well, wi' candles and decorations.'

Jeannie's mother had never had a Christmas tree, saying that there was never enough money to pay for such luxuries. But Jeannie, Tom and their mother had always enjoyed Christmas, although there was no money for anything but simple presents, perhaps a knitted scarf or a hemmed handkerchief. Mary cooked a small chicken, its cavity stuffed with onion and sage, but her speciality was the cloutie dumpling her Scottish mother had always cooked at Christmas. It was made with flour and suet and packed with fruit, sugar and spice, wrapped in a cloth and boiled for two hours, and served with hot custard.

When Dot had invited her, Jeannie wondered if she could contribute by making the dumpling; she'd never made one but had often helped her mother to stir.

'Yes, you can,' Dot said when she asked her. 'But I'll buy the ingredients. I don't want you to be out of pocket. I'll put the order in at the grocer's.'

Jeannie gratefully submitted. Buying the ingredients herself would have taken her last penny.

'Should I ask Harry, do you think?' Dot went on. 'Or will he be eating elsewhere?'

Jeannie shook her head. She didn't know. He

would be home in time, she knew that, but would he prefer to spend the day with Connie?

'I'm going to ask Auntie Dot if she'll invite Billy,' Rosie whispered to Jeannie one day. 'His mother allus has plenty of company and won't miss him.' She seemed pent up with eagerness and nervous excitement.

'They'll know it's serious if you do,' Jeannie told her. 'Is that what you want?'

'Yes,' she admitted. 'I do. Uncle Sam's allus saying I should marry somebody in business. They know Billy but've never expressed an opinion about him. I don't know if they like him or not.'

Jeannie smiled. 'You're old enough to do what you want,' she said. 'Billy doesn't have to ask permission.'

Rosie gave a little shrug. 'He doesn't say much,' she said. 'I don't even know if he wants to marry me at all.'

'Maybe he's not sure about you,' Jeannie commented. 'You sent him packing once, didn't you?'

'Yeh,' Rosie sighed. 'That's cos I was jealous.'

At night when she returned home it was bitterly cold and Jeannie hugged Jack close to her. Dot hadn't said she could use the pram for the journeys back and forth between the two houses and she hadn't asked, thinking that perhaps Dot wanted to keep it at her place for her own convenience.

The shops along the road were brightly lit and there was nothing that couldn't be bought or sold there. Grocer, butcher, draper, tailor and pawnbroker were all open for business, hoping to catch the fishing community, the railway workers, the tram drivers and the mill workers on their way home. The pubs, clubs and institutes were throbbing with customers and Jeannie heard the hum of conversation and an occasional shout of merriment as she passed by their open doors.

Dot had pressed her to stay the night or at least leave Jack as the weather was so bad, but Jeannie didn't want to, although she felt it was kind of Dot to suggest it. Her greatest and only pleasure was to have Jack with her, to feel his warm little body curled next to hers, to see his cheeky smile when he explored her mouth with his fingers or pulled on her hair. She loved him more than life itself and knew with an absolute certainty that he loved her.

If there were times when she had fleeting thoughts of Ethan, she didn't admit them even to herself. They had no future together, not now that she had made such a terrible mistake. An error that would last for ever, for while it was possible that Ethan might one day make a life with someone else she was tied to Harry whether or not he lived with her. Emptiness, bare and desolate, stretched before her, and although her circumstances had improved since she had found work she could see nothing but hardship and struggle ahead, lonely and alone.

'I want to ask you something, Mary.'

On a Sunday morning in Scarborough Josh had come to Mary's door and been invited in. She was wearing a white apron which came to her ankles and her thick hair was tucked beneath a bonnet. On the table was a large mixing bowl, a bag of flour, a bowl containing dried fruit, a lump of suet and a grater. A pan was simmering on the fire, its lid rattling.

He wrinkled his nose. 'What are you making? Christmas pudding?'

'Cloutie dumpling.' She smiled. 'My mother's recipe. It's something like Christmas pudding. I'm cooking one now to try and preparing another for Christmas morning. You can have a taste when it's ready, if you like.' She busied herself about the table, wondering what he was going to ask that was so important that it couldn't wait for when they next met. 'Will you be going to Susan's for Christmas?'

'I've been asked,' he nodded. 'We all have. I don't know if Ethan will accept. He says he's not up to company and he's a lot of last-minute particulars to see to before January.'

'You'll be sure of a feast,' she said, thinking of the butcher who had married his eldest daughter.

'Aye,' he agreed. 'Robin's a good chap. Our Susan couldn't have done better.' He sat down as invited. 'What'll you do? Are Tom and Sarah coming?'

Her face clouded a little. 'They'll come over, but Sarah wants to cook dinner in her own home. Understandable, as this is their first Christmas together,' she said, adding quickly, before he could announce that he would forgo his day with his children to spend it with her, or invite her to join them, 'I'm going to cook dinner here and take it up to Aggie's. She's failing fast. She might not make another Christmas.'

Ever considerate, she always made sure that her mother-in-law had everything she needed, including her company.

'I wanted to ask you something, Mary,' he repeated. 'Though you must say no if you think you can't do it.'

Josh seemed anxious, and she wondered, not for the first time, if he was totally committed to this new

381

venture of Ethan's. He wanted to support his son, she knew that, but she questioned privately whether his reasoning for doing so was sound. He was worried about Ethan; that much he had confided in her. Ethan was dissatisfied with his life. Off-shore fishing made little money and it seemed that Ethan was determined to establish himself in a bigger way, especially now that he had attracted capital from a Hull businessman.

Ethan had sought her out after his return from Hull and told her he had seen Jeannie. She'd asked him how she fared, and how her grandson was. He'd hesitated for only a second, but that was enough for her to know that not all was well with her daughter even though he had gone on to add 'Jack's a fine boy' and 'Jeannie was having dinner with relations of her husband's', implying that she was surrounded by family. But it hadn't escaped Mary's notice that he didn't mention whether Jeannie looked well and happy.

'Is it Ethan?' she asked Josh now. 'Is he doing the right thing?'

'Oh, yeh,' he answered vaguely. 'The capital's secure and the ship's almost ready, or will be by January.'

'And you feel you have to go with him?' She raised her eyebrows. 'You used to believe that fathers and sons shouldn't sail together.'

'I still do,' he said glumly. 'That's why I won't let Stephen come on this trip, even though he wants to. And that's what I want to talk to you about.'

Mary waited patiently whilst Josh took his time to explain what was bothering him.

'I'm only sailing with Ethan on this first trip to

show that I'm behind him in this venture. He seems to think that he's failed since the paddle steamer project didn't come off, though why he should think that I don't know. He's got his own smack and a half share in another, or he did have until he sold it for this new ship. But it's not enough; it's as if he has to prove himself.'

He sat staring at the pan bubbling on the fire. 'But it's Stephen I'm bothered about. Ida and Nancy would go to Susan if anything happened to me, but Stephen'll need a firm hand for a few years yet.'

'You don't have to go,' she said gently. 'Ethan is well able to manage without you. He'll have a good crew.'

He looked up at her. 'I know. But don't you see, Mary? By going with him I'm telling him that I believe in him, showing him that I'm confident this company he's forming will go from strength to strength.'

'Fishing is a hazardous occupation which ever way you look at it,' Mary said. 'No matter how much money you put into it you're still at the mercy of the sea.'

He nodded slowly. 'That's why I'm asking you.' He stood up and caught hold of her floury hands. 'Mary! If I don't come back, and I'm as sure as I can be that I will, will you have Stephen?'

Mary caught her breath. Once before she had thought he was going to ask her to marry him, but he hadn't. Some sixth sense perhaps or maybe something in her manner had told him that she would refuse him; and now she had mistakenly come to the same conclusion. Strangely, she felt a stab of disappointment. He wanted her to watch over his youngest motherless son, the infant she had held in her arms when his mother had died and since then had discreetly watched over as he grew into the rough and tumble of adolescence.

She gave him a warm smile. 'I will be very angry with you if you don't come back, Josh,' she said. 'But you know that I will always take care of Stephen. He can depend on a home with me.'

CHAPTER FORTY-THREE

An icy fog hovered over Hessle Road as Jeannie pushed Jack in the pram towards the Boulevard on Christmas morning. From the estuary came the low haunting shivering moan of ships' horns as vessels sent greetings to one another. Church bells rang out and people hurrying towards church or chapel, friends or relatives, greeted others as they passed.

'Good morning. G'morning. Season's greetings. All 'best.'

Jeannie responded to each passing stranger with a forced smile or a nod and a mouthed, inaudible 'Thank you, same to you'.

She did not feel full of seasonal cheer and it had taken a great deal of effort to get herself and Jack ready to come out. She had looked in on Mrs Herbert who was sitting in front of her fire, not knitting, not sewing, not reading, but merely contemplating the flames.

'Will you be cooking dinner today, Mrs Herbert?' Jeannie had shouted, for the old lady's deafness was getting worse.

'No, dear,' she replied. 'I've got a drop of stew left from yesterday. There's enough for me. I don't eat much.'

To see her sitting alone on Christmas Day had depressed Jeannie. Yet her landlady had responded with a positive smile as if she were content with her lot. I suppose she's used to being alone; having a roof over her head and sufficient food she'll consider to be luxuries, Jeannie thought.

But the overwhelming lowness of spirit, the fear even, which gripped her was that it might one day be her sitting alone on a Christmas morning, and the reason for that fear was that Harry had hammered on her door the night before, demanding to be let in.

He wasn't drunk – she could perhaps have forgiven him if he had been – but he had been drinking and he berated her when she refused his advances.

'There'll be no money for you if you don't,' he'd slurred, bending his face towards her.

'And if I get pregnant again, what then?' she rebutted, backing away from his beery breath. 'Will you run to Connie like last time?'

He'd shaken a fist at her. 'Don't you talk about Connie,' he bellowed. 'She's my friend. Allus has been.'

He'd thrown a few coins on the table and walked out of the door, leaving her shaking and afraid for her future.

As she walked towards the Greenwoods' house now, she chastised herself for her ineptitude and spinelessness, telling herself that she could survive without him; that in fact she would have to survive without him and that she was very lucky to have kinder people around her. Dot had admonished her a few days before for not taking Jack home in the pram. 'For heaven's sake, girl. Am I such an ogre?'

she'd said. 'I'd hardly keep it in 'hall as an ornament, now would I?'

Jeannie had been ashamed of herself for the misunderstanding. It was such a generous gift that she had felt she shouldn't take advantage; now she realized that Dot was big-hearted to her very core.

Jack's bright eyes looked out at her from beneath the pram hood, and his likeness to Harry struck her so forcibly that she wanted to weep. His eyes were now as brown as his father's; his hair was dark like hers and Harry's. He clapped his hands as they reached Dot and Sam's house, and Minnie opened the door and ran down the steps to help Jeannie with the pram.

'Has anybody else arrived yet, Minnie?' Jeannie asked.

'Onny Billy Norman,' Minnie said, bending to tickle Jack under his chin. 'I don't know who else is coming apart from Mr Greenwood's sister. We've enough food for an army so it doesn't matter who comes, cos there'll still be enough food for 'rest of 'week and into 'next decade, which Mr Greenwood is discussing this very 'minute.'

Billy shot out of the house and down the steps; he'd seen Jeannie and Minnie from the window as they struggled to lift the pram.

'Here,' he told Jeannie. 'You carry 'bairn and I'll fetch 'pram in. They could do wi' a ramp. I could mek one if Mrs Greenwood wants me to.'

'You're a marvel, Billy,' Jeannie murmured as she lifted Jack out from beneath his blankets and felt around for the cloutie dumpling, which she'd wrapped carefully in a clean cloth and placed at the bottom of the pram, well away from Jack's kicking feet. 'But Dot – Mrs Greenwood – might not want one on her front steps.'

'She's tekking care of 'bairn, isn't she?' he responded. 'That's what Rosie said, so she won't be bothered. But Sam might be, o' course. Lets 'tone down, you know!'

Jeannie smiled; a genuine smile this time. Billy was such an amazing tonic. She hoped that Rosie appreciated what a treasure he was.

Sam Greenwood was pouring sherry as she went into the large sitting room overlooking the street.

'Only a small one, please,' Jeannie said. She had never tasted sherry before and didn't know if she would like it. 'Is Rosie about?' she asked, for neither Rosie nor Dot was there to greet her. She unwrapped Jack from his blankets and shawls and placed him on the floor, where he sat gazing solemnly up at Sam and Billy.

'They're in 'kitchen basting 'goose. Been in and out all morning checking on it and draining off 'fat. Smells good,' he added.

The Greenwoods didn't have a cook. Dot liked to think she cooked her own food, but in fact it was the maid of all work Minnie who prepared the dishes ready for Dot to add the finishing touches to and put in the oven. Minnie also cleaned the house and washed the linen, but she seemed happy enough in her work and was paid well. She had her own room at the top of the house, and today because it was Christmas she would eat with the family after helping to serve.

Rosie came in; she looked very pretty, plump and rosy-cheeked from the oven's heat, Jeannie thought. 'The dumpling needs some more cooking.'

Jeannie handed the wrapped pudding over. 'Just to warm it through. I hope it's all right,' she added shyly. 'It's the first time I've made one.'

Rosie sniffed at it. 'Smells lovely,' she said. 'Do you want to come through to 'kitchen?' She lifted her eyebrows and gave a vague lift of her head towards the door, indicating that Jeannie should follow her.

Jeannie put down her sherry glass and picked Jack up. She smiled at Billy and Sam, saying that she wouldn't be long, and was surprised to see Billy give her a furtive wink.

'What?' she whispered to Rosie out in the wide hall. 'What's wrong?'

'Nothing, I hope, but Billy's going to tell Uncle Sam that he wants to mek an announcement.'

'About what?' It was clear to Jeannie that Rosie was excited about something, and whatever it was it was that and not the heat of the oven that was giving her the pretty flush on her cheeks.

Rosie pressed her fingers to her mouth. 'Billy's asked me to marry him! And I said yes! He's going to tell Sam and announce it at dinner time.'

Jeannie was thrilled for her, but felt a sudden rush of emotion; she swallowed down tears and said in a choked voice, 'I'm really happy for you, Rosie. Billy is so nice – and reliable. He'll never let you down.'

Rosie nodded. 'Not like somebody else that we won't name, eh?' She touched Jeannie's arm and said, 'If it hadn't been for you, I might not have come to my senses about Billy.'

Jeannie thought how very different Rosie seemed from when she had first met her, though she conceded that maybe it wasn't Rosie who was different but the circumstances. They had both been influenced by other people, Rosie by Nan's attitude and Jeannie by Connie's fabrication and lies about Rosie.

The doorbell rang as they were about to go into the kitchen. Rosie opened the door to a large lady warmly dressed in a coat with a fur collar and a large hat with fluttering feathers.

'Let me in then,' she snapped. 'It's cold out here.'

'You're well wrapped up.' Rosie opened the door wider, letting in a blast of freezing air. 'Nice coat. This is Jeannie, Harry's wife,' she said. 'This is Mrs Welburn, Jeannie, Uncle Sam's sister. She comes every Christmas Day.' She turned her head towards Jeannie so that Mrs Welburn couldn't see her face and cast up her eyes towards the ceiling as if looking for solace.

'I'd come more often if I was invited,' Mrs Welburn said, barely glancing at Jeannie as she shed her coat. 'Where's 'maid? Has she been given 'day off?'

Dot appeared to rescue them. 'No, she's in 'kitchen and she didn't want 'day off,' she answered her sister-in-law. 'She'd rather stop with us. Give us your coat, Bessie. Is it new? I'll hang it up. Hello, Jeannie love. Merry Christmas. And how's this fine boy today?'

Jack gave Dot a big smile and put his arms out to her; she took him and Jeannie felt suddenly bereft.

They all trooped back into the sitting room where Sam poured more sherry; Billy stood with his back to the fire and a tankard of ale in his hand, and moved over so that Sam's sister could sit nearest the blaze while she delicately pursed her lips and took a sip of sherry. When Jeannie glanced at him, he gave a little nod, and couldn't hold back a grin.

Mike Gardiner called in on his way to his son's

390

house to wish everybody greetings for the festive season. He said, 'How do, Bessie,' to Mrs Welburn and she gave him a frosty smile in answer.

At two o' clock they were seated at table waiting for the meal to be served. They were in a dining room with red flocked wallpaper, dark mahogany furniture, heavy curtains and a blazing coal fire. In one corner stood a Christmas tree with flickering candles. Jack crowed at it and clapped his hands as he sat in a wooden high chair that Dot had acquired from somebody she knew who had no further need of it.

It was incredible, Jeannie thought, how many people Dot knew who were about to get rid of something they didn't want any more that was just what Dot was looking for. The reason, she surmised, was that Dot, in spite of coming up in the world through Sam's endeavours, had kept her feet on the ground and stayed in touch with nearly all the people she had ever known.

'You are the only people I know who eat dinner so early,' Bessie commented sourly. 'Personally I never eat before seven.'

'We get hungry,' Dot said placidly, 'and it's 'way we all were brought up, in case you've forgotten, Bessie. Dinner was allus at dinner time, midday. We're late today cos it's Christmas. Pour everybody a glass of wine, Sam, and I'll give Minnie a hand to dish up. Rosie, come and help me.'

Sam's sister gave a rebuking sniff at another dereliction of what was right and proper and the casualness of the domestic situation. She almost fainted when Dot mentioned that Minnie would be eating with them.

'I cannot understand your wife,' she told Sam when Dot and Rosie had left the room. 'She has no sense of propriety or moral duty. The servant will abuse her position if she doesn't know her place.' She shuddered. 'And as for eating at 'same table!'

'She's been with us for six years, Bessie, and is 'daughter of one of Dot's best friends from 'old days,' Sam said mildly. 'We know who she is and she knows who we are and what we were. There's no reason for her to eat alone in 'kitchen when there's room at our table.'

Jeannie's opinion of Sam changed dramatically. She had thought him an overbearing man who had done well for himself and forgotten his roots, unlike his wife. Clearly she was wrong. I've been wrong about so many things, she thought as she waited and looked and listened and tried to keep Jack entertained, for he objected to being fastened in a chair when there were so many exciting things to explore.

'So where's Harry?' Bessie turned to Jeannie. 'He's never away on a trip at Christmas!'

'No,' Jeannie answered quietly. 'I don't know where he is, to be honest.'

Bessie hmphed. 'In some pub, I expect. That's where most of 'fishermen can be found.'

'Not all of 'em, Mrs Welburn,' Billy broke in, and found himself the object of hostile scrutiny. 'Most of 'em like to be at their own fireside.'

Jeannie became aware that Sam was looking at her, and when she met his eyes she thought she saw sympathy there before he transferred his gaze to his sister.

'Harry's not here cos he prefers to be somewhere

392

else, Bessie,' he murmured. 'You'll understand that more'n anybody. So we'll say no more on 'subject.'

Bessie's face flooded bright red and to cover her embarrassment she reached for a handkerchief and made a pretence of blowing her nose. Jeannie was astonished by the progression of meddlesome question to swift expressive answer, but the moment was over, done and finished with as Dot and Rosie, followed by Minnie, processed into the room laden with trays and dishes and an enormous platter holding a massive golden goose stuffed with sage and plum.

Sam carved at the table whilst Dot and Rosie put out dishes of crisp roast potatoes, buttered turnips, sprouts, parsnips, red cabbage and creamed leeks, and Minnie dashed back to the kitchen to bring in the plum sauce and onion gravy.

Jeannie had never in her life seen so much food served at one time, and Jack banged the tray of his chair with a spoon in his eagerness to try it.

'Here, give him a parsnip to chew on.' Dot deftly forked a sliver of parsnip to hand to Jeannie, who gave it to Jack to suck on.

When they were all served, Sam raised his glass. 'To all at our table and our brave lads at sea. God bless us all.'

As if on cue, the doorbell rang. Minnie got up to answer it. There was a murmur of voices out in the hall, and Dot called out, 'Tell whoever it is to come in, Minnie. Your dinner's getting cold.'

Minnie stood by the dining room door, pressing her lips together, and looked from Dot to Jeannie. 'It's Harry Carr, Mrs Greenwood. He's asking if his wife's here.'

CHAPTER FORTY-FOUR

Harry ran his finger round his shirt neck, clearly embarrassed at arriving as they were eating, but his gaze fell on the groaning table and involuntarily he licked his lips.

'Would you like to stay to dinner, Harry?' Dot asked. 'There's plenty.'

Jeannie hoped he would say no. She wouldn't be able to eat with him sitting at the same table and pretending that there was nothing wrong between them. As it was, his sudden appearance had curbed her appetite.

Jack looked up at Harry. He was still gnawing on the parsnip. 'Na na na na,' he chortled, holding up the wet and sticky vegetable towards Harry. Harry seemed confused, and clearly had no idea how to respond to the child.

'He's offering you some of his dinner, Harry,' Jeannie said softly. 'Can you pretend to take a bite?'

Harry gazed blankly at her and gave a shake of his head. 'I'll just have a slice o' meat, Auntie Dot,' he said. 'Is it chicken?'

'No, it's goose.' Dot asked Minnie to pass another plate. 'Would you like some plum sauce on it?'

'Yes please.' Harry watched as Sam carved two

thick slices of goose and put them on a plate. Everybody else sat with their cutlery suspended over their own meal whilst Harry was served. He sat down at the table next to Minnie, who shuffled up to make room.

'So, you're still wi' Humber Steam 'n' Fishing, I tek it?' Sam asked, filling what seemed to Jeannie a long-drawn-out silence. 'They're a good company to work for.'

The slightest of wavering on Harry's part as he paused with his fork to his mouth before answering 'Yeh' alerted Jeannie to the fact that he was not telling the truth. He's not! He's left or been asked to leave!

'So when's your next trip? Are they winter fleeting?'

'Yeh. I'm, er – I'm not going till 'New Year.' He said no more until his plate was empty, and then pushed back his chair. 'That were grand, Auntie Dot; thank you.'

He stood for a moment biting his lip and then looked at Jeannie, who hadn't touched her meal, and took a breath.

'I'll be off now and let you all get on wi' your Christmas dinner, but I just want to say – well, to thank you really, for havin' Jeannie and 'bairn here today, cos I don't know what she would've done otherwise. I called round to Strickland Street this morning but I hadn't got owt planned, so it would've been a dowly sort o' Christmas for her wi'out you.'

He came, Jeannie thought, and I'd already left. But what was his intention? After his outburst yesterday what else had he to say to me?

'And so, what I want to say,' he repeated, 'in front

395

of everybody' – Harry looked down for a moment before glancing again at Jeannie – 'is that after 'next trip I'll try to get myself sorted out. I've been a bit lost lately – well, since Nan died, I suppose, an' trying to get a decent ship an' all that – but come 'New Year I'll try to get some kind o' life together for us; an' that I'm sorry. Sorry for 'way I've behaved, Jeannie. You never deserved any of it.'

There was a momentary silence. Sam cleared his throat, frowning as if he didn't understand what all that was about. Dot rubbed at her nose. Rosie kept her eyes on Billy, who was staring at his plate, and Minnie continued eating as if she hadn't heard a word. Bessie's eyebrows were raised and she wore an expression of inquisitive interest.

Jeannie rose from the table. 'I'll see you out, Harry,' she said, as if she were the mistress of the house and not Dot, and walked out of the room ahead of him.

'I meant what I said, Jeannie,' he said in a low voice as she opened the front door. 'I'll do me best, but it's been awkward. You know what I'm saying, don't you?'

She nodded. It would be awkward with Connie in the threesome. Jeannie sighed. Connie wouldn't go easily, that was for sure, but that was Harry's problem and he would have to deal with it, not her.

'You don't believe me, do you?'

'I want to, Harry.' Her voice trembled. 'I want to for Jack's sake as much as yours and mine. I don't want him to grow up without a father. I had to, and I know it wasn't easy for my mother to manage alone.' She swallowed. 'But after your next trip . . .' the solution had come to her only as she thought of her mother's early struggle with two small children to bring up '. . . if you haven't sorted out your life and decided who you want to be with . . .' her breath was catching in her throat and it was as if a band was tightening round her chest as she tried to hold back her emotion '. . . then I shall leave Hull and go back to Scarborough.'

It was the only answer, she thought as she walked back towards Strickland Street. Billy and Rosie had come part of the way with her until finally, on her insistence that she would be all right now she was on the well-lit Hessle Road, they had turned back. Billy hadn't made his announcement after all. He said it didn't seem right, and Jeannie understood that. Harry's arrival had put a damper on the occasion.

'But you'll tell them, won't you?' she asked.

Rosie said they'd decided to wait until Bessie had left and Dot and Sam were alone. 'She's very nosy,' Rosie said. 'And she'd love to be 'first to spread 'news.'

A blizzard of snow came down as Jeannie went on, and Jack crowed with delight as the flakes landed on the pram but disappeared between his mittened hands as he tried to catch them. The sky was heavy with low grey cloud. Dot had said she could stay the night, but as ever Jeannie was afraid of taking any offer for granted, so that if, or more likely when, she was really in need she would feel she could ask for help without being thought to be taking advantage.

Yes, I'll definitely go home to Scarborough if Harry's intentions come to nothing, and if Ma doesn't mind. She'll help me with Jack, I know she will, and we can work together as we did before and pool our wages.

The fire was still warm when she stepped into her room and she thought that perhaps Harry had put on a piece of coal when he'd called earlier, but in fact it was Mrs Herbert who had done that, as she discovered when she put her head round the door to her room and told her she was back.

'There's been a young man looking for you,' the old lady said. 'I told him I thought you'd gone to relatives for your dinner.' She nodded amiably. 'I put a lump of coal on 'fire, I hope that was all right. Didn't want you coming home to a cold room.'

'Thank you, Mrs Herbert, that was kind of you,' she shouted. 'It's very cold out and snowing hard!'

'Would you like to sit in here?' Mrs Herbert asked. 'It's a bit warmer than in 'front room.'

Jeannie eagerly agreed. It was much warmer. The window at the front was frozen on the inside as well as out and patterned with shapes of iced flowers and leaves. Mrs Herbert had a bright fire glowing in her hearth and the kettle was steaming over it. Jeannie lifted Jack out of his pram and joined her.

'I've been thinking, m'dear,' Mrs Herbert said. 'You could live in here wi' me during 'day and just leave a small fire in your room for bed time. We could share 'expense of 'coal,' she added, and Jeannie thought there was an appeal in her expression.

It was quite a good idea, she thought. In Mrs Herbert's middle room a fireplace with a boxed-in grate and an ash can beneath it burned better and warmer and more economically than the one in the front. Two bars across it made it possible to boil a kettle or pan more easily than on her open fire.

'I'd like that, Mrs Herbert,' she shouted. 'It'll be warmer for Jack.' She was terrified that he would catch cold, which could so easily turn to pneumonia, and there was no cure for that.

They sat together by Mrs Herbert's fire. Jack was sleeping in a chair wrapped in a blanket and Jeannie was deep in thought about her future, a future which she felt would not include Harry. She couldn't envisage their patching up any kind of relationship. Connie was unlikely to let him go, and Harry, who, she admitted, was weak when confronted by emotion, wouldn't want to upset her. She jumped when Mrs Herbert suddenly stirred herself.

'I had a visitor,' she said. 'After you'd gone out.'

Jeannie nodded. 'Yes,' she said loudly. 'It was my husband, Harry.'

'No, dear. Not him. My brother.'

Jeannie expressed surprise. She hadn't known Mrs Herbert had a brother; she'd assumed she was without any relatives.

'Three brothers and two sisters I had,' she told her. 'But onny one brother left. He's younger than me. He married a woman from across 'river, River Hull that is, and went to live in Marfleet. Haven't seen him in a long time.'

Jeannie shook her head. She didn't know where Marfleet was, but she had gleaned from various conversations that 'across 'river', although the same town, was akin to a foreign country.

'Anyway, she died at beginning of 'year and he wants to come back to Hessle Road. He still thinks of it as home, you see, and as he's no bairns . . . well, he's found a house to rent and wants me to go and live wi' him. Says we'll be company for each other an' he doesn't like to think of me being by m'self.'

Jeannie's spirits dropped like a stone. She thought that she seemed to stagger from one crisis to another.

'So I've decided that I will,' Mrs Herbert went on, 'and what I thought was, when I flit, in 'New Year, then mebbe you could tek over me rent book. I'm not in arrears. What do you think?'

She didn't know what to think and tossed and turned in her bed that night as she went over various possibilities. She couldn't afford the rent for the whole house, that was certain. Perhaps if I found someone else to share with. Or perhaps I could let the upstairs rooms in the summer if they dry out. She had already explored the two bedrooms and found the walls running with water from broken guttering and loose roof tiles, and a strong smell of damp and decay. Mrs Herbert had told her that she'd reported it to the landlord's agent but he had only shrugged and shaken his head at the impossibility of getting it put right.

I have to get a better job with more hours, she thought as she lay wide awake. But what about Jack?

Jack whimpered beside her and gave a little cough and a cry. She held him close, giving him the little warmth she had. His arms and legs were cold, but his forehead was burning hot. She reached for her shawl; it felt cold and damp so she wrapped it around herself to warm it before putting it over Jack. He fell into a light sleep and she tucked him tightly beneath the bedclothes, then got out of bed and padded through Mrs Herbert's room into the scullery, which was freezing cold. Her toes curled on the bare floor. She picked up a jug of milk and a small saucepan and stole back to her room.

'*Please* don't let him be ill,' she muttered to herself. 'I'll die if anything should happen to him.' The fire was only just warm but she poured a little milk into the pan and placed it over the embers until steam rose.

She sat with the child on her knee, both of them wrapped in all the shawls and blankets she possessed, and holding him close to her body she spooned the warm milk into his mouth. He coughed again and she cringed at the husky rattling sound, but he opened his mouth for more milk.

'That's it, my precious boy,' she murmured. 'Drink it all up.'

He looked at her with his appealing moist brown eyes and his mouth trembled. She smiled down at him, reassuring him, touching his cheek with her finger. 'Your ma will make it better.'

CHAPTER FORTY-FIVE

The following day Jeannie huddled near the fire in Mrs Herbert's room with Jack on her knee. When he wasn't coughing, he lay lethargic and listless with his face pressed to her chest and she was distressed that her milk was gone and she wasn't able to offer him even that comfort. But then she looked down at his pale face and saw his little mouth sucking on her blouse as if he was feeding and she undid her buttons and put him to her breast.

Mrs Herbert kept her supplied with weak tea and slices of stale bread and sat with her, not talking, for which Jeannie was grateful. She had nothing to say. All she wished for was that Jack would recover, and soon.

When he fell asleep, she placed him in her chair, covered him with a blanket and went outside to the privy. The yard was thick with crisp unmarked snow and she padded across it feeling the cold seeping through her shawl and boots. We could be snowed in, she thought. I wouldn't be able to push the pram through this even if I dared take Jack out.

When she came back into the house she thought there wasn't much difference in temperature between the outside and the scullery except that the wind outside was keener than that which found its way beneath the wooden back door and swirled around her feet. She heaved on the pump handle over the sink to draw water to wash her hands, but it only creaked and groaned and no water came out. As she stood there, wondering what to do, Mrs Herbert opened the door and came into the scullery. 'Pump's been frozen since this morning. It happens every winter, so I had 'forethought to fill a bucket last night. So if you want a cup o' tea just ladle 'water into 'kettle.'

'I wanted to wash my hands,' Jeannie said. 'Is there enough to do that?'

Mrs Herbert shook her head. 'Can't waste good water,' she said. 'This is onny for cooking or drinking. Scoop up some snow into a pan for washing; that's what I usually do. Or sometimes I don't bother,' she added.

For three more days and nights Jeannie held Jack on her knee, letting him sleep if he could or when he was restless feeding him a drop of broth or sometimes warm water from a spoon. She thought he was worsening; his breathing was laboured, squeaks and gurgles coming from his chest, and she was frantic with worry.

'I don't know what to do, Mrs Herbert,' she wept. Tears ran down her cheeks. 'I wish my ma was here.'

Mrs Herbert pushed her shawl back from her forehead; beneath it she wore a woollen hat. 'I don't know what to tell you,' she said. 'I never had any bairns. If I could get out I could mebbe fetch a neighbour, but then what could they do?' She shook her head. 'But I'm afeared o' falling.'

Jeannie sniffed away her tears. 'No, you mustn't go

out. The snow's over the doorstep, and I daren't go out either.' She dared not leave Jack in Mrs Herbert's care; he might become worse whilst she was out, or fall out of the chair into the fire, or crawl into the cold scullery to look for her. Besides, whom would she ask for help? There was Mrs Norman, but what could she do that Jeannie couldn't? It would take too long to walk to Dot and Sam's house. No, she would have to manage as best she could, although already they were out of milk and bread, the water bucket was almost empty and they were rationing their tea. The only blessing was that there was still a little coal left and each day, when Jack had dropped asleep, Jeannie put on her work boots and warmest shawl and shovelled it from the coal house into a hod and brought it into the scullery.

'Where's 'babby's father?' Mrs Herbert asked at the end of the third day. 'Why isn't he here to look after you?'

Jeannie blinked. She had been so concerned about Jack that she hadn't given Harry a single thought. Yes, she thought, where is Harry? He won't have gone to sea yet. He said he was sailing in the New Year. Are we in the New Year? I don't know what day it is. I haven't heard the church bells or the sound of the ships' horns. It seemed a lifetime since she had spent Christmas Day with Dot and her family.

'He's left me, Mrs Herbert,' she said simply. 'I don't know where he is.' Though I can guess, she thought. 'Do you know what day it is?' She felt light-headed, unable to think straight. 'Are we in the New Year?'

'Not yet, dear. It's onny Sunday.' Mrs Herbert nodded her head and smiled. 'Somebody'll come lookin' for us now. I'll have been missed at chapel

404

and I dare say your family will come knocking to ask if you and 'bairn are all right. Where did you say your husband was? At sea, did you say? Funny time o' year to be away. Never known anybody go to sea at Christmas.'

Jeannie nodded. Sometimes that was all the response that Mrs Herbert needed: not an answer, just an acknowledgement that she had been heard.

And she was right. The next morning just after daybreak there was a knocking at the front door. It was Minnie, dressed in a long warm coat and shawl, and a woollen hat around her ears and another shawl on top of that.

'I couldn't get round 'back,' she said. 'Snow's half-way up 'gate.'

'I know.' Jeannie let her in and Minnie stood looking round the room.

'Don't you have a fire?' she asked in a shocked voice. 'How are you keeping warm?'

Jeannie led her into the middle room. 'I'm staying with Mrs Herbert,' she explained. 'We've been sharing the coal and the food, what little there was. Jack's been ill, and I haven't been able to get out.' She couldn't help the catch in her voice. 'I think he's still weak, though he's not as chesty as he has been.'

'Poor bairn,' Minnie said, and knelt on the floor to say hello to him where he lay propped up in the chair.

Jack turned his head away as if he didn't know her and then looked up at Jeannie, his eyes brimming with tears. She softly caressed his cheek.

'What are you giving him?' Minnie asked.

Jeannie burst into tears. 'Only warm water with a bit of sugar. We've nothing left – no milk, no

405

bread, and the pump's frozen so now there's no more water.'

Minnie opened her mouth on a breath. 'Right,' she said, getting to her feet. 'I'll go and do some shopping.'

Jeannie shook her head and burst into a fresh onslaught of crying. 'I've no money. Nothing!'

Minnie jingled coins in her pocket. 'Mrs Greenwood gave me some when she asked me to come,' she said. 'I'd have been here afore but everybody's been badly; Mrs Greenwood, Mr Greenwood and Miss Rosie. I'm 'onny one that hasn't gone down with owt. I've been dashing about like a scalded hen since Boxing Day, mekkin' hot drinks and keeping 'fires going.' She adjusted her shawl and turned up her collar. 'You wouldn't believe 'number of folks who are sick.' She pursed her mouth and looked at Mrs Herbert. 'And some old folk've succumbed to influenza. Parson's going to be busy.'

Jeannie felt as if a weight had been lifted from her shoulders and Mrs Herbert heaved a great sigh as Minnie went out. 'I was getting worried, I admit,' the old lady said stoically. 'I was onny thinking that I'd have to brave 'weather and go out and beg some bones from 'butcher to mek some soup.'

'We've no water,' Jeannie reminded her.

'No,' Mrs Herbert said. 'But we've got plenty of snow; we'd have had to use that.'

Minnie came back with bread, milk and cheese, onions and carrots and a slice of tender beef steak which she seared in a pan on the fire. Jeannie could hear her grumbling when she went back into the scullery to chop up the onions and carrots. 'Sweet Jesus, it's freezing in here.'

She came back into the room a few minutes later with the pan of meat and vegetables and a dollop of snow and placed it on the fire; she brought bread and cheese on a plate for Jeannie and Mrs Herbert, and for Jack a bowl of pobs, bread soaked in warm milk and sweetened with sugar. She knelt down beside Jeannie and gently urged Jack to open his mouth, which he did, like a little bird.

'Thank you.' Jeannie felt the tears welling up again. 'You're so kind. I don't know how I can ever repay you.'

'Oh, don't worry about that,' Minnie said, spooning another helping into Jack's open mouth. 'I'll think o' summat. Oh, and I've ordered a sack o' coal,' she added as a matter of fact. 'Stew'll tek for ever to cook on that fire. It'll be here later this morning.'

Billy called that evening after work, bringing a handcart full of wood for the fire. He'd been to see Rosie, who was still recovering from her bout of illness, and Minnie had told him about Jeannie trapped in the house with a sick child. He built up the fire with wood and coal and then suggested he should make a fire in Jeannie's room.

'It doesn't do to let 'room get too cold,' he said. 'It'll get damp.'

'It's damp already,' Jeannie told him. 'That's why Jack got ill.' She watched him as he knelt by the hearth, screwing up paper in the grate and then placing sticks and coal over it. 'Have you seen anything of Harry?'

'Not since Christmas Day. I was about to ask you 'same thing,' he said, concentrating on what he was doing. He lit a match and set fire to the paper. 'You might as well forget about him, Jeannie.' He didn't look at her but kept his eyes on the flame as it curled and blackened the edges of the paper and singed the wood. 'He was allus my best mate, even though I knew his faults, just as he knew mine.' At last he turned to look up at her. 'But I'm telling you now, he'll not come back. If he hasn't been to see if you and 'bairn are all right over Christmas, then he'll not be coming.'

'But he said – in front of everybody . . .' Her voice faltered. Why was she fooling herself?

Billy shook his head. 'He won't come. Connie won't let him.'

Billy told her that Harry had left the Humber Steam Company and signed on with a company called M and R. An old established company, he said, but not one that Jeannie had heard of.

'It used to be Masterson and Rayner,' he told her as he buttoned up his jacket. 'They were big in whaling at one time, so I understand, but 'name was changed a few years back to M and R. I think there's still a Rayner in 'company. They've got four or five ships.'

He changed the subject and told her that Dot wanted her to go and stay with them, but she quickly said she couldn't take Jack out yet.

'Not yet,' he agreed. 'But what about next Saturday? He should be a fair bit better by then – and you know what?'

Jeannie shook her head. Billy was always full of good ideas.

'What if I make a sledge for 'pram? You could wrap him up in warm blankets, put him in 'pram and we'll fit it on 'sledge and I'll pull it. 'Snow's deep in places but you could hold it steady by 'handle and we'd get there in no time.'

She laughed. Maybe it would work, but then she thought of leaving Mrs Herbert on her own and worried over that.

'You could fetch her as well, Dot wouldn't mind, but I doubt if 'old lass could walk that far,' Billy said, and he was right as usual, for when Jeannie asked her she said she'd be quite content at home now that she had coal and food, and would wait for the thaw.

'You forget, dear,' she said to Jeannie later, 'I've been through quite a few cold winters.' She paused for a moment. 'But I don't recall another quite as cold as this one.'

On the following evening, which was New Year's Eve, Jeannie and Mrs Herbert sat by the fire drinking tea whilst Jack slept peacefully in his pram, which Billy had brought through from the front room. At midnight Jeannie heard the ships' horns hooting and the sound of merrymaking out in the streets.

'It's the New Year, Mrs Herbert,' she said, her voice cracking. 'I wish you good health.'

'And 'same to you, m'dear,' the old lady responded, 'and to 'bonny bairn. Good luck in all you do.'

Jeannie swallowed hard and nodded, but couldn't help the tears which trickled down her cheeks. A new year and a new decade too. Surely things will change for the better. She gave a deep sigh. They surely can't get any worse.

CHAPTER FORTY-SIX

Dot greeted them effusively the following Saturday when Billy brought them to her house and Jack's face lit up when he saw her, though he was at first reluctant to go to her. Gradually, though, he climbed off Jeannie's knee and staggered unsteadily towards her. Dot lifted him up on to her lap.

'If he settles with me,' she said to Jeannie, 'why don't you go out for a walk? I know it's cold but you could do wi' some fresh air to sharpen you up.'

Jeannie smiled. 'I've just walked here,' she said. 'Through the snow!'

Dot nodded. 'What I should have said was why don't you take a walk and see who's about; like Harry for instance.'

Jeannie told her what Billy had said, and added that she didn't know where she would find him.

"Wassand Arms,' Dot said. 'It was allus his favourite.' She looked across at Jeannie. 'You could mebbe try, just one more time. Shame him if necessary.'

After their midday meal Jeannie grew restless. She had a headache; perhaps I should go out, she thought, I've been cooped up indoors for so long. Dot had insisted they must stay with them until after the thaw, which didn't appear to be imminent. It was bitterly cold, but the sky was blue and through the tall windows the sun was glorious on any unsullied snow, making it sparkle like crystal.

Jack had fallen asleep on Dot's knee and Dot herself was dozing. Jeannie lifted the child from her lap and placed him in a deep armchair, covering him with a shawl.

'I will take a walk,' she whispered to Dot, who nodded her head.

'He'll be all right wi' me,' she said sleepily. 'Don't worry.'

Jeannie told Minnie she was going out and asked her to keep an eye on Jack. Minnie gave her a warm coat and another shawl and a pair of woollen mittens, and told her to be careful not to slip as the footpaths were very icy.

The steps had been cleared and salted and once out on the Boulevard Jeannie took deep breaths which iced her nostrils and throat; her nose and ears tingled and she pulled the shawl further round her head. She reached Hessle Road and then hesitated, debating which way to go and wondering whether the choice she made would have any bearing on her future.

The heavy snow hadn't deterred anyone from coming out and the road was busy with shoppers and people going about their everyday business; horses pulling coal waggons were skittering on the packed snow and she heard the clang of heavy engines shunting in the railway yards. Men were shouting and there was raucous laughter coming from inns and hostelries. The laughter decided her. I will not be humiliated again, she thought, and hesitated only a moment more before heading towards St

Andrew's Dock, where she would enquire about M and R Shipping, the ships they owned, and when they would be sailing.

The fish quay was deserted on a Saturday afternoon, and she thought ruefully of the wages she had lost since Christmas and hoped she still had a job to go back to. Men were working on the ships, checking ropes and nets, swabbing decks, loading boxes and preparing for the next trip. There was ice floating in the dock, knocking against the hulls of the ships, and Jeannie shivered as she walked alongside. The vessels were mostly trawlers and paddle steamers, steam and diesel, and there were more than she could count; many tugs and coal barges too. She saw only two smacks, further along the dock, and curiosity propelled her feet in that direction.

One of the smacks was named the *Lincoln Maid* and two men were working on her; a little further along was the second smack tied alongside a trawler and her breath fluttered in her throat when she saw the name. The *Scarborough Girl*.

She stopped, huddling into her shawl and pressing her lips together. So Ethan had kept it after all, in spite of buying shares in another ship. Why hadn't he sold it and put the money towards the other? He's surely not sentimental over it? But of course, she realized, there'll be no market for smacks. The price of them would have dropped to rock bottom; there was no money in offshore fishing any more. Vessels were sailing further and further in search of a livelihood.

She walked on and came abreast of the trawler. She could hear men's voices from below calling to one another and some banter, then hammering and sawing. The ship looked as if it had been freshly painted and the deck was strewn with cables, blocks and nets, coiled ropes and fish boxes. Further along the dock was another trawler with the large letters M and R on the side and beneath it the name *Polar Star V.*

Curious, she walked on to take a look at it. So is this the ship that Harry is sailing on? She looks sound, as far as I can tell. Harry's been lucky if he's managed to get a ship with an old-established company. I hope he sticks with them this time. She shivered as the cold suddenly bit into her; she turned to go back the way she had come and found herself staring at the name of the trawler next to the coble. *Scarborough Girl.*

She swallowed hard. The same name. This must be Ethan's ship. There won't be anyone else's with that name. The smack was named for me, he said; she could hear his words clearly in her head. Is this ship named for some other Scarborough girl? Has Ethan named this for Pamela?

As she stood wondering two men came up from below. They were both dressed in thick clothing but one was head and shoulders taller than the other and wore a thick beard.

'Is that you, Jeannie?' Mike Gardiner called. 'Have you come to look at our new ship?'

She raised her hand in greeting. 'Hello, Mike,' she said, and then, 'Is it you, Ethan?' She forced her voice to be merry. 'I didn't recognize you beneath all those clothes and the long beard.'

Both men jumped ashore and Jeannie saw that Mike too was sporting a thicker beard than usual.

413

'I need a thick beard where we're going.' Ethan gazed at her. 'How are you, Jeannie?'

'I'm all right,' she said as brightly as she could. 'What about you? Ready for off?'

He nodded. 'Just about. Another couple of days. My da's sailing with us. He's coming by train on Monday.'

'Is he?' She was surprised by the news. She had thought that Josh would stick to local fishing. 'I'd like to see him – to ask him how my ma is.'

Ethan smiled, keeping his eyes on her. 'You could come and see us off,' he said.

'I don't think so,' Mike interrupted. 'They're a superstitious lot round here. They don't like their womenfolk anywhere near the docks when they're about to sail.'

Ethan raised his eyebrows. 'Jeannie was always on the harbour side when I was sailing,' he said softly. 'Remember?'

Jeannie felt herself blushing as she told him that she did. She recalled how she always used to watch for him bringing in his father's smack, even when they were children. She addressed herself to Mike. 'The M and R trawler,' she said, pointing over her shoulder. 'Is that their only one in the dock?'

Mike looked about him. 'No, there's another across on 'other side. *Arctic Star*, she's called. Why do you ask?'

'Oh, erm, Harry's sailing with them. I was curious, that's all.'

'Is he? Which ship? They're both ready to sail.'

'I'm not sure,' she said. 'I don't think he knows yet. He's – he's not sailed with them before.'

She saw Ethan's sharp glance at her and then at

Mike, and wondered if he would question Mike later as to why she didn't know the name of her husband's ship.

'They're a reliable company,' Mike said softly. 'Good strong ships and good company policy. They look after their men. They've had mixed fortunes over 'years, like everybody has, but they've allus survived. You don't need to worry, Jeannie.'

She knew from the way he spoke, so kindly and compassionately, that nothing escaped him. He probably knew all there was to know about Harry and Connie and even her own situation. She shivered again, feeling vaguely unwell.

'Would you like to come aboard?' Ethan asked. 'See what changes we've made.'

'It's going to mek our fortunes,' Mike said, grinning. 'It'll be a dynasty just like Masterson and Rayner. It had better be,' he added, 'for I've sunk everything I own into it.'

'I – I won't, thank you,' she said faintly. 'I'm feeling rather cold. I ought to get back.'

'Cold? You?' Ethan smiled as if disbelieving. 'That's not the harbour girl I once knew, out in all weathers. Where's your bairn, by the way? Is he well?'

'He's with Dot Greenwood. He's been ill,' she told him, pleased that he'd asked about Jack. 'They, erm, sort of rescued us and took us back to the Boulevard. Their house is warmer than mine – ours,' she added lamely.

She felt unsteady; her head pounded and the cold seemed to be creeping into her bones. She wondered if she had taken a chill. 'I'd better get off,' she muttered. 'He might be fretting for me, with him not being well, you know.'

Without any warning her knees buckled beneath her and Ethan and Mike both reached out towards her before she crashed to the ground. Ethan caught her, gathering her up in his arms.

'Jeannie! What's wrong?'

She couldn't speak; she had no breath and gulped down air, air so cold that it froze her throat and hurt her chest. She heard voices from a long way off, felt herself being lifted on board ship and taken below, where a blanket was wrapped round her and somebody put a cup to her mouth. She felt warm water on her lips and heard somebody say he'd fetch the waggon.

Everything that happened next was vague and insubstantial but she thought she was lifted up and carried back along the waterway; felt herself being placed in the back of a vehicle, her body protected by somebody else's, somebody's arms around her holding her safe.

She woke up later in a bed that wasn't her own. The bed was comfortable, much more so than Mrs Herbert's chair, the blankets were soft and against her feet was a warm brick, wrapped in a cloth; a bedside lamp was turned down, giving only a soft glow to the dark room.

She wanted to succumb to the comfort of it, but where was Jack? She called out for him and he was brought to her, but she wasn't allowed to hold him.

'Go to sleep now,' someone said. 'Everything's going to be all right. You've not been well, but you'll feel better in 'morning.'

'What happened?' she whispered. 'I was at the dock, looking at the ships.'

'You fainted, and Mike brought you home.'

Jeannie now recognized Dot's voice. 'He said he's allus rescuing you. Ethan was with him – he was right worried about you. Now will you go to sleep?'

Jeannie nodded her head. Sighing, she snuggled down beneath the sheets and submitted.

She wasn't allowed downstairs until two days later, when she was given a chair by the fire and Dot tucked a blanket over her knees. Jack was in the kitchen, being spoiled by Minnie.

'I feel such a fraud,' she said. 'I don't think I've ever been ill before.'

Dot looked at her wryly. 'We were fearful you'd caught influenza, but it turned out to be a chill and is there any wonder! You've never lived under such conditions before, I'll warrant. Nor been short o' food.'

'I came to you for Christmas dinner,' Jeannie countered.

'Except that you didn't eat it, did you? Harry put us all off our food. I hear he's sailed, by the way. Mike called in to ask how you were and said he'd seen Harry. He's gone on *Arctic Star*.'

Jeannie took a deep breath. Had he called at Mrs Herbert's to see her? she wondered.

'Mike told him you'd been took badly and Harry said to tell you he'll come when he gets back,' Dot said, a note of cynicism in her voice. 'And I said that pigs might fly.'

She's right, of course, Jeannie thought. Harry will be full of good intentions but they'll come to nothing. She took another breath, which caused some soreness in her chest. I must make plans whilst I'm sitting here like the lady I'm not. I can't expect Dot and Sam to be responsible for me and Jack.

She jumped when the doorbell rang, and Dot went to answer it. She felt a slight draught as the door opened again and she thought it was Dot returning until she heard Ethan's voice and looked up to see him in the doorway, twisting his hat in his hand.

'I – I wondered how you were, Jeannie,' he said diffidently. 'I didn't want to leave without knowing you'd recovered.'

'Will you sit down for a minute?' she asked, and he came and sat opposite her. 'I feel much better, thank you.' She wet her lips with her tongue. 'Thank you for bringing me here.'

He nodded. 'I'm pleased you've got such good folk to look after you. You've been neglecting yourself. Or at least' – his eyes narrowed – 'somebody else has been neglecting you.'

She shifted in the chair. 'You've heard about Harry? Did Mike tell you?'

'Aye, he did, though I'd already guessed something was wrong.' He bent his head as if he was thinking something over, and when he looked up she saw anger in his eyes. 'The man's a fool,' he said bitterly. 'As well as being a blackguard! How could he leave you to fend for yourself?'

Jeannie shook her head. 'No,' she whispered. 'I was the fool, Ethan. I was young and foolish and swayed by his promises and I believed them. But, you see, Harry lived by the rules that his grandmother laid down. She said he had to marry me, but once she was gone he had no rules to follow.'

'Don't defend him, Jeannie,' Ethan said brusquely. 'There are no excuses for his behaviour.' He stood up. 'I have to go; we're sailing on the morning tide and I've to count the men on board and do a hundred other jobs. My da has arrived. He said to tell you that your ma is well and that she would've come through with him, except that Granny Marshall is ill and she doesn't like to leave her.'

'Oh!' Jeannie said. 'I must write. I'll do it today.'

She shifted in the chair, but he put his hand on her shoulder. 'Don't get up,' he said softly. 'I'll see myself out.'

Jeannie swallowed hard and looked up at him. 'Good luck,' she whispered, a lump in her throat. 'God speed!' Tears which she had held back escaped and trickled down her face to her chin. 'Come back safely.'

He put a finger on her cheek and wiped away the tears; then he put his finger in his mouth and licked it with the tip of his tongue as if tasting the salt. 'I will,' he said. 'Be sure of it.'

CHAPTER FORTY-SEVEN

On returning to the house at the end of the week following her illness, Jeannie found Mrs Herbert packing; her brother it seemed wanted her to move as soon as possible. Jeannie had to make a quick decision about her own future.

During her convalescence she had given a lot of thought to what lay in front of her, and had realized that without some assistance she was condemned to a desolate and poverty-stricken life. She decided that the time had now come to be brave and ask for that help.

She asked Dot if she would look after Jack for one more day in the week if she asked for the extra time on the fish quay.

'It's just until I get some money together,' she said, 'and then I'll go back to three days.'

When Dot agreed, for she was fond of the child and so was Minnie, who helped her with him, Jeannie asked Sam if he would grant her a small loan so that she could take over the rent for Mrs Herbert's house. He said he would be happy to, but as she reckoned he was a hard-nosed businessman and she needed his friendship without conditions, she told him that she would naturally expect him to charge her interest as a moneylender would, but would pay it back within three months.

He'd given a wry smile, but she was in earnest and told him that she intended to clean the house, light fires in each room, including the two bedrooms, and sublet those within a month.

'A lick o' paint wouldn't go amiss,' he said. 'I'll lend Hicks to you for a couple of weeks, for free. He does odd jobs for me and I've nowt much for him to do at 'minute. Just give him some bread and cheese at dinner time and he'll paint or whitewash all your walls.'

Jeannie had heaved a sigh of satisfaction. Now that she'd actually made the decision, she was fired up to get started. Physically she still felt weak, but her head was buzzing with plans. The landlord's agent put her name on the rent book and she paid him two weeks' rent. She ordered coal and Billy brought her another handcart of timber, and she decided to make Mrs Herbert's room her own. It was warmer, being in the middle of the house, and she could cook on the fire as well as the gas ring in the scullery. Mrs Herbert had taken her furniture with her, so Jeannie brought her own bed and furniture into the room; she bought three cheap beds and second-hand chests of drawers and Billy made and put up shelves.

By the end of the first week, Hicks had white-washed her room, which brightened the sooty walls, and one bedroom, temporarily covering the damp patches, and lime-washed the scullery. She lit fires in all the rooms, swept and scrubbed the brick-floored scullery with soapy water and vinegar, washed the bedroom floors and donkey-stoned the front doorstep, something Mrs Herbert had done every week until the snow came. The snow thawed and froze again, but Jeannie's house was warm, and every day after work, having collected Jack and brought him home, she cleaned windows and put up nearly new curtains bought from a second-hand shop, and in the evenings she sat with Jack on her knee in front of her own fireside.

'I know somebody who wants a room, mum,' Hicks said, when he came the following week to finish painting the walls. 'My niece's daughter and her husband are looking for somewhere decent. They got married last back end and have been living wi' her ma. They're very respectable, and they're both in work.'

'Send them to see me,' she suggested. She had thought that the rooms would be taken by single people, but the larger upstairs room would easily accommodate a couple and so would the front room, the one she had previously rented. And, she thought eagerly, I can charge more for two.

The young woman, Doris, worked at one of the smoke houses and her husband worked at the Dairy-coates railway sidings. Both were earning good wages and Jeannie thought that they would eventually find a house for themselves. For the moment they just wanted to move from her mother's house and have some privacy.

'You wouldn't believe some of 'rooms we've looked at,' Doris said. 'You wouldn't want to keep a pig in 'em, never mind live in 'em yourself. Can we have use of 'scullery?'

Jeannie told them that they could, but they would have to put money in the meter if they wanted to use the gas ring. 'Or you can cook on your own fire if you want to.'

'We'll tek 'front room, then,' Doris said; she seemed to be the one who made the decisions. 'Can we move in at 'weekend?'

Jeannie laid down some rules first. They could come through her room to use the scullery, but must always knock first, and never after eight o'clock as she had to go to bed early in order to be up for her morning shift. They understood that as they too were always up early.

'Where's your husband?' Doris asked curiously, and nodded when Jeannie said he was at sea. 'Well,' she said, 'if you ever want any jobs doing, Jim's very handy. There's nowt he can't turn his hand to.'

Jeannie thanked them and wanted to whoop with delight when they paid her two weeks' rent in advance, covering the rent she had already paid the agent.

Sam gave her a cash book to write down the names of her lodgers and the rent they paid. 'Let them see you doing it,' he told her, 'then they can't say they gave it to you when they didn't. And give them a rent book wi' their name in it.'

Dot looked on approvingly. 'I can see we've got a businesswoman here. I think things are looking up for you, Jeannie. But have you thought of what might happen when Harry comes back? He might well want to come home when he sees what a cosy little house you've got.'

Jeannie chewed on a finger. 'Yes, it had crossed my mind,' she said. 'And he will have every right to do so.' But if he does, she thought, I know he won't stay. There's been too much disagreement for

423

us ever to make up and have a normal life. Aloud, she said, 'We'll have to cross that bridge when we get to it.'

Dot gazed at her. 'Yes. If in fact you ever do get to it.'

By the second week in February Jeannie had let all the rooms and paid Sam something back from the original loan. He'd said he could wait a bit longer but she'd insisted. She didn't want any debt in the new life she was creating.

Another week, or possibly two, and Harry's ship and Ethan's would be on their way back to port. She saw Mike Gardiner one day on her way back from the quay and asked if there was any news.

'Not yet,' he said. 'It's a bit early. I've heard there's been some rough weather, though. Two trawlers came in yesterday and they've sustained some damage.' He shook his head. 'They went too far for winter fishing, even though they got a good catch. They were tekking a risk, cos them islanders need their fish as much as we do. It's 'onny living they've got.'

'Why? Where've they been?'

'South-east Iceland. Brought back plaice and haddock.'

And that's what it's all about, she thought. Risking their lives to put food on the table.

Jeannie had seen Connie a few times as she went to and from work, but Connie acknowledged her only with a smug glance which she chose to ignore. She wondered if she was lonely whilst Harry was away and whether she had any kind of conscience, or if indeed she ever worried that he might leave her as he had left his lawful wife.

A week later the snow returned and the weather turned icy cold. Pipes, pumps and taps froze solid and on two occasions the women on the fish quay were sent home early as it was too cold to risk any accidents with cold fingers and sharp knives. Ships were arriving late and there were tales of vessels icing up in the North Sea as they made their way to port.

There was also some unrest in the town when it was announced that a conference was to be held in Hull during that year regarding the proposed legislation to ban summer fishing from grounds which had already been over-fished. It was mostly the wives of the fishermen who were up in arms, and there was many a debate on street corners as they complained that they didn't want their menfolk risking their lives with winter fishing and that they had to fish in summer in order to make a living. Those in authority argued back that some trawlers were catching young fish which were unfit to sell or eat from the foreign grounds and thereby depleting future stocks.

That an international agreement was needed was the one thing that all bodies were agreed on. But for the women who waited, the debates faded into the background and their concern deepened day by day as first one, then two, then five and six vessels were reported late home.

Jeannie heard the muttered gossip on the fish quay but refused to worry yet. The *Arctic Star* and *Scarborough Girl* were among those which were late. Ships were often late in winter, she told herself, and it was something wives and mothers had to live with, but there was an air of tension, broken only when a single vessel arrived home and told of one other ship, damaged, making her way up the Humber.

Families of those on board the other vessels started to gather at the dock gates as they awaited news. Women with small children huddled by their sides, pressing against them for warmth, waited for every tide.

The second ship arrived the following week and the skipper reported that several trawlers had been seen, but not close enough to identify. They were thought to be heading towards the east coast, but whether to Leith, North Shields, Scarborough or Hull couldn't be verified. One more trawler limped home a few days later; it had sustained considerable damage during a violent storm and one man had been lost overboard. It had seen nothing of the *Arctic Star*, *Scarborough Girl* or the *Mariner* since the four ships had left home port on the same day.

Jeannie took to walking beyond the end of the fish quay to gaze anxiously along the dock, hoping to be the first to see a late vessel entering from the estuary. She felt physically sick, unable to concentrate on anything, unable to talk, and at the end of another week she wrote a postcard to her mother: *Dear Ma, Ships missing. Please come. I need you. Jeannie.*

Her mother and Tom arrived two days later, bringing Stephen, Josh's son, with them. Mary, seeing Jeannie's pale and anxious face, gathered her into her arms and held her close. Tom kissed her cheek and then took Stephen with him in search of information.

Mary listened without a word whilst Jeannie poured out all that had happened to her. She told of Harry's leaving her for someone else, of losing the child she was carrying, of selling her wedding dress and being without money and what she was doing now in order to survive on her own.

'I'm so afraid, Ma,' she sobbed. 'I haven't told anybody how afraid I am. And I hate leaving Jack with somebody else, even though Dot is so kind and loves him like her own. I have to work to survive, I know that, and I know that there are other women in the same situation as me, but I'm so lonely and I feel so weak and helpless.'

She took a deep and shuddering breath. 'And it's not only Harry that I'm worrying over – he's my husband, after all, in spite of everything – but—' She burst into a fresh fit of sobbing. 'There's Ethan. I treated him so badly, and I didn't – I didn't realize – how much I miss him. And then there's Mike Gardiner's son, and Josh, and— Poor Stephen, how will he cope with the loss of his father and his brother?'

'Shh. All is not lost,' Mary murmured. 'We don't think the worst until the worst has happened.'

Jeannie looked at her mother and realized that she was suffering too. She had lost her husband to the sea, and now she might have lost a good friend and his son as well.

'Sorry, Ma,' Jeannie sniffled. 'I'm so – sorry. You must be worrying over Josh; he's been a good friend, hasn't he?'

Mary smiled and nodded. 'He asked me to marry him before he went away.'

'Did he?' Jeannie's eyes started to spout fresh tears. 'What answer did you give?'

'I said no,' her mother said, with a catch in her voice. 'And he was sad and disappointed, so I have that on my conscience.'

427

Tom returned to the house having found out nothing at all, and Jeannie thought how strong and purposeful he was and what a great support for her mother. Stephen was wide-eyed, not yet comprehending that his father and brother might not be returning home.

Tom returned to Scarborough the same evening; Mary said she would stay a few days longer, but promised to write if there was news. Given the option of returning with Tom or staying with Mary, Stephen decided he would stay.

'But I can't take too much time off,' her mother told Jeannie. 'I have a living to make too.' She put her arm around her daughter. 'You can always come home; you know that, don't you?'

'Yes,' Jeannie murmured, but wondered if she would or whether she would stay with the folk on the road who had treated her as one of their own.

She went to work the next morning, leaving Jack with her mother rather than taking him to Dot's, and as she reached the entrance to the fish quay she saw Connie standing as if waiting for someone. She came abreast of her, but kept her eyes in front and didn't glance at her. Connie turned and called her name.

'Jeannie! Jeannie, will you talk to me? Nobody'll talk to me. They're saying it's my fault.'

Jeannie looked at her. Connie's face was swollen with crying and her eyes were bloodshot.

'What's your fault?' she asked dully. 'I don't know what you mean.'

Connie began to weep. 'Harry's ship,' she wailed. 'Some of 'lasses are saying it's my fault it's missing.'

'You're being ridiculous,' Jeannie said sharply.

'Stop bothering me! Don't you realize what this is doing to me?' Her voice rose, the tension escalating. 'Have you no idea of my feelings? Are you so totally selfish that you don't care about anybody but yourself? Go away!'

She hadn't realized that she was shouting until she saw heads being turned in their direction. And then she saw that Connie was gasping for breath; she seemed to shrink and become the girl she had been when Jeannie had first met her, nervous and withdrawn and unsure of herself.

Jeannie stood staring at her. 'Are you ill?' she said at last.

Connie retched as if her throat was closing. 'No,' she whispered. 'I'm pregnant.'

Jeannie staggered at the news. Another child of Harry's to grow up without him.

'That's what I'm trying to tell you.' Connie's voice was choked. 'That's why it's my fault. I realized I was pregnant on 'morning Harry sailed and I chased after him to tell him. He was aboard by 'time I reached 'dock and they were already under way. I ran down 'side of 'dock shouting his name.' She wiped her wet cheek with her shawl. 'Some of 'men on 'deck were yelling at me to clear off but somebody else went to fetch Harry.'

She began to weep again. 'He came up on deck and I shouted to him that I was pregnant, but they were drawing away out of 'dock and towards 'estuary and he couldn't hear me, but – but I could tell what he was saying by 'way he was waving his arms.' She almost retched again as she continued. 'He was shouting *get back, get back*. It's unlucky, you see.'

429

Jeannie could barely hear her, but caught the last few whispered words.

'It's unlucky to see 'lads off on a trip. I was so excited about 'bairn that I'd forgotten. How could I? How could I forget when it's so important? And them other three ships; they were sailing on 'same tide an' 'men on board saw me as well cos I was stood on 'side of 'dock.' Connie took another trembling breath. 'And so it's my fault that they're missing.'

CHAPTER FORTY-EIGHT

Jeannie tried not to waken her mother, who was sleeping in the bed with her and Jack, but she tossed in an uneasy sleep for most of that night, thinking of a pregnant Connie, thinking of Harry somewhere out at sea, and thinking too of Ethan, the three of them in a bewildering tableau clinging to a broken mast and torn rigging; the scene set against heavy seas, with ships awash with fish and violent waves and herself on an open bridge shrieking orders that no one could hear. Timbers were crashing and fish boxes were sliding over the deck and then she was abruptly awakened by someone banging on the middle door. It was her lodger Jim, bare-legged, his hair tousled, dressed in his nightshirt with a jersey over the top.

'There's a young lad at 'front door wi' a message from somebody called Mike Gardiner,' he said. 'He says will you go to 'dock straight away.'

Jeannie dressed hurriedly and her mother got up to make her a hot drink. Stephen was sound asleep in a chair.

'We'll follow on,' Mary said. 'I'll give Jack his pobs and dress him and make sure he's warm.'

Jeannie nodded. She was so frightened she felt

sick and could barely answer, but she sipped her tea and reminded her mother to put Jack in the pram to save her carrying him.

It was not yet five o'clock and still dark when she left the house. There were other people, mainly women, going in the same direction, scurrying towards St Andrew's Dock. The streets were eerily silent but for the clatter of boots and clogs. The horse trams were not yet running and only the occasional butcher's shop or baker's had lights on as they prepared for the day's business.

The women did not speak to each other, simply hurried side by side with the same purpose, to learn the fate of the ships and the men on them, and facing the same uncertain future. The dock gates were open and they went through without hindrance, hurrying alongside the waterway, looking about them to find somebody who could answer their questions.

Jeannie spotted Mike and ran towards him. His face was grey and drawn and Jeannie knew how anxious he must be about Aaron. He drew Jeannie towards him and put his arm round her. 'There's a ship coming up 'estuary,' he said hoarsely. 'Onny one. There's no news of either of 'others so I fear they're lost. We'll find out when this one comes in.'

'Has nobody seen her name?' she asked. 'Surely . . .'

He shook his head. 'She's bearing no light or flag, but she's 'size of—' He swallowed hard. 'News is that she's 'size of *Arctic Star*, so it might be her. But we don't know for sure.'

Harry's ship. Jeannie took in the news and clutched Mike's arm. 'How long before she's here?' she whispered.

'Another hour, mebbe,' he said. 'Then there'll be relief and grief at 'same time.'

'The others might be safe,' she murmured. 'Or there might be more news.'

'Aye,' he said, without conviction. 'Mebbe so.'

They walked together to the dock entrance so that they might be among the first to see the ship approaching; half an hour went by and then another quarter. Jeannie shivered. It was so cold; she couldn't imagine how much colder it would be out at sea.

Dawn was breaking, long pencil-thin slivers of silver, red and gold breaking open the dark sky and heralding another day, when they saw the broken mast and ragged rigging of the advancing ship, escorted by the pilot boat all the way in through the huddle of vessels already docked. A thin cheer went up from the waiting crowd, which had increased in size as the news spread that a missing ship was homeward bound. But beneath the cheer was the wail of a plaintive keening.

'I can't look,' Jeannie gasped, and she couldn't see for her tears. Which ever vessel it was meant heartbreak for the families of those who were still missing. And for her, it meant she had lost either a husband or a dear friend and his father. 'Can you see which it is yet, Mike?'

He didn't answer, but squeezed her shoulder; she felt him shake and knew it was bad news. She heard the sob in his breath and then a gasp. 'I'm sorry for you, lass.' He couldn't keep the anguish from his voice or hold back the tears which poured down his face and into his beard. 'It's *Scarborough Girl* that's come home,' he choked. 'Not *'Arctic Star* after all.'

* * *

There were many tears and cries of grief when *Scarborough Girl* brought the news that the *Arctic Star* had perished in one of the worst storms that Ethan and his men said they had ever endured. They had seen the ship in difficulties and gone to her aid, but they were in trouble themselves as their vessel was besieged by battering seas.

'We managed to get a line aboard the *Arctic Star* before she went down,' Ethan wearily told the director of M and R, who had come to the dock with everyone else to wait for news about the company's ship. 'But she was swamped by massive waves which threw her over on her beam ends. We brought two men aboard, but one died of exposure. The other is safe and will be able to tell you what happened.'

The man nodded wearily. 'She was an old ship,' he said. 'But seaworthy. We won't replace her, and we can't replace those who were lost with her. It's a very sad day.'

'It is indeed. We too lost a man overboard,' Ethan told him. 'A young man on his first trip. I must find his mother to tell her how brave he was. This was our first voyage in *Scarborough Girl* and she's served us well in terrible circumstances.'

He sought out Jeannie, who was sitting on a fish box gently rocking Jack in his pram. Her mother was with her; Stephen had gone on board the ship to greet his father.

'I'm so sorry, Jeannie,' he said quietly. 'So sorry to bring you this news.'

Jeannie didn't answer. She felt numb, as if she was in yet another nightmare from which she would presently awaken. Then she said softly, 'At least I know what happened to Harry. There's no news of

434

the *Mariner* or its crew. Their families will always wonder and wait.'

'She's lost,' he told her. 'We saw her once before the storm hit, and then nothing.'

'Did you see Harry?' Jeannie asked. 'Before the ship went down? I suppose – I suppose you couldn't tell one man from another?'

'No,' he said. 'It was all confusion: great waves, thunder and lightning, and she was adrift and low in the water, probably heavily laden with fish. Her masts had been struck, I think; they were shattered, anyway. Ours were covered in ice. And it was quick, Jeannie.' He touched her shoulder. 'She went down in minutes; the men wouldn't have suffered for long.'

Rosie and Billy came to talk to her, and Ethan took Mary to see Josh and then went to join those who had lost men from the *Arctic Star* and the *Mariner*. Rosie was very distressed.

'I know we didn't see eye to eye most of 'time,' she wept, 'but he was my brother. Have you seen Connie?' she asked suddenly. 'She's on her own; she's crying.'

'I can't talk to her just now,' Jeannie said. 'I have my own sorrow to bear without sharing hers. I'm sorry for her, though.' She looked up at Rosie; Rosie who was once Connie's friend. 'She's pregnant,' she told her. 'She's expecting Harry's child.'

And so Rosie and Billy went to comfort Connie, who was crouched in a corner like a frightened animal. Dot and Sam arrived at the dockside. Sam was relieved that his investment was safe, but like Dot and Rosie he was distressed over the loss of life on the other vessels, especially Harry's. Dot said that when they were ready they must all go back to

435

their house for breakfast, and the men, Ethan and Josh, for a hot bath if they would like one.

Ethan thanked her but said he and his father would go back to Mike's, where he would be lodging for the foreseeable future.

'You'll not be expected at work today, Jeannie,' Dot told her. 'You'll come back, won't you?'

Jeannie said she would, and that she would bring her mother. She wanted someone to take care of her life until she found the energy and the will to do it herself. She waited with Ethan for his father and Stephen and her mother to appear, and saw Josh hand Mary down from the deck to the quay. She also saw how he held on to her hand and she didn't pull away. Stephen walked at her other side and put his arm in hers.

Jeannie glanced at Ethan, her eyes pricking, and saw that he had noticed too. Neither of them said anything, but when they joined them, and Mike and his son, they walked as a family might, but with one relative missing, out of the dock and on to Hessle Road.

CHAPTER FORTY-NINE

It was December and almost Jack's third birthday. He was a lively, happy child, chattering volubly and constantly getting into mischief. He loved his time with Dot and especially now that there were other children to play with, for Dot had found her vocation. She had never wanted children of her own but she was fond of other people's, mainly, she said, because she could send them home at the end of the day.

The daughter of a friend had seen how good she was with Jack and asked if she would take care of her little girl when she went back to work. Dot agreed, and one request led to another and before she had quite realized what was happening she and Minnie had cleared a room where they now looked after four children. It brought her in some money of her own, which she spent mainly on children's toys.

Jeannie had been promoted to forewoman of her team on the fish quay and been given a rise in wages. The rooms in her house were constantly occupied, although Doris and Jim had moved out as she thought they would, making way for an older single man who was quiet and well behaved and in regular work. All of her lodgers paid on the dot, none was in arrears and no one gave her any trouble. Perhaps the regular visits of Mike and Billy and the occasional appearance of Ethan assured them that as a young widow she wasn't friendless or unprotected.

The previous year she had heard through Mrs Norman that Connie had given birth to a son and had gone to see her. She found her in a miserable state, living in one damp dark room and reliant on handouts from the Poor Law. Jeannie had felt sorry for her and taken her some of Jack's baby clothes. She'd sat down to talk to her and suggested that as Connie had no contact with her mother she should write to her father in Brixham and ask if he could help her.

'The child is his grandson,' she said. 'And his – well, his wife, even if they haven't been able to marry, was Harry's mother, so young Harry here is her grandson too.'

Jeannie didn't hold out too much hope, as Rosie had told her that she had written to her mother to tell her about Harry's being lost at sea, and that he had been married and had a child. A postcard had come back with a few words expressing her sorrow and asking Rosie to send condolences to Harry's widow, but saying nothing about Jack.

Nevertheless, she helped Connie write the letter, guessing that she wouldn't do it on her own, and a reply came back from Connie's father within a fortnight to say that she was welcome to stay with them until she got on her feet and that there was plenty of work down there that she could do.

'A fresh start for you, Connie,' Jeannie had said, thinking of the relief for them both that they wouldn't have to meet or compare their children.

When she told Dot what had happened, she put up the money for Connie's train fare to Brixham.

During that first summer after Harry was lost, Jeannie scraped enough money together to take Jack on the train to Scarborough. She wanted to visit Granny Marshall who, although unwell, constantly asked Mary about her first great-grandchild. Jeannie wanted to visit old friends and Josh's family too, and more than anything to show Jack the sands and let him dip his toes in the sea.

She also wanted to re-evaluate her life. She needed to think about her past, and if possible decide what she wanted to do with her future. She knew that her mother wanted her to come back and live with her in Scarborough, but she told her she wasn't ready to make that decision, saying that she couldn't yet leave the people who had supported her when she was at her lowest ebb. She told Mary of the fish parcels she had found on her doorstep, the box that had held a potato, a carrot, an egg and a small screw of paper containing a scraping of tea. Gifts from people who had very little themselves.

In truth, though, she wanted to look out from the harbour walls, breathe in the salty air and remember her childhood when life had seemed so simple, when the days were long and sunny and without constraint. Did Ethan ever think of those days, she had wondered, now that he was living in Hull and making a hard though successful living? Does he remember them with affection, and – she had paused in her thinking as she'd watched the ships leaving the safety of the harbour and heading for the open sea – will he ever forgive me?

*   *   *

Jeannie was dressing Jack in the warm gansey and socks she had knitted for him, telling him that the next day was going to be his birthday and he would be having cake, when someone tapped on the back door. It was early for visitors, so she opened the door cautiously.

'Ethan!' she said when she saw his big frame filling the doorway. He was carrying a parcel. 'Will you come in?'

'Only for a minute,' he said. 'I thought I'd catch you before you went to work. I've brought a present for Jack. Isn't it his birthday tomorrow?'

'Yes,' she said, amazed that he had remembered again, as he had last year. She led him through into her room. 'I'm just about to take Jack to Dot's or I'd offer you a cup of tea.'

'No, that's all right,' he said. 'I can't stop. I'm leaving on the midday tide so I wanted to bring his present before I went. It's a wooden train,' he said, bending down to give Jack the parcel. 'I hope he likes it.'

'He'll love it,' she said with a catch in her voice. 'It's very good of you.'

Ethan smiled at Jack, who had taken the parcel from him and sat down on the floor and was now trying unsuccessfully to undo the string. Then he turned his gaze to Jeannie.

'How are you coping, Jeannie?' he asked. 'It's been a while since I came. It's not that I haven't been thinking about you, it's just that, well, I know you needed time to come to terms with the loss of Harry.'

That wasn't the reason, she knew very well. Being the man he was, he wouldn't have wanted her to be gossiped about because he as a single man came

440

calling too often. It was different for Mike, who was almost a surrogate grandfather to Jack, and for Billy, who occasionally did jobs for her, for he was now married to Rosie and they came together.

'I'm managing,' she said, looking back at him. 'I have to. But I manage very well with the support of my friends.' She smiled at him so that he knew he was included. 'Those who call and ask how I am.'

'We've all been concerned about you, Jeannie,' he said softly. 'Nobody more than me.'

'I know,' she said, 'and I appreciate it.' She glanced away, looking down at Jack, who having given up on the string was now struggling to tear the wrapping paper. 'But sometimes I'm lonely, even with Jack to comfort me. I need love to sustain me and I've been deprived of that. No, that sounds ungrateful. I don't mean that I haven't the love of friends and family. Without all of you who've been so kind and thoughtful I wouldn't have survived.'

She laughed then, as Jack with a great shout of triumph tore the paper and revealed the toy train. 'And Jack, of course, he'll always love me – his love is unconditional.' But there was a catch in her voice as she continued. 'It's being without someone special in my life that's the hardest of all.'

She saw Ethan's expression freeze and realized that he thought she was speaking of Harry.

'Harry wasn't that person,' she said softly. 'He only married me because his grandmother told him to. He was obeying the rules that she had laid down, but he didn't really believe in them, he told me that himself.' She paused, and when she went on there was regret in her voice for what might have been. 'He didn't love me, and I know now that I

441

didn't love him. I was young and foolish and was swept away.'

Ethan took hold of her hand. 'Is it too late for me? You know that I love you, have always loved you. My mistake was in not telling you. I was too shy to say anything and I thought you knew.'

Jeannie shook her head. 'I didn't know,' she whispered. 'I told you I was young and foolish.'

'You're still young.' Tentatively he stroked her cheek. 'And you haven't answered my question.'

'What was the question?'

'Is it too late?' He held her gaze with his blue-green eyes. The colour of the sea on a sunny day.

Jeannie moistened her lips. 'What about Jack?' she whispered.

'What about him?'

'Can you love him? Another man's child?'

'He's your child too, isn't he? I love him already.'

It was too soon for promises, they both knew that, but each felt a lifting of spirits as they parted. Ethan's trip would be a short one, for he said he would no longer risk his men's lives or his ship on a long winter voyage, and there was a spring in Jeannie's step as she walked to the fish quay after dropping Jack off at Dot's. A smile lifted her lips, the first in a long time.

A parcel came from her mother the following day containing a present for Jack's birthday, a soft toy she had knitted and stuffed which Jack clutched to him, crowing with delight, and a letter for Jeannie.

You already know that Josh is still waiting for an answer to his second proposal which came

442

after the ill-fated voyage. He's a persistent and patient man. He says that he will not leave Scarborough again – one voyage on a trawler was enough for him – and he's fishing successfully from the smack. Stephen goes with him at weekends and occasionally Tom plucks up the courage to go too, although he still prefers dry land, especially now that Sarah is expecting their first child.

So what should I do, Jeannie? Do I spend the rest of my days alone, or shall I take a chance at marrying again? Josh will make a loving husband, that I am sure of, and I would once again have a family to look after. Stephen is anxious for it to happen and so are his sisters. But what is holding me back, my dearest Jeannie, is not knowing whether or not you are going to return to Scarborough, for if you do, then more than anything I would want you and Jack to live with me in your old home so that I can help you in your life.

Jeannie folded up the letter and put it on the mantelpiece. She hadn't realized that her mother was waiting for her to make a decision about her life before making such a momentous one about her own. Well, she would write and tell her. But not yet.

A week later she waited at dawn in St Andrew's Dock for the *Scarborough Girl* to tie up. It was bitterly cold, though not as cold as it had been the morning they had waited for the missing ships. She felt a pang of sadness whenever she thought of Harry, and wondered how he would have coped with another son in his life. It would have been difficult for him. But

443

her memories of Harry were changing. She thought of how merry he had been when she'd first met him, as if he had not a care in the world to bother him, and it was this image she clung to when she looked at Jack, who looked so much like him.

'Jeannie! What are you doing here?' Ethan called as he jumped down on to the quayside. 'Aren't you cold?'

'Cold? Me?' She laughed. 'I'm a fisher girl, aren't I? I'm waiting for the sun to come up . . .' – she hesitated – 'and I've been waiting for my ship to come in.'

He looked at her, a puzzled expression on his face. 'Your ship?'

She nodded. 'My ship. The *Scarborough Girl*. Isn't she mine? Named after me?'

He nodded. 'Yes. They both were, the smack and the trawler.' His voice softened. 'There was never another Scarborough girl for me, even though she moved to Hull.'

Jeannie put her hand to his face. His beard was long and thick and bushy and she knew he would shave it off now that he was ashore again, just in time for Christmas.

'I loved you when I was eight years old,' she said huskily. 'How did I come to stray so far?'

Ethan put down his bag and took her in his arms. 'You were led up the wrong path, but you've found your way home again.'

'To you?' she asked, her eyes bright with tears and hope and seeing him clearly as the fresh new dawn broke over the horizon, painting the sky with streaks of gold and the blush of a rose. She heard the plaintive cry of herring gulls circling above them and on the breeze she could smell the sea. 'Where is home?' she whispered.

'With me,' he said lovingly, kissing her cheek, and then her mouth. 'Together. Always. Wherever we choose to be.'

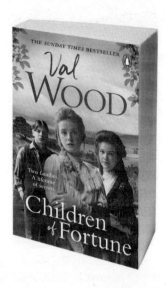

1864: Following the untimely death of her cold-hearted husband, Beatrix and her three children are finally free. While Ambrose has already determined his path in life, eldest son Laurie's future is less certain. With the responsibility of the family estate on his shoulders, Laurie must decide between staying in Yorkshire to farm the family land and following his dreams.

Meanwhile, headstrong and independent Alicia is defying expectation and excelling at school. There she befriends the enigmatic Olivia Snowdon and they quickly become inseparable. But Olivia's past is shrouded in mystery, and as the two families grow closer, secrets start to come tumbling out . . .

A powerful story of family ties, long-held secrets and the fleeting days of childhood.

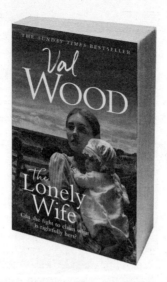

A powerful story about a woman's struggle to claim what is rightfully hers, from the *Sunday Times* bestselling author Val Wood.

1850: Beatrix Fawcett is just eighteen when her father tells her she is to marry a stranger. Hesitantly, but with little choice, she agrees to the match – in the hope of a good husband in Charles, and a happy new life together in rural Yorkshire.

As Beatrix sets about making their house a home, she falls in love with it and the surrounding countryside. But she does not fall in love with her husband . . . Charles has chosen her simply to meet the requirements of his inheritance and has little interest in his young wife.

Soon, the only spark in Beatrix's lonely life is her beloved children. But when Charles threatens to take them away from her, Beatrix must find strength in desperate times.

Can she fight against her circumstances and keep what is rightfully hers?

SIGN UP TO OUR NEW SAGA NEWSLETTER

Penny Street

The home of heart-warming reads

Welcome to **Penny Street**, your number **one stop for emotional and heartfelt historical reads**. Meet casts of characters you'll never forget, memories you'll treasure as your own, and places that will forever stay with you long after the last page.

Join our online **community** bringing you the latest book deals, competitions and new saga series releases.

You can also find extra content, talk to your favourite authors and share your discoveries with other saga fans on Facebook.

Join today by visiting
www.penguin.co.uk/pennystreet

Follow us on Facebook
www.facebook.com/welcometopennystreet/